Ship Happens

Lauren Biel

Library of Congress Cataloging-in-Publication Data

Ship Happens/Lauren Biel 1st ed.

Cover Design: Qamber Designs

Editing: Sugar Free Editing

Interior Design: Sugar Free Editing

For more information on this book and the author, visit: www. LaurenBiel.com

Please visit LaurenBiel.com for a full list of content warnings.

*This book is dedicated to a glass of bubbly. Bottoms up . . . in
more ways than one.*

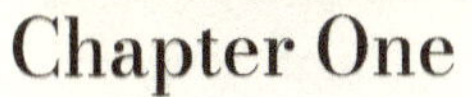

Chapter One

Frankie

My mother thinks this is a terrible idea. She's seated on the couch in her living room. The space is clinical—all-white everything—which is at odds with my mother's warm nature.

Yes, that was sarcasm. The woman is about as warm as a penguin's asshole, but she's my mother. It's just her way.

She worries her nails, not gnawing them off but running them through her teeth. Such a nasty habit, but I won't scold her this time. I understand her concern. A couple of agents going into a scenario filled with hardened killers is nothing to sniff at.

"Mama, I'll be okay," I say. I take her hands in mine to stop the incessant nail nipping. "I'm pushing forty, and I've finally been given a job in the field. Can't you be happy for me?"

She shakes her head, sending her gray hair into a flurry around her head. "Couldn't they send you to North Korea?

Frankie, I don't want you dealing with serial killers." She shudders.

My mother and I are in similar lines of work, though her dealings have been more on the documented side. The general American public hears about *her* accomplishments, especially after she studied some of the most notorious killers up close. My dealings, however . . .

I'm a ghost. Well, figuratively, and mostly from my office computer. I get in, I get out, and I try to leave as little trace of my existence as possible. There are no accolades, no public ceremonies to celebrate which dictator or crime lord I've toppled. It all happens beyond the public scope.

But it hasn't been enough. I've wanted to go into the field, just like my mother, since the day I got the job. I haven't been afforded this opportunity.

Until now.

"World leaders wield power and money," my mother continues. "You won't be swayed by that, but the killers, Frankie? They wield charisma, and that's a far more powerful weapon."

Another daughter would smirk at this, maybe even roll her eyes and tell her mother to stop being silly. But my mother speaks from experience, and I am the direct product of a difficult lesson learned.

"I'll be careful, Mama." I place my hand over hers, then rise to stand. "My meeting with Castle is soon, though, so I need to head out. I thought we could have dinner before I leave, but the plans have been moved up."

"This is all happening so fast," she says. Her hand rises toward her mouth again, and I lean down to place it back in her lap.

I pat her hand once more. "I'll be gone for two weeks.

The first week is the mission, and the second week is the debrief. Maybe longer if I discover something substantial."

"If you come back at all."

Now I roll my eyes. "I'll be back in three weeks at the most. Just plan to take me to dinner when I return. I want to eat at the Italian manor."

"Deluca's?"

"That's the one." I squeeze her shoulder and stand. "Make a reservation for the nineteenth at seven. I'm sure to be back by then."

"You wouldn't miss a dinner at Deluca's for the world," she says as her shoulders finally relax.

"Exactly, so you know I'll be back."

My mother relents with a nod, though she won't meet my eyes. She still isn't happy about this mission, but I don't blame her for her fears. I don't know many mothers who would want their daughter to plant themselves in a situation that puts them within a serial killer's grasp, let alone an entire ship full of them.

But that's exactly what I'll be doing, and Castle will join me. It's the first time our agency has required we work as a team, which means they want to hedge their bets. They expect to lose at least one of us, so they sent the second as an insurance policy.

Hi. I'm the insurance policy.

Castle was none too pleased when he learned I'd be accompanying him. He was supposed to head this mission alone. It's simple enough on the surface. Break into a rumored serial-killer retreat, then get evidence that can take down the suspected kingpin: none other than Jim Madigan, the Siesta Killer. He's been on our radar for years, but he's always one step ahead of us. If we can take him down, his entire murdery empire will go with him.

"The nineteenth at seven!" I shout as I open the front door. "Don't forget!"

"Don't fall in love!" she shouts back.

I scoff and shake my head with a smile. Not, *Don't die,* or, *Don't get hurt.* With the serial killers, she's most concerned about my heart.

No worries there. My contract demands I remain a lone wolf, and my job means more to me than a meaningful connection with a human being. If I have urges, I can handle them myself. I've never gotten off with any help from a man, anyway, so I'm not missing out on much.

As I slide into the driver's seat of my red sports car, the curtain beside the front door moves, and my mother's silhouette appears in the window. She slides the curtain aside and gives me a wave, and I return the motion. She's treating this like a goodbye instead of a see-you-later. The woman has incredible intuition, but she's wrong this time. I'll be back.

I'm like Ross Perot in the eighties. I always come back.

I adjust the rearview mirror and apply a bit of lipstick. Castle is intimidated by pretty women, and I just so happen to be both pretty and a woman. I'm no supermodel by any standard, but with my dark hair and blue eyes, I stand out in a crowd. My eye color came from my mother, but I can only assume the dark hair was passed down from my father. I've never met the man.

Spring sunshine blasts through my windshield as I pick up speed on a back road. My phone rings in the cupholder, and I glance at it. It's Castle, probably wanting to know where I am and why I'm nearly late. He's an uptight prick, and for that reason, I let it go to voicemail and ease up on the gas. I take my time and ignore the following three calls as well.

The traffic picks up as I near the airport. Richmond International is a bit busy today, but we have to fly out of here because Castle "knows a guy." If we want no record of ourselves or our movements, we have to operate this way. The right hand of the law doesn't always need to know what the left hand is doing, after all.

The parking garage eventually slides into view, and I tuck my sleek car into a spot for an extended stay. I hate leaving her exposed like this, but I don't rideshare. If I'm not in control of the car, I don't feel safe.

Once my luggage lies in a black pile at my feet, I swipe my hand down my black pantsuit to remove the wrinkles, then snag a quick glance of myself in my car's reflection. I'm certain to have Castle quaking in his boots. A pretty woman in a position of power will unravel him, and I am the picture of power and independence.

I don't want to overwhelm him for the sake of overwhelming him. There are two roles up for grabs, and we were told to decide who would best fit each role. We've been fighting about it for weeks, and King—our division's director—told us we couldn't board the planes until we come to a decision. That's why I'm bringing out the big guns.

I refuse to play the part of a killer at this retreat.

If that's even what this is. As I said, we've heard the rumors. We know of the whisperings. What we don't have is hard proof, and that's what we've been tasked with retrieving. Every attempt has been blocked thus far. We've had agents get as far as booking a place at the retreat, only for the information to completely disappear the next day. We've been good, but they've been better.

Until now.

I spot Castle at our terminal inside the airport. He paces

beside the massive window, his phone clutched in his meaty fist as he scowls at the departing planes. Sunshine blasts through the window and glints off his shining bald head. Skinny jeans hug his legs, riding a little too high on his ankles. His shirt is just as tight. Men with that much muscle should really wear looser clothing. He looks like he's shrunk all his laundry. What a chode.

I approach him and drop my black leather carry-on bag at my feet. "Been shopping in the toddler section again, I see. Those nut crushers don't look good on anyone, you realize."

"I've changed my mind," he says, jumping right to the meat and potatoes. "The more I thought about it, the more I realized you'd blow our fucking cover if you play the part of a killer. I can do what would need to be done. You'd choke."

My brain analyzes his words, parsing the potential meanings as quickly as he spits out each sentence. Maybe he's being serious. Maybe he believes I'll jeopardize the entire operation because I'm incapable of killing someone if I'm not under duress.

Or maybe he's playing the same game I'm playing after all.

Just as I've used his weaknesses against him—his weakness around pretty women in powerful positions—he could be using the same tactic against me. By challenging my abilities, he's hoping I'll defend my pride by swallowing the bait and demanding the position he's now requesting. Simple reverse psychology.

"We should let a randomizer decide." I pull a coin from my pocket. "Heads or tails?"

He licks his thin lips and looks at the coin. His skin is always a little redder than what's normal for any human being, but now he's turning maroon. "Let me play the criminal, Ghost."

I inwardly cringe at the stupid fucking name. By the time I joined their task force, all the chess-piece names had been given out, and I was stuck with a maneuver. Better than En Passant, I guess. Another chode.

"I'm perfectly fine with leaving it up to fate. I mean, unless you think *you* might choke." I move the silver dollar through my fingers, flicking the medallion over my knuckles with practiced ease. "Come on, Castle. You scared?"

He grits his teeth and shakes his head. "Fuck you. Flip the coin."

"Heads, you're the killer. Tails, I'm the criminal. Deal?"

The dumbass actually nods his head, and that's when I realize the error of my ways. If he plays the part of the killer, he will definitely blow our cover, but if he plays the part of the stupid criminal, we might actually pull this off. I'll just have to suck it up and become the thing I hate.

I stuff the coin back into my pocket and shake my head. "Fuck it. You can be the criminal."

He grins and pumps his fist in the air, but the smile and enthusiasm slide off his face seconds later. "Hang on, why are you giving it up so easily? Do you know something I don't?"

"We have the same intel, genius, so how would I know more than you?"

"Go over it again. Both sides."

I look around. There are too many nosy people milling nearby for me to lay out our mission so plainly, so I grip his shirtsleeve and pull him and his tight-ass pants into an alcove. Once I'm certain we're well out of earshot, I tell him all the things he should already know and has likely forgotten. The man has the brain of a goldfish.

"The criminal will meet with our operative to be placed inside the ship before the cruise is underway. The mission is to collect intel on how these criminals are housed, subdued, and transported around the retreat. The inner workings of the underpinning, if you will."

"Right. I just have to play the part of a bad guy and remember whatever I see."

"Exactly."

"And the killer?"

"The killer will be required to board as a guest. Their job is to get as close to Jim Madigan as possible."

"And kill people."

"If that's even required. We don't know that it will be."

Castle scoffs and folds his hefty arms over his chest. "Oh, it will be. Do you really think these sick assholes are out for a normal vacation?"

I shrug. "Maybe not for the past retreats, but they've done something different this time."

"Right. The *other* guests."

He's referring to the fact that not everyone on this cruise is thought to be a notorious killer. Slots were opened to the general public, which is a first, if the rumors are to be believed. We just don't know enough right now, but that will change.

Soon, we'll know everything.

"So what'll it be, Castle? We need to make a decision."

He mulls over the options that aren't really options at all. Looking at us now, I don't know how I ever thought it could be the other way around. He looks like a criminal and I . . . don't. It's shitty that society has placed a stereotype on the mere appearance of a person, but here we are.

"Why the sudden change of heart, though?" he asks, and it's a valid question. We don't really know the people we work with, after all. He doesn't even know my real name, nor do I know his.

I lean against the alcove wall and shrug. "Just pick whichever position you feel you'd do best with, and I'll take what's left over. I'm sorry to disappoint you, but there are no ulterior motives. I just want to get on with the job."

A voice crackles through an overhead speaker, letting everyone know that boarding is about to begin. We're taking separate planes, and the time for debating our decisions has passed.

"That's the criminal's plane," I say. "If you want that position, you'd better move those stubby fucking legs."

He hesitates before cursing beneath his breath and hurrying off. And just like that, it's decided. For the next week, I'm no longer Frankie Grant the Ghost.

I'm a serial killer.

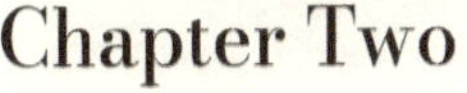

Chapter Two

Maverick

The limo pulls against the curb, and I hurry to open the back door for the special guest of the evening. Eve emerges from the shadowy depths, wearing a flashy purple top and flowing pants the color of a night sky. She's traded the box braids for a more relaxed look, allowing her thick curls to shine.

I offer her my arm. "How will the girls get any tips tonight when the entire room will be looking at you?"

"Not the entire room. Shit, *I'll* be looking at the girls." She slides her arm into mine and tosses her hair over her shoulder. "Let's get inside. I wanna see some titties."

Since the winter retreat, Eve and I have become best friends. She even moved in with me about a month ago, though neither of us is home very often. We're both workaholics . . . and killers.

"How was your flight back from Milan?" I ask as we hurry to the side entrance. As a celebrity, Eve rarely comes in through the front door. "Better yet, how was Milan?"

She blows out a breath. "Too rainy for my taste, and sort of cold. Beautiful as always, but the weather wouldn't cooperate for the show. We had to move it indoors, which sort of ruined the effect. I mean, we were supposed to embody Mother Earth."

I shudder when I recall Eve's outfit. She sent me pictures, and I've never seen a woman look so proud while wearing what equated to a ghillie suit. I wish I could say she still pulled it off, but I'm not sure anyone can pull off wet weeds.

Opening the side door, I usher her into the club before someone recognizes her. She turns to look at me as we step into a dark hallway.

"I'm a high-fashion model, Maverick, not a fucking pop star. You don't have to worry about me getting mobbed at a strip club."

"You're also my friend, and it's your birthday. I want to make sure you have a nice time without having to pose for pictures or scribble autographs." I open the next door, but I wait for her to walk through instead of hurrying her along. She just laughs and shakes her head as I lead her up a staircase to an elegant balcony overlooking the stages. It's the VIP area. Only the best for my friend.

A topless woman smiles at Eve as she clears the top step. "Happy birthday, beautiful," she says as she drapes a sash over Eve's slender shoulders. "If you'll just have a seat, I'll be right over to take your drink orders."

Eve's gaze doesn't linger on the woman's perky breasts, which is more than I can say for some of the men I've brought here. Though, since Bennett has become the object of Cat's affections, I've been coming alone.

We were all nervous for them at first, but Cat and Bennett have defied the odds. They've turned their little house into a home, complete with two cats. Bennett keeps begging for a dog, but Cat says no.

Speaking of Cat and Bennett, we're supposed to meet up with them for drinks at a nearby bar when we finish here. Ezra and Kindra are already in Miami, helping Jim settle the final arrangements for the upcoming cruise, so they won't be able to join us this evening.

Eve and I take a seat on an elegant leather couch overlooking the main floor. The waitress grabs our drink orders —something fruity and heavy on the vodka for Eve, and a beer for me—before the lights dim and the music starts. Our eyebrows pull together when the first few notes register in our ears. Instead of a sexy beat, a familiar song pumps through the speakers, and it's probably the least sexy song I know.

"Who strips to Tom Jones?" Eve asks with a laugh, and then her question is answered as Bennett and Cat slink onto the stage.

They're both decked out in hilarious 70s garb. They got the era wrong, but I think we'll let it slide. Some of the male patrons don't look too thrilled as Bennett begins stripping off his tasseled vest, however.

Cat grips the pole and spins around. Knowing Bennett, she won't be removing a damn thing, though her current outfit doesn't leave much to the imagination. It's essentially little more than a leather-tasseled bikini.

Bennett is truly a lucky man. Sometimes I think I really missed out, but then I see them together and realize it never would have worked. Even if I'd been open to the idea of dating someone, they were meant for each other, and it always would have turned out this way.

The song is short, and as it ends, they exit the stage and join us in the VIP lounge. They've traded their leather tassels for jeans and comfortable shirts. Bennett rocks a Hawaiian number with pineapples all over it.

"Is she dressing you now?" Eve asks as they take a seat on the couch.

"Every chance I get." Cat leans closer to Eve and brings her in for a hug. "Happy birthday, bitch."

Eve grins and hugs her closer. "It's happy now that you're here. I figured you wouldn't want to bring your man to a strip club, though. You know, since the both of you are so possessive and shit."

"I put down some ground rules, don't worry." Cat grins at Bennett, and Bennett groans. "Put them on, Benny Bear."

With his lips pinched together, he plucks a pair of glasses from his front pocket. A pineapple covers each lens. He slides them over his face, effectively blinding himself.

Is this what love does to a man?

Eve covers her laughter with her hand. "Very . . . stylish."

"It was this or letting her strip on stage," he says. "I didn't want to have to burn the joint down, so I chose the glasses. Fair trade, if you ask me."

Our waitress swings by again to take Bennett's and Cat's orders. Bennett looks to her right as he asks for a whiskey sour. He's clearly trying to pretend he isn't currently blinded by two plastic pineapples, and he's failing. Cat bites her lip to stifle a laugh before she asks for a Jack and Coke.

The lights dim again, and this time, a soft R&B number bubbles from the speakers. A spotlight focuses on a velvet curtain as a pale, slender leg pokes from the slit. Like water, a nearly naked redhead reveals herself, flowing from the curtain and moving toward the pole on the raised stage.

"Jesus fuck," Cat breathes. "She's so pretty. I don't know what I expected, but it wasn't this."

Bennett reaches for his glasses, but Cat swats his hand away.

The woman grips the pole and walks around as she sheds the shimmering wrap around her hips. Her full ass remains perfectly round as she hooks her leg around the pole and rolls her hips forward. She's perfection.

And yet, my dick doesn't move.

This is nothing new. It's a problem I've had since I was young. Since someone decided to teach my brain that sex is unsafe. The crossed wires can't be undone, and I can't get hard.

Well, I can, but it takes some work, and most women aren't prepared to provide what I require. I didn't pull the name Midnight Masochist from a hat, after all.

My little problem has created its own issues. Because I fear getting close to women, people automatically assume that means I prefer getting close to men. Not that I blame them, but I'm definitely into women.

And that's the thing. Women *do* turn me on. I feel all the signals, even now, as I watch the redhead remove her bra. My spine tingles, and my balls swell. My brain puts her in dirty positions, and I envision what it would be like to suck her pale nipples as she rides my cock.

But my cock refuses to respond.

I slide my hand into my pocket and pretend I'm looking for something. What I'm actually doing is giving myself a dose of pain. I snag my thigh's sensitive skin between my fingers and pinch as hard as I can. Water fills my eyes, but my dick refuses to listen. It's not enough.

Frustrated, I pull my hand out of my pocket before one of the security guards thinks I'm trying to play pocket pool.

The last thing I need before we go on this cruise is a Paul Reubens situation. God rest his soul.

"Hey, have you guys gotten your room assignments for the ship?" I ask the group.

"No, but Cat and I will be sharing a cabin. If not, someone will have hell to pay," Bennett says.

The girls are too busy watching the woman dancing on the stage to respond.

"I asked Jim to put me in a room with Eve," I say. "Nothing against Ice Pick, but he snores."

Eve sits back and looks at me. "Jim didn't tell you?"

Clearly not. I shake my head.

"Oh, honey. You need to talk to him. He didn't room you with Ice Pick, but he won't tell anyone who he roomed you with or why." Eve sips her drink, then places it on the low table in front of us. "He said he has a job for you. Something about keeping tabs on a newbie."

"And he told everyone but me? The person who's supposed to be doing the job? I don't even work for him. Why wouldn't he task Bennett with this?"

Eve shrugs. "I don't know, but he's already on the ship. I guess you won't find out until we board."

I sit back and run my finger around the bottom of the glass. What does Jim Madigan have up his sleeve? And why don't I feel good about it?

Chapter Three

Frankie

The luggage handle nearly slips from my sweaty grasp as I step onto the gangplank and board the cruise ship. This ship once bore the name Ice Princess Lenore, as it was commonly used in Alaskan cruises. Now she's been refurbished and renamed to the Bruise Cruise.

My nerves kick into high gear as I haul a bag containing a gun and handcuffs—among other things—onto a ship full of criminals and killers. No matter what happens, however, my focus must remain on Jim.

And not getting caught.

I glide into the atrium between a row of staff on either side of me. They clap their hands and smile as I make my grand entrance. Something looks a bit off about them, though. The smiles are too fake, and I don't mean the fake, sugary-sweet shit that normal cruise staff offer. These people look like they're the killers.

Is that the game? Are the staff the actual killers and the unwitting guests are their victims?

I keep my eyes wide open as I look around the spacious entry. It's your typical atrium, with grandiosity in every direction. The parquet floors gleam as sunlight pours through a wall of glass. A grand chandelier hangs above everything like some illuminated goddess. Luxury furniture in shades of pale blues and silvers dot the expensive paisley rugs.

An elderly couple stands beside one of the couches. The wiry man's gray hair pokes out around his head, and despite being on a cruise in Florida, he's wearing a gray suit. The woman, on the other hand, is dressed more casually. Her khaki shorts and loud Hawaiian shirt scream tourist. These people don't look like killers at all.

But then again, they rarely do. That's how they get away with it.

I approach the couple and offer them a smile, choosing to give my attention to the woman. Women find other women less intimidating when they steer their gaze away from the man they possess. It's basic psychology.

"It's a nice day for a cruise. Where have you two flown in from?" I ask.

The woman looks up at me and says nothing.

"I'm down from Ohio," I offer, hoping she'll open up if I do. Even though my cover story is a complete lie. "I just got out of a bad breakup and figured an adults-only cruise was just the way to break out of my shell again."

The woman turns away from me, grabs the man's hand, and looks into his eyes.

The man nods, then looks at me. "We are sorry for your breakup. Please do not speak to us again."

With that, the pair turns and meanders toward the other

end of the room, where they continue standing around. Serial killers are typically charismatic, which is how they disarm their victims. I can definitely scratch these two off the list.

A man approaches from my left. He's tall, well-muscled, and a pair of black frames perch on his nose. There's something hauntingly familiar about his face, but I can't put my finger on it.

"Excuse me," he says in the smoothest British accent I've ever heard. "The staff at the front are new, and it appears they forgot to remind you about your wristband. It's very important that everyone wears them while on the ship."

"Oh, right!" I lower my bag and dig around in a side pocket until I find the purple wristband. As I fasten the silicone strip around my arm, I realize it locks in place and can't be removed. "Do I have to wear this for the entire cruise?"

He checks my band, then smiles. "Yes. My name is Ezra Carter, and if you'll just come with me . . ." He turns and begins to walk away.

Gripping my bags once more, I follow the strange man further into the ship. His name doesn't ring any alarm bells, but I still keep my wits about me as we travel down a brightly lit hallway and end up at an elevator.

"Hold your band against the sensor." He motions toward the metal plate where the call buttons usually are. The plate is smooth and devoid of any buttons, depressions, or features at all.

I step forward and press my band to the metal, and a bell dings overhead. Seconds later, the elevator doors swing open.

"You're a VIP. To travel to the less accessible areas of

the ship, you'll need that band." The man—Ezra—steps inside the elevator, then motions for me to join him. Once I do, he leans forward and taps a button.

"Where are we headed?" I ask.

Ezra pushes his hands into his pockets and rocks on his heels, but he says nothing.

My stomach lurches as the elevator comes to a stop and spits us out in another hallway. The lights here are much dimmer, and the whites and silvers have been traded for dark woods and moody metals.

A bald man with a massive mustache wanders toward us. When he sees the man beside me, he smiles and raises his hand in a wave. When he sees me, he stops in his tracks and licks his lips.

"You got dibs on this one too?" the man asks.

Ezra shakes his head. "No, Ice. Kindra is the only one to lay claim to my heart, but that doesn't mean you can sexually harass every beautiful woman who joins our court. Have you tried masturbation?"

"I'm Frankie. Nice to meet you." I hold my hand toward him and offer a smile, then snatch back my hand when Ezra's question registers. It doesn't matter that I've used my real name. My birth certificate, social security card, and driver's license all say something different. I'm actually less discoverable if I use my biologic information.

Plus, it's easier to remember. You can't fuck up the truth, right?

As the bald man steps closer and takes my hand, I realize I've already forgotten his name. "On shanty, I'm sure," he says as he kisses my fingers.

"That's *enchanté*, you nit," Ezra says. "Follow me, Frankie, and I'll show you to your room."

The bald man looks so dejected as Ezra plucks my hand

from his and leads me down yet another hallway. I'm liable to get lost on this ship, what with all its twists, turns, and secret elevators.

My heart picks up speed as he stops in front of a cherry-stained door. He directs me to use my wristband on the door panel, so I do, and the door's lock clicks open.

I step inside and look around. The room is large—far larger than any cruise I've ever been on—and one massive white bed takes up a good chunk of the space.

"Do I have a presidential suite all to myself?" I ask as I turn to Ezra, but he's already gone. I step toward the doorway and look into the hall, but he's no longer anywhere. I hurry to close the door before the strange man with the mustache sneaks inside. Ice . . . something.

When I place my bag on the bed, I spy an envelope on the pillow. I snatch up the rectangular slip of paper and rip it open.

WELCOME TO THE BRUISE CRUISE!
PLEASE DRESS IN THE PROVIDED ATTIRE IN YOUR CLOSET AND MEET IN THE LOUNGE (DECK C) AT SIX P.M. SHARP. IF YOU DO NOT ATTEND, YOU WILL BE REMOVED FROM THE SHIP BEFORE WE SAIL TONIGHT.
ACCESSORIES AND REFRESHMENTS WILL BE PROVIDED. PLEASE ONLY BRING YOURSELVES.

I hurry to the closet and rip it open. Inside, two black garment bags hang from a rod. The name Maverick has been written across the tag on the first bag. I guess that's my roommate, though I don't know how I feel about rooming with a strange man who may also be a serial killer.

Not to mention sharing a fucking bed with him.

The second garment bag belongs to me, so I pull it from

the rack and carry it to the bed. After unzipping the bag, I reveal what I can only describe as a shiny silver hazmat suit, complete with a military-grade gas mask.

"What in the world . . . ?"

I pull the silver material from the bag and study the strange getup. This clearly wasn't manufactured by any official installation. None of the contractors we use would be caught dead crafting suits made from such a flashy material. And are those fucking rhinestones around the mask's blackened eye holes?

"At least it looks like it'll fit," I say as I hold the suit against my body. Now if I can just figure out why we're forced to dress like this.

I check my watch. It's late afternoon, so I have a little time to kill before I need to stuff myself into the mylar costume. Snooping around the ship would be a mistake, however. I know too little, and I'm more likely to fuck something up.

So I do the only thing I can. I sit on the bed and wait for my roomie to arrive.

Chapter Four

Maverick

The ship is immaculate. In true Jim fashion, he took a luxury cruise and made it even more luxurious. Most of the people aboard this ship don't even realize what's situated below deck, and they never will. If the Normies knew what was going on . . .

At least he gave everyone a wristband so that we can tell who's who at a glance. It wouldn't do for people to walk around in colored jumpsuits like we're some *Squid Game* knockoff. That would have drawn too much suspicion.

The Cattle wear their usual colors, though sometimes only on their wrists instead of their entire bodies—pink for the horrible pedos, red for the SA monsters, and yellow for the run-of-the-mill criminals. Purple is reserved for known killers, and orange signals someone as a member of staff. Blue is new. Blue means the wearer is a Normie.

Allowing normal people into our serial-killer retreat is risky. That's the understatement of the year. Granted, we thrive on risk, but still, inviting the Average Joe to wander so close to our secret doings is the most daring and dangerous thing we've done. Jim is either a genius or completely unhinged.

I guess we'll find out which one soon enough.

I spot Bennett a little further down the hallway. We've been tasked with ensuring the new arrivals wear their wristbands. Ezra was looped in as well, but his shift ended about an hour ago.

"We need to make sure none of the Normies catch a ride on the wrong elevator," Bennett says as he approaches me. "Two blue bands almost went to the Sinner suites because Grim and Rosie weren't paying attention."

I nod and look toward the elevators. The bands were a great idea, but they aren't without their flaws. "Jim should have kept the Sinner guest list closed to new applicants for this event. He still hasn't told me who I'm watching and why."

"Did you expect any fucking different? He's Jim. Secrets excite him more than murder, and that's saying something. If you want him to tell you something, you just have to act like you don't care. The more you ask him to tell you, the longer he'll make you wait." Bennett's watch beeps, and he looks down. "Our shift is over. Maybe you can figure it out when you meet your roommate."

"Yeah. Maybe."

Bennett glances at his watch again, then claps his hand on my shoulder. "Well, I'm off to check on Cat. She's already puked three times, and we aren't even at sea yet."

With that, he turns and heads toward the elevator.

Instead of following him, I take the stairs to the atrium. Bennett's advice is sound, and he's not incorrect, but I'd still feel better if I knew something about the stranger I have to sleep beside for the next week.

I don't spot Jim in the atrium, but I do see Ice Pick. He stands on the second floor, with his forearms draped over the balcony railing. In his right hand, he holds a beer. As he looks down, he gives me a little wave.

He's the only familiar face I see, so I start up the staircase. He's a bit of an odd guy, and I think there's some undiagnosed mental issues going on there, but he means well. I would say he's harmless, but his victims would disagree. He's just your typical lonely, middle-aged, awkward dude who enjoys killing people.

"Hey, Ice," I say as I approach him.

He raises his hand in a high-five, but I don't realize that's what it is until he's started to lower his arm. I thought it was another wave.

"You been to your room yet?" He takes a pull from the beer bottle in his hand. "Better yet, have you seen the dime piece that Ezra was showing around?"

"Dime piece?"

Ice Pick nods. "Yeah, total ten. Dark hair, blue eyes, and ass for days."

"You gonna go for her?"

"Me? Hell no." He laughs and drinks his beer. "Every time I try to put the moves on a chick, I end up pissing off one of my friends. First it was Ezra. Then it was Bennett. I'm steering clear this time."

"Don't give up on love, Ice. Your woman is out there. If you give up, you'll never find her."

He lets out a burp that smells like the inside of a cattle barn. "Maybe you're right. Thanks, Maverick."

"Anytime." I glance around the atrium, but I still don't see who I'm looking for. "I need to speak with Jim. Have you seen him?"

"Last I saw, he was heading toward the kitchen to talk to

Maurice about tonight's menu. Being the first night and all, you know how particular he is about the dinner." He looks at his watch and whistles. "Speaking of, we'd best go to our rooms and get geared up."

"Geared up?"

Ice downs the rest of the bottle. "Yeah, no formal attire tonight. Jim wants us dressed like spacemen."

Before I can ask what he means, he turns, tosses his bottle into the trash, and heads for the stairs. I guess I'd better go to my room if I want answers to all of my questions.

Using the special elevator that only responds to purple and orange wristbands, I head toward the Sinners' accommodations. I follow the numbered doors until I reach mine, then swipe my band. The lock clicks open, and I step inside.

Darkness shrouds the room. The curtains have been drawn tight, and all the lights are off. I don't even have time to feel for the light switch as the door clicks shut behind me. Standing still, I allow my eyes to adjust to the shadows. Despite the heavy-duty blackout curtains, a bit of fading sunshine squeaks through the outer edges and provides a little light. It's enough for me to make out the outline of the bed.

And the figure snoring on top of it.

With the thick blankets piled over the sleeping form, I can't tell if it's a woman or a man. The person makes use of the entire king bed, however, so I can already tell that our sleeping arrangement is less than ideal. Hopefully, Jim has a cot or something I can crash on to avoid the arms and legs currently stretched over every inch of mattress.

As I step closer, the loud snores reach a crescendo and stop abruptly, almost as if the individual choked on their tongue. Meanwhile, I'm amazed they can sleep through their own sounds.

"Is someone there?" a feminine voice asks.

I raise my hand in a wave she likely can't see. "Sorry for the interruption. I'm your roommate. My name's—"

The light beside the bed clicks on, and a dark-haired woman squints up at me. Though she's fully clothed, she pulls the blanket around her chest as if she's naked.

"My name is Maverick. There's no need to panic." I hold out my hands and take a step back. She looks terrified.

Then she blinks, looks around, and seems to remember where she is. "Shit, am I late?"

"For dinner? No. We still have about thirty minutes. That's why I came to the room. One of my friends said we have to dress like space people, and I wanted to see what that was about."

She looks down at her bags and things strewn across the foot of the bed. "Jeez, where are my manners? Sorry about the mess." After tossing the blanket aside, she begins pushing her things to the floor. Then she holds her hand toward me as she kneels at the foot of the bed. "I'm Frankie."

I grip her hand in mine and give it a shake, taking note of the purple wristband on her slender arm. Questions fill my head. If she's one of us, why does Jim want me to keep tabs? And what does he hope to discover?

And why is she so goddamn beautiful?

"Frankie, huh?"

"It's short for Francesca. Despite being incredibly unfeminine, my mother chose the floweriest name she could think of."

"So that she could call you Frankie," I say with a shrug.

Her eyes light up. "Oh my gosh, I've never thought of that before."

She lets out a laugh that is the sweetest sound I've ever heard. She looks like she might be older than me, but not by much.

Despite her beauty, and despite the fact that we'll be forced to sleep in the same room, I have no plans to fall into the same pits my friends have. Ezra and Bennett came out of these retreats in relationships, and I don't have time for that.

Hell, the moment we get back on dry land after the cruise, we were all supposed to head to Texas in search of the missing Carter sister. Ezra found a woman fitting the description, and he wants to get some sneaky DNA before we confront her. Bennett can't go because he promised Cat he'd help her get ready for college, and Ezra can't go because he has to be Kindra's arm candy for an upcoming press event.

That leaves me, the last man standing.

"Your friend wasn't so off about the outfits for tonight, though," she adds. "Take a look for yourself. Yours is still hanging up."

I backtrack to the closet and pull the garment bag from inside. Sure enough, the outfit looks like something from a 1950s sci-fi nightmare. Frankie pulls hers out as well, and together, we stare at the abominations.

"Is this normal for one of these retreats? The weird suits, I mean." Frankie looks up at me.

"No, we're usually required to dress for dinner, especially the first and last nights, but never like this. I don't know what Jim has up his sleeve."

But we're about to find out.

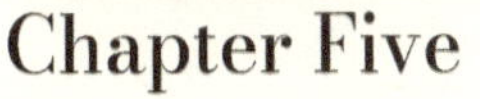

Chapter Five

Frankie

The purple wristband indicates a Sinner, which is code for a serial killer. The kind British man, the little elderly couple, and my handsome roommate all sport those purple bands, and I can't rationalize any of that in my brain.

Nothing feels right about this. That's what I keep thinking as I walk behind Maverick. I expected to be uncomfortable around these people. I expected my sixth sense to ping off the charts in the presence of serial killers. The reality is much different.

Maverick stops in front of the elevator and swipes his wristband over the metal plate. The elevator doors swish open soon after. We step inside, and he leans forward to press the button with a large glowing C in its center. My stomach lurches as the elevator car drops.

"So, what's your killer name?" Maverick asks. The gas mask muffles his words, making him difficult to understand. "I'm the Midnight Masochist."

"I'm the Fisher," I say with a little too much confidence.

Maverick's gas mask turns toward me. "The Fisherman?"

Drat. I've been alone with this man for less than an hour, and I've already made a misstep. I really need to be more careful. "Yes, the Fisherman. That's what I said. The mask . . . muffled it."

He shifts his weight between his feet and clears his throat, but he doesn't pry any further. Thank fuck. I had to memorize my cover story on the flight to Miami, and I made sure I picked the most obscure killer I could find. The online resources were few and far between, and something's wrong with the Wi-Fi on the ship, so I'm running on memory.

Thankfully, I don't need to utilize the Fisherman's MO. Our inside source explained that many of these killers choose to explore other avenues of murder while they're at the retreat. I can only hope I won't have to use any methods of violence at all. Despite being a government agent, killing isn't really in my wheelhouse. I'm not inclined to start now.

The elevator stops, and the doors open once more. We step into another dark hallway, and I'm beginning to see a trend. Silvers, whites, and other bright colors fill the areas for the average guests, and darker woods and moodier colors suffuse the serial killers' spaces. The strong visual differences make it much easier to discern what's what, and it definitely feels like two different worlds on the same ship.

Maverick looks around, but he seems to know as much as I do. No one else lingers in the hallway, and no signs point us in the direction of the lounge. Despite being thin, the hoods attached to our suits muffle all sound. If there's some sort of party going on nearby, I can't hear it.

A flash of silver emerges from a door behind Maverick,

and I tap his shoulder and point that way. He gives me a thumbs-up, and we head toward the other figure. Noticing us, the person waves and motions us toward the door.

Maverick begins talking with the stranger as we draw closer. They seem to know each other, which is all well and good for them, but I just want to see what's in the next room.

I mentally kick myself for not grabbing any of my gear before this first major event. My button cameras would have come in handy, and my service pistol would have put me more at ease. Though, I'm not sure how at ease one can be when you're trapped at sea on a ship filled with murderers.

As the men talk, I push open the door and step into the lounge. The name is apt, as the space looks like a stereotypical upscale jazz lounge. A small stage faces a cluster of tables, many of which already have silver-clad bodies seated in their chairs.

I step into the sea of tables and realize there are name placards at each setting. Ezra, Kindra, Cat, and Bennett are seated together, whoever they are. I only recognize the British man's name. After wandering through the rows, I finally find my name at the central table, right in front of the stage. And then I realize why I'm in such an important position in the room.

I'll be seated at a table with Jim Madigan.

Maverick and someone named Aven will also be seated with us, but it doesn't matter. This setup puts me directly inside Jim's circle, and that's all I need. An opening.

I slide into my chair and tap my gloved nails on the table as I look around the room. More silver figures fill the space with each passing second, and after a few minutes, nearly every table is fully occupied. I do some quick math in my head and determine there are roughly thirty killers seated in this room. The group is larger than King and Castle anticipated, but not me.

When I first heard about these retreats, I figured that—

"Excuse me, is this seat taken?"

I turn my head and face the source of the twangy Southern voice. "Oh, I think the seats are assigned, but you're welcome to hang out until the rest of my table arrives." I offer the man a smile he can't see, but I have to go through the motions. It's more convincing this way.

"We switch seats all the time at these things. I take it you're new? My name's Ice P . . . I think we met in the hall." His suit muffles the end of his name as he reaches across the table and grips Jim's name card, clearly intending to swap it for his own.

I lean forward and swat his hand without thinking. It's an instinctual reaction to the panic swirling through my guts. "Sorry, but I'd prefer to follow the host's intended seating arrangements. Being new, I'd hate to ruffle feathers. You understand, don't you?"

"Oh, sorry. I'm being too pushy again, ain't I?" He raises his hands to his gas mask and covers his "eyes" with his gloves. "I really suck at flirting. No matter what I do, women don't like me."

"Well, my rejection has nothing to do with you," I say. "In my line of work, relationships are sort of frowned upon, so I steer clear of flirtations. Maybe you're just picking the wrong sort of women."

"What do you mean?" He drops into Maverick's seat and leans forward, clearly enraptured by the topic at hand. "I don't really *pick* anything. It happens with all women. Skin color, body type, personality—I'm not picky at all."

I feel bad for the guy. I truly do. But I'm on a mission here, and this man's relationship woes aren't very high on my list of priorities. He's creating a distraction, and the last thing I need is something that takes my eyes off the prize.

"Listen . . . Ice Pig, I'd love to help you, but I'm the last person you should come to for relationship advice. I would rather step inside a church and risk bursting into flames than watch a romantic chick flick. I would sooner skinny dip in a lake of sulfuric acid than go on a blind date. Frankie and romance are like oil and water."

Ice Pig's shoulders seem to droop as his gas mask bobs up and down. "Okay, well . . . thanks anyway, Frankie. I'm really sorry I bothered you."

As he slinks away, guilt grips my lungs and squeezes. I feel like shit for running him off, but I wasn't lying when I said I fucking hate romance. Yeah, maybe that's because I'm jealous of the people who get to experience it, but I have an amazing career. My bed may be empty, but my heart is filled.

Mostly.

I turn in my seat and look toward the open doorway. A few silver suits mill about in the hallway, and a few more hover near the bar. We haven't been instructed to take off our masks, so I can only assume they're patiently waiting for the go-ahead.

The room darkens further, and the muffled voices drop to whispers as a spotlight illuminates the dark stage. Four people are led onto the stage by a person in a suit like mine, but it's all black instead of silver. The four people wear similar but different-colored suits as well. One is pink, one is red, and one is yellow. The fourth suit looks like an oil slick, with an array of colors gleaming on the metallic material. All of their ankles have been cuffed, and they're held together via a daisy chain that's also bolted to the floor.

The tall man in the black suit removes his gas mask, revealing his face. It's Jim Madigan.

"Sinners, please keep your masks in place for the time being," he says as he strolls to the front of the small stage. His voice booms through overhead speakers, so he must be wearing a mic. "We'll eat and drink and be merry very soon, but first, I wanted to provide a little pre-dinner entertainment and a hint at our secret game."

Spit gathers under my tongue, and a wave of unease moves over me. It's a collective feeling, shared by others in the room, and it charges the air.

Something isn't right.

I've never been to one of these retreats, and we don't have any intel on what occurs, but this isn't how things are usually done. I feel this more than I know it, but either way, I trust it. My anxiety blossoms for a very different reason, but I'm not the only one who feels it.

"By now, most of you know of the scavenger hunt I've arranged among the Normies," he continues, "but did you know there are other scavenger hunts to be had?"

He steps up to the first person in the line—a tall figure in a red suit. Jim lowers the red hood, then removes the gas mask to reveal a terrified man. Dried blood gathers around threads that hold his lips together. They've stitched his mouth shut.

I should be horrified. Disgusted. Completely aghast.

But I'm not.

I'm intrigued, and I can't tear my eyes away from the fear in that man's gaze. He knows his time on this earth is very limited, as is evidenced by the puddle of piss forming at his feet.

"Here we have a sad little man who thought it would be fun to slip drugs into a woman's drink before assaulting and strangling her." Jim smiles at the man. "You were due to get out of jail in a few months, weren't you?"

Tears stream from the man's eyes as he nods.

"Do you feel you've served enough time? You've only been in prison for what, twelve years?"

The man's eyes clench shut. He doesn't know how to answer. Not honestly, anyway. I'm certain he feels he's served enough time, but he doesn't know what answer is expected of him here.

"Kill him!" someone shouts, and a few other muffled voices offer the same sympathies.

"All in good time," Jim says to the crowd. He strolls to the next in line and pulls away the pink hood before looking out at us again. "How do we feel about child predators?"

The room fills with boos, and I join them. We can agree that these people are disgusting at the very least. It's too bad we can't agree on how to handle them.

Jim pulls off the mask and reveals an older woman with a short black bob. "She owned a daycare and thought it would be a good idea to line her pockets with the pain of her small charges. Millions of sick individuals tuned in for the abuse perpetrated at her hands. Should she die as well?"

The room fills with a loud cheer, and the woman collapses on stage. Jim steps to the side so that he doesn't slow her descent, and her head cracks against the stage floor.

"Whoopsie!" Jim says with a laugh. "I guess she's not used to being the one in the spotlight." He steps over her prone body and stops beside the yellow suit.

I'm seeing a trend here. Everyone on the stage was chosen for a particularly heinous crime. Sexual assault. Child predation. But what could yellow mean? Or iridescent? Surely they don't take down fellow murderers. What sense would that make?

Jim peels back the yellow hood and strips off the gas mask to reveal another woman. Blood coats her chin, and her lips are in tatters. Thin strips of skin dangle where she's ripped out the stitching.

"I'm not like those criminals!" the woman screeches. "Tax fraud! And I scammed some people, but that's it. I never hurt women or children."

Jim brings his finger to his lips, encouraging the woman to be quiet. Surprisingly, she listens.

Like some macabre game-show host, he turns to face the crowd once more. "She has a point, people. I mean, tax fraud?" His shoulders rise in a shrug. "Does she really deserve to be subjected to some of the horrific things we do to our victims?"

Mutters and mumbles fill the silence, followed by the shuffle of fabric as dozens of silver suits shift uncomfortably in their seats.

"No, she doesn't deserve it," a female voice calls from the back of the room.

"Ah, the Confessor," Jim says. "The crime is important to you, isn't it?"

"Yes, it's very important. I think it's important to most of us."

"So should we let this woman keep her gas mask?" Jim looks at the woman, who's been reduced to a quivering, crying blob. Snot slides into the lip wounds, and I want to puke.

Something shuffles behind me, and two silver-clad beings take a seat on either side of my chair as Jim and the Confessor continue to debate. The one on my left is Maverick, so the body to my right must belong to Aven.

"Enjoying the show so far?" Maverick asks, and I nod.

I am not.

The second figure—Aven—leans closer. "I'm a first-timer too. My name's Aven. Nice to meet you." He holds his hand toward me, and I shake it, noting the Scottish accent. "I spoke to Jim earlier, and he let it slip that the fourth person on the stage is going to be a doozy. I didn't want to miss it."

Biting my lip behind the safety of the gas mask, I turn my attention back to Jim. He's finished debating with the Confessor, and it appears he's going to let the yellow-clad woman live. After securing her mask and hood once more, he steps up to the final figure.

And as he pulls back the hood and mask, I want to scream.

It's Castle.

Chapter Six

Maverick

I don't know what game Jim is playing. Getting him alone before he had to go on stage was a near impossibility, and why I've been tasked with watching Frankie remains a mystery. But I'm beginning to get an idea.

She isn't one of us, that much is clear. When she told me her killer name—the Fisherman—I knew she was full of shit. The Fisherman died on Devil Horn Island several years ago. That's why the bridge is known as Fisherman's Bridge. What I don't know is *why* she lied, and I'm sure that has something to do with what I'm tasked with finding out. Or maybe it has something to do with whatever Jim is doing on stage right now. Not to mention, this is the first I'm hearing about a scavenger hunt.

"I wonder what this man has done," Jim says as he walks around the iridescent suit.

Unlike the other three, this figure shows no signs of fear. He stands like a soldier, tall and proud, with his shoulders pulled back. His eyes glare straight ahead.

Frankie fidgets beside me. She's either excited or uneasy about the impending kills, but either way, she can't keep still. Her feet shuffle under her chair, and her gloved hands grip the sides of the seat as she twists and writhes in her skin. Her gas mask turns toward me, and the fidgeting stops. She folds her hands in her lap and looks away from me again.

Interesting.

Back on stage, the man is still doing his best to look unaffected as Jim strolls around him and talks about parasites hiding among the wolves who hide among the sheep. The Normies are the sheep. We are the wolves. But who the fuck are the parasites?

The room falls deathly silent as we all tune-in to Jim's frequency.

"They want to take us down from the inside because the laws they've created to protect themselves have protected some of us as well. They want proof of our crimes more than they want their next breath, so I've chosen to deny them the latter." Jim's smile shifts from amused to satanic as he looks into the crowd. "Everyone, please ensure your masks are securely fashioned, and enjoy the show!"

"Entry of the Gladiators" blasts through overhead speakers as Jim lowers his mask, raises his hood, and hurries off the stage. Once he's seated with us at the table, the lounge lights cut out completely, giving the stage all the glory.

Beside me, Frankie's head twists on a swivel. As everyone else stares straight ahead and waits for the chaos to begin, she looks around . . . for what?

A loud bang reverberates overhead, and someone screams. I'm pretty sure it was Cat. Confetti rains down on the stage, followed by a loud hissing sound. The bang came from the confetti cannons, but that hissing . . .

The woman who collapsed earlier chooses a pretty terrible time to wake up. Her eyelids flutter open as a fluorescent-green gas overtakes the stage. The stoic soldier on the end doesn't lose his nerve. He keeps standing, staring out into the darkness as he welcomes death.

For nearly thirty seconds, nothing else happens. The Cattle in the red suit tries to get off stage, but the chain securing their legs together also secures him to the floor. He can't take more than a few steps before he's brought to a halt. With his hands bound behind his back, he can't even stop himself as he falls to the floor. Like the woman beside him, his head cracks against the wood, though I doubt anyone in the back heard it. The music is still so loud.

Speaking of the music, it's shifted to a softer part of the song. Two figures in orange PPE gear wander onto the stage and douse the four Cattle in a cloud of glitter shot from packs on their backs. They spin to the beat of the song, adding to the show.

Frankie leans closer to me and shouts, "What the actual fuck is happening right now? Are we supposed to kill them?"

"I don't think so," I shout back, though I'm not entirely sure what's happening. I can't remember Jim ever bringing government employees onto the killing fields, but it seems that's what he's hinting at with the fourth vic. He's either a cop, a fed, or, as I suspect, a soldier.

Is that why he wants me to keep a close eye on this woman? It would explain why she got so fidgety when the fourth Cattle was revealed. Is this part of Jim's scavenger hunt? She must be one of them too.

A loud retching sound comes from the stage, right as a

large hoop drops from the ceiling. Where the fuck did Jim find a criminal aerialist? But then the orange-clad figure tries its first high-flying maneuver, and down they go. They land on the stage in a writhing heap, and no one goes to check on them. We're all too busy laughing.

The retching sound returns, but it's doubled this time. Red Cattle and Pink Cattle sit up on their knees and gag until the blood vessels burst in their faces. Seconds later, Red Cattle vomits a puddle onto the stage that matches the color of his suit. Blood and thick chunks of pink material filter through the stitches.

The entire time, Soldier Cattle stands like a statue, and then I realize why. He's holding his breath.

Red Cattle finally collapses and begins seizing as Pink coughs up a chunk of lung. Literally. Instead of coming through the stitches, however, the chunks fly from her nose. She looks into the crowd, and several people cheer when she collapses onto her face.

Jim claps his hands and turns toward me, then points at the stage. He says something, but I can't hear him over the song. He smacks his knee and doubles over, laughing at the joke only he heard.

Back on stage, Red has stopped moving and Pink has begun convulsing. A frothy pink foam spills from her mouth as her legs thrash and spin her body in a circle on the stage. When the chain catches, she just lies there and jerks.

I look back at the soldier, who was forced to take a breath halfway through the song. The glitter brigade pumps one more sparkling cloud into his face, then hurries off the stage. I wait and I watch, but by the end of the song, he's still standing.

"Well, this won't do," Jim says as the music fades away. He

rises from his seat and climbs onto the stage again. After stepping over the two bodies—both of which are now still—he skips past the Yellow Cattle and goes straight for the soldier. "I had my scientists work for months on a new nerve gas, and you've defeated it by holding your breath. This won't do at all."

I chuckle to myself. When Jim killed that doctor who was abusing his elderly patients, he inherited the man's entire legacy via a bit of legal sleight of hand. That came with the care homes and an entire scientific branch. He kept the teams that were working on cures for cancer, but he added a new team of his own to work on highly illegal chemical agents. Now we know why.

Jim places his hand above his gas mask, as if he's shielding his eyes from the sun, and "looks" into the crowd. "Frankie? Where are you, dear child? You're new here, and I'd *love* to give you the honors."

I turn to look at Frankie, but her chair is empty. She's no longer seated beside me, and even if she's somewhere in the room, I'd never know. Not with all these gas masks.

"She went to the restroom," I shout, and I don't know why I'm covering for her. Especially not when Jim already knows the score. Hell, he knows more than I do at this point.

Jim's mask slants as he tilts his head. "Did she, now? Well, then I guess we'd better put the games on pause for the time being. We'll get this Yellow Cattle trained for staff work, and we'll send this other fellow back to the brig." He turns toward the soldier. "For now."

A few workers in orange suits and gas masks hurry onto the stage. Some drag the dead bodies away, while the others lead the two living Cattle off stage right.

"As for the rest of you," Jim says, "please exit into the

hall, strip out of your suits, and meet us in the Sinners' dining room in fifteen minutes."

The lights click on, and I file out of the lounge with everyone else. Once we're in the hall, Ice Pick is the first to strip out of the suit. I think the rest of us are a bit nervous about the potential for immediate death.

"You'll all be just fine," Jim says as he joins us. He's already removed his mask. "In reality, there was no need for the suits at all. It was all for show. Red and Pink were injected with a substance several hours ago, and that substance reacted with the gas we released."

Cat rips off her mask. "You mean to tell me that I've been suffering in all these shitty fucking textures for *nothing*?"

Fabric rustles, and annoyed grumbles fill the air as everyone begins undressing. Everyone except Bennett. He only takes off his mask as Jim tootles to another group of people.

"Aren't you ready to get out of these hot suits?" I ask Bennett.

His cheeks flame red, but he doesn't answer me.

Cat chuckles as she steps out of the suit and kicks it away from her. "Mister Genius over here thought he'd go commando under the suit, so now he's forced to wear it to dinner."

"It was hot, okay?" Bennett starts down the hall toward the dining room, and Cat follows him.

I shake my head and go back to the task at hand. Once the shiny suit is on the floor, I turn and spot Frankie a few feet away. The mask is off, and her face is a few shades paler, but she's still wearing the hideous outfit.

"You can take that off now," I say as I step closer.

She looks down at her outfit and seems to remember

where she is. "Oh, right." After gripping the first glove, she stops and looks at me. "Are we sure it's safe? Nerve gases can remain effective by—"

"It wasn't just a nerve gas. It required a catalyst. That's why Yellow and the solider didn't die."

"The soldier?"

I mentally kick myself for calling the guy by the nickname I coined in my mind. "Yeah, that guy on the end. He held his breath and looked into the face of death like a soldier. Well, he spit in the face of death. That's more accurate."

"He didn't die?"

I shake my head and notice when she seems to breathe a sigh of relief. I thought she was thrown off by the nickname, but in reality, she was only concerned with his fate. Something is definitely off here.

She grips the zipper and lowers it, completely unaware that I'm beginning to suspect her. And that's good. If I want to discover whatever it is Jim wants me to discover, she needs to think I'm on her side.

"Here, let me help you with that." I step closer to her. "Hold on to me so you don't fall. The fabric kind of clings to your legs."

She unfastens the straps securing the pants around her ankles, then stands and grips my shoulders. I'm a fairly tall man, and she's a fairly short woman, but never in my life has a woman seemed so delicate and small as she stands before me. Like something I need to protect.

Fiercely.

Then she nibbles her bottom lip as she tries to pull her legs free, and I have to look away. When she does cute shit like that, it makes me want to protect her even more. And something tells me that's a horrible feeling to have.

If she's a cop—or worse—then I need to keep a safe distance.

Once she's out of her spacesuit, we start down the hallway. Most everyone has already undressed and headed toward the food, but a few people still struggle with their suits. I don't recognize any of them, and my suspicion grows as I study each face. How many "soldiers" did Jim let into our midst?

"Ah, Maverick! Just the man I wanted to see," Jim shouts as he spots us coming down the hall. He leaves his post beside the dining room door and comes toward us, grabbing Frankie's hands as he reaches us. "Dear girl, I hate that you missed the grand finale of the first event. We'll have to do better next time, hmm?"

Frankie smiles up at him, completely unbothered by his little jab. "Sorry about that. I have a tiny bladder, even for a woman, and I have to listen when nature calls."

"It's okay, dear. Just hurry inside and find your seat, and we'll be along shortly." He smiles and rocks on his heels, holding his hands behind his back as he waits for her to walk away.

She looks back at me, and that's when I know that she sees me as her lifeline. Which is exactly what Jim intended.

"He'll be seated right beside you, not to worry," Jim says with a smile when he notices her hesitation.

Frankie's head jerks back toward the dining room, and then she hurries inside. I go to follow her, but Jim grabs my arm.

"Just a moment. A word, if you will." With his grip still firmly fastened around my bicep, he drags me away from the doorway. We don't stop until we're far enough that not even a listening device could hear us. "You have a special mission on this retreat," he whispers.

"So I've heard."

"Oh, don't be annoyed with me. Isn't it more fun this way?"

I raise an eyebrow. "No, not really."

Jim scoffs and folds his arms over his chest. "Would you prefer I give the assignment to someone else? I'm sure Ice Pick would be more than happy to trade rooms."

"No, I can do it." My agreement comes a little quickly, so I dial it back. "I'm not happy about it, but I can do it. It would be helpful if I knew what *it* was, however."

"I knew you'd see sense." He clamps his arm over my shoulder and leans closer. "All you have to do is convince the girl that we aren't so bad."

"So I'm correct to assume that she's part of some sort of legal agency that could bring everything crashing down around us?"

"Yes, son. You have the long and short of it, as it were. She's a fed, but I don't just want you to keep an eye on her. I want you to convince her that we aren't worth the paper our warrants would be printed on."

"Feds? As in multiple?"

Jim nods.

"How many?"

"The exact numbers aren't important, but—"

"How many, Jim?"

He drops his arm from my shoulder, shakes his head, and sighs. "Five of the Cattle, four of the Sinners, and one of the Normies."

"Ten total?" My eyes widen.

"Eleven, when you count your little stowaway."

"You want us to convince eleven federal agents that serial killers aren't *so bad*? Jim, have you lost your fucking mind?"

Jim looks around as if someone might have heard me, but we're the only people in the hall now. "Keep your voice down, and no, I don't expect the others to be convinced of anything. Only Frankie. The rest are for the Sinners to find and dispose of."

"This is insanity."

He smiles. "Isn't it glorious?"

"No, not really. How do you expect me to convince her we're the good guys? You just put one of her people on stage in front of her, and I'm pretty sure she knew it."

"She has to know the truth of who we are, Maverick. She can't be convinced with tricks and deception. If she's going to accept us for who we must be, she has to know exactly what we do."

"Why? Why this woman?"

"Just keep her safe and bring her around to our way of thinking. That's your mission, and this is your final chance to hand it to someone else."

I stuff my hands into my pockets and stare down at the black carpet. Keeping her safe won't be an issue, but am I really the person to convince someone that murder is okay?

"Fine. I'll do it."

Jim claps his hands together. "That's my boy! After dinner, we'll participate in our first activity. Make sure she's in your group."

Before I can ask anything else, he starts toward the dining room, leaving me in the hallway, alone and confused.

Chapter Seven

Frankie

Gripping the edge of the porcelain sink, I try not to vomit up the suspicious-tasting meat I had for dinner. The dark-haired woman beside me tried to encourage me toward the veal, stating the option I chose —honey-basted man—wasn't a misprint. What I received definitely wasn't ham, so I have to believe her now.

I close my eyes until the wave of nausea passes. This wasn't mentioned during any briefing I've ever been to. I thought this job would be a cakewalk, but it's becoming increasingly clear that I'm in over my head.

A light tap comes through the bathroom door, followed by Maverick's voice. "Everything okay? You've been in there for a while, and I haven't heard you retching for several minutes. You didn't die, did you?"

I push the door open and look up at him.

He clears his throat. "No offense, but you look a little . . . Maybe we should skip the games tonight."

"I know how I look. After eating human body parts, I look how I feel, and I feel like shit."

I struggle to my feet, push past him, and go to the bed, where I flop down and regret ever boarding this ship. This is the closest I've come to living in a nightmare.

"Here, drink this." Maverick holds a cold bottle of water toward me, and I take it. At least one of the monsters in my nightmare is kind. And dangerously good-looking.

"Do all of you eat human meat? Maybe I'm just weird, but I've never felt the urge." I twist off the bottle's cap and chug the cold liquid.

Maverick sits on the edge of the bed. "No, most of us prefer to eat normal stuff. The chef is just . . ." He shakes his head. "If we aren't going to the game, I'm going to head to the lobby to—"

"We are definitely going to the game. I didn't come all this way to spend my time in the cabin." I place the empty bottle on the bedside table and lean back on the pillows. In reality, I'd love nothing more than to skip their sick games. Perhaps it isn't too late to leap from the side of the ship and swim to shore. "When are we due to set sail?"

Maverick glances at the bedside clock. "The Bruise Cruise officially pulled out of port around an hour ago."

My heart sinks. "Seriously? I didn't feel a thing."

"The stabilizers on these ships are pretty state-of-the-art. Unless we hit some very rough seas, you shouldn't feel much of anything." He turns and looks at me, and only now do I notice just how green his eyes are. Seafoam and glitters of gold swirl around his black pupils. "Are you sure you're okay to go to the games?"

I get off the bed and step toward my bag, if for no other reason than to put a little more space between us. Looking into his eyes is the only game I need to avoid.

"I told you, I'm fine. Stop mothering me. What with our age difference, it should be the other way around." I pull a t-shirt and jeans from the bag. "How should I dress for this event? Is there some sort of app to tell me what we'll be doing?"

Maverick steps around the bed, putting himself in my personal bubble again. "Hang on. Back up to what you said before that. You can't be more than five or six years my senior."

"How old are you?"

"Twenty-two."

I smirk. "I'm thirty-eight. That's a sixteen-year age difference, and I'd say that's pretty substantial. But only if we were trying to fuck—"

"Which we aren't," we say in unison.

That moment breaks the surface tension, and we finally laugh. I'm glad we're on the same page about that. Now if I could just get my fucking vagina to think rationally . . .

"If Jim doesn't tell us, we can just wear whatever we want," Maverick says.

"So he doesn't micro-manage every aspect?"

Maverick shakes his head, but his short blond hair doesn't budge from the styled hard part. Does he use product? "Nah, he mostly lets us have free rein. He's only funny about the first and last nights. Usually."

An opening presents itself, so I take it.

"Could you spin around while I change?" I ask, and he does. Personally, I could give two shits about my modesty, but I want to gauge his body language when he answers me, and that's easier to do when he isn't looking directly at me when I'm looking directly at him. "Tell me a little more about Jim. What does he do when he isn't organizing retreats for serial killers?"

His shoulders rise and fall in a shrug. "Nothing much to tell. We don't know a lot about him." He pauses, then clears his throat. "Look, I know this is your first retreat, but we don't exactly have sharing circles where we talk about ourselves outside of these events. I'm afraid I won't have much info on most of these people, if that's what you're looking for."

"Sorry, I wasn't trying to pry. Just trying to make conversation while I strip directly behind a stranger."

He turns to face me. "Would you feel more comfortable if I stepped into the hall?"

"I would feel more comfortable if you didn't turn around when my tits are out." I scramble to put on my t-shirt, which is a bit too baggy and hangs off my shoulder, but I'm not really bothered that he turned around. The fact that his eyes never strayed below my chin is a little annoying, though.

He smiles and turns to face the door again. "My apologies."

The uneasy feeling returns, and my heart picks up speed. He didn't appreciate me sniffing so close to Jim, and by saying they don't really talk much at these things, he was quick to put an end to all future questions about anyone at all.

As I fasten the button and raise the zipper on my shorts, I make a mental note to grab my gun while Maverick is asleep tonight. I'll feel a lot less jumpy once my gear is close at hand. I'm essentially walking around naked, and that's making me anxious. Without my service pistol, badge, and other tools of my trade, I have only my brain, and that bitch is betraying me at every turn.

"Okay, you can turn around now," I say once I'm dressed.

He faces me and gives me a once over before uttering a low whistle. "You dress down good, sweetheart," he says with a laugh, and that little pet name makes my heart flutter.

"It's still better than the space costume."

"I dunno. Before, your face was covered up. Now we all have to look at it. Gross." He makes a gagging face, and I swat his arm. "I'm kidding, I'm kidding. You look . . ."

As he hesitates and searches for the appropriate word, I hang on that pause. Will he go the safe route and say I'm cute? Or will he try flattery and tell me I'm beautiful?

"You look really familiar, now that I think about it." His eyebrows pull together, and he leans closer. This went in a direction I didn't anticipate, but okay. "I can't put my finger on it, but I feel like we've met somewhere before. Do you spend any time in Florida?"

I shake my head.

"New York City?"

I shake my head again, though I actually spend a good bit of time in the Big Apple.

He squints and studies my face, then steps back. "No big deal. I'll figure it out eventually, but we need to get going. You ready?"

"I need to freshen up a bit, but you can go on ahead. I'm sure I can find my way around."

He nods and heads into the hall, leaving me alone in the room. I step into the bathroom and run a brush through my hair, then dab a bit of matte lipstick on my lips. The corner of my mouth rises in a smirk as I recall him thinking we were closer in age. I may be pushing forty, but I've still got it.

The bags under my eyes can't be helped, however. I

need an entire night of restful sleep, and that isn't likely to happen until I retire. Which I will never willingly do.

I shove my things away in a small bag and join Maverick in the hall. He stands beside a shorter man with dark hair and eyes as blue as mine. When the man notices me, his lips push together, and the whispers stop.

"Sorry to interrupt," I say. "Is it time for the next game now?"

"I'll let you two get on with it," the man says. He nods toward me with a pinched smile, then turns and strides down the hallway.

"Who was that?" I ask, hoping the question sounds innocuous enough to his ears.

"Just Bennett."

"What's his killer name?"

Maverick's green eyes pin my feet to the floor. "Why do you want to know?"

"Curiosity," I say.

When he takes a step closer, my feet still refuse to cooperate. "You're curious, huh?"

I nod. "Yeah."

"You know the saying, don't you? Curiosity killed the cat." He stops and looks down at me, and I have never felt this small and inconsequential. "Satisfaction brought him back. What would it take to satisfy you?"

He means my curiosity, but my pussy doesn't get the memo. I nearly blurt out that about five minutes with his dick should do the trick, but my lips clamp shut before I can embarrass myself.

"There you are!" a woman shouts from down the hall, and we turn toward a tall beauty in a beige pantsuit. Gold jewelry shimmers on her fingers, and her makeup is so flawless that her face looks like a living photo filter. "Jim was able to arrange a flight a day early, so I didn't have to miss the first game. Just dinner."

Maverick pulls her in for a hug, then turns her toward me. "Frankie, this is—"

"Eve," I say. I hold my hand toward her and try to hide my shock when I spot her purple wristband. "I know who she is. My mother and I attended the show in Paris last spring."

Eve's dark eyes widen, and she smiles. "The show for Florenz Francesi? Wasn't Vlad's cape to die for?"

"The one made entirely from beach plastics?" I nod. "How does Francesi come up with that stuff?"

"Honey, I don't know, but the man is a genius. He's hosting another showing this winter, but it's by invitation only." Eve raises one perfectly sculpted eyebrow. "Lucky for you, I know a guy."

This woman is an icon. Even in the least fashion-forward circles, she's a household name. She's the face of numerous charities, including one for breast cancer research and another for victims of childhood abuse. Two years ago, she received international recognition for her humanitarian efforts in war-torn areas.

And she's a fucking *serial killer?*

"I hear it's a team game," Eve says as she slips her arm through mine and starts down the hall. "You and I *must* be on the same team. I won't have it any other way. The ladies have to stick together."

Footsteps join ours, and Maverick says, "Excuse me, but she's *my* roommate. If she'll be on anyone's team, it's mine."

"Chill, Casanova. I'm not trying to move in on your woman. I actually met someone recently." Eve turns her head so that she can look at Maverick. "Her name is Silo, and she can do some nasty things with her tongue."

"Silo?" Maverick asks. "What sort of name is that?"

Eve chuckles. "That's the kind of name you get when you go viral after stuffing an entire granary worth of corn inside your—"

"She didn't!" I say, and my eyes must be saucers. In reality, I've seen far stranger things in my line of work.

Eve flashes a knowing smile. "Oh, she did, and I got to witness it live. I doubt it will go anywhere, as neither of us is searching for something serious, but it's nice to have an orgasm provider on speed dial."

I wouldn't know what that's like. The only orgasms I've experienced have been from my own hand. Or the detachable showerhead. And once with a very girthy cucumber.

Don't judge me.

The three of us file into an elevator, and Maverick works the buttons to get us to the correct level, which is B this time. B for blood? Fuck, I hope not. When the elevator comes to a stop, we file out again.

We step into a hallway that must be for Sinners only, as the darker colors are present. The elderly couple from earlier walks several yards ahead of us. They stop in front of a pair of wooden doors, check the placard on the wall, then head inside.

That's our destination, but what will we have to do once we enter? There's only one way to find out, so I steel myself as Eve grips the doorknob and flings the door wide.

Chapter Eight

Maverick

Much like the lounge, tables litter the floor in front of a small stage in this room. The tables here are larger, however, and the lighting is much brighter. A microphone stands in the center of the stage. Behind it and to the right, something large and rounded at the top broods beneath a white sheet.

Eve plucks a blank name tag from a table against the wall beside the door. She bends at the waist to fill out her name, and Frankie follows suit. I look around the room and try to figure out what Jim has up his sleeve, but there isn't much to go on.

Bennett and Ezra catch my attention, and I start toward them, but then Jim appears out of nowhere and pulls me off to the side.

"How are you getting along with your charge?" he whispers.

I peer past his shoulder. Frankie hasn't noticed my absence as she peels the backing from her name tag and sticks it to her baggy shirt. She glances around once, but she doesn't seem to be looking for anyone in particular.

"We're getting along fine, but I don't understand this setup. Could you shed a little light?"

"All in good time." He pats my shoulder and smiles. "You'll hear more about the scavenger hunt shortly, but I need to be sure you understand that your little package is different from the rest. While the other flies in our potato salad can be squished, she must be protected. In fact, no one else can even suspect she's not one of us."

"Jim, they'll know. Hell, within the first few minutes of meeting her, she already fucked up her backstory. She said she was the Fisherman."

Jim winces and gives his head a half-shake. "Damn, that's a sorry business, but that's what you'll need to fix. Help her fit in."

My head turns toward him at a pace so slow that I feel the creak of every tendon in my neck. "You want me to help her . . . fit in. A fed. Amongst serial killers."

"Now you're catching on." He glances from side to side, then leans closer. "And if you can pull it off, if you can convince her that we aren't the droids she is looking for while convincing everyone else that she belongs, you'll receive a very handsome prize."

If he's insinuating an invitation to a sad pizza party in the basement of his island mansion, I'll pass. Still, the challenge will give me something to do while I'm here.

"Okay, Jim. I'm in."

"Glad to hear it. Now, there's just one little rule. Frankie can know that you know, but if anyone else finds out, the game is over."

I glance back at the table, where a few more participants

have gathered to fill out name tags. Eve and Frankie chat off to the side.

"Not even Eve?" I ask. "She's a close friend, and I trust her with my life."

"Not even Eve."

It's a tall ask, and I doubt I can pull this off, but I nod my head. "Okay, I think I've got it."

"Good, now go make sure she's on your team for tonight's festivities. I'd hate to think of what she might slip up and say if you aren't there to help her." He raises his eyebrows and looks over at the table. Cat and Kindra have joined the . . .

Cat and Kindra.

I rush away from a cackling Jim—the man lives to torture us, I swear—and hurry to the group of women. When Kindra notices me, she steps in front of me before I can reach Frankie.

"Where have you been hiding this enchanting woman?" Kindra asks as she points to Frankie. "First you hog all of Eve's time, and now you're determined to keep this one away from us as well? Maverick, sharing is caring."

I hold my hand toward Frankie and motion for her to come with me, but Cat swats my hand away.

"Back off, blondie. We're forming an all-girls team, and you can't steal one of the few pairs of tits in this sausage fest." Cat weaves her arm through Frankie's, and Eve does the same on the other side. "We only need one more, and I think I can convince Rosie to join us."

"Or," I drawl, "you could put me on your team and up your chances of winning. You don't know what Jim has planned."

"And you do?" Kindra asks. "Not even Ezra knew, and he's become Jim's party planner extraordinaire."

"Okay, no, I don't know what Jim has planned, but neither do you." I cock my head and wait for a response.

Eve places her hand on Kindra's arm. "He has a point, honey. If we want to win, we might benefit from having some male energy on the team. Besides, it looks like Rosie and Grim have already teamed up with your men."

We follow Eve's pointed finger to Bennett, Ezra, Grim, and Rosie, who have taken a seat at a table.

"He could always join them," Cat says. "They have an opening, and there are a few other women around here. Somewhere."

But then an unfamiliar man takes a seat beside Ezra.

"Oh, fuck it," Kindra says. "Maverick, welcome to the team. If we don't win, it's your fault."

"Noted," I say.

I scribble my name on a name tag, then peel the backing and stick it to my gray t-shirt. The girls start toward a table, and like a little pull-string puppy, I follow them. I take a seat between Cat and Frankie, but then I feel eyes on me. When I look across the room, Bennett is leveling me with a death glare.

"Frankie, could we swap seats?" I whisper, though I've leaned a little too close. When she turns her head to address me, our lips nearly touch.

She leans back to avoid the kiss of death, then nods. "Uh, yeah, sure."

Once we've swapped places, a hush falls over the room as Jim climbs the few stairs to the stage. From his inside pocket, he pulls a stack of notecards, then adjusts his tie. He clears his throat and steps up to the mic.

"Sinners, I'd once again like to welcome you to the Bruise Cruise. After the little show before dinner, several of you approached me with questions and concerns revolving around the scavenger hunt. I'm here to squash all the rumors and explain the game in detail."

He drones on for the next ten minutes about the scavenger hunt, and unease grows as we learn that there are multiple federal agents among us. Every rank has been invaded: Sinners, Cattle, Normies, and the crew. Our job is to find them and get rid of them without alerting the Normies on board.

Kindra's hand rises. "What if we fuck up and kill an actual newbie Sinner on accident?"

She brings up a good point. During past retreats, killing a fellow Sinner came with steep consequences, up to and including death. Jim's little plan sounds interesting, but there is a very large margin for error here.

Jim nods. "That's the unfortunate bit of business, but before dispatching a Sinner, a Normie, or a member of staff, you must first bring your suspicions to me. The members who drew the short straws and were doomed to become Cattle are destined for death, regardless. If they aren't killed during the games, they will be offered no quarter in my staff, I'm afraid."

Shuffling sounds come from under the table, and when Frankie's leg bumps mine, I realize she's causing the sound with her incessant fidgeting. She looks up at me with a sheepish smile, and once again, the fidgeting stops.

And it's no wonder she's fidgeting. Jim has just issued a death warrant for all of her pals, and she believes her name is on the list as well. I'm tasked with ensuring that doesn't happen, though.

But am I the only one?

I look around the room and study the unfamiliar faces. Have Ezra and Bennett been tasked with caring for a fed?

Cat, Kindra, and Eve? Are we all competing against each other?

I turn back to Frankie. If that's the game, I plan to win.

Leaning closer, I whisper in her ear. "For the rest of this cruise, don't leave my sight."

Her blue eyes widen, but she doesn't speak.

"Now that we've gotten that business out of the way, let's get on with tonight's game, shall we?" Jim pulls the mic from the stand, then strolls over to the large sheet. With a wide grin, he grips one corner and snatches the material away, revealing a large randomizer wheel. Each slice of the colorful, glittery pie has something written on it, but it's too small to read from this far away.

Murmurs rise from the crowd. Speculations swarm, but Jim shushes us.

"Quiet, quiet. All will be revealed in time." He shuffles his notecards, then prepares to read the first one. "For the first game of the cruise, let's play a little trivia, shall we? Table one, we'll start with something easy. Tell me, which infamous killer was known as the Co-ed Killer?"

Cat shoots from her seat. "Edmund Emil Kemper the third!"

"Thank you, Miss Novak," Jim says, "but you are seated at table *two*."

"Whoops," she whispers as she takes a seat.

Jim clears his throat and shuffles to the next card, then tries again. "Table *one*." He pins Cat with a pointed stare, and she makes a zipping motion over her lips. "Who was the first to coin the term 'serial murderer'?"

Table one puts their heads together and begins discussing their options.

"You have thirty seconds to answer," Jim says through the mic.

"That's so easy," Kindra whispers. "Everyone knows Robert Ressler said it first."

Frankie turns toward Kindra. "Actually, Robert Ressler popularized the term serial *killer*, but Ernst Gennat, a German criminologist, used the term serial *murderer* first. I'll save you the German pronunciation."

Fuck, that's exactly the sort of shit a fed would know.

"What did you say your killer name was again?" Eve asks.

Frankie opens her mouth to answer, and my life flashes before my eyes. If she tells anyone else she's the fucking Fisherman, she'll be dead before the clock strikes midnight.

"She's the Mona Lisa," I blurt, "because she always wears a smile while killing."

Frankie looks geared to argue, so I'm grateful when a stranger stands from table one.

"That would be Ernst Gennat," the man says.

A mischievous twinkle glints in Jim's eyes as he smiles down at the man. "Mark Lewis, isn't it?"

The man nods.

"Well, very good job, Mark Lewis. Who on your team knew the answer was Ernst Gennat?"

"That was all me, sir." Mark blasts Jim with a proud smile, looking and sounding every bit the government agent.

Sir? Ha.

Aven—one of the new guys—stands at table one as his teammate sits. "Jim, permission to kill Mark Lewis?"

The pitifully doomed Mark Lewis jumps to his feet and runs for the door.

"Permission granted," Jim says.

Aven glances around the room. Seeing no good weapons, he settles on the newly empty chair. His thick arms and barrel chest are so massive that it looks like he's plucking up dollhouse furniture when he grips it and lifts it into the air. In a few quick strides, he's reached Mark Lewis, who struggles to open what must be a locked door. Jim really thought of everything.

"He's going to kill him here? In front of everyone?" Frankie whispers, and I'm glad I'm the only one who heard her.

"Yes," I whisper back. "We're all killers here, remember?"

She sits back, but I don't miss the way her hands can't keep still in her lap.

A loud *thunk* comes from the other side of the room, and I turn in time to see Aven bring the chair down on the fed's head for a second time. A red freshet burbles from a split running through his scalp. Mark goes down, but Aven doesn't stop. Even once a chair leg flies off and puts a large hole in the wall, he keeps swinging until Mark Lewis' skull is reduced to pulp and bone shards. His job finished, Aven returns to his seat, and the game resumes.

Our table is next, and I can only hope that Jim doesn't ask a question that could blow Frankie's cover. Then again, she's so busy gawping at the twitching body by the door . . . I nudge her leg, and she schools her face, finally wrenching her gaze away from death.

"Table two, not all serial killers are created equal," Jim says into the mic. "The most notorious killers are not even of our ilk. One of the most disgusting and vile monsters to ever don the title of serial killer was known as the Werewolf of Wysteria. What was his actual name?"

"Albert Fish!" Frankie opens her mouth and blurts the answer before I can stop her. That glazed look in her eyes tells me she's entirely unaware of what's about to happen.

"That is correct!" Jim shouts. "Get up here and spin the wheel!"

She looks to me for help, but the girls encourage her to get up. There's no telling what that wheel entails, but I can bet it's murder. I stand, half-expecting the girls to yank me back into my chair, but Jim is the one who stops me from approaching the stage.

"Now, now, Maverick. Frankie answered the question, so Frankie gets to spin the wheel." His eyes glint with the pleasure of his mischief as he motions her toward doom.

And I can only sit here and watch.

Chapter Nine

Frankie

Well, fuck. My cover is about to be blown, and I have no one to blame but myself. Is it too late to hope that a new car is on the prize wheel? Ugh, fuck me for being such a smarty pants. The answer just came out of me, and I was still shocked from witnessing a brutal murder. I didn't consider what my prize might entail.

On shaking legs, I rise and head toward the stage. I risk one backward glance toward Maverick, who clearly knows more than he's letting on. He has me pegged as a fed, that much is clear.

So why hasn't he killed me?

"Come on, come on." Jim waves his hand through the air, encouraging me to move my legs. "No need to be shy, Frankie. Everyone will get a chance to make a kill, so you don't have to feel bad about earning this one."

The room falls silent as I grip the narrow metal railing and climb the first step. I steel my nerves as Jim clutches my arm and hauls me toward the wheel of disaster. As we draw closer, my brain tries to understand the words written within each glittering triangle, but it's as if I've forgotten how to read. The letters jumble together.

This isn't who I was trained to be. I have nerves of fucking steel. I was chosen for this mission for a reason, and that reason is my skill. Since arriving on this ship, I've gotten everything incorrect, and that shook my confidence. If I want to survive the next few days, I need to find that confidence again.

I step up to the wheel and grip the edge for one hell of a spin, but Jim places his hand over mine and smiles down at me.

"This one's a little eager to make the kill, isn't she?"

The crowd offers an obligatory chuckle in response to his weak-ass joke.

I smile at the crowd and fake a laugh, then lean closer to the mic. "We came here to kill these assholes, didn't we?"

A few cheers rise from the tables, including the women seated at mine. But Maverick doesn't cheer. He doesn't even smile. He just sits there with his arms folded over his chest, watching me with a straight face. I'm glad I've gotten the girls back on my side, but something tells me Maverick is far too suspicious now.

"Very well. Spin the wheel, my dear." Jim takes a step back and stretches his arm toward the monstrous circle.

With an entirely falsified grin, I step forward and grip the side of the wheel once more, then give it a spin with all my weight. The metal tines poking from the center of each slice slap against the plastic arrow that points to the words I can't read. The ticking sound slows, and the wheel comes to a stop on a glittering red sliver.

"Russian roulette! How exciting!" Jim shouts into the

mic, and now we're deaf. "Please bring a red Cattle and the revolver to the stage."

The curtain behind us rustles, and two men with orange wristbands wrestle a man in a red jumpsuit onto the platform on which we stand. Another staff member appears with a chair, and the three of them set to work. Within only a few minutes, they've strapped the man down.

Metal bindings secure his wrists, ankles, and neck to the thick wooden beams that make up his death throne. The seat looks suspiciously similar to an antique electric chair, minus the metal cap. One of the workers scurries behind the curtain, then returns with a revolver, which they place into my hands. I study the worker's face and notice tiny scars around his lips, almost as if his mouth had been sewn shut at some point.

Do they allow some of their victim pool to become workers? I file this question away for later. If there is a later. Maverick is cute, but he's going to throw a big wrench into my plans if he tries to kill me.

Which means I'll have to take him out before he can take me out.

I test the heft of the gun in my hand, then step toward the Cattle. *It isn't Castle.* That's what I keep repeating in my mind as I press the gun's barrel against the man's temple.

He pulls his head away and screams through his nose. His lips have been glued shut instead of sewn shut, but the effect is essentially the same. Sweat gathers on his forehead and drips into his eyes.

"What did he do?" I ask Jim.

He waggles his eyebrows and looks into the crowd. "Oh, do we have another Confessor in our midst? She wants to know what this vile creature has done." Jim walks around the seated man. "This monster kidnapped his sixteen-year-old niece and assaulted her for three weeks before police discovered her body. He's been in prison for ten years, and he's up for parole in twenty. Thirty years for taking a life and abusing a corpse. Do you think that's fair, Frankie? Our government certainly does."

I'm not here to debate our penal system and where it fails. My job is to get the bad guys off the streets. I can't stop them from getting out again. If this is his gripe, he'd do better to pack the scavenger hunt with defense attorneys instead of federal agents.

In answer to his question, I aim the gun and pull the trigger.

Click.

The man strapped to the chair squeals and braces for impact, but no bullet jets from the gun. A sprig of disappointment blossoms inside me, disgusting me. I need to be careful that their sickness isn't catching. I'm not a fucking killer.

With a shrug of my shoulders, I offer the gun to Jim, but he shakes his head.

"No, dear child. You get to keep going until the gun fires." Glee glimmers in his eyes as he pushes the gun against my chest. "You can drag this out for as long as you'd like, but he will die by your hand. That's your prize for answering correctly."

"Lucky!" someone shouts.

I don't know. I don't feel very lucky. And neither does the Cattle.

Shit. I mean the *man* in front of me. Now I'm starting to think like one of them.

He strains against the restraints until the thin metal edge cuts into the top of his left wrist, sheering the skin from his hand as he pulls it free. With no blood going to the flap, the skin turns a sickly whitish-yellow as it dangles and flops over tendons and flashes of bluish-white bone.

Remembering Maverick's new cover story—and fuck him for that—I smile before I step forward and pull the trigger multiple times. This has to end, and quickly.

Click. Click. Click.

On the next pull, fire explodes from the barrel, and my wrist snaps backward. The Cattle's head jerks in the opposite direction, and a bloody waterfall flows from the side of his skull facing away from me. His chest rises and falls a few more times, weaker and weaker, before he stills.

A hand clamps over my shoulder, and another raucous cheer erupts from the people seated before me, but I hear, see, and feel so little. Everything is a blur or a murmur or a numbness.

On robotic legs, I march off the stage with my fake smile held before me like a shield. My fist rises in the air in a show of feigned triumph, and they cheer again.

But not Maverick. Still not Maverick.

The girls rise from the table and surround me, welcoming me into the fold, my previous misstep forgotten. As far as they're concerned, I'm one of them. Only Maverick seems to be outside of my spell.

"Settle down, everyone. Settle down," Jim says from the stage. He turns to the next table with their question.

I'm deaf to all of it. My ass slides into my seat on autopilot when all I want to do is run down the hallway and warn every agent to head for a lifeboat. This ship is sinking, and we don't even have a life vest.

The game continues, and a few more Cattle—*human beings*—are dispatched. As each new victim comes out, I study the face, searching for Castle, but he isn't among the dead by the end of the third round. Meanwhile, my anxiety continues to rise. Maverick studies me each time someone makes a kill, likely looking for a crack in my veneer.

Cracks run through me, but he won't see them. I'm careful to keep my nervous fidgeting to a minimum, now that I know he's wising up. If I can avoid killing him, I'd prefer that, but if he forces my hand . . .

If he forces my hand, I'll end him without hesitation.

A loud bang pulls my attention from the maze of thoughts I've lost myself in, and I turn toward the stage. Aven's team landed on Russian Roulette, and they've just claimed their prize. I wish I felt worse about watching someone get murdered for fun, but it's hard to mentally defend people who've done some pretty indefensible things.

As the staff drags the body away, our team focuses on the stage. Our turn is next.

Jim clears his throat and steps around a large puddle of blood as he shuffles the notecards. Then he raises the mic to his lips and looks at us. "Table two, before the I-90 killer went dormant, the feds postulated that it was actually the work of three men, not one. What tipped them off?"

This is a tricky question. King, our division's director, believed it was the work of three men because of the bodies —the bodies we've discovered, anyway, and there haven't been many. It wasn't so much the condition they were left in, however, which was the same every time: dressed to impress, and clean, despite several victims coming back as known vagrants. What struck King as odd was that while the majority of the victims were buried in the same manner, on rare occasions, we'd discover flowers left on the dirt mound, and in one instance, piss.

But King only shared his suspicions with our team. No one else.

I'll have to play dumb this time. As the girls begin to formulate theories, I just nod and agree. Maverick stays silent, watching me as the seconds tick down.

"I've never even heard of the I-90 Killer," Eve whispers, "so how the fuck am I supposed to know what tipped off anyone to anything?"

The pretty blonde—Cat—leans forward, sending a lock of hair into her eyes. "He picked up sex workers and killed them. No rhyme or reason other than that. They've only found five of his victims, but there are believed to be about four times that many."

"Answer?" Jim prods.

"Give us a moment?" Kindra pleads. "This is kind of a tough one."

"Frankie, do you have any input?" Eve asks me, her voice low. "You seem to have a pretty deep knowledge base here. I guess I slept through Serial Killer History in school."

"You and me both," Kindra whispers.

Maverick leans forward. "Kindra, considering your line of work, I'd think you'd know more than you do. How does Cat have all the answers?"

"Are you saying that because I'm blonde?" Cat squeals.

Maverick sighs. "Cat . . . I'm blond as well."

I lean forward, breaking Cat's line of sight to her intended target. "Guys, let's focus. How specific do we need to be here?"

Eve looks up at Jim, then repeats my question.

"Just ballpark." Jim rolls his hand through the air. "If you get anywhere near the vicinity of correctness, I'll be a magnanimous host and let you have it."

I can't give them the answer, but maybe I can guide them in the right direction. "Okay, let's consider what we know about how they profile us," I whisper. "Usually, they nail us with a common way we kill, but sometimes there are other tells."

"Like the location," Kindra says.

I nod, then raise my finger as if I've just had an epiphany. "Or the way the bodies are disposed of."

"Ooh, what about Satan's Fury?" Cat says. "He's a Japanese serial killer who got his name because of the mask he wears."

"And the brutality of his kills." Eve shivers. "I met him at Rakuten Fashion Week in Tokyo, and—"

"Table two?" Jim taps his wristband. "Time is wasting."

Maverick finally speaks. "Maybe it has something to do with the time of day when he takes his kills."

"Or when he disposes of them," I say, trying once more to lead the horses to water.

Cat slaps her palms on the table and stands. "It has something to do with his M.O., but there are too many things that make up a killer's profile, Jim. This is the sort of question that *only* a government agent would know, and we clearly don't have one of those at our table. This game is rigged."

Jim smiles and looks directly at me as he raises the mic to his lips. "I'm sorry, Catarina, but that answer is incorrect. Thank you for playing."

As he turns to the next table and asks their question, a nail runs up my spine. It's clear Jim knows I'm a fed, especially if he set up this scavenger hunt. I might be in more trouble than I realized. I have to get off this ship.

I'll make my escape tonight, when Maverick falls asleep. A little fake snoring should do the trick, and once he's out, so am I.

Chapter Ten

Maverick

As we wander back to our room after the game, there's no denying the heavy blanket of tension weighing down the air in the elevator. She likely suspects I know her secret. That's fine. After a good night's rest, I plan to lay everything out for her, anyway. It's the only way I can keep her safe (and win).

She begins readying for bed the moment we step into the room. Kneeling on the floor, she digs through a bag until she finds what she needs, and then she scurries off to the bathroom. Seconds later, the shower kicks on.

I try to stop my mind from going places it shouldn't, but it's useless. The woman is just too damn pretty for her own good, and I bet she's even prettier when she's wet.

The lighter in my pocket calls my name. It speaks in a sing-song voice and begs me to flick the wheel until a spark ignites. Once the flame heats the metal, I'll hold it to my skin and lose myself to visions of a dark-haired woman touching herself in the shower.

I pull my hand away from my pocket and stand before I do something stupid. The last thing I need is for her to walk in to me furiously beating my dick while intermittently burning myself.

After stripping down to my boxer-briefs, I call down to room service and request a cot. Minutes later, a bug-eyed man appears at the door. Burn scars cover his face, along with several long scars that look like the work of a blade. Thinning hair stands in short spikes on his head, letting his scalp shine through.

"Here's the cot you wanted, sir," he says as he hands it to me with a smile. He cranes his neck to look up at me. "You don't plan to sleep on it, do you? You're so tall!"

"I'm not that tall." I place the cot against the wall, then turn back to the man. "You're just a bit short, pal."

The man laughs like I've just told the joke of the year. "You're right about that."

My eyebrows pull together as he wanders off. It's odd enough that he's this chatty, as most of the staff don't mingle with the Sinners, but it's incredibly strange that he would laugh that hard at what I said about him. Almost as if he were trying to get me to like him.

With a shake of my head, I begin setting up the cot as I commit his face to memory. Maybe he's another agent. Whoever he was, he wasn't wrong to worry about how I'll fit on this cot. Was it made for a child? When I lie on it, I feel like Alice in goddamn Wonderland after she outgrew the house.

The bathroom door slides open, and Frankie emerges from a thick cloud of steam. I forget all about my awkward sleeping arrangement as I watch her step toward the sink to begin her routine. A routine which turns out to be very in depth, explaining the lack of wrinkles on her face.

She swipes, smooths, wipes, and rinses for the next fifteen minutes, and not once does she realize I'm watching her. If she's truly a fed, she's not a very good one. Aren't they supposed to have a killer sixth sense? I'm openly fucking staring at this point.

I begin to wonder if perhaps she's just pretending she doesn't notice me, but then she leans forward and I'm sure. No one would clean nose gold while someone was watching. Yet . . . she's still so adorable as she takes a cotton swab and swipes inside her nostril. Tipping her head upward, she holds her mouth in a downward position to get a better look. That's when the laugh springs out of me.

Frankie jumps a solid foot in the air, then pretends to busy herself with whatever she's strewn all over the sink. With a huff, she shoves bottles and tinctures into a small leather bag. "I don't know what's so funny. I didn't laugh when I came out of the bathroom and was greeted by fucking Gulliver trying to lie on the townsperson's bed."

I pull my knees to my chest so that nothing hangs off the cot. Touché.

"Just take the bed, Maverick. It makes more sense." She pushes the leather bag to the side of the sink, then steps closer to the cot. "Is it comfortable, at least?"

"When I was in high school, I spent the night in a field after a party. I was too drunk to care when I fell asleep, but I woke up with a cow patty as a pillow. Rocky earth served as my mattress. My back and ribs ached for a week. Despite all of that, I can confidently say I'd take that over the cot. So you take the bed."

Frankie slicks her dark hair into a ponytail, then motions for me to get up. "I'm not putting you through that. If you don't want to share the bed, I'll sleep on the cot."

"I was never opposed to sharing a bed. I just figured—"

"That I'd be more comfortable if we didn't?" She smiles and shakes her head. "I'm older than you, but I'm not a pearl-clutching Goody-two-shoes who subscribes to the ways of the past. My morals aren't at risk just because I'm forced to share sleeping quarters with an attractive man."

"What if I'm worried about *my* virtue?" I smirk up at her. "After all, I'm not the only attractive party in this scenario."

"Oh, so you're cocky? Consider my loins officially girded. Get in the bed, Maverick." Frankie strolls closer to the bed, then sits on the edge and pulls the blanket over her. "To fully protect your precious penis from my vagina, I'll even sleep on top of the comforter. Wouldn't want you to slip inside me while I'm sleeping."

The mental image is more than I can stand. If I weren't so damaged, I'd have gotten one hell of a boner from thoughts of fucking her as she sleeps. My brain takes the fantasy further, imagining how she'd look up at me when she wakes up so full of me.

"Are you coming or not?"

I fucking wish.

Not wanting to look too eager, I sit up and offer an exasperated—but very fake—sigh. She thinks she's pulling teeth to get me in bed with her, but I want nothing more than to get a little closer. Her chosen profession is acting as more of an aphrodisiac than a deterrent. The aspect of danger makes any situation more exciting, and none more so than sex.

And nothing would be more dangerous than letting the long arm of the law reach out and grab me by the dick.

I ease beneath the comforter on the empty side of the bed, and my body immediately thanks me. The luxury mattress far surpasses the thick swath of canvas that supported me minutes ago.

Frankie shuffles around under her thin blanket on top of the comforter until she's facing me. She lies on her side with her hands tucked under her head. "See? Isn't that better?"

"Yes. Much."

"You forgot to turn off the light, though." She opens her mouth with a wide yawn, which she quickly covers with her hand. "I can't sleep if there's any light. Once I'm out, you can do whatever and I won't budge, but falling asleep is the hard part for me."

Just last week, I made fun of Ezra for getting the remote for Kindra when it was closer to her, yet I stand and go for the light switch mere feet from her side of the bed without so much as an argument. Maybe our ancestors weren't so wrong about witches being a threat, because I certainly feel like I'm being put under a spell right now.

On my way back to my side of the mattress, my pinky toe collides with one of the bed's metal legs. Pain sears up my shin, and I'm not convinced the toe is still attached. The tiny digit hurts to the point of numbness.

I clamp my teeth together as water fills my eyes. The woman in the bed probably already thinks so little of me, what with me being so much younger than her. And the fact that I'm a serial killer. If I start crying about a stubbed toe, she'll think I'm a fucking child.

My mouth opens in a silent scream as I grip my ankle and lean against the foot of the bed. As long as my voice doesn't betray me, she'll never know I'm fighting for my life over here. Not with the total darkness in this room.

"Everything okay?" she asks.

I hold my breath, count to three, and plead with my

vocal cords to cooperate. "Yep, just trying to find the bed." My voice cracks on the last word. I clench my eyes and silently scream again before patting the mattress and saying, "Found it."

I hobble the rest of the way, using the bed as a support, then climb back under the comforter. Several silent minutes pass as Frankie tosses and turns. Finally, she settles, and I begin to drift to sleep.

"Can you go jiggle the handle?" Her voice cuts through the darkness, and my eyes pop open. "The toilet keeps running, and it's all I can hear."

"You know, if you're asleep, you won't have to hear it."

"Please?"

With a sigh, I get out of bed once more. I'm careful to use the mattress as a guide this time, though, and I make the trip to the bathroom without incident. After a jiggle of the handle, the toilet finally quiets, and I make my way back toward the bed. Unfortunately, I forget to feel my way through the room on my return trip, and my big toe collides with the corner of the wall.

I grit my teeth and hold my breath so that I don't scream. Bracing myself against the wall, I suffer in silence as my toe throbs in time with my heartbeat.

"You may want to consider wearing shoes at all times," Frankie says. "I've never met anyone who stubbed their toe twice in one day, let alone twice in the span of ten minutes."

Wearing a cloak of embarrassment and cursing under my breath, I hobble back to the bed. Since she's a government agent, I'm not stupid enough to want to impress her and make her like me, but if I could maybe not look like an incompetent toddler for the rest of the cruise, that would be great.

Once I'm under the comforter, Frankie performs her

toss-and-turn ritual again. Now that I've silenced the noisy toilet, I can only hope she'll go to sleep. When I'm rewarded with soft snores ten minutes later, I smile to myself and close my eyes, happy to finally put this day behind me. Tomorrow . . . Well, tomorrow will sort itself out eventually.

Chapter Eleven

Frankie

I wake the next morning to the sound of Maverick brushing his teeth, which fucking sucks because it means instead of pretending to fall asleep, I *actually* fell asleep. And that means I'm still stuck in this nightmare. Whoever designed these beds should be shot for creating something so comfortable.

Rolling onto my side with a groan, I glance at the bedside clock and am shocked to see it's only five in the morning. Why the fuck is he up so early?

The sink cuts off, and I close my eyes and pretend I'm still out. Maybe I'll actually fake-sleep correctly this time. Footsteps shuffle around the bed. The closet opens and closes, and then the bathroom door slides open and closed. Seconds later, the shower starts.

This is my chance.

I fling the blanket off my body and hurry out the cabin door, making a break for the elevator down the hall. Now I just have to find the exit. Or another agent. Anything.

"Don't tell me you're another morning person."

I spin on my heel and face Eve, who covers her mouth as she yawns. In her other hand, she holds a paper cup. The skin around her eyes is still puffy with sleep.

"No, not particularly." I offer her a disarming smile. At least, I hope it's disarming. For all I know, I look absolutely maniacal, which would fit with how I feel. "My stomach keeps grumbling, so I thought I'd get up and search for some food. Would you happen to know where the kitchen is?"

"The kitchen?" Eve looks me up and down. "Honey, no. When we are on vacation, we don't look for the kitchen. We look for the room service number. Live a little! Go back to your comfy blankets and have the staff bring whatever your heart desires."

Before I can argue, she spins me around and pushes me toward my room. On any other day of the week, I'd be in awe of the beauty spiriting me away, but I need to get off this ship. I place my hand over hers and try to stop this train, but she's on a mission.

"Room service sounds great," I say, "but I enjoy cooking in my spare time, and I really wanted to see what the ship's galley has to offer."

"Oh, then the cooking class would be perfect for you! I didn't do it at the winter retreat, and I hadn't planned to try it this time, but it's around lunch if you want to go?"

"I, um . . ." Warning flares prepare to fire, but then the cabin door swings open and Maverick steps out wearing only a towel draped over his waist. Whatever I planned to say evacuates my head as my eyes fill with dips and ridges and so much gloriously damp skin.

And the smells. I can't even name them, but it's the distinct and stereotypical scent of man.

His hand closes over my wrist, and he snatches me into

the room. "Where did you go? You shouldn't be wandering the ship alone! Something could have happened to you."

Eve is all but forgotten as I take my scolding, and why is he so upset? I'm a grown woman. If I want to wander the ship, I will.

I snatch my hand away and step toward Eve. "My stomach woke me up, so I thought I'd pop down to the kitchen and find something to eat."

"And that's when she found me." Eve peers around my head and gives Maverick a wave. "I get why you're worried, honey. Jim's little scavenger hunt makes this a dangerous game for all of us, but Frankie's a big girl. She can hold her own without you babysitting her. In fact, she already has plans to attend the cooking class with me at lunch, so you can quit worrying. I've got her."

Maverick glares down at me, but there's no malice in his gaze. He looks concerned more than anything, but why?

"On second thought, maybe that room service doesn't sound so bad." I take a step toward Maverick, then turn to face Eve. "I'll meet you in the galley for the cooking class, okay?"

"Suit yourself, but if his little White Knight act gets to be too much, you're welcome to hang out in my room. I'm just down the hall." She gives my arm a squeeze, then walks away with her coffee held elegantly to the side.

I don't have time to process what just happened as I'm yanked into the cabin. Maverick closes the door behind him while gripping the towel above his hip. Considering the dangerous way that fabric dangles, I'm at risk of a peep show if he doesn't maintain his hold.

I put some distance between us and step toward the bed before I turn to face him again. Part of me wants to air everything out right now, but I need to be smart about this.

Eve mentioned something about Maverick's White Knight routine. If he has that sort of complex, I can use it to my advantage. White Knights have one weakness . . .

The damsel in distress.

"I didn't mean to worry you." I bat my eyelashes and look up at him with what I hope are the most innocent doe eyes he's ever seen. "You were just in the shower and . . . and I'm sorry."

Instead of falling for my guise and comforting me, he adjusts his weight and appraises me. "You need to dress. And stop doing whatever it is you're doing. You're prettier when you aren't pretending."

Then he turns and steps toward the bathroom, leaving me feeling foolish. Minutes later, he emerges once more, having traded the towel for some pink board shorts and a neon-green tank top that the 80s would like back.

My lip curls. He wasn't even alive for the 80s.

"Why aren't you dressed?" He glances at the clock. "We have to be on deck in ten minutes for an event."

"I figured I'd just stay here. Won't I be safest in the room?" I have no intention of staying in this fucking cabin, but it won't hurt to have him think otherwise.

He bends over, grabs my bag, and chucks it into my lap. "I said to drop the act. We don't have time to talk right now, but we can skip lunch and have a much-needed conversation after this event."

"The cooking lesson?"

His eyes close, and he curses under his breath. "After the cooking class, then. Just stick by my side and try not to talk."

I make a zipper motion over my lips and turn my attention to my bag. Maverick definitely knows I'm a fed. There's no question of that now. He plans to confront me after the cooking class, but why? And why not now?

Is it because he needs time to get Jim's permission for the kill? Maybe he freaked out when he saw me in the hall because he thought someone else might snatch the opportunity away from him. Drat.

"Can I at least know what activity we'll be partaking in?" I ask, trying to calm my nerves. "I kind of need to know how to dress."

"Wear a bathing suit. We'll be getting wet."

"At six in the morning? Who goes swimming this early?"

"Who said anything about swimming?" He glances at the clock again. "I'll be in the hall."

With that, he leaves me alone to dress. He plans to confront me, and when that happens, I want to be sure I have my gun. He can't kill me if I kill him first. Once the cooking class is over, it's bye-bye Maverick.

Chapter Twelve

Frankie

When the morning event is canceled due to bad weather, I'm happy. When Jim encourages me to explore the ship a little, I'm ecstatic. But then my joy comes crashing down as Jim, Maverick, and I stand by the glass doors overlooking the deck.

"I think we'll probably just go back to the room and get some more sleep," Maverick says. "How does that sound, Frankie?"

It sounds like I don't have a fucking say in the matter, but I just smile and nod. "Yeah, I'm still pretty tired. I can always explore the ship later."

"Nonsense. Did you come on this cruise to sleep?" Jim rocks on his heels and smiles at me in that weird way that's one-part comforting and two-parts creepy as fuck. "Go explore the ship, Frankie, and when you're done, meet your new friends for the cooking class. I'd hate for you to miss it."

The round muscles at the corners of Maverick's jaw tense, and his hands clench into tight fists that leave his knuckles white. "Are you sure that's a good idea? I mean, considering your little *twist*, Jim?"

"Not to worry, son. I'm sure she can hold her own, hmm?" His head tips slightly to the left as he appraises me, waiting for a response.

If I go along with Jim, I can potentially touch base with another agent and feel a little safer, sure, but that will also piss off Maverick. He's practically daring me to defy him as he and Jim stare me down.

But I'm not here to make friends.

"Well, if you insist," I say, aiming my smile at Maverick. "You're welcome to join me if you're worried. I'm a very capable woman, but I wouldn't mind the companionship."

"Sure, I'll tag along," he says with a smirk, and my heart sinks into my ass. I didn't expect him to accept.

Jim claps his hands and smiles at me. "Then it's settled. The two of you can have a nice stroll through the ship, and then you can enjoy the festivities at the cooking class. Make sure you aren't late. You know how Chef is about timing."

We say our goodbyes and head toward the elevator. Despite offering to accompany me as I explore the ship, I have a feeling Maverick has no such intentions. For either of us. My suspicions are confirmed when he presses the button to take us back to the Sinner cabins.

I want to tell him to cut the crap, but again, not wise. Not until I have my gun in my hand, which will be possible in only a few minutes.

Arriving at the cabin door, he swipes his wrist over the panel and steps inside. I follow him through a haze as I recall how he looked in that towel. I'd much rather fuck him than kill him, but if he pushes the issue, I'll do what I have to do.

Either way.

Rain and wind batter the door leading onto our balcony. It feels like each droplet is a thought thrust against my brain. I flop onto the side of the bed and try to remember what my mother warned me about.

He's handsome, yes, but he's dangerous.

The man lives by a different set of rules.

The man lives by no rules at all.

And I like rules.

Granted, the rules state that I shouldn't murder someone without good reason, and I'm planning to do just that as I bend and grab my bag from the floor. Maverick is at the sink just off the bathroom. He won't even know what hit him.

I pull the gun from the bag and clutch it to my chest. In equal measure, the cold steel comforts me and makes me feel like I'm heading toward a cliff's edge. Just like a base jumper, I'm about to take a leap of faith. My parachute will open. Or it won't.

With a steeling breath, I stand and step toward Maverick. He leans over the sink, repeatedly splashing cold water against his face. His eyes are closed.

And he looks so tired for such a young man.

I'm busy second-guessing my plans when his eyes pop open and he sees the gun in my hand. Instead of wheeling around with a look of panic, he sighs and shakes his head.

"We don't have to do it this way," he says. "We could use words instead of weapons, Frankie."

"If that's my real name."

"Oh, it is."

"How would you know?"

He smirks. "What you do for a living and what I do for a living aren't so different. We profile people. I'm just better at it than most, and I know when you're lying. You have a tell."

"The fidgeting?"

He shakes his head and reaches for the hand towel by the sink as if my finger isn't beside the trigger guard. Doesn't he know that I'm about to end him?

"Go to the bed," I command with a flick of the pistol's barrel.

Instead of obeying me like a good boy, he turns and sits against the sink. "Frankie, sweetheart. I told you. It doesn't have to be this way. You don't have to shoot me."

"Don't call me sweetheart," I say, though I don't add that it bothers me because gentle words are more dangerous than the gun I now aim at his skull. "If you want a chance to talk, fine. I'll give you ten minutes. But you'll do the talking while cuffed to the fucking bed. Now move."

He takes his bottom lip between his teeth, tips back his head, and lets out a low groan that sounds more like a growl as his eyes close. "Fuck, you have *got* to stop talking down to me. You're playing a game you don't have the rule book for."

As I stand here in disbelief—all while I have a locked and loaded handgun aimed at him, mind you—Maverick grips the hem of his shirt and pulls it over his head. My brain empties as my eyes fill with tan skin, rippling muscle, and the . . . the V. The godforsaken Adonis belt. That horrifically tantalizing dip of shadow.

God, I want to use him as a champagne flute.

"Don't get distracted now, sweetheart. Boss me around some more." He groans again, and his green eyes practically beg me to pull the trigger. Then, before I know what's happening, he steps into me and presses the gun's barrel below his chin. "Pull the trigger, Frankie. Fuck, I want it so bad."

"What is your fucking damage?" I whisper. I meant to yell the words, but my voice won't cooperate.

He leans closer, until our lips are only a breath away. "Wouldn't you love to know?"

Before I fuck up and kiss him—or shoot him—I thrust my knee between his legs. It's a cheap shot, but he has the size advantage, and despite wanting to kill him, I can't do it. With a grunt, he cradles his junk and drops to his knees.

I hurry past him and reach for my bag. My fingertips glide over a stack of passports, a few knives, and my badge, but where the fuck are my goddamn handcuffs? I remember packing them. I know I did.

Didn't I?

Surely I didn't forget a key part of my kit. But as I dig and dig and find everything but cuffs, that appears to me my fucking reality.

Maverick is regaining his composure. He's on his hands and knees, and his face has gone from carmine to coral. That vein on his forehead still squiggles and throbs, but he'll be on his feet in the next thirty seconds. I won't have another chance to subdue him.

I rip back the zipper on a hidden side pocket, then squeal when I'm rewarded with a glint of shiny metal.

Unfortunately, I'm out of time.

Chapter Thirteen

Maverick

Now that I can finally draw a breath that doesn't feel like it's directly connected to my testicles, I get to my feet and lunge toward her. I don't want to hurt her, but I need to get her to calm the fuck down so that we can talk.

Then she wheels around, and I know talking is off the table.

Her icy eyes land on me. There's a wildness there that concerns me. She lacks the control of her counterpart, looking more like a feral cat than a stoic soldier now that her back is against the wall. In this way, she's far more dangerous than that soldier. She's something to fear.

I raise my hands and take a step toward her. "Hey, I don't want to hurt you. If we can just talk about this and—"

"I prefer to converse with people who share common interests. Something tells me we are *nothing* alike." She rises to stand, the cuffs held in her left hand and the gun gripped tightly in her right. It's no longer aimed at me, but the threat remains. "Get on the fucking bed, Maverick."

Yeah, that ain't happening. She'll have to shoot me if she wants to cuff me to the bed.

I take a step back, toward the cabin door. "I have a better idea. I'll head to the atrium and give you some time to cool off, and you—"

"Get on the fucking bed!"

Fuck, she's leaving me with no choice. She's the one who needs to be handcuffed to the damn bed.

The solution comes to me like a lightning strike. I just need to wait for an opening, then get the gun out of her hand. After that, it's as simple as cuffing her to the bed and explaining why she needs me on her side. She'll have to see reason after that.

Thunder booms as the ship travels through the storm. A strong gust of wind pushes a sheet of rain against the balcony door again, but it makes a much louder sound this time. Frankie's head whips to the side, and there's my opening.

I lunge forward, keeping my entire focus on the gun. With a quick chop to her wrist, I disable her grip, and the gun drops to the carpet.

"Ow! What the fuck, Maverick?" She shakes out her hand, then steps toward the gun.

My foot rushes forward and kicks it under the bed. "Are you ready to listen now?"

The little minx is too quick for me, and she shoots forward and straps the cuff around my left wrist before I know what's happening. It's too bad that she won't get the chance to secure the other side to anything else. That's my job.

I band my arm around her waist, then lift her into the

air and slam her onto the bed. The wind evacuates her lungs, and I regret the force I used, but she did this. This is her fault.

Taking her right arm, I drag her body toward the head of the bed and then loop the remaining cuff through the decorative gap in the headboard. Before she can regain her composure, I yank her arm once more and slap the cuff over her right wrist.

Now she can't get away.

Neither can I, but where there are cuffs, there are keys. Once she finally sees sense, I'll set both of us free.

I lie back on the bed and catch my breath as Frankie does the same, though I toss Frankie's light blanket over my crotch to hide the arousal that isn't directed at her. It's merely a product of the pain and the struggle. The risk. But she doesn't know this, and if she fears I'll lose myself and take advantage of her, there's no chance in hell she'll ever trust me.

It's not that I want her to trust me for my own selfish reasons alone. Fuck, I'm trying to protect her too! Jim wants her kept alive, and I want to keep her alive. She's just making this more complicated than it has to be.

Frankie grabs a pillow, shoves it over her face, and screams.

"Are you ready to listen to me now?" I ask.

She raises the pillow. "You're so fucking stupid," she wheezes. She lowers the fluffy fabric over her face and screams again. If she says words, I can't make them out.

"You clearly aren't ready to *talk*," I mumble.

Frankie throws the pillow against the wall and blows the hair out of her face. "Where is the key, Maverick?"

"Uh, in your bag, I guess?"

"And where is my bag right now?"

I peer over the side of the bed. "On my side. Near the footboard."

"And how will we reach it?"

I look at the handcuffs. I analyze the short chain connecting our wrists. My brain calculates the length of my arms versus the length of the bed. All of these things happen in the split second it takes my plan to come crashing down around me.

"I don't know," I whisper.

"No, you don't know. And neither do I." She sits up and tries to cram her hand through the headboard gap, but it's no use. Her hand won't fit unless she can dislocate some bones. "Well, I can scratch 'live through a Stephen King plot' from my fucking bingo card."

"You read?"

She scoffs. "Yes, I fucking read. Well, I listen to the audiobooks, but it's the same thing."

"Listening to an audiobook is definitely still reading. A few months back, I was in a heated Facebook debate about the veracity of audiobooks versus consuming books the traditional way."

"Veracity? Consuming books the traditional way?" Her head slowly turns toward me, and her brows push together. "Facebook? Isn't that more for people my age?"

I shift uncomfortably. "I'm an old soul. Fucking sue me."

"On the contrary. I find it refreshing to meet a twenty-something who isn't talking about crypto or Taylor Swift's newest album."

I won't mention that Eve and I attended the Eras Tour. We all have our guilty pleasures.

"Don't get your hopes up, though," she adds. "Even if we find common ground, I have a mission to complete. The only way to stop me from disclosing everything I discover is to kill me."

"That's not what we want."

"We? Who's in on this? And what exactly *do* you want from me?"

"Jim and I know who you are." My cuffed wrist begins to ache, so I sit up to take the pressure off. "No one else does."

"You didn't answer the third question."

I snatch on the cuff, my frustration building. "Because I can't. Because I don't have all the answers. I was given a mission, same as you."

"That's where we differ. I know why I'm here. My mission means something to me because I swore an oath." She scoffs and shakes her head. "There's no honor in what you do."

Arguing right now is futile. She fully believes she's making a difference through her work, but I need to show her that she and I can coexist, that her goals aren't so different from ours. Our solutions are just more . . . permanent.

I also need to reach that bag at the foot of the bed. Once that's accomplished, I'll think of an alternate plan.

"Take off your bra."

Her head whips to the side. "Excuse me?"

"I'm going to use it to fish for the bag. If the hooks on the bra's fastener can catch that mesh pocket on the side of the bag, we'll be free."

Her drawn-down eyebrows rise. "That's . . . actually a pretty good plan. But turn your head."

She doesn't need to tell me twice. The temptation is definitely there, but her inability to listen to reason is one hell of a mood killer.

Several quiet seconds pass. Well, they're quiet aside from Frankie's huffing and grumbling. I can't imagine it's easy to unfasten a bra using only one hand, but she's making it sound like a struggle of epic proportions over there. The bed bumps and rocks, and she finally lets out a single whimper.

"I think I'm stuck."

I blink at the wall. "Stuck? Like . . . how?"

"My bracelet is caught on a thread on my shirt."

"So rip it?"

"The bracelet was a gift from someone, and it means a lot to me, so I'm not ripping the bracelet." She grunts again, and the bed squeaks as she struggles. "I don't care about ripping the shirt, but since someone prevented me from using one of my fucking *hands*, I can't exactly pick and choose."

"Look, just rip the bracelet. I'll pay for the repair." My hand rises, yearning to push through my hair and release the tension crawling over my scalp, but I stop before I fuck anything up. The style strategically hides a scar I don't want to talk about. "The only other solution is to allow me to help you."

Frankie's legs thrash on the bed. I assume it's her legs, anyway. It could be her entire body for all I know. Then she stills. "Fine. Just don't get any fucked-up ideas. Sex is tied to damn near everything where you sick assholes are concerned."

She's wrong, but now isn't the time for correction. If anything, I can remain a complete gentleman and prove that serial killers aren't oversexed maniacs.

I turn my body, and my left shoulder thanks me for coming around to a more natural position. Frankie tries to scoot and angle her back toward me. By the time she stops squirming and twisting, I can see where the bracelet has snagged her shirt.

I can also see acres of smooth skin. My eyes are drawn to the dark freckles that occasionally accentuate her body. Is this what men feel like when they step into territory that hasn't known human interference in eons? I imagine it's similar. Like I shouldn't be seeing this, and I definitely shouldn't be allowed to *touch* what I see.

She's a living, breathing liminal space.

"Unless you possess magical powers, I don't think you're going to untangle this mess with your fucking eyes," she says, snapping me out of the trance.

I lean forward and grip the bracelet between my fingers, providing an anchor so that it's supported. She was right to worry. The frail gold chain would have snapped long before the shirt gave way. A single charm dangles from the thin chain, but I can't make out what it is.

Frankie looks over her shoulder. "Do you have a good hold on the bracelet?"

"Yeah."

She twists her body, and the fabric rips, tearing a large hole from the middle of her back to her armpit. Her wrist comes free, complete with a flailing fabric souvenir.

"We'll have to work together to unfasten the bra. I can't do it with one hand," she says, and I nod.

Again, I don't feel like I should be touching her, but here we are.

I slide my fingers beneath the band, providing support on one side as she pushes and pulls the other. Her muscles and skin warm my hand as they writhe against me. I imagine her writhing for other reasons, and a familiar ache steals my breath.

The fastener slides free, and Frankie breathes a sigh of

relief. She and I work together to unhook the right strap from the band, then get it off her body. Unfortunately, it then proceeds to tangle itself within her torn shirt.

"Can nothing come easy for me?" she screams at the ceiling. "Maverick, turn around. I'll have to remove my shirt to untangle the bra."

The ache intensifies as I turn and imagine what her breasts look like. I can't help it. She was talking about them, and now they're all I can think about. It feels wrong, like I'm violating her privacy by imagining her tits, but I can't stop my mind from squeezing and licking and sucking every fantasized inch of them.

Frankie mutters something under her breath, and I turn to ask her what she said, completely forgetting that she's currently disrobed. She lets out a scream that I hear loud and clear, and then she slaps me hard enough to put a hadron collider to shame.

I let out a groan of ecstasy as blood finally fills my cock and dampens the ache. The throbbing urge to empty my balls is much more tolerable than the desperate discomfort my entire being feels when I can't get erect. But I'm definitely hard now. It doesn't get much harder than this.

Unfortunately, Frankie notices.

"You *are* a sick pervert! I knew it!" She snatches up the thin blanket and covers her chest, but the damage is done. I've seen them, and they're beautiful.

I grab her bra and turn away from her to begin fashioning our fishing line. "I'm not a pervert. Pain gets me hard, that's all. It doesn't mean I'm not in control of what I do with my dick."

"You have no impulse control. Shocker."

She's really starting to piss me off, which is a feat. My

patience has known no limits when tested at every turn in my life, but Frankie has finally found the boundary.

"We aren't who you think we are, and that's what I need you to grasp." I test the weight of the fishing line, then decide to add some heft and length via the bedside clock. "I'm not asking you to agree to anything immediately, but couldn't you stop being a close-minded bitch for like, ten minutes?"

Frankie chokes on her indignation, scoffing and huffing until she finds her voice. "Close-minded . . . bitch?"

"Good. We've established that you aren't deaf."

Like a wild creature, she lets out a scream akin to the sound a mountain lion makes when it's pissed. She lunges forward as much as the chain will allow as she goes on the attack. She thinks she's tough, and I'll admit that these little slaps of hers sting like hell, but I could break her in half with little to no effort.

Then the pain registers, and my cock is an iron bar.

I lie back and yank her body over mine, pinning her left arm under her body and stopping the onslaught. This position also pins her breasts against my chest, but I'm trying not to think about that.

She struggles against me, thrashing and screaming and making this so much worse. It's been so long since I've indulged in the pleasure of a warm body. If she keeps up this thrashing, I'm liable to come in my fucking pants whether I want to or not.

"You have to stop beating me up, sweetheart," I say, trying to keep my voice calm. Instead, it comes out all low and gravelly, like I'm trying to seduce her. That only makes her panic more.

"I won't let you take me!" she screams at the top of her lungs.

It's fine. I didn't need my right eardrum.

Her thighs press against my cock as she squirms in my hold. I'm past the point of needing pain, so the erection is here to stay and the end result is inevitable if I can't get her to be still. I grip her tighter with my left arm and squeeze my legs together. Her thighs fall to either side of my hips, and I don't know if this is better or worse.

"No . . . that will fucking split me in half," she whimpers, and fuck her for that. And fuck her for how warm she is between her legs.

"I'm not going to do anything to you, but you need to be still." I move my arm to adjust my grip, which gives her room to wiggle.

Repeatedly.

With a grunt, I hold her against my body as I come in my board shorts.

Frankie seems to realize what's happening. Either from the horror or the finality, she finally relaxes against me.

"Did you just come in your pants?" she squeaks.

I push her off me and go back to situating the fishing line. "Yes, but that was your fault, not mine. I asked you to stop moving. Trust that I got zero pleasure from it."

That's enough to shut her up. For now. I'll have to answer questions later, I'm sure, but right now, I just want to get free so that I can tell Jim the deal is off. He can kill her for all I care, but I refuse to spend another minute with a woman who can't listen to sense or see reason.

I fasten the alarm clock to the bra, then rip out the electrical cord from the lamp so that I can extend my line. Once everything is hooked together, I toss it out. It takes a few tries, but Frankie stays quiet as I reel in the bag.

"The keys should be in the side pocket," she says as I hoist the bag onto my lap.

I don't respond. After what just happened, I never want to speak to her again. Part of it is the embarrassment, but it's mostly the frustration. I allowed her to get me this upset.

With my jaw set, I turn and unlatch my side of the cuff, then hurry to fasten it to the bedpost. As I slide the key into my pocket, she finally realizes I have no intention of setting her free. That's when the panic sets in.

"Lots of guys nut fast," she says. "It's nothing to be ashamed about, and it's certainly not a reason to kill people. Is that why you do it? Because you're sexually frustrated?" She yanks on the cuff.

"The profiling only works when the killers slot nicely into your predesignated boxes. We don't fit your boxes, so stop trying to cram us in there. That's why you've had to resort to these measures to find some of us."

I stand and go to my bag so that I can get a clean pair of pants. Though I didn't come a gallon, it's enough to leave me uncomfortable in more ways than one.

"You can't just leave me cuffed to the fucking bed," she says as I gather my things.

"Oh, I can and I will. But it won't be up to me. I'm telling Jim I need to switch rooms." I start to leave, then decide to give her a parting shot. "Whoever comes after me may not be so kind, you know. Not all of us are sexual sadists, but not all of us aren't, either."

She tugs frantically on the cuff and lets out a low growl as I exit the cabin in search of Jim. Good fucking riddance.

Chapter Fourteen

Frankie

The hours pass, though I can't track them. Not with the clock lying on the floor, unplugged and lifeless. I judge the time by the light along the edge of the blackout curtains. Lunchtime comes and goes, and still I remain chained to the bed. I guess the cooking class is off the table.

By the time the sun begins to set, the bottle of water I've rationed has run dry. It's also run straight through me, and I've needed to piss for too long at this point. If I were a man, this wouldn't be a problem. I'd just hold the tip of my dick to the bottle's narrow opening and release the floodgates. Meanwhile, with my current plumbing, I struggle to piss in a cup at the doctor's office without wetting my hand.

When I get out of this predicament, I'll have Maverick's head on a platter. Fuck discovering Jim Madigan's little secrets. I want a peek behind a different curtain.

I could have done both if I hadn't embarrassed blondie.

How was I supposed to know his broken dick came with a high-pressure valve? It's not my fault he gets off from dry humping.

It was kind of hot, though. Not gonna lie.

"No, no, no," I whisper to myself. "We aren't going there, Frankie. Get your mind out of the gutter."

But my bag *is* right there . . . and it's not like I'm going anywhere anytime soon . . .

I haven't masturbated in months. There was a time in my life when I would rub one out twice a day, but as my career took off after years of being overlooked, I couldn't find the energy. I've neglected pleasure in favor of pursuit.

But now that I'm chained to the bed, pursuit is off the table. "Fuck it."

I dip over the side of the bed and pull my bag into my lap. The little silicone toy is tucked away in the false bottom. It's probably dead and this is all for nothing, but I ease it out of its hiding place, anyway. As I depress the button, I'm surprised when it buzzes to life.

I click the button again, and it goes to the alternating vibrations. Why is it so loud? Has it always sounded like a horde of bees? If anyone hears me preparing to pollinate my flower, I'll be mortified.

With another click, the toy shuts off. I stuff a pillow over my lap, followed by my light blanket. My shirt is already off, but I have no plans to strip further. It's been so long that the slightest touch to my nether regions will send me spiraling into oblivion. The shorts won't be an issue.

Closing my eyes, I warm myself to thoughts of a faceless man. He has blond hair, but like I said, he's faceless, so it isn't Maverick. The stranger leans over me, nipping my skin and getting closer to my breasts.

The toy buzzes to life between my legs, and I press it against my shorts. Vibrations travel through the fabric. It's not enough, though, so I spread my legs and press harder.

In my mind, the blond stranger peers up at me with green eyes. *Wait. No. Make them brown . . .* And the headboard knocks against the wall as Not Maverick thrusts into me.

Knock, knock, knock.

My eyes pop open. That sound didn't come from my fantasy. Someone is knocking at the door.

And apparently, this person is a doctor, because the door opens before I even have a chance to invite them in. Or shut off my fucking sex toy. My finger scrambles to find the button as footsteps stomp nearer, but it's as if the damn thing ceased to exist. Finally, my finger lands on the small depression, and I press it and shove the toy into my shorts. I've just gotten my hand above the blanket when Jim rounds the corner.

I pull the blanket higher on my chest. He doesn't seem shocked to find me in my current position, so I have to assume Maverick went straight to him to pawn me off on someone else, just as he said he would.

"Whatever game you're playing, you can't win," I say. "Do you know who my mother is? What sort of power she wields?"

Jim offers a pinched smile as he sits on the edge of the bed, careful to avoid touching my legs. His hands clasp in his lap, and he stares at the wall. "I know of your mother, yes. I know that she's a decorated veteran in her field of study. The better question would be, do *you* know who your mother is?"

I don't dignify his stupidity with a response. Of course I

know who the fuck my mother is. I've known her for my entire existence.

"What about your father?" Jim continues. "What do you know of him?"

"Seems like you have more answers than I do. Why don't you tell me?"

His smile strengthens now. "Oh, I plan to. By the end of this cruise, you'll have answers to questions you never thought to ask."

I roll my eyes. I can't help it. It's comical that he believes I give two fucks about whatever he knows. Still, I'll play along for a little longer. "And what questions would those be?"

"It's not that simple, Frankie. If you want something from me, you'll have to give me something in return."

"Money won't do you any good from behind prison walls, Madigan. Whatever you want from me, you won't be free long enough to enjoy it."

"Money? You think I want money?" His head tips back as he laughs. "Child, money is meaningless to me. I'm at the age where I've grown bored with money and what it brings."

"Is that why you kill? Boredom?"

"My reasons are my reasons. If that's the question you want answered, I'll grant you that. I'll even allow you to place me in handcuffs and lead me off the boat on the final day."

"And what do you want in exchange?"

He spreads his hands and looks at me. "It's quite simple, really. Just play my game. For the rest of the cruise, pretend you're a Sinner. Participate in the games, get to know your fellow participants, and at the end of the cruise, you can have me."

"Just like that?"

"Just like that."

I take a moment to consider his proposition. It would be stupid to deny him, but it might also be stupid to accept his offer. After all, serial killers aren't exactly known for their honesty. Their notoriety stems from their uncanny prowess in the art of lies and manipulation. Agreeing to his plan might mean walking right into the gaping maw of a hungry beast.

But my intuition says he's telling the truth.

"Is my safety guaranteed? Meaning, if someone learns my identity, will you permit them to kill me? Better yet, let's make agents off-limits entirely."

Jim shakes his head. "We both know I can't give you the latter, but you will be safe as long as you play by the rules and listen to your handler."

My handler. Since Maverick chose to push me off on someone else, I wonder who that will be. And I wonder if the devil I know might be better than the devil I don't know.

Beneath the blanket, my left foot begins to tingle. I'm sitting with my legs crossed beneath me, tailor fashion, and the limb has fallen asleep. I straighten my legs while keeping the blanket over my chest.

Buzz . . . buzz . . . buzz, buzz, buzz.

Even if Jim doesn't hear the toy currently assaulting my poor labia, he has to feel it. I feel it in my fucking teeth. My thighs must have put enough pressure on the button to turn on the toy, and now I'm being forced to masturbate against my will.

Jim's eyebrows pull together, and he looks around. "Do you have phone signal in here? The ship has no Wi-Fi, so I don't know how you're receiving a call right now. I'm afraid you'll have to hand over your phone and anything that's giving you a signal."

I wish it was my fucking phone. I'd hand over everything, including my gun and badge, if it would just end this embarrassing moment birthed from the womb of my most vivid nightmares. Clearing my throat, I attempt to shut off the toy by moving my thighs again, but that only changes the pattern. Instead of morse code, the fucking thing is bellowing a low, steady bass note.

It's unmistakable now.

Jim's cheeks blaze red, and he stands from the bed. "It appears I've intruded on a private moment. My apologies. If you don't have any more questions, I'll let you . . . get back to it."

"No, wait," I say through clenched teeth. I can't help it. I'm about three seconds from crying out in ecstasy as Jim looks on, mortified. Same, buddy.

I cram my hand into my shorts and search for the button, much to Jim's ever-increasing discomfort. And mine. From his angle, it probably looks like I'm trying to finish the job while he's standing there. My nervous whimpers must sound like restrained passion to his reddening ears.

After torturous seconds that seem to stretch into years, I finally disarm the device and remove it from my shorts, though I keep the damned thing beneath the blanket. It's bad enough that he heard it. He doesn't need to see it too.

"Will Maverick be my handler?" I keep my voice level, trying to pretend what just happened didn't actually happen. Fuck diamonds. Denial is a girl's best friend. "We don't exactly mesh well, but I'm at least familiar with him."

Jim sighs, but he won't look me in the eye now. That's probably best. "Maverick seems to think you'll do better with someone else, but I chose him to be your handler for a reason. Frankie . . . not all of the Sinners are good people, but some of them are the best people. You'd do well to remember that instead of allowing preconceived notions to cloud your perception."

He walks away and leaves the room without answering my question. Or unchaining me from the fucking bed.

"Wait!" I call as the door clicks shut. "I really need to pee! Please!"

Seconds later, the door opens again, and Maverick comes around the corner. Much like Jim, he won't look me in the eye. He stares at the carpet and says, "Do you need more time to . . ."

"No! I don't need any time for that. I wasn't—" I close my mouth and take a deep breath. "Whatever Jim said, he was mistaken."

Maverick lets out a deep sigh, then nods. "Jim asked me to give this another shot. He's been good to me and my friends, so I'm doing this as a favor to him, just so we're clear. If it were up to me, I'd have handed you off, but he didn't feel you'd be safe with anyone else."

"Well, at least we're both in this for our own ulterior motives. You want to be a good friend, and I want to take down the white whale."

"So, he's agreed to give himself up at the end if you agree to play nice?"

"In so many words, yes."

He shakes his head and looks at the floor. "I told him you'd have your own conditions."

I rattle the handcuff. "Any chance you could set me free so that I can dress? This conversation would be a lot better with eye contact."

"Why? So you can profile me some more?" He stands and fishes the key from his pocket, then tosses it into my lap.

"Enough with the sad-sack routine. I agreed to play nice, and I will. My part of the bargain will be upheld without reproach." I free my wrist, then rush for the bathroom while gripping the blanket around my naked torso. Before I pop behind the door, I lean around the corner and look Maverick in the face. "I'm going to shower and dress. Meet me in the atrium bar. We have so much to talk about."

Chapter Fifteen

Maverick

Jim might be a weird man, but he also has one of the biggest hearts I know. That's what I would have said before this cruise from hell. Now? Now I'd say Jim is an asshole and a half, and his good deeds aren't so altruistic. When he helped me clear my mother's medical debts a few years ago, I never realized it would come back to bite me in the ass.

Both cheeks.

Repeatedly.

I close my eyes and sip the glass of ice water in front of me. Times like these call for clear heads. Well, *my* head has to be clear. What Frankie does is her own business. Hell, she might be more tolerable with a few shots in her.

The bartender looks past me as he wipes the bar with a white cloth. He lets out a low whistle under his breath, remarking on the "piece of ass" that's currently climbing the stairs. Not one to pass on the chance to admire an attractive woman, I turn to see who he's referring to.

As I suspected—and feared—he was referencing the one and only Frankie. Her fingertips barely grace the handrail as she clears the final step, though I'm not sure how she even walked up the stairs in that tight beige pencil skirt. Strappy tan heels hold her dainty feet in a death grip, and a flowing cream top gives the faintest hint of cleavage.

"I bet she smells good," the bartender whispers as he licks his lips and stares openly. "Fuck, I bet she tastes good too. Not that I'd eat her rich-bitch pussy."

I turn on my stool and motion the bartender closer.

"What can I get for you, bud?" He smiles at me as he turns a glass in his hand.

I smile back as I place my forearms on the bar and lean forward. "I'm just curious about something, *bud*. How old are you?"

"Me? I'm—"

"Old enough to know how to treat women with respect?" I cock my head and drop the smile. "Yeah, you're old enough for that. How about you keep your disgusting sexual commentary to yourself."

He opens his mouth to pop off with some asinine comeback from his grade-school days, but then his eyes fall on my wrist. As a member of staff, he knows his place.

"Sorry about that. W-won't happen again," he says with a tight smile.

I take another sip of water to wash down the heat rising in my chest. I remind myself that I would have defended any woman in that situation. This isn't some protective feeling toward Frankie. It's just not.

Fabric rustles beside me as she slides onto the stool. The faint scent of mint mingles around her, prying into my nose. I hate that I like this smell.

"Damn, is that vodka?" She turns my glass, then leans closer and sniffs. "Nope. That's definitely not vodka."

I pull the glass in front of me again. "I'm not a big drinker."

"Or a big talker, apparently." She waves down the bartender, who wisely keeps his eyes above her neckline as she orders a white Russian.

I close my eyes and swallow my frustrations. If I want to hold down my end of Jim's deal, I'll have to let my guard down again, like it was in the beginning. I'll have to give her a chance if I expect her to do the same.

A water droplet races down the side of the glass and fades into the napkin beneath it. I've never wanted to be a water droplet so badly. "Talking isn't easy. You need to see it from my side. You want to destroy the people I care about. And for what? So that you can have your picture in the newspaper? Serial killers murder for fame too, you know."

"But I'm not murdering anyone. I'm simply putting them behind bars." She twirls her slender fingers through the air. "What you people do is wrong, and I'm just calling for the past-due bill."

"Just . . ." I search for the right words, but no matter what I say, she'll bat it right back to me. "Just open your mind, even if it's only a tiny crack. You might even find you like the fresh air."

"Doubtful."

I grip the edge of the bar and grit my teeth. "Just fucking *try*."

"Okay, okay." She heaves an exasperated sigh and sips her drink. "I agreed to this, so it's only fair that I give this a shot. Must I kill your victims, though?"

"Shh!" I look around to be sure no one heard her. Then I lean closer. "They aren't victims, sweetheart. You need to change that way of thinking real quick. They're Cattle—here for our use."

She grimaces and traces the rim of her glass with her finger. "I can't think of people like that. They've done some horrible things, but what gives us the right to punish them so finally?"

"So you're against the death penalty?"

"I didn't say that."

"Then what are you saying?"

She turns her head, looking me fully in the face. "I'm saying that it isn't our place to make these decisions. We have a legal system. We aren't animals."

"Our legal system is flawed."

"So you've said, but I never claimed it was perfect." Frankie sips her drink and spins on the stool, stopping once she's facing the banister overlooking the atrium's first floor. "If I have to kill them, I'll only take out the pinks and reds."

The tight knot in my chest loosens a little. "It's funny that you mention that because there is a tight little collective of killers who run on that same fuel."

"Is Jim one of them?"

Fuck. "Well . . . no, but—"

"What about you?"

I don't want to answer this question, but I have no choice. "I'm a contract killer, so I've probably made some questionable decisions, but when I kill for sport, it's a red or a pink."

"Kill for sport? Do you hear yourself?" She shudders. "I don't think I can get into your headspace. I just can't. Maybe fifteen years ago when I had a malformed brain, but I'm a mature woman now. I have sense."

"And crow's feet," I mutter. It's a lie, but I know it will cut deep. Her two-hour beauty routine is proof of that.

She opens her mouth to blow me down with a cheap shot, I'm sure, but I hold up my hand and silence her as I spot the time on my watch.

"Save it for later. We have to be on deck in less than thirty minutes, and you aren't dressed appropriately for the activity." I slide off my stool and look back at her. "Have you ever been swimming with sharks, sweetheart?"

Judging by the stunned silence and widening blue eyes, the answer is no. Oh, this is going to be fun.

Chapter Sixteen

Frankie

I stare at myself in the mirror and sigh. Is this really better than being handcuffed to the bed while topless? God, that would almost be hot if the circumstances were different, but no, I'm not sure this is better. Not as I stand below deck on a small fishing vessel and prepare to commit murder under a sea of stars.

Eve steps beside me and offers a kind smile. "If you're nervous about the sharks, don't be. Yeah, it's possible for them to get into the cage, but you're more likely to be struck by lightning."

"They can get into the cage?" I blink a few times and try to steel my nerves, but it's no use. That wasn't what I was nervous about, but it sure as fuck is now.

"You'll be working with Maverick, right?"

I nod.

"Then you definitely have nothing to worry about. Honey, he is the definition of Mister Nice Guy. If the shark squeezes into your cage, he'll throw himself into its jaws to save you."

"The Maverick you know and the Maverick I know are two very different people, it would seem. To be honest, I don't think he likes me very much." I pretend that this bothers me. And it kind of does. "He and I don't see eye to eye on killing, and it's creating a bit of a disconnect."

"Because he's a hitman?" Eve nibbles her lip. "I hate to break it to you, but I'm no different from him. Kindra and Cat struggled with it at first too, but our friendship came first, so that helped them cope. Maybe that's how you need to look at it. See Maverick for who he is as a person and how he treats others."

I mean, he kills others, but okay. Maybe she has a point. Maybe I should try to silence my rational mind and be a little more open. Hell, maybe I should even cut loose a little. It's not like anything can come back to haunt me. King gave us license to kill.

"Yeah, maybe you're right," I say, and that earns a smile from Eve. I'm grateful. I really like her. And maybe I don't have to rat on *everyone* after this.

We help each other into our wetsuits. The only other woman in the changing room is the little old lady from the first day, but she hasn't said peep since we boarded the ship. She picks up the wet suit, grimaces, then hurries up the steps.

"What's her deal?" I ask when the upstairs door shuts behind the woman. "I met her on the first day, and she didn't speak then, either."

Eve gathers her hair and ties it back with an elastic, then hands one to me. "Don't take offense. Her ex-husband slashed her throat and damaged her vocal cords, so she can't talk. Well, she can, but only in a language she and Grim understand fully."

"Grim . . ." Realization dawns, and the blood freezes in my veins. "*Der Sensenmann?*" I whisper.

"Honey, you don't have to whisper," Eve says with a chuckle. "We're all a little infamous here. The Abattoir Adonis, the Heartbreak Killer, the—"

"The Abattoir Adonis *and* the Heartbreak Killer are here? Where?"

Eve laughs again, a little harder this time. "You're starting to sound like Cat. She was obsessed with serial killers before she became one of us. I can't lie, though. I was a little starstruck the first time I met Kindra, but I played it off well."

"Wait, I thought the Abattoir Adonis was a man!"

"He is. That's Ezra, the hot British guy with glasses." Eve pulls the rubber hood over her head, leaving only her face exposed. "Kindra is his fiancée. The Heartbreak Killer. Cat, her best friend, is the Confessor, and *her* boyfriend, Bennett, is the Chaos Killer."

Jesus fucking Christ! Who needs Maverick when there are Eves in the world? I feel like I've met God at the pearly gates, and he's giving me the answers to all of life's mysteries.

"Do you know who killed JonBenét too?" I ask, though I'm only half-joking.

"No, but Jim promised that as soon as he learns of the killer's identity, he'll pay five million to the Sinner who brings him to Devil Horn Island."

My ears perk up, and I log that tidbit away for later. Devil Horn Island doesn't sound familiar, which means it hasn't been on our radar. I plan to change that.

We start up the stairs, which means I'm running out of

time to ask questions. If Maverick gets wind of the sort of conversations I'm having when out of his grasp, he'll keep a tighter hold.

"Have you been to Devil Horn Island?" I ask.

Eve shakes her head. "No, my first trip was last winter, and that wasn't on the island. Jim hosted the first winter event in Alaska, and I had a break between shows, so I decided to give it a go. I'm so glad I did because I've made some incredible friendships."

"Alaska, huh?" I close the door behind me as we reach the top of the stairs, but the questions come to a swift halt when I spot Maverick's tall figure a few feet away.

He stands at the ship's edge, gripping the railing as gentle waves rock us back and forth. Ice Pig stands beside him, and both men stare out at the open water. Stars gleam in a clear sky, only sharing the stage with a sliver of moonlight.

To our right, the deck stretches out and widens. A large spotlight shines on the water, where some of the crew has already dumped chum to stir up some sharks. I've never been cage diving, so I don't know if this is normal, but it feels dangerous. Why send the sharks into a frenzy before putting people in front of them?

A few Cattle also stand on the deck. I can tell them apart from the others because they don't wear wetsuits. Aside from the glittering red or pink bikini bottoms, they don't wear anything at all.

Two more men in wetsuits join Maverick and Ice Pig as Eve and I approach. I recognize both of them. One is Grim, the notorious killer from Germany, and the other is Aven, the Scottish man who sat at my table on the first night.

"He's definitely one of them," Aven says, and my ears practically twist like satellites to hear more. "He said he came cage diving to swim with sharks, not murder people. I don't know what more proof we need than that."

Maverick's gaze flicks to me. "Jim isn't here, so we can't sanction an agent kill right now. You'll have to save it until you get back to the ship."

"I have to get in a fucking cage with the guy," Aven whispers. "What if he tries to take me out?"

I study Aven's beefed-up frame. He looks like he eats steroids for breakfast and shits pure creatine in the afternoon. What does he have to fear?

"Could you switch with me?" Aven asks Maverick, and my heart picks up its pace. "You seem like you're pretty close with Jim. If you kill the guy, he probably won't excommunicate you."

Maverick shakes his head, and my heart rate returns to normal. "Can't do it. I have to look after my roommate. It's her first trip, and she's a little nervous."

"Perhaps Rose will switch with you, Aven. If you feel unsafe, you can get into my cage with me." Grim is completely serious, despite standing before us in little more than a shiny silver banana hammock that struggles to obscure his massive balls. "Rose will not hesitate to put an end to funny business, so she will be safe." He turns to me. "Please do not stare at my genitals. It is rude."

"He can't bring that much hanging brain to the table and expect people to be unaffected," Eve mutters. "His nuts could have their own zip code."

I cover my mouth to stifle a smile.

"You'll be fine, Aven," Maverick offers. Then his gaze travels upward, and his jaw slackens.

We turn as a group to see what has him so flustered. At first glance, I can't figure it out. It's just the older woman descending the steps from the wheelhouse, and aside from her attire—which is no attire at all now—I see nothing out of the norm.

That's when the spotlight catches on the blade in her hand. As she steps closer, streaks of red also become more visible. They paint her in random places, as if she's been slinging a paintbrush at a canvas.

Or a knife into a body.

She steps closer to the old man and traces symbols on his palm, leaving red lines behind. He smiles at her, then faces us.

Grim clears his throat. "The matter is thusly concluded. Rose severed his femoral artery and allowed him to bleed out."

"But why is she naked?" I ask.

He turns toward me, his face a mask of serious offense. "Because she wishes to be." With that, he grips her arm and leads her back to the wheelhouse.

The five of us who remain watch silently as they ascend the steps and disappear once more. I have so many questions.

"Do they normally just . . . take each other out?" I whisper to Eve.

"Honey, I have no idea. This is only my second trip, and it's nothing like the winter retreat. With these people, you just need to put your wheels down so you can roll with things." She cracks her neck and shakes out her hands. "Any chance we could get this show on the road?" she asks Maverick.

He nods and leads the way to a small table covered in weaponry. The Cattle stand chained to the deck a few feet away. Now that we're more in the open, I can see the two cages dangling just below the ship's edge. I step a little closer and peer into the water. Flashes of silver-brown skin catch the light and disappear into the depths.

Maverick and the others study the weapons. I'm assuming we'll each take Cattle to use as bait for the sharks, and I feel absolutely sick about it. The four men on deck may be criminals, but they have a right to due process and a punishment that fits their crimes.

I step closer to the weaponry. I need to understand the *why* here. "Eve, how do you pick who you want to kill at these things?"

Eve shrugs and runs her fingers along a harpoon. "I just tell Jim to bring a red or pink for me. That's all the motivation I require."

"But what if they're innocent? I mean, what if the court got it wrong?"

Ice Pig chuckles and gathers a few large fishhooks from the table. "Well, then I guess that's on the court, ain't it?"

"What if we kill innocents, though?" I pick up a filet knife and pretend I'm testing its heft. Feeling like a fool, I put it down. "Does that ever bother you?"

Maverick is staring at me with that look again. Like he's over my bullshit. When he opens his mouth, I prepare for some sort of admonishment, but then his eyes soften. "Come with me."

He grips the filet knife and tosses it once before jerking his head toward the Cattle. When he starts walking, my feet stupidly follow him. I blame how cool he looks while doing literally anything. We stop in front of the Cattle, who've been so quiet because their lips are glued shut.

"They can't even plead their case if they have a case to plead," I whisper, motioning to the four men. "Do you really see no problem with this?"

Maverick steps forward, toward the first man on the

end. "Mind if I cut your lips loose, pal? It won't hurt as long as you don't move."

The man shakes his head, then raises his face, offering his lips to Maverick, who steps forward and gently slices through the layer of glue. And part of the man's lips, but we'll pretend it was as painless as he promised.

"Oh, thank you," the man whimpers.

Maverick holds up his hand. "Don't thank me just yet. I'm going to give you an opportunity right now. What you do with it is up to you." He looks down the line. "In fact, I'll give all of you the same opportunity. One of you will get to live today. The others will die."

He pushes me forward, and I peer at him over my shoulder. What the fuck is he doing?

"This is your judge and jury. Her name is Frankie, and she's very fair. She values honesty above all else, however, so your best chance is to tell the truth, no matter how horrible that truth may be. So, if any of you would like the chance to live, step forward and plead your case."

The first man needs no more convincing. "I did it. I said I didn't, but I did. I'm guilty. Please let me live, and I won't do it again. I won't, I won't, I—"

"That's a good start, but it's not enough." Maverick places his hand on the man's shoulder. "What are you guilty of?"

"Oh, fuck. Fuck. Is she the Confessor?" The man squirms in his pink undies. "Oh man, yeah. It was bad. I'm sorry. I'm sick."

My insides twist into knots until I fear I'll vomit. "No, I'm not the Confessor. That's enough."

But it isn't enough for Maverick. He goes to the next man, then the next. Both men cry guilty, and because they wear red or pink bottoms, that's enough for me; I don't want the details. Then the fourth man gets a turn.

"I didn't do it," he says. His voice is flat, emotionless, and unlike his peers, he doesn't squirm and beg for his life. "They said I raped my friend's cousin, and then they put me away for twenty years. I didn't fucking rape her. She came into my room in the middle of the night and started sucking my dick. The bitch started it."

"She told the story a little differently, but it doesn't really matter." Maverick turns away from him and faces me, as if he's proved his point, but that doesn't prove anything. He is prepared to end a man's life over a belief, not a fact.

"Was she intoxicated?" I ask. "Drugs, alcohol? Anything that could damage her ability to make decisions? A drunk yes isn't the same as a sober yes."

"No shit, lady." The man rolls his eyes. "No, she didn't drink or nothing."

"Probably because she was so involved with her school's D.A.R.E. program." Maverick turns to me. "The *bitch*, as he called her, was a seven-year-old girl, and no, she did not *start* anything. This man stumbled into her room in a drunken state and—"

I hold up my hand. "I don't need to hear any more. I've made my decision, and I want that one." I point to the man who claimed his innocence.

"This is the one who gets to live? Seriously?" Maverick throws his hands in the air and shakes his head. "I give up."

"There seems to be a misunderstanding," I say. "This isn't the man I want to save. This is the man I want to kill."

As Maverick unhooks my chosen Cattle, I wage a war inside myself. Instead of talking myself into the kill, however, I'm talking myself out of enjoying it. Because I want this a little too much. The sickness is catching. The bloodlust fills every cell until I'm shaking with rage.

I'll never admit it to Maverick, but I get it now. The anger. The need to end someone. In this situation, when presented with the option to feed that feeling or deny its meal in favor of righteousness, I'm going to go against everything I am and feed the beast.

"She wanted it, you bitch." The Cattle turns his head and spits in my face.

Maverick tenses, and the Cattle stumbles forward and goes over the side of the boat. It happens so quickly that neither of us has time to react. The Cattle doesn't even scream before a loud splash breaks the quiet.

I rush forward and peer over the railing. Seconds later, the man's head pierces the white foam, and he sucks in a gulp of air as he floats on his back and gloats up at us. His arms are still fastened behind him, but his legs are free to kick and keep him above the waves.

He smiles and screams something up at us, but I can't hear him over the spray.

"What?" I shout down at him as I cup my ear.

He repeats himself, but I still don't hear him. Not that it matters.

Maverick comes up behind me and dumps a bucket of guts into the water. Realizing what's about to happen, the man spins onto his stomach and tries to kick away from the chum.

It's too late. There is no soundtrack to play a steady two-note theme, and the telltale fin never breaks the water, but when the surface tension explodes in a spray of silver and white, we all know what happened. The man's brief scream disappears below the water, followed by the flood of a sickening shade of red.

I turn to Maverick and shrug. "He was asking for it, right? I mean, he went into the water with sharks, so he must have wanted to be eaten. Isn't that the logic?"

For the first time since I forced him to come in his pants, he smiles.

"Damn," Eve says as she hurries to peer over the side of the boat. "Fucking cold, Frankie. I love it! You pushed him right over the edge."

I don't correct her. Neither does Maverick.

"I guess it doesn't matter that we lost one, since Grim and Rosie won't be diving. We only needed three." Eve looks back at the remaining Cattle.

Maverick winces and rubs the back of his neck. "Yeah . . . about that. I kind of promised one of them that they'd get to live. I can't go back on it now."

"Well, then I guess you guys won't be cage diving." Eve turns to me. "Sorry, honey, but if you want to saddle yourself with Dudley Do-Right, you'll have to deal with the consequences."

I think I'm okay with that. And I think I'm starting to see Maverick—and his hobby—in a new light.

Chapter Seventeen

Maverick

After our eventful cage-diving outing, we were too exhausted for dinner, so we went back to the room and crashed. We woke up this morning, had breakfast together in the dining hall, then separated for lunch. She had plans to eat with Eve and the girls, and we would meet up when they finished.

So please tell me why I walked into the atrium and spotted Frankie and Ice Pick as they sashayed toward one of the lounges? And day three had started out so well.

I hurry to catch up to them before Ice Pick spills too many beans. He's denser than fruitcake, so I'm not necessarily concerned that he'll discover Frankie's secret, but he's bound to reveal all of ours. I catch them just before they enter the lounge.

"What are . . ." I gulp air. The mad race down the flight of stairs left me winded. "What are you two . . . up to?"

Frankie slides her arm from the crook of Ice Pick's elbow, and my blood pressure lowers slightly. "As the girls and I were finishing lunch, Ice Pig showed up and asked if we'd like to go to a speed dating event with the"—she glances around—"Normies. The girls are all in relationships, so they declined, but I'm free as a bird and figured it might be fun."

"I don't know if that's such a good idea." My gaze slides from Frankie to Ice Pick, then back to Frankie. "I mean, the Normies are . . . and we are . . . You get what I'm saying, don't you?"

Frankie cocks her head. "No. That would require you to use words."

Ice Pick chuckles beside her, and what a team these assholes make as they turn and start into the lounge.

I reach out and grip Frankie's arm, stopping them from entering. "Do I really need to explain why it's a bad idea to mingle with the Normies? Jim intended for us to do just that, but I'd prefer to stick to our own."

"Don't be a killjoy, Maverick." Frankie rolls her eyes. "I can't believe I'm saying this, but act your fucking age. Live a little. Throw caution to the wind and give a middle finger to the consequences. What's good for the goose is good for the gander, yeah?"

I don't know how I feel about this new version of Frankie. The experience last night seemed to unlock some unhinged part of her, and I think I'd like to shove it back in its box now. I wanted her to loosen up, not completely come undone.

But it doesn't matter what I think, because she wrinkles her nose in a snarky smile before turning back to the lounge and stepping inside. Speed dating isn't my idea of an afternoon well spent, but if I want to keep an eye on Frankie, I guess this is what we're doing.

I catch up with them at a table lined with pens and

paper name tags. Ice Pick scrawls his name on a tag and slaps it on his chest. Only then do I realize that he's gone with his government name, which is . . .

"Chad Smith?" My eyebrows rise up my forehead. "I never really pictured you with a name at all, but Chad Smith?"

He pulls me aside as Frankie searches for a working pen. "I didn't want to write Ice Pick and make the girl feel bad for calling me the wrong name. She seems nice, and I don't want to embarrass her."

"So you made up a name?"

His mustache twitches as his lips curve into a smile. "Nope, that's my name. It's a family name, you see, passed down through the generations. My great-great-great grandaddy, Chad Smith, was pretty famous. If you're wondering if that's who I'm named after, it sure is!" His grin widens as if he's just told me a sneaky secret.

Meanwhile, I have never heard of Chad Smith. Or rather, I've probably heard of so many Chad Smiths that the name is synonymous with familiarity. For his sake, however, I widen my eyes and act impressed.

"No shit? I never would have thought."

"Well, I don't like to tell many people. I'd hate for someone to think I was bragging." His expression sobers. "Let's just keep this between us, though, okay?"

I zip my lips. "Your secret is safe with me."

Frankie joins us, and I snag a quick glance at her name tag.

"Gina Tagliano?" I lick my lips and read it again to be sure.

"If he can be Chad Smith, I can be Gina Tagliano." She flicks her finger toward Ice Pick's name tag, not realizing that this is his actual name and not the most generic thing he could come up with.

"You gotta pick a funny name too," Ice whispers. "We can make a game out of it."

And now he's playing along. Fuck my life.

"If I have to loosen up a bit, so do you." Frankie nibbles her bottom lip and nudges me toward the table.

Yes, fuck my life indeed, because that flirty look is all it takes for me to bend at the waist and scrawl the name Leviticus Deuteronomy. "Weird enough for you?"

"Leviti—you just wrote books of the Bible, jackass. Here, give me that." Frankie snatches the pen from my hand and sets to work. Seconds later, I receive my new name.

"Chester . . . Copperpot? Why does that sound so familiar?"

She slaps the nametag onto my chest as Ice Pick giggles like a schoolgirl beside her. Before she can answer my question, feedback squeals through a microphone and a perky blonde steps to the front of the room. We listen as she squints and grins and gives us her spiel.

"If she pours on that sweet act any thicker, we'll drown," Frankie whispers beside me.

"Sure as hell beats pretending to be Chester fucking Copperpot, whoever that is." I shift my weight and continue "listening" to the rules of the game. "What was the Sinner activity this afternoon? I'd rather be doing that."

Frankie turns to face me, no longer caring about the woman at the head of the room. "Remember when you wanted me to try? Just a little? Maybe you could do the same. Maybe we can both benefit from seeing how the other half lives, hmm?"

She keeps her voice low so that Ice Pick can't hear her, though I don't think that's an issue. He's actually entranced by the blonde. And now that I think about it, maybe this wasn't the best activity to take him to. He doesn't exactly have the best track record when it comes to wooing women.

It's too late to back out now, though. The doors swing shut behind us and the lights dim as the blonde jangles a little bell and instructs the men to take a seat. My heart squeezes in my chest as Frankie—*Gina*—gives me a flirty wink before joining a gaggle of women near the blonde.

Ice Pick and I do as instructed. The little tables are far enough apart that the private conversations remain private, but he and I sit as close as we can. I fully understand the risk we're undertaking, and Ice Pick seems to at least grasp the need to stick together. Frankie, on the other hand, chats with the women as if she belongs with them.

And that's when I remember that she does.

She isn't one of us, and Jim's little science experiment won't change that, even if she's playing nice now.

A lavender sheet of paper rests on the table. This is how I'm meant to keep track of my dates, but it might as well be Frankie's vagina because I have no plans to do anything with it. The little bell rings again, and the women take their positions at the various tables, with instructions to move counterclockwise around the room. I'm not surprised to see that we have a surplus of men, but that means Ice Pick and I will need to wait a bit before any ladies swing our way. I turn my attention to the room. While I'm just sitting here, I might as well make use of my time.

We haven't taken out any of the Normie agents yet. They don't stick out like sore thumbs in a crowd of Normies, though. It's much more difficult to spot them in this setting.

While analyzing the men and women, my gaze keeps returning to Frankie. She offers easy, relaxed smiles to the first two men, but her eyes hold no interest. As she scrawls something on her notepad, I'm dying to see what she's written. What does she think of these men?

Why the fuck do you care, man?

I don't know. But I do. And that's a fucking problem.

I nearly jump out of my skin as a woman drops into the seat in front of me. With a reluctance that scares me, I tear my eyes away from Frankie and give this person my full attention.

A laugh springs into my chest, but I shove it down with sheer willpower. If Eighties were still alive, this would have been his perfect partner. Her red hair belongs firmly in a Whitesnake video, and that electric-blue eyeshadow isn't doing her any favors. The woman smacks a wad of spearmint gum that fights for its life amid a cloud of cigarette aroma as she holds a hand toward me and offers a breathy, "Hey, I'm Twilight."

Twilight might want to lay off the Pall Malls.

I accept her handshake—and make a mental note to find the nearest hand-sanitizing station—before offering my fake name.

"Chester Copperpot?" She smacks the table and giggles. "You're funny."

Unsure how to respond, I blink at her. "Yes. So what do you like to do in your free time, Twilight?"

"We don't really want to talk about hobbies, shug. Let's swap room numbers and move things along." A puff of stale air accompanies her hoarse southern twang. "I take it in the ass, shug. Raw."

She grins, putting her yellowed teeth on display, and I want to run away. Far, far away. Instead, I clear my throat.

"As tempting as that offer is, I think I'd rather shove my

dick in a flaming pile of elephant shit." I smile at her. "Raw."

Twilight jerks backward as if I've slapped her. This isn't a shining moment for me, and I'm usually more polite, but this woman repulses me. The sooner she moves out of my orbit, the safer we'll all be. Thankfully, she rises to her full height—which extends by an extra three inches, thanks to her hot-pink heels—and storms out of the lounge.

I lean over my sheet of paper and scribble my thoughts.

Twilight aka Peggy Bundy: Not interested. Smells like a smokestack and looks like a nightmare. 1/5

The man Frankie is seated with stands from his seat and excuses himself. He probably wants to chase after that raw anal. Some of us need it more than most. She looks at me and shrugs, and we share our first telepathic joke with stifled giggles.

I lean over my paper and scribble something else.

Frankie: Interested against my will. Smells like fresh mint. Looks like

I can't finish the sentence on the paper, but I can in my head. She smells like fresh mint, and she looks like something I struggle to put words to.

She looks like my downfall.

Chapter Eighteen

Frankie

I hum a little song under my breath as I rifle through the clothes in my bag. For the life of me, I can't figure out why Maverick is so pissed. All I did was speak with the speed date organizer after the event so that I could set up dates with our matches. We're supposed to be having fun, but he looks prepared to set the cruise ship on fire to get out of this evening. I'll just have to keep the matches out of reach.

He rubs the back of his neck as I try to decide what to wear. "You're supposed to be seeing things from our side of the fence. If you're skipping all the Sinner activities, how can we achieve that?"

I fling a dress onto the bed. "Does this look too slutty? I don't want him to think he's actually got a chance, but I want him to want me."

"Are you even listening to me?" He glances at the bed. "Don't wear that."

"I'm listening, but that doesn't mean I agree with you. Besides, we still have four days on the water. I'm sure I'll be forced to kill again, don't you worry." I roll my eyes and pluck a baby-blue romper from the pile of clothes in my bag. "What about this? It'll give some leg without revealing everything."

"Yeah, the color goes well with your eyes." Maverick sighs and goes to the closet. "What about Ice? Have you thought about how this Normie woman might affect him? He probably sees this as a real date. Are you going to break it to him that we're all just having a bit of fun? And what about the guy you're seeing? At least I'm not stringing anyone along."

"Oh, you'll have a date too. What fun would this be if you weren't in on the joke?"

He walks toward the bed with a pair of khaki shorts and a gray polo. "You can't be serious."

My lip curls. "Neither can you with that grandpa outfit. If you must wear a polo, at least pick one with some color."

I go to the closet and look through his clothes, but most of the nicer things are also very drab. I feel like I'm rooting through my mother's wardrobe.

"Jesus, could you borrow something from a friend? What about that British guy? He's always well-dressed."

"We're roughly the same height, but he's a bit bulkier. I'll look like I'm playing dress up with Daddy's clothes if I borrow anything from him."

"What about the really crass dude who wears the fun Hawaiian prints?"

"Bennett?"

"Yeah, that guy." I grab the romper and head toward the bathroom. "Go see if you can wear something of his. The funnier, the better. I need a good laugh."

"No fucking way," he says, but the cabin door opens and closes seconds later. Even if he won't wear a silly shirt, maybe he's at least off to find something presentable.

Not that it matters. Ice Pig and I handpicked our dates, but Maverick's date was handpicked by me, and I can't wait for him to meet her.

I smile to myself as I strip off my clothes.

After dressing and touching up my makeup, Maverick still hasn't returned. He'd better not back out of this. I'm toying with the idea of letting him leave the ship without handcuffs, but if he spoils my fun, that could change.

The list of people I'm willing to turn over to King is shrinking by the minute. When I first stepped foot on this boat, I was prepared to shout every name and pull back every curtain. Now I'm finding it difficult to imagine doing that to any of these people. Even Jim.

"Remember why you're here, girl," I whisper to myself as I slip a pair of dangly silver earrings into my ears. "This is your chance. You have to give them Jim."

And isn't that why I've thrown myself so fully into this mess? Jim made a promise, and if I hold up my end of the bargain, he'll be forced to hold up his.

I drop my strewn makeup into a small bag, then cut off the lights as I leave the room. The dark hallways have started to feel more familiar to me than the bright spaces for the Normies, so I'm glad we'll be spending the evening on Normie turf. While I'm having fun, I can't let myself fall too deep into this den of iniquity.

After a quick elevator ride, I'm deposited on one of the upper decks. I still have a half hour to spare before I'm supposed to meet Ice Pig and our dates at Boogie Woogie Woo—the ship's version of a 70s night club—so I stroll to the side deck to take in some sea air.

A man stands a few feet away from the door, and when the light catches his side profile, I realize it's Jim. His hands clutch the railing as he looks out at the black ocean. Shadows cling to the few wrinkles on his face. Despite knowing who he is and what he's capable of, I find myself almost sorry for him. He looks sad.

The door snicks shut with a click, and Jim turns at the sound. When he sees me, he smiles. "Hello, dear child. Where's your friend this evening?"

You mean my babysitter. That's what I want to say, but the venom doesn't fill my fangs the way I'd hoped. Taking a jab right now feels . . . wrong.

And I can't put my finger on why.

"Unless he backs out, Maverick will be joining me shortly for a date," I say instead.

The sadness in his eyes is replaced by a glint of something else. "Oh, a date? I didn't realize you two would so easily jump the hurdles in your path, but I'm pleased."

My eyelids nearly retract into my skull as I realize what he thinks I meant. "No, no. You misunderstand. We aren't going on a date together. We're going on a date with others. Well, technically, a triple date."

"I find the act of lovemaking more pleasurable when it's one on one, but if you enjoy group activities, I'm happy Maverick and your third are on board."

Jesus fuck. I'd try to set him straight, but I'll probably end up in a bukkake ring if I keep going.

"I'm just glad you're finding things to enjoy on this trip," he adds. "You're special, Frankie. Untouchable beyond your own understanding. When we dock at port on the final day, you'll face a decision unlike any you've faced before." He takes a deep breath, his smile fading. "And when you make that decision, I want you to do it with your heart instead of your head."

I scoff and join him at the railing. "That's how you get into trouble, Madigan. The heart wants. It feeds on irrationality and chaos. The brain needs. It runs on logic and willpower." I lean my forearms on the railing and shake my head. "You can live with only needs, but you can't survive on wants. And there are—"

"Laws," he says, finishing my sentence. He nods his head and smiles again. "Yes, there are laws, aren't there?"

"Right."

"Where there is good, there is bad."

"Exactly."

"And those two things can't coexist in the same space, can they?"

I shake my head softly. "They cannot."

"Can you blame an old man for wanting the impossible? Some of us haven't mastered thinking with their heads." He offers a light laugh, then stands to his full height and pats my shoulder. "I hope your evening is wonderful, Frankie. Thank you for holding up your end of the bargain. You can trust that I will do my part as well."

"I'm counting on it," I say, but as he retreats into the ship's interior, I'm not so sure I mean it.

I lean against the bar and nurse a lukewarm beer, checking my watch for the third time in five minutes. Ice Pig and Maverick still have a few minutes before they're due to arrive, but our dates are already on the dance floor. I can't keep making excuses.

The song shifts from a current pop tune to something slow, and the people file off the dance floor and crowd the bar. Only a young couple remains beneath the glittering disco ball. They look into each other's eyes, completely unaware that someone is likely being murdered on this ship at this very moment. I saw the Sinners' evening itinerary, and if I had to miss an event, I'm glad it was the one titled Conga Line.

My date slides against me, his hand wandering over my waist as he yells for the bartender to bring him a beer. The two women for Maverick and Ice crowd me on the other side.

"Where are our boys?" the brunette asks in her nasal voice. "I wanna meet the man of the hour!"

Because there were so many men and so few women, not every lady had the chance to meet every man in our allotted hour of speed dating. Rhonda here was very displeased about missing out on Maverick, so I figured I'd help her out.

"They said they'd be here. Maybe they want to show up fashionably late?" I shrug my shoulders.

"I'm not so sure about the fashionable part," Rhonda says with a curl of her lip.

I follow her gaze to the doorway, where Maverick and Ice Pig step into the swirling laser lights. Ice hasn't changed a thing. He still sports the same t-shirt and jeans he wore earlier, complete with an unknown stain just below his left nipple. Maverick, on the other hand, is a new man.

He strolls toward the bar with a confidence he has no business displaying while wearing such an atrocious ensemble. He seems to have taken my advice to heart, as he now sports a loud Hawaiian shirt that looks a couple sizes too small. He's left it unbuttoned, revealing peeks of his toned chest and abs. The bright-pink board shorts and flip-flops with socks just seals the deal.

But the hair. The hair is like nothing I could have conjured in my wildest dreams. The perfect hard part has been cast aside for the most hideous and unbecoming pompadour I've ever witnessed. And is that a gold cross dangling from his left ear?

Maybe it's the hideous outfit or maybe it's the beer, but I start laughing and can't stop. By the time they reach us, my mascara has probably cut black tracks down my face from the tears, but the laughter pours out of me. He'll be furious when he sees me losing it, and I don't care.

But he isn't. As he draws nearer, he spins and holds out his hand with a playful grin. I step forward to take it, but Rhonda gets between us. That's when I remember he isn't my date.

"I didn't have the pleasure of meeting you at the event," he says over the music. "The name's Chester Copperbottom."

"Copperpot," I correct.

He nods and turns back to Rhonda. "That's what I said. Copperpot."

"I thought you got lost while looking for One-Eyed Willy's treasure," Rhonda says with a laugh, and that's when the realization dawns in Maverick's eyes.

He pins me with a look before embracing the chaos. "Yeah, my mom loved that movie." He raises a fist. "Goonies never say die."

I'm shocked he knows a movie that's more from my era than his. Shocked, but not displeased. "You must do an excellent truffle shuffle," I say. "Why don't you get on the dance floor and show us?"

"With pleasure, but I never dance alone." He reaches

past Rhonda and offers his hand. When she huffs, he spares her a glance. "Sorry, but you aren't my type. That guy looks interested, though." He points to my date as he drags me onto the dance floor.

When he pulls me against him, I finally get a good look at his eyes. That's when I realize something is very wrong.

Chapter Nineteen

Maverick

"Have you been taking *drugs*?" Frankie whisper-screams as her hands rest on my shoulders. I hardly hear her over the music.

The music. It's really good. I don't know this song, but I like it. My hips rock to the beat as Frankie's fingers brush over my skin. I'm so sensitive to her touch. It's really good too. The hairs on my neck are like guitar strings, and Frankie strums them as we spin on the dance floor. Is that where the music comes from?

Her finger taps against my head, but it feels more like she reaches beneath my skull and taps my brain. "Hello? Anyone in there? What drugs have you taken?"

"I don't take drugs. I don't smoke. You won't find a single tattoo or piercing on my body. Not my style, sweetheart." I lower her into a dip and nearly drop her on the floor.

Frankie rights herself with a scowl and grips my hand, tugging me off the dance floor. That's probably good. I'm fucking thirsty. I can't remember the last time I wanted water so badly.

But instead of leading me toward the bar and the pretty lights and the music that's trying to meld with my soul, she drags me to a dark, quiet(ish) corner. How very lame of her.

"Come on! Loosen up and have some fun!" I jump up and down and pump my fist to the beat.

Frankie grips my thrusting fist and lowers it as she glances around. "Dude, you're currently party rocking to Hozier's 'Work Song' like it's your job. What the fuck did you take?"

I look at the dance floor. The figures are a little blurry, but they're holding each other and swaying slowly. Why does the song sound so different to me? I hear the backfill, the hidden melody. It's a fucking *banger*!

The chorus hits, and I tip my head back and shout the words. When Hozier's honeyed voice drops low and soft again, I smile at Frankie. "Fuck, I love this song!"

She takes a step back and studies me as I keep bopping to the bass notes. Starting at my feet, she travels upward until she reaches my hair. With squinted eyes, she steps forward and wipes sweat from my brow.

"Shit," she mutters before gripping my hand and leading me away from all the fun. When we get to the hall, she spins around to face me. "The date is officially cancelled. We need to get you in bed."

"In bed, huh? Are you thinking what I'm thinking?" I step into her and take her into my arms. "This chemistry between us . . . you feel it too, don't you?"

"What? No!" She fights her way out of my hold, but her back is against the wall. Literally.

"Frankie baby, we could have so much fun if you'll just put the badge away and take up the knife." I make a stabbing motion as I step closer, then pull her against me again. "You are *so* soft. Your skin is made of fucking velvet, sweetheart. I want to wear you like a coat."

My god, I have never felt something so soft. I just want to keep feeling it. I want her skin on my skin more than I want my next breath.

She ducks out of my arms and grips my hand. "Come on, Romeo. We need to get you back to your right mind before you do or say something you'll regret."

"What about Ice Pick? We can't leave him alone in there."

Frankie freezes. "Ice *Pig*, you mean?"

"Oh, shit. I forgot." I don't want to laugh, but I can't help it. I feel like I'm both telling the joke and receiving the punchline. "Yeah, you've been calling him by the wrong name since day one. Wow . . . your eyes are *really* blue."

She blinks up at me before gritting her teeth and resuming her mission to drag me to the elevators. That's okay. The colors here are pretty too. And they're moving! Man, Jim really spared no expense.

Once we're on the elevator, she crosses her arms over her chest and glares up at me. "Which room is Bennett's?"

"He's in S-404 with Cat."

"Were they going to the Sinner activity?"

I shake my head and smile. "Nope. They were staying in for the evening because Cat was feeling queasy again. Cat. That's a funny word. Cat, cat, cat—"

"Maverick, focus! Did you eat or drink anything while you were in their room?"

I think back to what feels like happened years ago. "Bennett picked my outfit. Cat styled my hair and let me borrow this clip-on earring. I thought you'd like it."

"You thought I would like . . . this?" She motions to all of me.

The elevator dings, and the doors slide open. Why is it so warm in here? I pull off my shirt and drape it over my shoulder. Frankie grips my hand again, and tingles shoot through my muscles as she hauls me down the hallway.

"I'm putting you to bed, and I don't want you to move a muscle. Do you understand?" She swipes her wrist over the door's lock, then opens the door. "I won't be gone for more than five, ten minutes. While I'm gone, I want you to lie in bed and drink water. Lots and lots of water."

With a groan, she deposits me at the side of the bed and heads toward the mini fridge.

"How can I drink water if I can't move a muscle?" I flop onto the bed with a smirk. Fuck, this blanket feels so good on my skin. I strip down to my boxers so I can feel more of it.

"Don't be an ass," she says as she stands and pushes a water bottle into my hand. "And stop writhing on the bed like that. You look like a worm on the sidewalk in summer."

"Would you still love me if I was a worm, sweetheart?" I bat my eyelashes at her. "Ooh, that feels kind of good too. I wonder what it would feel like to have more eyelashes. What if we had *ear*lashes? Wouldn't that be fucking weird?"

She opens her mouth to respond, then closes it. "I'll be back in ten minutes. Don't. Move."

With that, she leaves me alone to enjoy the bliss that is this blanket. Blanket. What a weird word.

Chapter Twenty

Frankie

I raise my fist and knock on the door to room S-404. My voice nearly goes into the pitch—federal agent, open up—but then I remember where I am. I wait silently until the door opens.

Cat stands on the other side. Her hair is a disheveled mess, and she's nearly green with nausea. She holds a bag of ice to her wrist as she motions me inside. "It helps with the seasickness," she says before bolting to the trash can by her bedside.

I stand patiently as she dry heaves, glancing around the room for any sign of the man. How could he leave his woman alone in such a state?

"Bennett went down to the—" Her voice is cut off by another guttural gag. "Bennett went down to the—"

"Maybe just give me the second half of the sentence on your next breath," I say with a gentle smile.

She nods and wipes a string of drool from her mouth. "Infirmary. Motion-sickness patch."

"Ah, got it." I look around the room for a place to sit, but the cabin chair stands on their balcony. I step closer to the bed, prepared to sit on the edge, but that's when I notice the dildo sinking up to its silicone ball sack in a glass bowl of mashed potatoes. "What the actual fuck?"

Cat flinches as she follows my gaze. "Sorry. We like to play with our food."

"Do you . . . eat it after you fuck it?"

She nibbles her bottom lip and wraps her arms around the metal trash can resting on her knees. "Sometimes."

Note to self: decline any food from these two.

"I wish I could be more hospitable, but I can't stop gagging long enough to fix you a drink." She pushes the trash can away from her. "I think I'll be okay if I just stay still."

My gaze darts around the room as I look for any clue as to what might have been given to Maverick, but aside from the mashed potatoes, nothing is amiss—and my god, I hope he didn't eat those potatoes. It feels too accusatory to ask, but I don't have another choice, and I want to help Maverick.

"Um . . . when Maverick was here earlier, did you guys . . . give him anything?" I choose my words carefully. I don't want her to feel as if I'm wagging my finger at them.

"Bennett loaned him a shirt. I styled his hair and—"

"Gave him the clip-on earring. Right." I dare to sit beside her on the edge of the mattress. "No, I mean anything that might have loosened him up a little. He's acting strange. Sweating, remarking on how everything feels."

"Fucking Bennett," she mutters with a shake of her head. "He keeps a little pharmacy on standby, and I wouldn't put it past him to slip something to Maverick, especially with how he was acting."

I cock my head. "What do you mean?"

"I only caught bits and pieces because they were having a boy-talk sesh on the balcony, but the gist was that he wanted to make you laugh and didn't know how. He wanted our help."

"So Bennett drugged him?"

"Probably." Her eyebrows pull together as she bites her lower lip again. "Actually, yeah, he was drugged for sure. Probably shortly after they spoke on the balcony, because by the time we got to his hair, he was willing to let me style it. He's very particular about his hair."

"So I've noticed. It never moves."

"I don't know why he's so funny about the style." She holds up a finger, then heaves into the trash can again. When she's done, she flops backward on the bed. "Bennett should be back any second. He can tell you what he gave him."

I shake my head. "No, I'm fairly certain he micro-dosed him with MDMA. His high should pass in a few hours. I'll just keep him hydrated until then."

"You want some too? The sex is pretty amazing, not gonna lie."

I don't know whether to laugh at her assumption or set her straight, but I settle on the latter. "Maverick and I aren't intimate. To be frank, I think he'd rather stick his dick in a light socket than me."

"I disagree." She sits up and brushes a stray lock of blonde hair from her forehead. "He's kind of mean to you, right?"

"I wouldn't say mean, but he certainly doesn't treat me like he treats everyone else."

"Yeah, that's my point. Take it from someone who pined after him for months. If he's acting different toward you, there's a reason."

She's right. There is. It has nothing to do with some imagined affection for me, though. He treats me differently because I'm a fed.

"Thanks, Cat. I'd better get back to the room before he starts wondering how it would feel to leap off the balcony, but I appreciate your help."

"Anytime. And if you spot Bennett in the hall, tell him to hurry the fuck up." She reaches for the trash can again as I take my leave.

I close the door behind me, silencing the retching on the other side. If Maverick ingested the ecstasy when he went to change, that means he should start coming down soon. It's been nearly three hours.

When I open the cabin door, Maverick is still where I left him. He's polished off the bottled water and even gotten another. The empty bottles stand on the bedside table.

He looks up and smiles when he hears me come in. "I tried not to move, but I had to get more water. Have you ever tried sitting still for hours on end? It's more difficult than you think." He tips his head to the side, and the ridiculous cross earring drapes over his shoulder. "I think my head is starting to clear a little, though. I'm not sure what's wrong with me."

"You were drugged." I go to the sink to fetch a cool washcloth. When I return, he looks so confused.

"Drugged? I don't partake."

I motion for him to scoot over a bit, and he does. I sit beside him and dab his forehead, which is much less sweaty now. "When you went to Bennett's room, he gave you something to help you loosen up a bit. Cat said you told them you wanted to make me laugh, so they were just trying to help."

He closes his eyes and grimaces, then opens one eye to look at me. "Did it work, at least?"

I smile down at him. I can't help it. "Yes, you made me laugh."

"Good. You're so much prettier when you smile. I mean, you're pretty anyway, but when you smile, it makes me want to smile too." He relaxes into the pillows. "Wanna cuddle?"

"I mean, if that's what you need right now, I guess I can do that."

Confused as hell, I sit on the mattress, then stretch out beside him. I rest my head on his bare chest, and the awkward feeling fades with each beat of his heart against my ear, each inward breath he takes. His arm bands around my shoulder, and he sighs.

"Damn," he says.

"What?"

"This is actually really nice. I've never done this before, so I didn't know what it would be like."

"You've never cuddled?" I ask with a laugh. "I'm the Ice Queen, and even I've cuddled."

He chuckles, and the movement bounces my head slightly against his chest. "I'm not some innocent flower or anything, but no, I've never cuddled like this. I, uh . . . I don't really get close to women."

"You and Eve seem close."

"No, I mean intimately."

My eyes widen, and I panic internally. "Is this intimate to you?"

"Well, yeah. If my shit worked, I'd be rock hard right now." His fingers trail over my shoulder. "Something tells me your skin would be this soft even if I wasn't coming down from a high." He lowers his voice until I can hardly make out the whispered words when he says, "Something tells me I'd never come down if I were to get inside you."

I skate on thin ice. If this had happened on day one, I'd have leapt for shore. Now I'm considering plunging beneath freezing waters just to feel a little of his warmth.

His fingers trail lower on my back, and the ice cracks a little more.

This isn't the same as before, when I teased him until he came in his pants. Now I want to tease him until he comes inside *me*.

"Maverick, maybe I should see if Eve could come take care of you. I'm afraid of what might happen if I stay in this room tonight."

He sighs again, this time sounding more forlorn than relaxed. "Yeah, I know what you mean. But you don't have to worry about us crossing any lines. My dick doesn't work, remember?"

I nibble my lip, wanting to ask why that is, but the question dies in my throat. It feels too personal.

He must sense this, because he points to a thin white scar that runs along his hairline. "See that line? That's why I'm so particular about my hair. I style the swoop so that no one can see it."

"So that you don't have to talk about how you got it."

"Bingo." He pauses, seeming to consider something before he says, "That part isn't important, but it left me with a gnarly case of erectile dysfunction. Once I get it up, I'm good, but the initial erection can prove elusive."

I shift, placing my hand on his chest, then resting my chin on the back of my hand so that I can look at him. "Is that why you don't get close to women?"

"To be honest, I always thought it was because I cared so much about my career. Now I'm not so sure. I mean, what does working have to do with shutting myself off from connecting with someone like—" He stops, unable to finish the thought, so I do it for him.

"Like what we're doing now."

"Yeah."

I raise my head slightly and trace lazy circles on his abdomen. Goosebumps rise on his skin, and I hate myself for wanting to run my tongue over all of them.

God, what am I doing? He's practically a kid. At twenty-two, I doubt he'll know my clitoris from my urethra.

And he's a murderer, Frankie. Let's not forget that.

Instead of turning me off, the thought of Maverick standing over a body as blood coats his bare skin does something disgusting inside me. I imagine what it would be like to slide against him, both of us covered in that awful metallic scent. A low whimper squeaks out of me, and I freeze.

"Frankie?"

I close my eyes. "Yeah?"

"What the fuck was that?"

With a squeal, I press my forehead against his chest and mutter into his warm skin. "I don't fucking know. My brain went somewhere really weird, and that sound just happened."

"What were you thinking of?"

"I don't wanna say."

"Come on, sweetheart. Judgment-free zone, yeah?" He

slips his finger under my chin and eases my head upward so that I'm forced to look into his green eyes. "We're having a moment. Just let it happen."

Okay. I'll fudge it a bit, but I'll tell him. What's the worst that could happen?

"I was thinking about a dream I had. You were . . . naked."

He tips his head back and laughs. "That's all? Hell, I've thought of you naked a few times myself. At least a dream is involuntary." His expression sobers. "That was rude of me, and I apologize."

"Apology not accepted," I say with a giggle, "but that wasn't the worst part. You were covered in blood. And I liked it."

His hand firms on my shoulder, like he's hugging me the only way he can in this position, and my insides begin to tumble. "Nothing weird about that."

"I'm getting wet to thoughts of our bodies coated in blood as we fuck. I'd say that's the *definition* of weird."

His fingertips loosen, and his hand dips below my romper. Gentle warmth brushes over my bare skin. "Maybe we could try something tamer first."

"Maybe . . ."

We're dancing around a fire, both of us too scared to get close enough to feel the heat.

"Can I tell you a secret?" he whispers.

I nod against his chest.

"I didn't want you to go on that date tonight. I wanted it to be me."

"I know."

He looks down at me. "You did?"

"Not at first, but when Cat said you wanted to make me laugh, I kind of thought something seemed odd." I swallow around a lump in my throat. "And I wouldn't say the curiosity is exactly one-sided."

That's when Maverick dives into the flames headfirst. Before I realize what's happening, he's shifted and pulled me into a sitting position. And with a force and passion I've never felt, he kisses me.

Chapter Twenty-One

Maverick

Light fizzles and ignites like sparklers in my nerve endings. She sighs into the kiss, a gentle moan gripping the tail of that soft sound, and I'm melting. I'm drifting. Pieces of me break apart and splinter in the best way. The walls collapse as if she's pulled a string.

Frustration follows the pleasant feelings because I can't *do* anything with them. This woman is quickly becoming putty in the hands of an incompetent artist. Instead of molding her body to mine, I can only look and imagine what it would be like to be part of her.

I lean back and look into her eyes. "Slap me, sweetheart."

The lust-haze clears from her gaze, and she blinks. "Huh?"

"I don't mean a little love tap, either. You really have to give it all you've got."

She looks at my crotch as realization dawns in her eyes. "Oh. Right." Looking back at my face, she nibbles her bottom lip and raises her hand. "Are you sure? I mean, you're under the influence, and I don't want to take advantage of you."

"I'm clear-headed enough to tell you that I want you more than you can understand. More than even *I* can grasp. I'm also clear-headed enough to know this is a bad idea." I lean forward and run my hands through her dark hair until I reach the back of her scalp, where I squeeze and pull her closer. "It's a *terrible* idea, but fuck the consequences. Hurt me, Frankie. Hurt me so that I can please you."

I pull her lips to mine, and she relaxes in my hold as our mouths move as one. Her hands drift to my biceps, where she explores each muscle as if she's mapping me out. She breaks the kiss and straddles my waist.

"I've made worse decisions," she whispers against my lips. Then she raises her hand and delivers one hell of a slap to the side of my face.

Fuck, the pain is delicious. Heat blazes over my skin, and my cheek begins to swell. My eye even waters. But it's not enough.

"Treat me like one of your interrogation suspects," I offer, hoping it gives her some ideas.

"The slap wasn't enough?"

I shake my head.

Whap!

My skull rocks to the side, and I see stars.

"How about now?" She reaches back and cups my semi. "Jesus, what the fuck do I have to do, shoot you? If this is what it takes to get hard, it's a wonder you're still alive."

The insecurity nibbles at my insides, and I try to ease her off my lap, but she fights to stay seated.

"Hang on," she grunts. "I'm not ready to give up just yet."

Without any warning, she drops against my chest and sinks her teeth into my trap. With the bite force of a fucking alligator, she clenches her jaw while also driving her nails into my ribs. Glorious pain sings through my muscles until I'm forced to cry out.

She releases her hold and looks at me. "Too hard?"

"If you mean my cock, yes." I smirk at her. "Keep it going until we're in the heat of battle, sweetheart. Dose me with little shots of pain."

I reach up and tear down the romper top, not caring as the fabric rips. Frankie hurries to pull it off the rest of the way, followed by her bra and panties. As she stands beside the bed, I can see every beautiful inch of her body, and it's magnificent.

"Lie on the bed," I demand. "I need to taste you."

As soon as her back hits the mattress, I'm on her. Need was the right word, and I can't even blame the drugs now. This desire springs from a hunger I've endured for far too long. I'm starving for her, and I don't know where to start. My tongue lashes over her relaxed breasts, and my fingers revel in their softness. I suck her hardened nipple into my mouth and nibble that delicious bud until a soft moan rolls out of her.

Despite all the glorious feedback from Frankie, I'm unable to maintain the erection, and my cock softens as I nip and nibble my way down her soft stomach. That's okay. I'll focus on her for now. The important part is that I know she can deliver the push I need.

"Do you have any kinks, sweetheart? I can't be the only one." I nip her thighs and move closer to the warmth between them. "Hopefully it's not submission. Not sure how that would work out."

She laughs, and that sound coupled with the sweet

scent of her desire is almost enough to get me hard. I don't wait for her response. I can't. If I don't press my tongue to her and taste that beautiful pussy, I'll die.

A moan drifts on the air as my mouth connects with her. Heat rushes over my tastebuds in waves, and my tongue must feel so cool against her warm skin. Her hips jerk when I find her clit and give it a light flick with the tip of my tongue.

"God, this is so fucked up," she moans. "Maybe that's my kink. Doing what I shouldn't."

I keep eating her, refusing to stop long enough to reply. Once I've made her come, we can continue the conversation.

Her thighs quiver against my head, but she doesn't come. Even when I slip my fingers into her warmth and tease that sensitive place deep inside her, she teeters on the edge of oblivion but refuses to fall.

"I need you to fuck me," she begs through a whimper.

Well, damn. I didn't see this coming.

I reach into my pocket and pull out the trusty lighter. As I eat her pussy and finger her with my right hand, my left hand flicks the wheel until a flame appears. I allow the heat to linger before dousing the flame and pressing the metal against the back of my ear. While I don't enjoy leaving a mark that someone might see, needs must.

Pain sears through my skull, and I'm just glad Frankie is too lost to the moment to realize what I'm doing. Blood rushes to my cock at the same speed. I pull away long enough to yank off my shorts, hurrying before the pain recedes and my brain figures out what we're doing here.

As my cock springs free, Frankie's eyes widen. She licks her lips and swallows, then closes her legs. "On second thought—"

I stop mere centimeters from her entrance. "If you've changed your mind, we don't have to continue. I want you, but I've never been turned on by forcing a woman to do something she isn't comfortable with."

"Why do you have to say something so perfect when I'm trying to be a good girl?"

"Because I like you better when you're bad." I lean forward and kiss her as my erection begins to fade. *Maybe this is for the best*, I think as she pulls away, but then her teeth sink into my bottom lip.

I harden instantly and jerk forward, pushing against her pussy. She opens her mouth to cry out as I enter her, and I've never felt more like a beast in rut. I interpreted the bite as an invitation, but was I wrong? Judging by the way she looks up at me, I might have been.

"Fuck," she whispers. "I don't think I've ever been so full. Go easy on me."

"Sweetheart, I will do whatever you tell me to. If you want it gentle, I'll show you gentle."

I ease forward, pushing myself deeper before easing out of her again. She breathes with me, matching the motion, sighing a little harder with each thrust as her eyes drift closed. Her breasts rise and fall, and her lips part as she loses herself to the feeling.

"Can I go a little deeper?" I ask, and she nods her head. Dark hair falls over her cheek as she whimpers, and I lean forward and brush it away as I maintain that slow, deep rhythm. "I want to see you. You're so beautiful, so familiar to me. When you come, I want to watch you lose control."

She moans and rocks with me now. Her hands move to her breasts, where she squeezes the mounds and tweaks her nipples between her fingers. Watching her play with them makes me want to suck them. Bite them.

"I want you to ride me," I say as I ease out of her. "Use me until you come."

We swap positions, and she straddles my waist. Before she puts me inside her, I pull her down so that I can nibble her breasts. As I willingly suffocate, she grinds down on my cock to the point of pain, which is perfection. Each moan that slides out of her chips away at my patience a little more, and when she finally slips me inside of her, I nearly come.

This isn't how this is supposed to go, and I start to panic internally. First she made me come in my shorts, and now I'm about to nut before she's had a chance to get hers. Ain't happening.

But fuck, now she's speeding up. Her hands plant on my chest, and she grinds down, taking me all the way. With a long, low moan, her head tips back. She's a fucking goddess.

"Fuck, I think I might actually come," she says, and her pussy clamps down on my cock. "I'm so close . . . so . . ."

My hands shoot to her hips, keeping her steady as her pussy creates a friction burn on my pelvis. The speed with which she moves, the hunger that permeates every gasp for air, tells me she wants this orgasm more than she wants a fucking promotion in her department, and that is a very dangerous thing to know.

Because as she moans and shakes and explodes on my cock, she's losing a piece of herself. And as I release inside her, so am I.

Chapter Twenty-Two

Frankie

Realization doesn't dawn on me until I'm seated at breakfast the following morning. I spent last night in a haze, wrapped in my lover's arms. The fog lifts as I look down at a human ear resting atop a bed of scrambled eggs. Faced with a literal appendage on my plate, I can't pretend anymore.

I fucked a serial killer.

Eve sets down a glass of orange juice, then grimaces at her plate. She received a finger, which she flicks off the eggs before scooping up a yellow forkful. Across from me, Kindra looks down at what I think is a nose. The skin has shriveled, making it hard to discern exactly what it is. She grimaces, and I'm glad to see I'm not the only one who can't stomach this chef's particular brand of what the fuck.

"Where's Cat?" I pluck up a strip of bacon, which seems safe enough, I guess. "She was sick last night, and I wanted to check in on her."

Kindra pushes her plate to the side. "She must be

feeling better, because she went with Jim and Ezra to set up for today's big event. The Normies will have a day on a private island, where they'll get to watch a pirate show."

I spit the glob of meat onto my plate and cover it with a napkin before pushing the plate away. That definitely wasn't pork. "Sounds fun. Sign me up."

"You're already signed up, honey," Eve says. "Who do you think is putting on the pirate show?"

I meant sign me up to sit on a private island where I can sip Mai Tais while watching some riveting entertainment, but it was stupid of me to wish for something so simple.

"Where's Maverick this morning?" Eve asks. "You two are usually connected at the hip. The man never lets you out of his sight."

"He wanted to sleep in. Bennett drugged him last night, and he's got a touch of a hangover."

Kindra shakes her head and rolls her eyes. "It's always something with that one. If he wasn't Ezra's brother and my best friend's boyfriend, I'd kick him off the boat. If he ever comes at you sideways, just mention the pineapple incident and he'll shut up."

Before I can ask about this incident, the dining hall doors swing open, and Maverick and Bennett shuffle into the fray. I wish I could muster Kindra's annoyance at Bennett, but I'm kind of thankful he drugged Maverick like he was at his first rave. If he hadn't, I never would have seen him in a new light.

And now we get along so well that I let him get on a first name basis with my fucking *vagina*. Jesus fuck, what is wrong with me?

My mother was right to worry. I don't like where my head is at right now.

Maverick sits beside Kindra and across from me, and

Bennett sits beside him. Despite joining us for breakfast, they don't have anything to eat. I glance back at the serving station.

"Don't worry about us," Bennett says as he realizes where I'm looking. "We ate with the Normies so that we could avoid Chef's little surprises."

"Thanks for inviting the rest of us," Eve quips.

Bennett grins. "Don't mention it."

"How are you feeling?" I ask Maverick as I push my glass of water toward him. "Drink this. Hydration helps."

"Don't fucking mommy him," Bennett says with a hard eye roll. "I mean, you're old enough to be his mother, but you don't have to act like it. That just makes the sex weird."

I bite the inside of my cheek to stop the scream from breaking out of my chest, but I can't contain my voice. "Maverick! You told him we had *sex*?"

"No, but *you* just did," Bennett says.

Okay, *now* I want to strangle him.

I feel the girls' eyes on me, but I'm too embarrassed to look up. Instead, I stare down at my eggs and wonder how long it would take me to choke to death on them. Probably a lot less time than it will take for me to squash this developing infatuation with someone I absolutely cannot be with.

An arm wraps around my shoulder, and Eve pulls my ear to her mouth. "Don't let him get to you, honey. Bennett is a special brand of stupid, but his heart's in the right place. Still . . . if you want him to stop, you know what to do."

"Now, now," Bennett says. "No secrets between friends. Say it loud enough for the entire class to hear."

I clear my throat and pin Bennett with a glare. "She was just telling me about an interesting incident with a pineapple. I'd love to hear the dirty details."

Kindra, Eve, and Maverick cover their mouths to hide

how pleased they are with my little jab. I'm being so serious, though. I want to know what the fuck the deal is, and why the mention of a pineapple has Bennett's cheeks turning seven different shades of red.

"It's not unusual," Kindra says through a giggle.

Eve loses it now, uncovering her mouth and letting out a musical laugh. "The fuck it isn't. It's the *most* unusual thing."

"Says the woman who's enamored with a chick who shoves objects into her ass and shits them out for fun." Bennett scoffs and stands from the table. "Fuck all of you. I'll see you assholes at the event, where Cat and I will soundly beat all of your asses in whatever games Jim has up his shitty sleeve."

He storms off with his fists clenched at his sides. We sober as we watch him leave.

"I think we hurt his feelings," I mutter.

Kindra scoffs. "He'd have to have feelings if we wanted to hurt them."

"You guys are too hard on him sometimes. He fucked a pineapple." Maverick shrugs. "So what? Women fuck weird shit all the time, and we say fuck all about it."

"I once read a book about a woman who liked fucking a snowman," I offer. "I guess a guy fucking a pineapple isn't that weird." The unwanted images fill my brain, and I shake my head. "No, never mind. It's definitely weird."

Eve's eyes widen, and she turns her head toward me. "Wait, back up to the lady fucking the snowman. What did she do, craft an icicle dick?"

"No, she used a carrot."

Kindra laughs and stands from the table. "I don't know if that's better or worse, but it doesn't matter. If we don't get a move on, we won't have time to get into character before we head to the island."

The rest of the group stands, and we follow her out of the dining hall. I pick up the pace to walk beside her.

"Character?" I ask.

"Bennett brought our outfits to the room after you'd gone to breakfast," Maverick says behind me. "They're certainly . . . interesting, if his description is to be believed. Very authentic."

"Great," I mumble under my breath. "Can't wait."

We walk as a group, parting ways as we exit the elevator on the Sinner level. I shuffle along beside Maverick, trying to keep pace. His legs are so long that he takes one stride for three of mine. Thankfully, he notices that I'm practically running to keep up, so he slows down.

"About last night . . ." he says, and my blood runs cold. Sure, part of me wants to talk about what happened, but a much larger part of me wants to pretend that everything is normal. "No one has seen Ice Pick since we were with him at the lounge, and I'm starting to worry."

Okay, not what I expected to talk about, but I think we're on the same page about pretending things are normal, at least. "He's an adult, isn't he? Is there a reason we should be concerned?"

Maverick smirks and shakes his head as he lets us into the cabin. "I'm not so sure. Maybe it's nothing."

He stops beside the closet and pulls two garment bags from inside. God, I hope it's not another fucking spacesuit. I'll roast to death in this sunshine. He hands one bag to me, then goes to the bed, where he drops his bag and sighs.

I place my hand on his arm until he looks at me. "It seems to be bugging you, so it's definitely something. The girl he went on a date with seemed nice. Are you worried she might be a fed?"

"I'm not sure. It's just . . . it's not like Ice to go missing at breakfast. He loves food. Bennett and I ate with the Normies, and I didn't see him, and you guys were at the Sinners' breakfast, and he wasn't there either." He leans down and unzips his bag, then stands up. "What the fuck? Jim can't be serious."

I drape my bag over my arm and step closer so that I can peer around his tall frame. Inside the bag rests a pirate costume, but it's so much more extravagant than I pictured. I expected a cheap getup, with a plastic-hook hand or maybe a fake parrot, but this? As he pulls the long captain's coat from the bag, I'm in awe. This sort of detailing must have cost a fortune.

I hurry to open my bag, excited by what I might find. My mother wouldn't let me participate in trick-or-treat when I was growing up, and dress-up wasn't a game in our household. She sent me skydiving at five, but Halloween was off-limits. Probably because the chameleon aspect of our lives wasn't something to play with, but still, it's exciting to finally wear a costume.

My ensemble is just as detailed and expensive-looking—and feeling—as Maverick's attire. I begin stripping immediately. The sooner I can slide my body into this outfit, the better. I start with the top—a white linen shirt that drapes off my shoulders and trails down to flowing sleeves. The skirt is to die for, with all its silky purple ruffles. It stops at my upper thighs in the front and trails to my calves in the back.

I turn to see how Maverick's getting along, and my jaw nearly hits the floor. He's gotten as far as the loose brown pants and ankle-high boots, and honestly, he could stop right there. He looks like he walked out of a period piece, and nothing is sexier than a man right out of 1829.

"I feel like an idiot," he laments as he lifts the white shirt from the bag. The frills at the ends of the sleeves give me a chuckle.

I pluck the black corset from my garment bag and cinch it around my waist. "If it's any consolation, you certainly don't look like an idiot." I give him my back. "Little help?"

He steps behind me, and his cologne teases my senses with hints of leather and sin. His fingers work quickly, pulling the strings until my rib cage shrinks three sizes. With each tug, he asks if it's too tight. It is, but that's okay. I want to look snatched.

With the last stay in place, I grab the black knee-high boots and a feathered cap that I'm a bit iffy about. Hats and I don't tend to mesh well. Maybe once my makeup is on, it won't be so bad, so I hurry to do that while Maverick busies himself with the rest of his outfit.

While I don't normally wear much makeup, this event calls for some flair. I pull out the big guns and set to work, contouring my face until I look like a starlet. I finish off with some fake lashes and red lipstick. After running a curling wand through my hair to give it some oomph, I try the hat again. I'm surprised when I look in the mirror and like what I see. This doesn't happen very often.

Maverick lets out a low grunt of approval as I come around the corner. "Shiver me fucking timbers. You clean up well, sweetheart."

"If you ever say shiver me timbers again, I will stab you." I smile at him. "But thanks. You look pretty swash-buckling good yourself."

"Oh, you haven't seen the best part yet." He turns back to the garment bag, digs around, then spins to face me once more. In his hand, he brandishes a cutlass. "Son of a bitch is sharp, too. I sliced the fuck out of my finger because I thought it was fake or at least dull, but no. Jim got the real deal."

My stomach sinks as I realize what that means, but I should have known we'd have to kill people today. Drat. Suddenly, this outing doesn't seem like such a good time.

"Hey . . . is there a possibility you could, maybe . . . help me avoid having to kill anyone today?" I nibble my bottom lip as I wait for him to slot his sword into the hilt at his hip. "It wasn't so bad when we accidentally sent the guy over-board, but I'm having second thoughts about it now."

But then he shakes his head, and my stomach hits my feet. "Frankie, I wish I could, but you have to remember the other game we're playing here. If anyone learns you're a fed, they have a right to your head."

"So you've changed your mind about offing me?" I say as I sit on the edge of the mattress.

"I never wanted you to die. Even when I wasn't so sure about you, I felt the urge to keep you safe." He sits beside me and drops his hands into his lap as he looks at the floor. "But yes, I suppose I feel differently now. Haven't things changed for you?"

"Of course they have, but I still don't know what that means."

"Meaning you still plan to turn all of us over at the end of the cruise."

My mind searches for the right words to explain my situation, but I don't know how to help him understand. This is my career. If I don't give them Jim at the very least, I'll be in the unemployment line by the end of the month. My sports car. My apartment. My life.

I would lose everything.

But if I turn in Jim or any of Maverick's friends, I lose him. He doesn't have to tell me that. It's an unwritten rule.

"Right," he says with a pinched smile when I don't say anything. "Well, at least we still have a few days left to have some fun."

He stands and heads for the door. With each step he takes, my heart beats a little harder. Three days stand between me and a difficult decision, and I wish I could stop time. Better yet, I wish I could go back in time and refuse this assignment. Maybe then I could spare myself the impending heartbreak. Whatever I choose, I'll suffer a loss.

Chapter Twenty-Three

Maverick

The Jolly Roger waves in the wind on the pirate ship's stern, and I have to give Jim credit where it's due. This vessel is a scaled-down replica of Queen Anne's Revenge, the very ship commandeered by Edward Teach himself. Jim explained he had to scale it down because the original Revenge required a crew in excess of three hundred men. If we put that many Cattle to work on this boat, we'd have no one left to kill.

And much to poor Frankie's displeasure, killing is definitely on today's to-do list.

She rests her forearms on the railing and peers at the open water, looking but not really seeing. Cat stands beside her. Well, she leans more than stands, but I'm proud of her for staying upright. She tried to sit this one out, but Bennett begged her to come.

The ship creaks as the waves bump against it. At least they're gentle. Jim wanted it to be as authentic as possible, and stabilizers weren't a thing in the late 1600s. Neither were bathrooms, and I'm thankful Ezra stepped in for us there.

Frankie leans closer to me so that Cat can't hear her. "Where does he keep the victims on this thing?"

"Vic—" I grip her arm and pull her out of Cat's earshot. Not that she's paying attention. "Cattle, sweetheart. Call them Cattle. If anyone hears you refer to them as victims . . ."

"Right," she says. "I forgot."

I try to soften my expression. "Just think of it like culling sick animals from a herd. These people hurt others for fun, so we're just evening things out."

"Yeah, I get that, but what if we get it wrong?"

"What do you mean?"

She shakes her head, but Eve and Aven approach before she can formulate her thoughts.

"Arr, mateys! Batten down the hatches and . . . whatever the fuck pirates say!" Eve pulls a dagger from the belt on her hip and aims the blade skyward. "Thar be treasure!"

Aven looks at me. "Is it normal to be forced into costume for every bloody event? I came here to kill shit and take out some frustration, not play Jim's real-life version of Dress to Impress."

"How the fuck do you even know what that is?" Eve asks. "Isn't that a game for kids?"

Aven's cheeks pinken, and he walks away.

"He's so talkative," Eve says with a shake of her head. "But you guys will find out all about it, because we're on a team. Jim said it was a random draw, but I don't know what's so random about you two always ending up together." She wiggles her eyebrows at Frankie.

"Do you know how we'll be dispatching the . . . Cattle?"

Frankie asks, and I'm proud of her for using the proper term.

Eve shrugs her slender shoulders. "No clue, honey. I think Jim wants to keep the playing field even. We're competing for a grand prize this time."

I let the girls continue talking as I stroll down the deck toward Bennett, Ezra, and Kindra. When I reach them, they're all smiles and excitement.

"Did you hear what we're competing for?" Kindra asks, and I shake my head.

"Half a million," Bennett says with a laugh. "Can you fucking believe it?"

Yes, easily. Jim shits bigger piles of cash on a regular basis. We have no clue where he gets it, but the well seems never ending.

"If I win, I'll use my cut to set Cat up at the best fucking college. She'll be an Ivy League nurse." Bennett looks around. "Shit, where did she go?"

"Probably to the nearest loo, if her green skin was any indication." Ezra clears his throat and turns to me as Bennett shuffles off to find his ailing girlfriend. "They're with Kindra and myself. One of Jim's 'random' draws."

"Yeah, I'm with Frankie, Eve, and Aven." I peer around the deck, spotting Grim, Rosie, and two strangers talking near a cluster of barrels. "Hey, Ezra, have you seen Ice Pick? He's been missing since last night."

"That's what Kindra said, but no, I haven't seen him. Do you think we should be concerned?" Ezra's expression sobers. "I trust you, Maverick. If you think something isn't right, just say the word. We'll cancel the pirate show and find him."

"Yeah," Kindra adds. "He's part of the inner circle. He's groped all the women at least once, then apologized to them and their men at least thrice for it. The man is our annoying older brother, and we have to look out for him. God knows he can't look out for himself."

My heart beats a little faster. "He was supposed to go out with a woman he met at the speed dating event. What if he got too handsy? I know he wouldn't take it too far and do something to end up in a red suit, but . . . she doesn't know that."

Frankie and Eve join us, catching the tail end of what I said.

"Who doesn't know what?" Eve asks. "Don't leave us out of the tea. It's hot out here, and bitches get thirsty."

"Yes, bitches do," Frankie says with a smirk, and I'm glad to see she's making friends.

I catch the two of them up to speed, and by the end, we all agree that this is wholly unlike him.

"At the summer retreat on Devil Horn, he went MIA with food poisoning," Kindra says. "Who here's eaten what he's eaten?"

We look around and compare notes. Between all of us, we've shared every meal with him, and there's not one runny asshole to be had.

"What about Cat?" Frankie asks. "She's been sick since last night. Maybe it isn't seasickness. Maybe she has food poisoning."

"She has a very good point." Ezra rises onto his toes and looks through the people on deck. "Where's Jim? We need to bring this to his attention immediately. It's already been twelve hours since anyone last saw Ice. If he's in trouble, we can't afford to lose another blasted second."

"Fan out and search for Jim," I say. "If anyone knows where Ice Pick is, it'll be him. We'll find him faster if we split up. The ship may be a smaller version of the original, but she's still a beast."

Ezra nods, and we scatter in different directions. Only once I've taken a few paces forward do I remember that I'm not supposed to let Frankie out of my sight. I peer over my shoulder and spot her purple feather bobbing beside Eve's brown captain's hat. Gritting my teeth, I spare a tenth of a second to debate with myself, then decide she'll be safe. Eve won't let anything happen to her. I'd trust that woman with my life.

I race toward the ship's stern. Jim had the captain's quarters built there, and while he isn't the captain of this ship, he's claimed the room as his. A navy-blue door leads down a few steps and into an antechamber, beyond which stands the wooden door to Jim's quarters. I approach and knock, and I'm shocked when Jim's voice bellows for me to enter; I neither expected his presence nor the bass in his voice.

Easing open the door, I step into the candlelit shadows and blink a few times, not sure I'm seeing what I'm seeing. But no matter how many times I flutter my lashes, the image remains. "Jim?"

He's seated behind a large wooden desk that probably weighs as much as the central mast. Gold coins spill from a small chest atop the desk, clinking and rattling as the vessel creaks and sways. To my right, a kingly bed lies unmade. Which means he slept here. And when I take in the man himself, I can only assume he did so to get into character.

The man who sits before me is almost unrecognizable. His all-black captain's attire is so at odds with the three-piece fashion statements he usually wears. That's difficult to rationalize, yes, but my brain can't even compute what is happening with his *head*. Jim's usual salt-and-pepper hairstyle and clean-shaven face are no more. Unruly black locks hang to either side of his head beneath a weathered tricorne, and whoever applied the facial prosthetic deserves a fucking award. Not only does the haggard beard look realistic, but he has an entirely different nose and chin.

I pinch my arm to make sure I'm awake. "Jim?"

"Come, my boy. Blackbeard won't bite ye . . . too *harrrd!*" He tosses his head back and laughs.

I wish I could find the humor, but I'm still processing.

When he's finished, he wipes his eye. "Did you hear tell of the buried treasure? Half a million doubloons, boy. You could buy a whole lot of painted ladies with that sum, eh?" He laughs again, then waves me closer.

Despite his encouragement, I do not step closer. I don't need to get anywhere within the vicinity of whatever is happening here. "Jim, Ice Pick is missing."

Instead of tensing with concern, Jim relaxes into his chair and kicks his leather boots onto the desk. "There be skullduggery afoot," he whispers, with a devilish glint in his eyes. His face contorts beneath the makeup, making him look almost gleeful.

"Why the fuck are you smirking like that? Didn't you hear me? Ice Pick is *missing,* Jim."

He waves me off. "Who is this Jim you speak of, boy? My name is Edward Teach, and as one of the most trusted men in my pirate crew, you should know that best. But please, call me *Blackbeard.*"

"Drop the fucking act, man. I'm serious. We're all very concerned."

Jim rolls his eyes and finally breaks character. He pulls his boots off the desk, then leans forward on his elbows as he steeples his fingers beneath his chin. Some of them disappear into the coarse hair.

"The only person you need concern yourself with is Frankie." He sits a little straighter and peers behind me. "You didn't leave her to her own devices aboard this ship, I hope. A few of her compatriots are tucked away below deck, and I'd hate for her to run into them. All of your hard work could come crashing down if they remind her that she isn't one of us when she's just starting to think she might be."

"Could you stop focusing so hard on *her* and put some of that energy toward some concern for our *friend*?" I close my eyes and squeeze the bridge of my nose. "Please . . . can some of us go back to the ship so that we can check the security footage? If we can figure out where he last was, we can figure out where he went."

Jim sighs. "I'm sure he's just fine, but if it will make you feel better, we'll organize a search party the moment we're back on the Bruise Cruise. Satisfied?"

No, not really. We're wasting valuable time here. Like Ezra said, every second that passes . . .

But Jim won't be moved, and this is the best I'll get. Plus, what he said about Frankie is starting to worm its way into my head. I don't think Eve would have been silly enough to take her down to the brig, where the Cattle are being held, but I'll feel better if I can lay eyes on both of them.

I leave without responding to him. He yells something at my back, something about getting my group together on deck, but I ignore him. If his little games cost Ice Pick his life, I'm not sure any of us will ever forgive him.

As I pass through the antechamber, a bell tolls somewhere on the ship. Orange-banded crew members hurry to their positions, leaving only the Sinners on deck. It's much easier to find everyone now, and I spot Frankie and Eve standing with Grim and Rosie by the barrels. Frankie waves me over, and I hurry to join them.

"Grim saw Ice Pick this morning," she says.

The wiry German turns to me. "He was following a woman. He said something about taking her out."

"He's going to murder a Normie, Maverick," Eve says. "If we don't stop him, he'll get himself into a mess. "

I raise my hands to silence them. "Hang on. He was with a woman and said he planned to take her out, but that doesn't necessarily mean he's going to *kill* her. Maybe they hit it off and he's taking her out . . . on a date."

Rosie shakes her head, and Grim nods.

"These behaviors were not courting behaviors," Grim says. "The man was stalking his prey. He hid behind a plant until she passed, though he was much larger than the plant and poked out from all sides. Once she turned a corner, he continued hunting."

"Could she be a fed?"

We all turn toward the Scottish accent and spot Aven behind us. He steps into the group.

"Madigan said he hid some of the shits in the Normie population." Aven shrugs. "Maybe he's making sure before he asks for the kill."

"Possibly," Eve says. "That doesn't make me feel any better, though."

We all agree, but there's nothing to do about it right now. The anchors have come loose, and the ship is on the move. The games are about to begin.

Chapter Twenty-Four

Frankie

When I was seventeen, I went to the county fair in a little town in West Virginia. I arrived in early afternoon, and by the time the barkers started hollering for everyone to spend their tickets and get the hell out, I'd eaten my weight in turkey legs and funnel cake. I had three tickets left. That was exactly what it cost to ride the Tilt-A-Whirl, so I grabbed an extra-large cherry slush and chugged it while I waited in line.

All of that to say this: Despite the involuntary expulsion that occurred on that day, I have never felt as sick as I feel at this moment. I have never felt the urge to exist without insides, but with each dip and sway of the ship, I pray for this lifetime to end. A small piece of my soul vacates my being, and I'm certain I'm dying.

Cold water crashes against my neck and spills down my top, soaking my chest and back. My hands release the railing, instinctively flying upward as the icy shock drives down my spine. The ship rocks again, and I'm tossed sideways.

Before I crash against the deck and break open my skull, I land against something much more forgiving. Still so hard, though. His thin garments do nothing to hide that lean muscle.

"I've got you," Maverick says as he steadies me.

"Thanks."

I blink to clear my head as I'm held upright. When the wave of dizziness recedes, I grip the railing and glance behind me. Eve wiggles a small metal bucket, which is now empty.

"Sorry, honey, but being overheated won't help with the motion sickness. Just trying to help."

I give her a nod, too sick to form words.

Maverick releases my arm, keeping one hand on my opposite hip. I can't tell if he's trying to get handsy or be helpful, and I'm not sure it matters. I'm happy either way. A smile bubbles out of me, and I can't stop it.

Maverick looks down at me, giving me a lazy half-smirk.

Oh god. Oh god, no.

Something else bubbles out of me. And I can't stop it, either.

With one hand on the railing, I turn my head and projectile vomit into the sea. I hope the fish enjoy the hot ham sandwich we ate on the tender ride to this pirate ship.

Now that I've vomited, the cold sweat finally passes. I turn back to Eve, who seems to be one of the few people completely unaffected by the ship's motion.

"What's your secret?" I croak.

She shrugs and tucks the bucket under her arm. "Good genes, I suppose. Same as Rosie, Maverick, and Bennett. We seem to be the only three who aren't affected."

She's right. Kindra and Ezra huddle by one of the masts, both of them slightly paler than normal. Bennett tends to

Cat, who hasn't stopped dry heaving since we set sail. Rose flits between Aven and Grim, who sit on the deck with their heads hanging between their bent knees. She places a damp cloth to their necks, periodically wringing it out in a bucket of ice water.

"This is a fucking mess," I say. "How are we supposed to put on a show when seventy-five percent of us are down for the count?"

Jim approaches from our right. Even though Maverick warned us about his transformation, it's still a surprise to see Blackbeard in the flesh. I'm thankful he uses his normal voice when he talks to us, though. A straight face would have been an impossibility if he'd spoken in the voice Maverick described.

He raises his hands in a placating gesture as he steps closer. "I understand the seasickness is a bit of an issue, but you should all feel a bit better once we come to a stop. We're going against some rougher waters, so it feels a bit bumpy."

Cat raises her head. "A bit bumpy? Jim, this isn't a fucking HPV outbreak. It's hell! Would it have killed you to allow this piece of shit to have stabilizers?"

"Hear, hear," I add, though only loud enough that Maverick can hear me. He rewards me with a smirk.

Jim's shoulders droop, giving him the appearance of a wilted flower. "They're about to drop anchor. As soon as we clear the side of that island, we'll be in view of the Normies, who've just settled at their tables for lunch. Then we can begin."

The fact that I feel compassion for this man is a bad sign, but I do. He was clearly excited about this event, and it's not working out as he anticipated. And dammit, I want to help him.

"It's okay," I say. "Like you said, once the ship comes to

a stop, most of us will feel better. All the murdering will take our minds off this shitty feeling."

Jim's eyes soften as he looks at me. "Thank you for the vote of confidence. It means more than you know."

Oh, I know what the fuck it means, and I'm struggling with it.

I look out at the water. A large patch of ocean creates a barrier between the ship and the island, so I'm not certain how entertained the Normies will be. We'll look like ants fighting for a bread crumb from this distance.

Jim must realize what I'm thinking, because he pulls a spyglass from an interior pocket and hands it to me. I extend the lens and peer through the eyepiece. The device eats up the distance, and I can make out leaves on the island trees. A few small birds huddle amongst the rocks lining the shore on this side.

"The guests on the island will have something similar, though not so powerful. We want them to be close enough to see some action without realizing what's actually happening." Jim takes the offered spyglass and passes it to Eve, who tries it out, then passes it to Maverick. "They won't get them until after the first event, however."

"Why is that?" Maverick asks as he stares at the island through the lens.

"I tried to figure out how to make keelhauling look less authentic, even from a distance, but it was unmistakable in our test runs. A living person goes in, and a dead person usually comes out." Jim shakes his head. "Blood helps sell real death as fiction. Without the set dressings, it's clear that we're just hauling up drowned men and women."

"Keelhauling?" I look at Maverick. "Test runs?"

"Yes, well, we couldn't very well have the big show be our dress rehearsal, could we? I needed to know if this would work, and it does." Jim clears his throat and looks into the distance. "Just not as well as I'd hoped. Some of them survive."

Maverick turns to me, ready to explain. "Keelhauling is where a rope is tied to—"

"I know what keelhauling is," I say. What I can't say is that I'm not okay with this sort of torture. It's cruel and unusual in all the worst ways.

But at least there's a chance of survival, I guess. Maybe I can help our Cattle make it through to the end. I'll find out soon enough because the island's forest-enclosed beach eases into view, and the pirate ship comes to a stop.

"Don't get any ideas," Maverick whispers as Jim hurries away. "You can't save them."

"Who said anything about saving anyone?" I look out at the water, unable to meet his eyes.

"For a fed, you sure suck at lying."

I grit my teeth and grip the railing tighter. "I'm struggling with this, okay? It's not easy to let go of my morals."

"You don't have to let them go. You just need to adjust them."

"Then I'm having trouble *adjusting* my morals. Happy?" I groan and tip my forehead against the backs of my hands. "I'm sorry, but this is incredibly stressful. Can't we just try to help our Cattle stay alive? For me?"

"I don't know how that will work, but . . ."

I push out my lower lip as he looks at me.

He sighs and shakes his head. "I'll do what I can."

That will have to do, because it's time. The anchors have dropped, and our Cattle have been led onto the deck. They're dressed in period clothing as well, though they look like their outfits came straight from a Chinese sweat shop. I highly doubt pirates ever wore neon-green spandex leggings.

Crew members work to fasten thick rope around each man's waist. Their hands are bound behind their backs, and their legs sport metal shackles around their ankles, preventing them from running or kicking. Colored bands circle each wrist. One man sports a yellow band.

"That's the one I want," I tell Maverick as I point to the yellow-banded man. "We don't have to feel bad for keeping him alive."

He sighs and takes my hands in his. "Compassion is a privilege that has been ripped away from most of us, either through genetics or experiences. Be glad that you know it so intimately, and please don't ever change." With a sigh, he looks at his feet. "We'll take the yellow guy for keelhauling, and we'll pull the rope as quickly as we can. At the next station—"

"Next station? How many murder *stations* do we have to go through?" I hold my hand to my forehead and close my eyes. "I've died and gone to serial killer preschool. Are we going to fingerpaint with blood and stack body parts as we count them?"

Maverick doesn't laugh.

"I'm sorry. It's just . . . a lot. I know I've already killed, but this isn't getting any easier for me."

Having caught this bit of our conversation, Cat stumbles over. "Are you struggling with it too? I had a hard time at the winter retreat, so I know where you're coming from. What's your MO again? Maybe I can help."

Maverick and I lock eyes, and I kick myself for speaking so loudly. And fuck, I can't remember my MO! I know that the Fisherman story is incorrect, but it's been days since

Maverick made up the lie to replace it, and now I'm fucking screwed because I can't remember the new tall tale.

Maybe the department was right. I'm not cut out for field work, and I never have been. The curtain is about to come crashing down.

But then Maverick steps in and saves the day. "She was seen smiling before taking a kill, so they call her Mona Lisa, but she's still kind of new to this. Her previous kills were personal, and she's struggling to find the motivation here."

"Oh, I see," Cat says with a nod as she turns to me. "It helped me to learn what they did. I'd get so pissed off that murder was the only option. When you think about their victims, it's kind of hard to see any other solution."

I want to say that recidivism is lower than it's ever been, but that would be a lie. It would also out me as a fucking fed, so I just smile at her.

Is she correct? Have they had it right all this time? Maybe their solution to our first-world problem isn't so terrible, but who decides which people are vile enough to become Cattle?

"Don't overthink it," she adds. "I see the wheels spinning in your mind, and that's—" Her stomach lurches, and she covers her mouth with her hand before running to the side of the ship.

Don't overthink it. Okay.

I'll try.

Chapter Twenty-Five

Frankie

Maverick, Eve, Aven, and I take up our positions on the deck. All six teams will participate in keelhauling at the same time, so our little groups are dotted at regular intervals. The Cattle have been lined up on the opposite side, with ropes fashioned around their midsections.

The task is simple enough. Crew members will hoist the Cattle overboard on that side, and we'll haul them in on the opposite side, dragging them under the boat and across the keel. That's keelhauling in a nutshell. They didn't even need to put a sick twist into the activity because it's already twisted as fuck on its own. The risk of drowning is high, but even if they survive the ordeal, they'll be beaten to fuck and back by all the pulling.

Maverick is at the head of our rope, followed by me, then Eve. Aven takes up the slack at the end. He's our powerhouse, and I only hope he'll pull with all his might.

Judging by his mounds of muscle, there's plenty of might to go around.

"Are we really trying to do this as fast as possible? Seems a bit counterproductive, if you ask me. What's the fun in saving them?" Aven asks as he tests the rope's heft in his hand.

"So that we can torture them later," Eve says. "Have you never given your victims a little hope? It makes it that much sweeter when you end them."

Aven scoffs. "Jim hasn't even said how the winner will be decided. What if it's the group who kills the most Cattle? If we're trying to keep ours alive to the end, we'll lose."

"You started working for Jim a few months ago, yeah?" Maverick asks, and Aven nods. "Then you have more than enough money for all the hookers and blow you can afford. Grab the rope and haul as fast as you can."

Aven sets his jaw and solidifies his grip on the rope. He isn't pleased, but it's three on one. I'm glad Eve and Maverick are in my corner.

Speakers hidden around the ship begin playing the same spiel the Normies hear on land. It starts with a rousing orchestral song that sounds like a sea shanty, minus the raucous voices. Instead, Jim's voice pipes over the music, using that same deep voice Maverick described earlier.

"*Arr, landlubbers! Cast your eyes toward the horizon, for thar be pirates!*"

Eve and I share a glance, then turn our attention toward Jim, who beams near the deck's center. He's like a proud director watching his third graders prepare to put on a show for their doting parents. Too bad the parents won't realize the dead bodies aren't stage props.

"*The naval commanders tried to board their fine ship, and now the pirates must teach them a lesson. For your first course, please enjoy the Keelhauler appetizer: a fresh pairing of cocktail shrimp with a side of bloody cocktail sauce to dunk them in!"*

"Everyone get ready!" Jim shouts, and we situate our grips on the rope.

Boom!

The boat lists to the side as a cannon fires somewhere below. Jim topples to his ass with a laugh, his hand clutching his hat to his head. The slack behind us tightens as the crew dumps the Cattle into the drink, and seconds later, we're rewarded with a splash.

"Pull!" Maverick shouts, and we all pull back as we planned. "Pull!" he shouts again, and we give it everything we've got.

The struggle is immediate. I don't know why I thought it would be simple to pull a human body from one side of the ship to the other, but I grossly underestimated the difficulty. Instead of water, it feels like we're pulling him through wet cement.

I count the seconds in my head, holding my breath right along with the Cattle. By the time I reach thirty, I'm forced to suck in air, and it feels like we've made no progress.

"Longer pulls!" I shout. "We're losing progress each time we adjust our grip. Hold tight and walk it backward on my word!"

Everyone nods and firms their grip.

"One, two, three, *heave!*" I yell, and we all step backward as a unit. "*Ho!*" I shout, and everyone instinctively adjusts without being told. "*Heave!*"

We pull with all our might, taking a few steps backward, and we practically feel the boat shudder as our Cattle strikes the underside.

"Okay, maybe a little gentler this time!" I shout.

We continue on for what feels like forever but is probably only about two minutes. Finally, the dead weight of a body out of water slows our progress. I'm tempted to rush to the railing and gawk over the side to see if he's still alive, but there will be time enough for that once we get him back on deck.

After a few more pulls that make me feel like I'm going to shit my pants, the man finally clears the side of the ship and lands on the deck. The outcome is immediately obvious. If his pale lips and skin weren't enough of a sign, the ability to see part of his spine through the gaping wound in his neck tells me everything I need to know.

"Shit, we damn near took this bloke's head off." Aven whistles, then laughs. "I was wrong. We can listen to Frankie from here out."

My insides recoil, and I want to puke. Where is the motion sickness when I need it?

Maverick's hand lands on my shoulder, and he gives it a squeeze. He can't exactly comfort me in this moment, so he's doing the best he can. And I'm grateful. I feel like shit.

"Six points to Maverick's team!" Jim shouts. "They were the first to haul their catch aboard!"

Kindra groans and releases her section of rope, sending the other three members of her team stumbling forward. "What's the fucking point? How can we compete if we don't know what we're trying to do?"

"She's a touch competitive," Eve whispers beside my ear.

Despite Kindra folding her arms over her chest and refusing to help, her team pulls their Cattle onto the deck next. Unsurprisingly, he's also very dead.

"Five points to Ezra's team!" Jim yells.

A team of unfamiliar people come in third, followed by

Grim's team in fourth. The last two teams are eliminated when they can't get their Cattle above the waterline by the game's end.

"Better luck next time," Jim says as they're ushered to a waiting area below deck.

The dead bodies are removed from sight as servers piddle around the tables on the island. I know this because Jim left the spyglass in my care. Its strap currently hangs around my neck as I stare through the eyepiece and wish I was eating whatever the fuck sort of meat that is.

The pirate music blasts from the speakers again, followed by Jim's voice. "*Looks like those soldiers paid dearly for stepping in harrrm's way. Let this be a lesson to ye. When you mess with Blackbeard, you'll get very familiar with the briny deep. Please enjoy your next course, a plank of beef served with a side of soldier-shaped mashed potatoes.*"

I turn to Maverick. "Planks . . . like walk the plank? What the fuck will we have to do this time?"

Maverick looks around, as curious as I am, though for a very different reason. I see the excitement in their eyes. All of them. They're practically frothing at the mouth for what comes next.

Jim motions us closer as the crew starts setting up actual fucking planks off the side of the ship. Four of them, to be exact. Yet again, this is something that is survivable, so I'm not sure what sort of wicked twist Jim has up his sleeve.

And I don't want to find out.

Before everyone else reaches him, I hurry toward Jim. "Hey, I *really* need to use the restroom, if you catch my drift. Lunch isn't sitting so well in my stomach."

"We can't stop the show now," Jim whines. "What about all the guests? They'll be so disappointed if we take an intermission, and their next course might get cold."

Is he fucking pouting?

No matter. I have to get out of this.

"Yeah, I understand if you need to keep going. I'll be back before the next game." I raise two fingers. "Scouts honor."

He doesn't need to know that two more fingers are crossed behind my back. After all, diarrhea can be very unpredictable, especially when it's fake.

Jim sighs and clenches his fists at his sides. "If you must, but please return by the final game. I wouldn't want you to miss the special guest."

"Wouldn't dream of it," I say with a wink.

He shouts something at my retreating back about staying away from the brig, but he doesn't have to worry about that. I have zero desire to go anywhere near the criminals.

I hurry to the staircase before Maverick realizes what's happening. If he follows me, Jim will surely halt the games before I return. I can only hope that Maverick didn't spot me wandering off in all the hubbub.

Shadows linger below deck. Glass lanterns along the wall provide the only light as I hurry down a long corridor until I reach the bathroom at the end. Whoever designed it did their best to make it look like it belongs in the same time period as the ship, so I'm grateful when the toilet flushes after I step into the small space and try the handle. Not that I actually need to use it. I close the lid and sit down.

Almost instantly, the door springs open and a man backs inside, completely oblivious to my presence. My fear is quickly replaced by relief when I realize I could overpower this man with my pinky. He's quite short.

I clear my throat, and he whips around with wide,

bulging eyes. It takes a second to realize that his appearance isn't due to shock. This is just how he looks.

"Oh, so sorry," he says as he hurries to avert his eyes. "I didn't realize this one was in use. Um . . . can you give me just a second?"

I stand and smooth the front of my corset. "You can turn around. I wasn't using the facilities, just . . . taking a break."

"I'm hiding, but please don't tell Jim."

I glance at his wrist, where an orange band circles his skin.

He holds out his hand. "I'm Gary, by the way. Some guys brought me to an island by mistake, so Jim lets me work for him now. If he finds out I snuck aboard . . ." He looks to the side and shakes his head, and his smile finally breaks. "I'm grateful for Jim. We travel a lot, and I have food and a bed. As long as I stay out of Chef Maurice's way, I do fine. I wasn't supposed to be on the pirate ship today, but the crew was short due to seasickness, so I volunteered. If Jim knew, he'd be upset."

"He doesn't normally assign you to the games?"

Gary shakes his head hard enough to make his jowls waggle. "Nuh uh, no way. He knows I don't like the . . . the bodies. He also doesn't want the guys to see me. It's our little secret." His lower lip quivers, and his eyes bulge a little more. "When Jim found me in the basement traps, crying in a corner and begging to be spared, he saved me, but he made me promise to never go around the guys who brought me here. They can't see me."

I offer him a soft smile. "Why not hang out in here for the rest of the voyage? It'll be *our* little secret."

"Do you mean it?" His face lights up, and the smile returns. "Gosh, you sure are nice." He licks his lips and peers around as if someone might hear him. Meanwhile, we're in a three-by-six room, very much alone. "I'll do something nice for you too. You know those feds you guys are hunting?"

My heart stops in my chest, realizing what he'll say before he says it.

"Two of the Cattle on this ship are feds, and they've owned it outright. They'll tell anyone who'll listen, in fact. They've said some other shit too. Shit so bad that Jim made us change one of their bands when he substantiated the claims." Gary shakes his head. "The red guy is the worst. The shit he's done to women is sickening. I'm glad you guys are killing him today. I can't stomach hearing more of his stories."

I move toward the door, a cold sweat slicking my palms. "Thanks for that, Gary. I'll keep it in mind."

"Anytime. But you won't tell anyone you saw me here, right?" He looks down at his feet. "Probably don't say anything to the guys, either. It was a stupid idea to come on this ship."

"Scouts honor," I say, and this time, I don't cross my fingers. I don't know which guys he speaks of, so it's an easy enough promise to keep.

I close the door as I step into the hall, and the lock fastens behind me. I didn't plan to visit the brig while I was down here, but sometimes, plans change. Spying a sign for the cells, I aim my feet down a dark hallway and head for the truth.

Chapter Twenty-Six

Frankie

The brig smells much like I'd expect it to. Stale urine and fresh vomit are the prevailing aromas, with gentle notes of fart cloud and B.O. woven through. Men and a few women cling to the metal bars, decrying their situation as I pass. I find myself studying their bands more than their faces, judging their perceived crimes.

I'm no better than any of the killers aboard this ship, and I'm losing my humanity by the second. If I can speak to Castle, maybe I can remember why I'm here.

My brain rushes back to what Gary said in the bathroom. One of the feds claimed to have done horrible things to women, and that can't be the truth. Agents are pushed through rigorous screenings. My psych eval took months, and I'm pretty cut and dry. I can only assume the agent said those things to fit in. The alternative makes my skin crawl.

Despite checking each cell twice, I don't see anyone I recognize, and I can't exactly wander down the line playing pin the tail on the fed. The sting of defeat nips at my heels as another cannon blast rocks the ship.

The second game is underway, and I'm running out of time.

I start down the aisle a third time, checking each face a little more closely. Some of them hide in the shadows, making it difficult to see who they are. It isn't so difficult to see what some of them are doing, however. The lightning-quick faps are hard to miss. I guess furious masturbation helps pass the time.

But Castle isn't here. When I reach the end again, I have to accept that.

"Let me the fuck out of here! Do you know what my boss will do to you when he finds out how we were treated? You'll all burn for this! All of you!"

My ears practically swivel toward the familiar voice. It sounded muffled, as if the speaker was behind a closed door instead of locked inside these barred cells. I make my way to the other end of the hall and find a door hidden within the shadows. I open it and step inside.

This must be the ship's medical area. Three Cattle sit strapped to seats lining the wall closest to the door. A fourth lies on a metal table, his hands and feet held in place with leather straps as a man hunches over him. When the man realizes he has an audience, he stands upright and blinks at me behind thick glasses.

"You aren't supposed to be here," he says. "Crew and Cattle only."

I push ahead, hoping my authoritative tone is enough to convince him. "Are these the Cattle for the third game?"

"The fourth," the man says. "I already stitched up the shits for the third game."

I peer at the table and see that I interrupted his sewing

class. A thick strand of thread hangs from the long needle in his hand. Blood drips from the pinprick wounds surrounding the Cattle's mouth.

I turn back to the three Cattle sitting by the door and spot Castle.

"Perhaps you aren't aware, but I'm the Confessor. As such, it's important that I understand their crimes. I can't kill them otherwise. Could I possibly take this one into a private room so that we can have a chat?" I grin and bat my eyelashes at the man as I try to push my cleavage a little higher. "I sure would appreciate it."

He eyes me, then looks past me, at the door. "Maybe I should talk to Jim first. How do I know you aren't one of those feds?"

I'm a bit shocked by his question. Shouldn't he want the feds to help him escape this death trap? Instead, he views us as the enemy. Come to think of it, Gary seemed pretty content with his current situation as well, and he wasn't even a criminal.

Stop it, Frankie. This is why it's so important to speak to Castle alone. You're losing your grip, girl.

"Would a fed do this?" Without flinching—and that is a fucking feat, let me tell you—I grab the needle from his hand, hold it between my fingers, and turn the Cattle's crotch into a pin cushion. I drive the pointed end past the fabric until it meets skin a sickening number of times before I toss the needle onto his writhing stomach. "Satisfied?"

The man gulps. "Almost . . ."

Oh fuck, he's got a boner. It's hard to mistake in those fucking spandex pants. The fact that it's so aggressively straining toward me doesn't help.

"Well, let this be a lesson to you. Don't fuck with the Confessor," I say before motioning for him to free Castle.

The sooner I can get away from his fleshy dowsing rod, the better.

He looks at the door once more before huffing and releasing Castle's waist from the chain. Once he's double-checked his wrist and ankle bindings, he nods for me to take him away.

Keeping my composure—again, massive feat—I calmly exit the room with Castle in tow. Once the door closes behind him, he tries to speak, but I silence him with a look. As he slowly dies inside, I turn and keep walking. Deferring to a woman isn't his bailiwick, but he's about to learn today. I'm not the Ghost he left at the airport four days ago.

I walk down the hallways like I know where I'm going, but by the time I've tried the third locked door, it's clear I'm lost. Isn't there a single fucking place on this godforsaken ship where we can get a little privacy? Finally, the fourth door comes open, and we step into a supply closet filled with janitorial offerings. The door clicks shut, and I lock it for good measure before turning to Castle.

"You dirty fucking bitch," he grinds out between clenched teeth. "You knew all along. That's why you let me play the criminal. You wanted me to die so you could finally rise up the ranks."

"Castle, I assure you, I had no idea."

"Bullshit!" He flails his shoulders. "Untie my fucking hands."

"I can't do that."

"The fuck you can't. I refuse to die on this ship. Untie my fucking hands, and we can take them out together. I met a guy here. He isn't from our unit, but I trust him. With his help, we can make it out of here."

What he's saying sounds good, and there's a chance a few feds are playing Sinners on deck as well. If we all worked as a team, we could overpower damn near everyone on board, save for the big Scottish guy. And the big British guy. And his feisty fucking brother.

And Maverick.

Okay, maybe his plan isn't a plan at all.

"No," I say.

His eyes widen when he hears no indecision in my voice. "You can't be fucking serious. Ghost, they'll kill me. You've seen what they do."

Yes, I have, and I'm not okay with it, but I don't want Maverick to get caught in the crossfire. If I finish the mission and take Jim peacefully, no one else has to get hurt. Maybe not even Castle.

"Jim said I had a special guest appearing for round four. I think that's you," I say. "Once I know what the game is, I can try to find a way to keep you alive. The first round was keelhauling, and the—"

"Keelhauling? You can't survive that shit!" He thrashes around again, knocking several rolls of toilet paper from a shelf. I've never had or witnessed a panic attack, but this is a pretty textbook freak out. I have to stop him before someone comes to find out why there's a goddamn velociraptor in the mop closet.

"Shh!" I take a deep breath. "Keep it down. I'll untie your hands while we talk, but you have to let me tie you up again before we exit the fucking closet. And you have to be quiet, okay?"

He clenches his jaw, but nods. With a scowl, he gives me his back, and I unfasten the rope around his wrists, revealing raw skin beneath. He's been hard at work, trying to break out of his confines. A lot of good it's done him.

But as the rope falls to the floor, I notice the band on his wrist. I lick my lips to wet them, but my mouth is a desert.

My soul tries to evacuate my body as I stare at that silicone band, but I gather every ounce of strength and keep my composure.

I'm beginning to understand panic attacks a little better now. Because that band is not yellow.

It's red.

Chapter Twenty-Seven

Maverick

Eve flops onto her ass, followed by Aven. They drop back on the deck with their arms outstretched as they fight for each breath. I'm just as winded, but I manage to stay upright.

"That could've been a touch easier with our fourth," Aven says. "I dinnae get a break."

His accent is thicker when he's tired, making him difficult to understand, but I get the gist. He's irritated that Frankie wasn't here to help, and I concur. We were forced to saw through the plank as the Cattle inch-wormed his way toward us, and it's a race we almost lost. Unlike the other teams, we couldn't take breaks in pairs. Eve and I just repeatedly switched with each other.

"Sorry, boys. My career doesn't exactly encourage strength training." Eve sits up. "Not many models walk about with guns for biceps, you know?"

I swat the brim of Eve's hat, sending it over her eyes. "No worries. You did great, and we weren't last."

Aven sits up and drapes his arms over his knees. "Would've been, if that old geezer hadn't kicked off about the guy on his team."

I glance down the deck, to where a pirate lies in a pool of blood. Another fed has been ferreted out and dispatched, and the noose tightens around my neck. Well, it tightens around Frankie's neck, but it might as well be mine. Despite the absolute irrationality of it all, I've grown entirely too fond of her. I see her as an extension of myself, much as I see my other friends. The fierce need to protect her began as an assignment but has turned into something much more complicated.

Speaking of protecting Frankie, I haven't seen her since before the second game started. Worry nips at my heels as I glance around for that purple feather and find it missing. Jim said she went to the bathroom, but she should have been back by now.

I hurry over to Jim as the crew cleans up the deck for the next game. Well, they remove the bodies, but the blood-stains remain. Jim said it "gives the old girl character." He stands at one of the smaller masts, with his arm around the tall wooden post as he stares at the distant island.

"Frankie still hasn't come back. Do I have time to check on her before the next game starts?"

Jim pouts and leans his head against the mast. "I'm starting to think you people don't appreciate my games."

"We love the games, but things have a habit of happening during them. But hey, the sooner I find Frankie, the sooner we can start the next one."

"Don't bother. I'll need to adjust the next two games to make them work for two people, anyway. I didn't expect Grim to discover his teammate so quickly." Jim sighs and hugs the pole a little tighter. "Just make sure you're back in time for the fourth game, hmm? I've brought along a surprise for Frankie, and my day will be positively ruined if she isn't here to see it."

"She could be hurt, Jim. Don't you care about that?"

He pins me with a look as the melancholy leaves him. "If you felt she were in real danger, why on earth would you require my permission to save her? Have you ever tried thinking for yourself, son? My indifference is a direct result of your lack of concern."

I'll tend to my bruised ego from that tongue lashing later. He has a point. Why am I wasting time when she could be in trouble?

My heart hammers a little harder in my chest as I turn for the stairs. I pick up the pace as worry nests like a bird in my chest. Wing beats flutter against my ribcage, and I realize the bird isn't nesting. It's trapped. It's panicking.

"I wish I were a bird," I mutter under my breath. "I'd fly into the first window I saw. Repeatedly. Anything to end this."

I'm about to turn toward the hallway lined with cells when I pick up a feminine voice in the other direction. It's hard to make out, and it could be a crew member, but I want to believe it's Frankie. It has to be her because the sooner I find her, the sooner this growing ache in my chest will recede.

When I reach the door, I spot a small sign to the left that says it's a supply closet, and there's no mistaking that the voice on the other side belongs to Frankie. Her cadence rings through, easing my worry. I raise my hand to knock on the door separating us, but I freeze when a male voice reaches beneath the door and grabs me by the throat.

"So you're buddying up with these shits?" the man says.

"Castle . . . it's more complicated than that. Look, I

appreciate the intel, but I'm just trying to fit in so that they don't kill me. The moment we dock at the end of this cruise, I'm turning in every single piece of shit I've laid eyes on."

This isn't new information, but it hits me like a slap in the face. I was wrong to worry she was getting too comfortable in her new role. She certainly fooled the fuck out of me.

"I saw you with that pretty boy," the man—*Castle*—says. And what a dumb fucking name. I'd love to meet his brothers: Skyscraper, Townhouse, and Quonset Hut. The man scoffs, and the disgust in his voice makes my skin crawl. "I saw the way you looked at him, Ghost. Typical whore moves, using your dirty snatch to get your way. King will hear about this shit. You're fucking the enemy, and it's gonna cost you the job."

Despite feeling destroyed about what Frankie said, I hold my breath as I wait for her to tear this asshole a new one. She can be a real bitch, which I find refreshing.

So imagine my disappointment when she self-flagellates instead.

"You're right," she says. "I agreed to be the killer because I thought I could use my femininity to my advantage. I was wrong, Castle, and now I need your help. Let me tie your hands so that we don't get caught. Once you're on deck, I'll cut you free so we can kick all their asses. Regardless of what you told me, we're still federal agents."

So that's her fucking game? And I fell right into it.

The blood heats in my veins and rockets upward until my head feels like a furnace. Castle says something else, but I can't hear him over the thunderous rush of my heartbeat in my ears. How could I have been stupid enough to believe we were getting closer?

Something bumps against the door, and a whimper from Frankie clears my head in an instant.

"Castle, personal space, dude," she says, but the slight quiver in her voice betrays her. She's scared. "Just turn around and let me tie your wrists."

"What, you think you can just fuck everyone else over and avoid getting fucked yourself? It doesn't work that way, slut. I've hated you since the moment King brought you into our division, and I'll continue hating you while I choke you to death with my fat cock, you filthy cunt."

"Doubtful. You'd need more than two inches to accomplish that."

Castle chokes on air. "What the fuck did you say?"

"I hear you've been hiding a little secret of your own, Castle. I don't know the details yet, but when I figure them out, I'll bring them to King's attention. I never even thought about taking your position, but if it's as empty as your fucking head, I might as well."

When Frankie finally delivers the heat I expect, I'm overjoyed, but that joy is short-lived. Muffled bumps, bangs, and grunts filter through the door. She might be a federal agent trained in the art of hand-to-hand combat, but she's also shut in a confined space with a fucking bull. The horns are bound to gore her.

But when I try the door, I realize she isn't just shut in that space. She's locked inside.

With no room to gear up for a running start, I ram my shoulder into the door. As I repeatedly beat my body against the unyielding slab of wood, I feel so helpless. I have to get her out of there.

A bug-eyed man emerges from the bathroom further down the hall. He's a member of the crew, so I can only hope he's high enough in Jim's ranks to have a key to this fucking door.

"Little help!" I shout toward him.

He looks to his left and right, then points to his chest. With raised eyebrows, he mouths *Me?*, and I want to scream.

"No, the little green man behind you," I bellow. "Yes, you! Do you have a key to this door?"

The man hurries closer, stopping a few feet from me when he hears the commotion.

"Not the lady with the purple feather," he says. "Not her."

"Yes, her. Now help me help her!"

Frankie screams, and that seems to get him into gear. He hurries forward again until he's at my side.

"On three, we'll ram the door," I say. "Ready?"

He nods, then shakes his head. "Wait, *on* three? Or after three? Like, one, two, *ram*? Or one, two—"

"The fucking first one! One, two—"

We push into the door with all our might, but it still isn't enough. We manage to knock the doorknob slightly loose, but that's about it.

The cannon blasts, adding to the sounds of the struggle happening just out of sight. I squeeze the back of my neck and fight the urge to panic as Frankie's whimpers intensify. I hope she realizes I'm not up on deck, playing a game as she fights for her life. I'm down here with her, trying to save her. And when I get my hands on this man, there won't be anything left of him.

The door rattles again, shaking the dangling doorknob, and I have an idea.

"Can you get a hammer?" I ask the bug-eyed man.

"Anything metal and heavy, really. A few blows to that doorknob should have us in there in seconds."

His eyes bulge a bit more. "I don't know about a hammer, but after Jim found me, part of my skull had to be replaced. Is titanium strong enough?"

The man doesn't realize what he's offering. The force it would take to dislodge the doorknob would likely kill him in the process. Despite being who I am and doing what I do, I can't bring myself to take advantage of his ignorance.

But then he says, "I know I might not survive it, but she was so kind to me. In the bathroom, she—"

I grip the side of his head and slam it against the doorknob.

"The plate's on the other side," he says so matter-of-factly, as if I didn't just bash his head in. As he stands upright, blood drips into his eye from a large gash, but at least the scar will go well with the dozens littering his face. "I don't feel much pain, so don't worry about—"

My hand takes the other side of his head and rams it onto the doorknob. This time, the metal gives way and crashes to the floor, followed by the man.

There isn't time to tend to him. I knock the mechanism loose from inside the door, then yank open the useless slab of wood. Castle currently straddles Frankie's prone form, his hands coiled around her throat. Her nails dig into his wrists, but she's fighting a losing battle. Her glassy gaze rises to mine, pleading for me to help her.

With a hop step, I slam my shin into Castle's side, but the brute is immovable. I repeat the action until something cracks, and only once he grips his side and grunts do I know it was his rib cage. Intense pain radiates through my leg, but it was worth it, now that his hands no longer close Frankie's airway. She gulps oxygen and coughs beneath the lug groaning on top of her. I take the opportunity to land another kick, this time aiming for his head. His skull rocks to the side, and then he crumples against the shelf as Frankie scrambles out from under him.

"You son of a fucking *bitch*!" she screams as she rises like a phoenix. I can practically see the tendrils of smoke curling from her ears. When she raises her foot and stomps her boot heel on his crotch, I damn near get a boner. "You're a sick piece of shit, and I hope they blow out your asshole in prison!"

He won't make it to prison. When I see the red finger marks on Frankie's neck, coupled with her swollen lower lip and puffy right eye, rage overcomes my senses.

"What the fuck did he do to you?" I bellow as I search the shelves for something sharp. "If he violated you, his death will be so much more fucking painful."

"It's not enough that he beat the fuck out of me?" she says. "I think that's grounds enough for torture."

"I agree," says a voice from the hall.

"Gary? Are you okay?" Frankie squeezes past me and hurries to help him stand. "Jesus, what happened to your head? You're a mess!"

I snap a wooden mop handle in half, giving me a nice pointy stick. That'll do. "Take Gary to the medical bay. I'll deal with this piece of shit."

"Stop!" Frankie shouts.

My hand freezes mere milliseconds before driving the sharp end into his neck. "What am I stopping for, sweetheart? This man just tried to take something that doesn't belong to him. So please, tell me why I should stop when I have never wanted to continue more in my fucking life."

"I've had a change of heart," she says. The glassy haze clears from Frankie's eyes, an unrecognizable look replacing it. She plucks her hat from the floor, situates it on her head, and looks down at the unconscious asshole. "It's time for round four, and I'm ready to play the fucking game now."

Chapter Twenty-Eight

Maverick

I stand off to the side on deck as Eve and Kindra fuss over Frankie's wounds. When Jim saw her state and heard what happened to her, he finally came to his senses and offered to call off the final round so we could get her back to the Bruise Cruise. Frankie would have none of it. She's bound and determined to play the fourth game, and she's adamant that Castle will be our Cattle.

When she said that, Jim couldn't have looked more pleased. I should feel the same.

So why don't I?

The goal was to get her to turn against her own and side with us, and for all intents and purposes, that has been achieved, but I can't pat myself on the back for this. I don't feel as if I've accomplished anything. The only thing I feel is awful. The kill she made before served a purpose—an unavoidable means to an end—but the bloodlust lighting her eyes ablaze is different now. This is personal. I've taken an incredible woman with proper values and ironclad morals and turned her into a fucking psychopath.

When the girls have had their fill of the retelling, they meander back to their respective groups to prepare for the final round of the game. I take this moment to pull Frankie aside. I haven't had a chance to check on her fully, and I want to be sure she's up for whatever game Jim has in store. Though it goes against my mission, I almost hope she's had a change of heart and wants to back out.

I pull her against me and embrace her openly, not caring who sees. "Are you okay? Truly?"

"The swelling is already going down in my eye, and at least I now know that lip fillers are definitely not for me. My lip looks worse than it feels, though." She smiles up at me, looking adorable in a scruffy, beaten-to-hell-and-back kind of way. "My throat is a little worse for wear, not gonna lie, but I think I'll be okay. Thank you, by the way."

"If you want to thank me properly, I gladly accept blow jobs." I lean closer to her ear and drop my voice to a whisper. "In fact, we could skip out on the last game entirely and head back to the ship. Think about it, sweetheart. You could knock me around a little, and then I could replace every ounce of pain with double the pleasure." I nip her earlobe and revel in the way she shudders against me.

"That . . . actually sounds really nice."

My spirits rise as her hand secretly gropes the front of my pants. Maybe I can get her out of this mess yet.

She squeezes my limp cock, sending a spike of pain through my groin. "But I'm not skipping the game, Maverick. Whatever fucked-up shitshow lies in store for Castle, I don't want to miss a second of it."

I smile down at her and hope she doesn't see the way

I'm breaking inside. This isn't who she is, and I feel responsible for her coming into her villain era. It's not a nice feeling.

"Hey," she says as she places her hand on the side of my face, stroking my cheek and offering a wan smile. "This new way of thinking isn't a bad thing. If anything, it's the *best* thing because it's pretty much what you wanted. I get it now. I understand why you people kill, and you were right. Some shit stains are too dirty to run through the wash. Instead of wasting resources on scrubbing what can't be cleansed, it makes more sense to toss out the ruined garment."

I search my brain for something that will snap her out of this. "What about your career?"

The smile shifts, looking sadder by the second but still remaining on her face. "What career, Maverick? Didn't anyone tell you?" She utters a wry laugh and shakes her head. "There was never a mission to hand over any of you. This was a suicide trip. We weren't expected to return. None of us."

"Wait, why would you think that?"

"Castle said as much."

I hold her at arm's length and stare into her eyes. "You can't be serious. How can you believe anything that came out of that asshole's mouth? He just said that to hurt you."

"No, it tracks. When I went to the bathroom, Gary, that weird little man who helped you out, told me Castle had been running his mouth about some vile shit he's done. Castle didn't know that, but when he mentioned that we were set up, he said it was because a higher-up demanded a hard cull of any agents with skeletons in their closets. Vile shit sounds like skeletons to me."

"Then why are you here? Are you secretly a mass murderer?" I shake my head and drop my hands. "It doesn't make sense."

"No clue. I have no secrets. I guess King grew tired of me trying to climb the ladder, so he figured this was the best way to be rid of me." She keeps her voice steady, but the hurt shines in her eyes. "I just don't know how I'll tell my mother. This was her greatest fear."

"That you'd give up your government job?"

"No," she says with a laugh. "That I'd fall in love with a serial killer and abandon my scruples." Her eyes widen and her lips clamp shut. "Not that I'm in love. That's not what I'm saying."

"Sure it's not," I say as I drag her against me again. She struggles to pull away, but I just hold her tighter. "It's okay, sweetheart. I tend to have this effect on women."

She lands a punch to my side. How cute. "I'm not in love with you. I just like you." She punches again, a little weaker this time. "A lot."

I lean down and kiss the top of her hat. "I like you too. A lot. And that's why I don't think you should do this."

Leaning back, she looks up at me. "You don't think I should kill Castle?"

"No, I don't. I think you should let me do it."

The pirate music cranks up again, and Jim shouts for everyone to man their stations. Still locked in an embrace, Frankie and I watch as people scurry to and fro, some setting up for the event and some preparing to play.

The crew drags pieces of a small metal stage to the middle of the deck, where they begin a speedrun assembly of the multiple pieces. Another group rolls the barrels up a shallow ramp and onto the stage. This must mean they were part of the games all along, not just set dressing.

"What's in the barrels?" Frankie asks.

Eve steps up beside us. "No clue, but what the fuck is happening on the island?"

Frankie and I turn toward the blip of land. Most of the Normies still sit at their tables, but toward the right end of the line, some sort of commotion has broken out.

I motion for Frankie to hand over the spyglass, and she does. As I peer down the long metal tube, I can't believe what I'm seeing.

"It's Ice Pick," I say. "He's fighting one of the . . ." I lower the spyglass. "Shit."

"What?" Eve squeals. "Don't leave us hanging like this, honey! Spit it out!"

I push the device into Eve's hands and motion for her to see for herself. She ends up as speechless as I am as she passes the spyglass to Frankie. They had to see it for themselves. No one would have believed me otherwise.

Because on the island, Ice Pick is currently refereeing a vicious cat fight, and they appear to be fighting over *him*.

"Oh, the money I would pay to be the fly on that potato salad," Frankie says. "I want to know what they're saying."

Eve takes the spyglass from Frankie and holds it to her eye again. "I don't know, but the brunette is finally walking away. Well, hobbling away. She's missing one of her Red Bottoms, so she's moving a bit funny."

"Damn, I was rooting for the brunette," Frankie says.

"Seems like you prefer blondes, though," I say with a wink, and she swats my chest.

"Yall's little fling ain't no secret, honey," Eve says with a flick of her wrist. "No need to keep playing coy when you already announced that you're fucking him."

Frankie's cheeks blaze red, but she smiles before cracking her knuckles and looking around. "Where is everyone? It seems there aren't as many people out here now."

"Since Grim killed the fed, they were down a man, so their team bowed out. Rosie joined up with Bennett, Ezra, and Kindra because Cat had to go downstairs to die. I don't know where the other team disappeared to," Eve says. "Aven went to use the bathroom and hasn't come back."

A woman approaches from our left, and we turn to look at her. Her gray hair says she's over forty, but like Frankie, her face and body could easily pass for much younger. I've seen her here and there in passing, but we haven't spoken before, and this is definitely her first trip with us.

"Hello," she says with a wiggle of her fingers. "Jim said I should join you guys because Aven no longer wishes to play. Something about being too hot. I'm Anne, by the way."

Frankie looks her up and down and cocks her head. "What's your designation, Anne?"

Anne blinks, her head slightly rearing back. "Pardon? I'm not sure what you mean."

"What's your assignment, then, if you feel the need to play dumb?"

I grab Frankie's arm. "What are you doing, sweetheart?"

She snatches out of my grip, her eyes still trained on the woman. "Did they tell you to catch one of us big baddies? Did you believe you would have the opportunity to work your way to the top rather than sucking your way there?"

"Oh shit," Eve says through a laugh. "Do you think she's a fed?"

"What? I'm not one of them!" Anne says as her hand flies to her chest. "What makes you think that?"

Yeah, I'd like to know too. The alternative is that Frankie has truly lost her fucking mind.

Frankie glances around, finds what she's looking for, then yells, "Jim! Permission to kill Anne . . ." She looks at the woman.

"Wilcox," Anne says.

Frankie's eyebrows rise, and she smiles. "Wilcox . . . really? My grandmother on my mother's side was a Wilcox."

"I married into the name," Anne says. "My maiden name is Smith."

"Anne Smith. What a tragically mundane name." Frankie shakes her head and turns again. "Wilcox!" Frankie shouts toward Jim.

"Permission granted!" Jim shouts back.

And the chase is on.

Anne takes off toward the other side of the deck, but she soon realizes she's trapped. Frankie and Eve take off after her, the latter having the forethought to find a weapon on the way. Eve snatches a broadsword from Ezra's side, but it isn't needed. Anne takes one look back at the women rushing toward her before hoisting herself over the side and disappearing. Her scream cuts off abruptly when she smacks against the water.

I hurry to join Frankie and Eve as they peer over the side of the ship. Anne resurfaces seconds later, though one of her arms dangles in the water as she pinwheels the working limb to compensate and stay afloat.

"Fuck, she survived," Frankie says. "Where's a bucket of chum when you need it?"

A crowd gathers, and we watch as Anne treads water for several minutes before finally disappearing below a rogue wave. She doesn't resurface.

"How'd you know?" I ask Frankie as Jim yells for us to prepare for the game.

"I'll tell you later," she whispers. "Right now, I want to prepare for what I'm about to do. That wasn't satisfying enough, so this one has to be better."

"Didn't they teach you about the desire for escalation in fed school?" I whisper back. "This isn't you, sweetheart. You don't have to do this."

Frankie stops walking. She faces me as she thrusts a pointed finger toward the railing Anne threw herself from. "No, Maverick. *That* isn't me. I have never been accepted as one of them, but here on this ship, with all of you, I finally feel like I belong somewhere. I've been in my line of work for most of my life, and do you know how many friends I've made? Zero. Not a single one. I've been telling myself that I don't have relationships because of work, but it's because of me. I've crammed myself into spaces where I didn't belong, and now that I've slotted in so nicely here, I can finally see that."

"Frankie—"

She holds up her hand, silencing me. "You broke down a fucking door to save my ass, but the people I was supposed to trust put me in that room."

"You don't know that. He could have been lying."

"He wasn't."

She looks down at her feet, and the cracks in her veneer show through. The woman is angry, hurt, and betrayed. Whether her emotions stem from fact or fiction doesn't matter because the emotions are very real, and I've been an ass. She doesn't need a lecture. She needs comfort.

"Come here," I say as I pull her into me, and I'm pleased when she lets me. "If you need to kill Castle, then I'll support you. Just don't let this change who you are, okay?"

She looks up at me, and my heart breaks when I see the

tears forming in her eyes. "At nearly forty, you'd think I'd know who I am, huh?"

I lean down and kiss her forehead, and she sighs.

"If I kill Castle, can I still knock you around and get fucked stupid when we get back to the room?"

Smirking against her skin, I close my eyes and accept defeat. "Definitely."

Chapter Twenty-Nine

Frankie

I sit on the edge of the bed in the cabin on the Bruise Cruise. I stare at the wall and mentally relive every glorious second of the kill. We came in last because I took so long to end Castle's life, but I wanted to keep going. A wave of disappointment washed through me when he finally stopped screaming.

My lips curve into a smile at the memory of his muffled pleas.

He was surely shouting to everyone that I'm a fed, but he's wrong. I *was* a fed. Now . . . I don't know what I am.

I flop back on the bed and stare at the ceiling as the shower kicks on in the bathroom. Maverick wanted to clean up after sweating to death in that costume. I don't exactly feel fresh and clean myself. Maybe I should join him.

Nibbling my bottom lip, I imagine getting under the warm spray and rubbing my slick skin against his. The heat. The slippery feeling.

The water in my fantasy turns red, coating our skin as

we kiss beneath the vermillion rain. Instead of being disgusted with myself, I run with the fantasy, imagining the way he'd smash me against the wall and impale me until I can't stand.

All while covered in blood.

I can practically feel his fingers running over my body, touching and teasing. I've forgotten how nice it is to receive pleasure from a hand that isn't my own as Fantasy Maverick slips two thick fingers between my pussy lips.

"Getting started without me?" Maverick says, and I pull my hand from my pants and sit up.

I didn't even realize I'd been touching myself, let alone how much time had passed, but with this glorious sight in front of me, I want to keep going. Maverick rubs his head with a towel, and another winds around his waist. A few scars poke from the edge of the fabric tucked against his left hip.

"What happened there?" I ask.

He looks down and rubs his thumb over the faint white lines. "These?"

I nod.

"Desperate times called for desperate measures. I needed the pain to perform, and I hadn't yet discovered ways to harm myself that didn't leave lasting marks."

My stomach knots when I think about him sleeping with other women, as that's essentially what he's implying. I'm not dumb enough to think he's never had sex before—his skills in bed tell me he's had plenty of experience in his twenty-two years—but I still feel so angry that anyone else has enjoyed his donkey dick.

And I have no right.

Maverick isn't mine, and he never will be.

Why not? a voice whispers in the back of my brain, and

that bitch has a point. My career isn't holding me back from exploring new hobbies now, so it certainly won't stop me from exploring a new relationship.

"How do you feel about commitment?" I blurt.

Maverick's eyebrows rise, and he sits on the edge of the bed. "Wow, you're just going for it, huh?" He rubs the back of his neck and looks at the carpet. "I'm not seeing anyone else, if that's your concern. I'd be open to something when we get back, but . . ."

But?

The wind leaves my sails. "Is it my age?"

"I want you to have the space to make a clear decision, that's all," he says with a shake of his head. "What you want right now may not be what you want in six months, but what I want . . . that won't change."

"And what do you want?"

He turns his head, piercing me with his green eyes. "You."

Cupping the back of my head, he pulls me closer. Our lips meet, tentatively at first, almost as if we're both unsure. But as his hand wanders beneath my t-shirt and his fingertips glide along my stomach until he grips my hip, our confidence grows. We deepen the kiss, sighing together as our hunger ignites.

Maybe this is his way of shutting down the commitment talk, and I'm okay with that. I can badger him later.

His lips move to my jaw, and then he nips and nibbles his way down my neck. When he reaches fabric, he grips the hem of my shirt and pulls it away, exposing my breasts.

"You are fucking perfection," he whispers as he lays me back.

He leans down and pulls my nipple into his mouth. Sparks of pleasure travel between my legs with each pass of his tongue across that sensitive bud. I drive my hands through his damp hair and pull him closer, wanting more.

Castle's face pops into my mind. Specifically, the way his eyes bulged as I slowly lowered him into the barrel of acid. I imagine him here now, forced to watch me receive pleasure as his skin melts from his bones for eternity. It's a small price to pay for trying to assault me.

Warm breath fans across my chest, cooling the places Maverick bathed with his tongue. "I want to be inside you more than I want my next breath. It's painful, sweetheart. My desire hurts. Please . . . give me relief."

He lies on his back, letting the towel fall away. Despite limply resting against his thigh, his cock still intimidates me. I know what he's asking for, but I'll choke to death on that thing.

I can think of worse ways to die, though.

I slide off the bed and drop to my knees with my hands on his thighs. With my left hand, I grip his balls and give them a gentle twist. "Are you okay with this?"

"Sweetheart, I'm more than okay with it. Fucking hurt me."

My wrist turns, ratcheting the pressure. Maverick sucks air through clenched teeth as his eyes slam shut, and like a magic trick, his dick begins to levitate. Before my very eyes, it thickens until it's practically menacing. Keeping his sack painfully contorted, I lean forward and grip his dick with my other hand, then run my tongue along the underside of his shaft.

"Fuck," he breathes. "You're teasing me now. I want to feel your mouth around me. Take me into your throat."

I squeeze his nuts in my fist. "Don't demand things from me. When I'm ready to suck your dick, I will. Until then, enjoy what I give you."

"I like it when you're bossy," he grinds out.

Good. I don't know how to be any other way.

I run my tongue up his shaft again, then nip the underside of his cock. His body jerks, and his hand shoots toward my head. I swat it away.

"Don't—" he starts to say, but I put my teeth on his dick again, and he quiets.

"That's right. Be a good boy, and if you're quiet, I might let you come in my mouth." I dip a little lower and drag my tongue over his sack. "I might even swallow."

His hand moves toward my head again, and it gives me an idea.

I stand and go to the closet. When I return to the bed, Maverick looks confused.

"What the fuck are you doing with those?" he asks.

I wiggle the handcuffs. "You can't seem to keep your hands to yourself, so I'm going to help you with that."

He licks his lips, a moment of uncertainty flashing through his eyes. "I don't know about this. We don't have a good track record with handcuffs."

I clamp the cuff around his left wrist and motion for him to lie in the correct orientation on the bed. Despite voicing his concerns, he does as I ask, and I loop the second cuff through the headboard before securing him fully. I step back and look at my handiwork.

Biting my lip, I smile. I can't help it. "I could leave you like this, you know. Nothing is stopping me from walking out that door."

"Not even the promise of pleasure?"

"Okay," I say. "Maybe that."

He uses the tension from the cuffs to sit up a little more, and the sinews pull taut around his muscles. I need a napkin to wipe the drool from the side of my mouth. Nothing should look this good.

I get on my knees on the bed and take his cock into my hand once more. It's gone slightly soft, so I try tweaking his nuts again, but he almost seems to get softer.

"I might need a little more . . . encouragement," he says softly. "It's not you, Frankie."

His reassurance is nice, but I can't help feeling like my relaxed breasts and laugh lines are biting me in the ass. My skincare routine is great, but aging is a natural process I haven't exactly tried to adjust via the surgical route. Now I wonder if that was a mistake, but how could I have known I'd fall for a man nearly twenty years my junior?

"There's a knife in the blue bag in the closet," he continues. "It's very sharp, so be careful when you—"

"Whoa, whoa, hold the fucking phone. I wanted to give you a blow job, not do a goddamn Ginsu demonstration." I liked this better when the problem was self-loathing.

"You aren't going to go deep, but a cut is the best way to keep me where I need to be. It's easier to show you than try to explain it."

I nibble my lip, but without the grin this time. What he's asking is something I don't know I can give him. But fuck it, I'll try.

The knife is easy enough to find at the bottom of his bag, tucked beneath neatly folded jeans and a few pairs of khaki shorts. The handle looks worn from years of use, and the blade hasn't fared much better. Nicks and scratches mar the metal, but when I run it over the fine hairs on my forearm, I see that he was correct. It's sharp as fuck.

"So . . . how do I do this?" I ask as I stand over him. "Is there a particular spot, or . . . ?"

"The hip, sweetheart. Press lightly and drag the blade from my hip toward my groin. The skin is sensitive there."

I feel like a topless doctor about to perform a kinky surgery as I bend at the waist and hold the sharp edge against his skin. Even as I apply pressure and begin to move my hand, my brain screams that this is wrong.

Maverick cries out and winces, and I snatch back the blade.

"Sorry!" I shout. "You fucking told me to!"

He shakes his head, sending a bead of sweat into his eye. "No, you're doing great. This is what I need. But bend a little lower so your tits swing by the blade. I've had this fantasy for so long, and you're the living embodiment."

"Wait, so you haven't done this with anyone else?"

His eyebrows pull together. "No, I haven't shared this part of me with anyone else. You're the first. I usually just pop to the bathroom, singe my ball sack with a lighter, and carry on."

"I just thought—"

"The scars are there because that's what I would do when I was alone. Before I found better ways to masturbate." He shrugs as best he can when cuffed in that position. "The fantasy wasn't as good without the girl."

I lean forward and look into his eyes as I press the knife to his skin. "Oh really? And how is the fantasy now?"

His eyes snap to my chest, and he licks his lips. "Better than I ever imagined."

I pull the blade downward, but I don't stop when he cries out this time. I complete the motion, bringing an alarming amount of blood to the surface. Maverick must notice the concern on my face, because he starts reassuring me again.

But I'm not concerned for his safety. While he's

bleeding pretty good, it isn't a dangerous amount. No, I'm concerned because my thoughts keep going to a very dark place. First the bloody visions, then Castle, and now—

Fuck it.

I drag my palm through the blood pooling in the dip above his hip, then swipe it over his stiffening cock. When he realizes what I'm doing, he groans and watches as my hand slides up and down his shaft, painting it red. Looks like his fantasy isn't the only one we'll be fulfilling today.

After gathering more blood, I lather my chest with crimson as I continue stroking Maverick. When my breasts are good and slick, I lean forward and smash his dick between them. He rocks his hips upward with a moan that vibrates the mattress. His head tips to the side as he fucks my crimson tits. His eyes are glued to the place where we join, and the unbridled pleasure on his face has me dripping. He meant what he said. He wants me, relaxed breasts and all.

As the blood begins to dry, it grows more difficult to slide his dick through the tight space, so I release my breasts and drop my mouth to the head of his cock. The metallic taste rockets over my tongue as I take him to the back of my throat.

The headboard groans as Maverick's arms jerk downward, but his hands stay in place. "God, I just want to touch you."

I twist his shaft with one hand and move my mouth in the opposite direction. I want him to touch me too. But not yet.

"If I can't feel you with my fingertips, can you at least angle that ass toward me? I want to view your perfect pussy while you please me."

Using my free hand, I lower my shorts and kick them

away, then reposition to give him the view he desires. All the while, I keep sucking his dick like my life depends on it. It's a delicate balancing act, but I manage it.

"Oh, fuck," he growls. "You're so wet for me."

His cock jumps in my mouth, an involuntary twitch of excitement when he realizes how much I want him. Meanwhile, I'm just trying to pretend I don't have a butthole he's probably looking at. I've seen the TikToks.

"I'm close, sweetheart. If you keep up that rhythm, I'm going to come."

I squeeze the base of his shaft in a death grip as I break the suction and lick the blood from my lips. "Don't even think about it. Not until I've gotten mine."

He tips his head back, and he curses under his breath as I stroke his shaft. "I can't hold out with you. I'm trying, but you've turned me into a fucking minute man."

"Good thing I only need a minute, then."

I take his cock to the back of my throat again, fully realizing I'm forcing him to disobey my command by doing so. As I bob on his cock, I'm dragging him closer and closer to detonation as he claws away from the impending explosion.

My fingers run over his abs as I keep sucking him. I feed on the way his stomach jerks with each ragged breath he takes. He doesn't want to come. He wants to do as I've asked, and I'm making that impossible. Sweat dampens my fingertips as I splay my palm and drag my short nails down his chest. His hips jerk upward, ramming his dick down my throat.

My stomach clenches, and I gag. I can't help it. While I'm pretty good at controlling the reflex, it's not easy to do when I have a fucking meat log rammed in my windpipe. But it gets so much worse, because the moment I suck air through my nose, a spurt of come jets out of his dick.

I pull back, but the inches of penis I remove from my mouth seem never ending. All the while, Maverick uncontrollably comes, choking me in a really alarming amount of semen.

My brain does her very best to fight the urge to cough, which would send a gooey spray all over the bed, but she can't do two things at once. The urge to gag overpowers me, and I nearly piss myself as my stomach heaves again. The glob of warm goo sitting heavily on my fucking tongue isn't helping matters.

Keeping my lips pinched shut, I cast my gaze around the room, searching for somewhere to leave my offering. The orgasm-haze clears from Maverick's head, and he realizes what's happening.

"The mini bar!" he shouts as he flails his foot toward the tiny fridge. "There's a vintage Bollinger in there. You can use it to wash it down."

With my cheeks puffed out, I give him a thumbs-up before diving for the fridge. But this is no longer a wash-it-down situation. It has become a get-it-out-of-my-mouth moment. I wish I could be a trooper and swallow, but now that I've tasted it and felt the large quantity, there is no other option than evacuation. It also doesn't help that I still need to cough the initial spurt out of my left lung.

I find the bottle right in the center of the fridge. It's hard to miss, as it's the only occupant. After snatching it up, I rip off the foil, remove the wire cage, and gently ease the cork free, careful that it doesn't pop off and put out my good eye. I debate going with the wash-it-down plan after all, but my stomach immediately disagrees. To prevent making more of a scene, I do what I must and ungracefully offer my deposit to the bank of Bollinger before stuffing the cork back in place and setting the bottle on the long desk below the television.

With flaming cheeks, I grab the handcuff key from my bag and hurry to release Maverick. I toss the cuffs into the small waste bin once he's free, all while coughing myself into a stupor.

"Why'd you throw them out?" he asks as he rubs his wrists.

"You were right. Those handcuffs are bad luck, and we are never using them again." I grab my shirt from the floor and look for the arm holes.

Maverick smirks and sits up a little straighter. "There's no need to get dressed. Who said we were done?"

I lower the shirt and look at him, still mortified by what just happened, but the look in his eyes washes that feeling away. He smirks up at me and motions me closer, and like the horny slut I am, I obey.

Chapter Thirty

Maverick

If she thinks I'm going to get mine without making sure she's satisfied as well, she's sadly mistaken. Orgasms feel great, but nothing compares to giving Frankie that same sweet release. As she steps closer, I feel a sense of relief. Now I won't have to strap her down and force the orgasm out of her.

"My issue has its downsides, but it has its benefits as well." I fist my softening cock in my hand, gently stroking as I speak to her. "All it takes is a little more pain, and I'm ready for round two."

Her pupils dilate as she watches my hand creep toward the cut on my hip. With gritted teeth, I speed up my strokes and prepare for a sharp dose of anguish as I drive my thumb deep into the gash. She snags her lower lip between her teeth, and it's the last bit of assistance I need. My dick hardens in my grip.

"You gave me what I needed, sweetheart. Tell me what you need. How can I please you?"

She steps closer to the bed and sits on the edge. With a gentle touch, she guides my hand away from the cut and onto her bloodstained breast. I cup the soft flesh and stare into her eyes as I stroke myself.

"I want you to fuck me slowly. I want to feel every inch as you push and pull your hips. I don't want you to speed up until I tell you to."

I nod, then kiss her bloody fingers. "Whatever you need. Now place your hands on the bed. I can promise to move slowly, but I can't promise I'll be gentle."

As she leans forward and positions herself, I slide off the bed and get behind her. My hands glide up her back, catching on her wide hips as I come back down. She fits so perfectly in my grasp. I could toss her around, but I won't.

Not unless she asks me to.

I position the head of my cock against her glistening entrance, reveling in the way her thick lips spread over the shining skin. When I push forward, her hips ease back, swallowing me. She's so greedy for me, and I fucking love it. Watching my cock slowly appear and disappear, inch by agonizing inch, is a mistake, but I can't tear my eyes away. It doesn't matter where I look, anyway. Everything about Frankie is a feast for my eyes.

Like the way her hands grip the sheets at the apex of every thrust.

Or how she boldly looks back at me and whimpers as I take her wrists in my hands to hold her in a better position.

I leverage her ass against my pelvis, crushing the cut against her skin each time we meet. Each sharp ache rushes into my cock, and I punish Frankie for giving me so much perfection by pleasing her to the point of delirium. I catch a glimpse of her eyes rolling back in her head before she pushes her face into the mattress and lets out a low moan.

"Harder," she groans when she finally turns her head to the side.

I pull back on her arms and thrust into her, keeping the tempo slow but using more force at the end of each push. I bottom out each time, and I can't imagine it feels good.

Unless I'm not the only one who enjoys a little pain . . .

Releasing her wrists, I move my grip to her hips. My fingers sink into her flesh, biting deep enough to feel the bones beneath the scrumptious layer of soft flesh. Frankie's back arches and she cries out, but she doesn't tell me to stop.

"Is this too much for you?" I ask, punctuating the question with another driven thrust.

"No, give me more," she says. "Harder."

I pull out of her and flip her onto her back. She spreads her legs, eager to have me inside her again, but I push her thighs together and toss her calves over my left shoulder. Without warning, I enter her once more.

Frankie's eyes clench shut, and she grips the comforter by her head, breathing in through her nose and out through her mouth in time with my strokes. But I quickly realize it's the other way around. I'm matching tempo with each breath. As she speeds up, so do I. She eventually loses control and drives her hand between her legs, but I keep the steady pace.

I lean forward, fucking her hard and fast as her fingers fly over her clit. How comedians can make fun of this moment, I'll never understand. There's nothing comical about the beautiful act of a woman working so diligently to come. It's so beautiful, in fact, that it's bringing me close to my edge again too.

"If you keep working your pussy like that, you're going to make me come," I whisper down at her. "I love to see you pleasing yourself. Come for me, sweetheart. Come for me so that I can get some relief."

Her back arches and her mouth opens as her pussy squeezes my dick to the tempo of her heartbeat. The rhythm against her clit stutters, so I rapidly flick my thumb against that sensitive nub to work her through the momentary paralysis. The backs of her thighs quiver against my stomach, and I don't know how it's possible, but she gets even wetter.

"I'm coming," she breathes. "Fuck, I'm coming."

"Oh, I know." I smile down at her as the orgasm wanes, but I have to get mine now. The dull ache at the base of my shaft is bordering on anguish.

I ease her legs apart, draping one leg over each shoulder as I pull her closer to the edge of the bed. With her ass hanging at a slight downward angle, I can push even deeper inside her. I slow my pace a little, watching as her breasts move like water with the motion. Reaching out, I grip one and squeeze, and the gasp from Frankie is enough to send me into a blackout.

My brain ceases to function, and I lose myself inside her. I fuck her without regard, relentlessly. If she cries out for me to stop, I don't hear it. I don't hear anything aside from the slap of skin against skin. The pain sings from the cut, drowning out all thought, and with a groan, I fill her.

Gripping her thighs, I hold still as come jets from my cock. She's still trying to catch her breath, looking up at me with wide eyes as her chest rises and falls. The fact that she's looking at me sends my balls into overdrive, and I fear I'll never stop unloading inside her.

As I pull away, I also worry Frankie's upset with me for losing control like that, but then she laughs and says, "I don't know where that came from, but I'm going to need more of it."

"Sorry. I'm usually more controlled than that." I grab the towel lying by the pillows and hold it between her legs. "Hang on and I'll grab something so that you can clean up."

She grips the towel against her pussy as I ease out of her and head to the bathroom for a washcloth. "Losing control isn't such a bad thing. I let go of control, and look at me now, lying on a bed, satisfied."

"I don't know about that. You were pretty controlling." I smirk as I run the rag through warm water, then wring it out. "Not that I mind. I kind of like it when you treat me like your sex toy."

"Say less," she says with a laugh.

I bring the warm washcloth to her, and she cleans herself up before waddling to the bathroom to piss and shower. I go to the closet to dress. While I'd love to stay in the room and continue fucking her all evening, I haven't forgotten about Ice Pick's little situation. The sooner I can find him and get him back to the Sinners' side of the ship, the sooner my worry will lessen.

Standing beside the bathroom door, I let Frankie know my plan. I'm shocked when she yells back and asks me to wait, saying she'd like to go with me. It's not something I'm used to, having a lover tag along for my day-to-day shit.

But it's kind of nice.

She emerges from the bathroom a few minutes later. After she dresses in a pair of black shorts and a loose blue top that hangs off her shoulder, she looks at the bottle of champagne. "What do we do with this?"

"Just put it back in the fridge. I'm not really a drinker, so you don't have to worry about me accidentally partaking."

"Yeah, me neither," she says as she stuffs the bottle into

the ice box. She stands and pulls her hair into a loose, dark mess on top of her head before securing it with an elastic. "Do we have any events tonight?"

"No." I pull a collared shirt over my head. "Does that disappoint you?"

She shrugs and sits on the edge of the bed as she pulls on some flat shoes. "Kind of. But we could always make our own fun. Maybe we could hunt for feds while also searching for Ice Pick. We'll already be on the Normie side, and Jim said there is one over there."

"Frankie . . ."

"Don't *Frankie* me. I like it better when you call me sweetheart." She stands on tiptoes and plants a kiss on my cheek before skipping out of the room.

I slide my feet into a pair of sneakers before hurrying to join her. In her current state of mind, there's no telling what sort of mess she might get into on her own. I can only hope I can shift her way of thinking once more before the end of the cruise, even if it means losing the best thing to ever happen to me.

Chapter Thirty-One

Frankie

After scouring the atrium, a few lounges, and the upper-deck celebration for the Normies, we're forced to admit defeat. Wherever Ice Pick is hiding, he's doing a damn good job of staying below our radar. It's almost dinnertime, and we haven't even caught a glimpse of his shining head.

"What about the surveillance cameras?" I ask. "Won't Jim let us check them out?"

Maverick shakes his head. "Before we spotted him on the island, maybe, but now that he knows Ice Pick is essentially safe, he'll want to let the chaos run its course."

"But what if that gets Ice Pick in trouble? Doesn't he care?"

"He won't let it get that far."

I don't miss the slight quiver in his voice. He believes himself as much as I do.

"Come on," I say as I wind my arm through his. "Let's

check the dining hall. There's a buffet, and I'm kind of hungry."

He smirks and matches my steps as I start down a hallway. "You don't want to see what's on Chef Maurice's menu tonight?"

"I'll pass on the man meat, thanks." I look him up and down. "Unless you're on that menu."

"You want Chef to kill me and serve me on a plate?"

"Okay, I didn't think that one through."

Our laughter is cut short as the elevator opens and Ice Pick emerges. Before he has a chance to scurry away, Maverick grips his arm and drags him back into the elevator. I hurry to join them as the door whispers shut behind me.

"Let me go, man," Ice Pick shouts as he tries to yank his meaty arm out of Maverick's hand. "I've got a date, and she's very funny about punctuality!"

"What do you think you're doing? She's a Normie, Ice! Aren't you concerned she'll figure out who the fuck you are?" Maverick releases him and takes a step back to give him some space. "We saw the cat fight on the island. You're drawing a lot of attention to yourself."

Ice Pick swipes over the wrinkles in his Bud Light t-shirt. "We hit it off. I can't help that the drunk brunette wanted a piece of old Ice Pick too, but I only have eyes for Amber. And for the first time, someone only has eyes for me. I don't care that she's a Normie. I've already decided to give up killing."

"Give up . . . killing?" If Maverick's jaw drops any lower, we'll have to have it surgically reattached. He steps closer to Ice Pick and takes his shoulders in his hands. "Do you hear yourself? Ice, you can't change your entire way of life because you think you're in love with this woman. This might only be a summer fling for her."

His words get under my skin. It's as if he's speaking in subliminal messages meant for me. Is that why he's so adamant that I keep my federal job? Is this just a fling for him?

I step closer and place a gentle hand on Maverick's shoulder. He looks back at me, then steps aside to let me talk sense into Ice Pick.

"Not you too," Ice Pick mutters as he looks at his feet.

"No, not me too," I say, and Maverick practically gasps behind me. "I think you should go for it. If Amber makes you happy, go be happy. If you don't want to kill anymore, don't."

Ice Pick looks up at me, his mustache curving slightly as he smiles. "Do you mean it?"

I nod and smile back at him as Maverick groans and tries to walk away, only to remember that we're in an elevator. When he can't escape, he starts mashing buttons. The doors open with a ding, and he steps into the hallway.

Stepping backward so that the doors stay open, I wave for Ice Pick to join us.

"You can't be fucking serious," Maverick says as he swipes his hand down his face. "You want us to join him for dinner with his Normie girlfriend? When he's about to throw his life away? And you expect me to say *nothing*?"

I turn away from Ice and face Maverick, still keeping my hands on the doors. "Yes. If this is your friend, you will support him. Even if it's just a *fling*."

His eyes widen, and his frustration shifts to sheepishness. "Oh, I didn't mean . . . You thought that . . . Frankie."

"Save it." I hold up my hand. "We are going to dinner with Ice Pick and Amber, and we will have a nice time. Got it?"

Maverick pinches his lips shut and nods, and Ice Pick

finally emerges from the elevator. As a trio, we start toward the dining hall. Ice walks a few feet ahead, occasionally glancing back to see if we're still following him.

"Do you guys really have to tag along? What if you embarrass me?" He stops just outside the open doors and glances at his watch. "I told her I'd meet her at eight, and that's in fifteen minutes. Could we hang out afterward?"

He has a point. Maverick and I are like parents attempting to chaperone their tween's first date. It's not a good look for him, but it's an even worse look for us. I look up at Maverick.

"I guess we could eat at a different table?" I say.

"Or in our room," Maverick mutters. I give his side a sneaky pinch, and he jumps. "We'll eat at a different table," he says to Ice Pick.

Knowing this is the best he'll get, Ice Pick turns and heads into the dining hall.

Once he's out of earshot, Maverick whispers, "I didn't mean what you thought I meant. This isn't just a fling for me."

I firm my grip on his arm and rest my head on his shoulder. "And maybe this isn't just a fling for them, either. Let the poor guy have some fun."

"I'm just worried about him. Ice is one of us, but he's different. We have a support system of close friends, but we only see him on these trips, really. He goes missing the rest of the year, and we only know he's still alive because we'll see news blips about his kills in Texas." He shakes his head and swallows. "If he gives up killing, how will we know he's okay?"

Now I see that this goes deeper than I realized. He's worried about his friend, sure, but he's more worried about losing the friendship. If Ice Pick gives up killing . . . they may never see him again.

I consider how that translates to my situation. By giving up my career, I'll be forced to say goodbye to my colleagues as well. A momentary flame of regret flickers to life before my brain douses the fire in a spray of reality. My colleagues were sent to die, and I was collateral damage. The man I trusted, the man I admired and viewed almost as a father figure, sent me to my death. So no, our situations aren't so similar after all, but that doesn't mean Ice and I shouldn't come to the same conclusion.

That sometimes change is a good thing.

I grip Maverick's hand and give is a solid squeeze. "Sometimes we have to let people we care about make the scary decisions. We have to trust that they know what's best for them."

"And you think *he* can tell what's best for him?"

I follow his gaze to a line of people standing alongside the buffet table. Ice Pick mills about with his plate piled to the brim. A Swedish meatball rolls from the edge and splats on the carpet in a spray of wetness. He bends at the knees, plucks it from the carpet, and puts it back on his plate. Then he licks his fingers.

"Okay. Maybe you're right. But maybe it's best to let things run their course. I mean, what harm could it do?" I squeeze Maverick's hand again. "Let him have this. For me."

He looks prepared to concede as we step into the dining room, so I shut my mouth and leave it right there. Nothing is more annoying than someone who keeps on once they've made their point.

We grab a warm plate from the station and stand in line. When I say the plate is warm, that's a gross understatement.

The ceramic feels as if Satan dragged his fiery asshole over everything my fingers touch. Maverick and I play hot potato with the white disks, looking as foolish as everyone else.

"It looks like we'll lose feeling in our fingertips by the time we reach the mac and cheese," I mutter, and he struggles to keep a straight face as he stares down the line.

Ice Pick has reached the end. He grips a drink in his left hand as he makes his way to his table. Unfortunately, he chooses this moment to glance at his watch, which sends the entirety of his sweet tea to the floor. I internally cringe and hope Amber wasn't here to witness this.

But then a blonde appears at his side, materializing out of thin air. With wildly apparent mother-hen energy, she begins helping him. She takes the plate from his hand and ferries it to their table before returning with a clump of napkins, which she uses to pat the damp area near the bottom of his jeans. Instead of looking frustrated or embarrassed, she's all smiles and sweetness.

But that's when I notice the bracelet on her wrist, and my world comes crashing down. Ice Pick has made a huge mistake. Because as it turns out . . . he's fallen for a fed.

Chapter Thirty-Two

Maverick

Frankie and I place our plates on the table, and Ice Pick's gaze flies to my face as we slide into the booth seats directly across from him and the fucking *fed*. When Frankie told me what she suspected, sitting at any other place in the dining room was no longer an option.

Frankie knew Amber was a fed the same way she knew the woman on the pirate ship was a fed: the bracelet. Her director gave it to her as a gift before she left for the assignment, and it appears she wasn't the only recipient.

"Change of plans, buddy," I say as I pick up my fork. "Looks like we were able to join you after all. Why don't you introduce us?"

Ice stutters and stumbles over his tongue, but Amber holds a dainty hand toward me. "I'm Amber. It's *so* nice to finally meet some of Chad's friends."

Frankie sputters on a gulp of sweet tea. I pat her back, wishing I could choke too. To death, preferably.

"*Chad's* friends?" I hope I don't sound as flabbergasted as I feel.

Amber waves my comment away. "Oh, I know you guys call him Ice Man or something, but he's just my Chad." She wrinkles her nose at him, and I want to puke.

"So, what do you do for work, Amber?" Frankie lifts a sauce-laden rib to her lips. "If you don't mind me asking."

Amber's cool demeanor slips, but she straightens her mask. "Oh, just a little office work. A button masher, if you will."

"Right," Frankie says after swallowing a glob of meat. "Me too."

With my knee, I nudge her beneath the table. She needs to be careful. If this woman doesn't recognize her from their division, that misstep goes in her favor. But if this woman realizes who she is, this could blow up in our faces.

"What do you do for work?" Amber asks me. "Chad here works in construction. Oh, but you already know that."

I want to ask if they've talked about favorite hobbies, but I bite my tongue.

Frankie saves the day by changing the subject. "I'm glad you two hit it off the other night. We looked for you guys but couldn't find you."

"Can you blame me for wanting this hunk all to myself?" She bats her fake eyelashes at Ice Pick. "I mean . . . lovers can't exactly share secrets when they're surrounded by everyone. You get what I mean, don't you?" She turns her fluttering lashes on Frankie.

"Do you have something in your eye?" I ask, and Frankie returns the nudge.

Amber clears her throat and sips a glass of wine. That gives me an idea.

"Hey, would you two want to come to our room after

this? We could share a drink and swap war stories about this guy." I lean across the table to pat Ice's shoulder. "We could even play a little strip poker, if you ladies are bold enough."

Amber's panic bleeds through her eyes. "Oh, I don't—"

"Texas hold 'em?" Ice asks. "Shit, I think we could stop by for a few hands."

"Baby," Amber whines quietly, as if we aren't close enough to hear. Her wheedling voice and grabby fingers make my blood boil.

"It's all right, sugar," he whispers back. "Don't you worry that pretty little head. I'll give you all three inches when we get back to the room."

Again, we are close enough to hear every stomach-churning syllable.

Frankie's rib bone drops to her plate. "I think I've had enough of that," she mumbles.

"Right, well, we'll go up to the room to get things ready. See you shortly!" I say, and we squeeze out of the booth with full plates of food, our appetites destroyed.

As Frankie and I exit the dining room, I just have to hope that Ice Pick's love for poker will overpower his newest infatuation.

"You were right, and I was wrong," Frankie says as we step into the elevator. "We have to get him away from her. I don't think she's that into him."

"Really? You don't think so?"

She responds by pinching her lips together and scowling at me. "I said I was wrong." Her finger flies to the elevator buttons, and she mashes our floor repeatedly. "Why isn't this thing moving? We have to find Jim so we can get permission to—"

"Whoa, Jim? Who said anything about involving him?"

The doors finally close, and the elevator begins to

descend. "We can't very well kill her without getting the okay first, and I definitely want to kill her. How dare she toy with his heart like that. You saw the way he looked at her. Maverick, he's in love."

Yeah, I saw it. That's why I don't want to kill her. I just want her to admit the truth to Ice Pick so that *he* can kill her. I explain this to Frankie, and thankfully, she gets it.

"We should still get the okay from Jim. That way, when the mean reds take hold, Ice Pick doesn't have to pause the festivities for permission."

"Mean reds?"

"You've never seen *Breakfast at Tiffany's*?"

I shake my head.

"I see a movie night in our future."

The elevator comes to a stop, but my stomach lurches for a different reason. Mainly the fact that she sees a future with me in it. I have to find a way to show her that she can't give up everything for me. Her life was meant for something more, and I can't be the reason she gives up on her dreams.

"The mean reds. It's the moment of hopeless despair," she says as she uses her purple wristband to let us into our cabin. "He'll feel it when she tells the truth, and I know just the thing to loosen her tongue. You go find Jim, then meet me back here."

I nod and start down the hallway as an uneasy feeling nips at my heels. While I hope it won't come to it, if I can't convince Frankie that I'm not worth the sacrifice she intends to make, I'll have to take drastic measures. I'll have to hurt her to save her.

In the meantime, I'll try to enjoy what time I have left.

Jim stands with his back to me as I enter his office. He stares out a window overlooking the star-filled sky, a glass of something dark and dusky in his hand. He swirls the glass, then tips the edge against his lips.

"We've got a problem," I say as I close the door behind me.

He turns and smiles. "What else is new?"

"The woman Ice Pick fell for? Turns out she's a fed. Frankie figured it out, and now we need permission to kill her."

Jim chuckles and sips his drink again before turning away from the window. He strolls to a massive desk and takes a seat behind it. After folding his hands in his lap, he nods toward the leather chair in front of the desk.

"I don't have time to sit. Frankie is currently preparing something so that we can get her to tell Ice the truth. Then we want to let him kill her."

He tips his head to the side. "And what if he won't?"

"What if he—" I squeeze the back of my neck and close my eyes. "Jim, she's betrayed him in the worst possible way. She doesn't actually want him. She wants whatever information he can give her."

"How is that any different from your situation?" He sits forward and taps his finger on the desk. "Frankie's goal is the same as hers. To get intel on us. How much have you given her in exchange for a little attention?"

"That's an entirely different matter, and you know it. Even without all the strings you've pulled to turn her against her own, that Castle asshole did the hard work for you. He's put it into her head that her division was out to kill everyone they sent to this ship."

"Yes. That's correct."

All thought flies from my head, and I forget why I came here in the first place. "Excuse me?"

"You heard me correctly, son. All eleven agents were sent here to die. They're a black spot on the government records, and they need to be disposed of. Quietly."

"I-I don't understand. Why Frankie? What the fuck did she do that was so horrible?" Now I sit in the chair. If I don't, I'll collapse. I never imagined Castle's little death confession would hold an ounce of truth.

"It's not my place to say, but all will be revealed. In time." Jim sits back in his chair again. "For now, continue to be her friend. She's going to need one when everything comes to light."

I grip the arms of the chair and fight the urge to raise my voice. "Jim, we're talking about her life here. I know you like to play these stupid games, but I'm not willing to put her through hell just so you can get a little entertainment."

"Well, well. Looks like someone's gotten a little more invested, hmm?"

"Cut the shit."

His smile drops to something sad, and he spins his chair around with a sigh, giving me his back again. "Permission granted. As for the rest, you'll just have to trust that my interests lie in the same pit as yours."

I stand and hurry out of the room before I leap across the desk and strangle him with my bare hands. My temper doesn't usually flare like this, but I'm not usually this terrified, either. If Frankie was sent here to die, what is she hiding?

And why don't I care?

As I rush down the hallway, I look for the stairs. The elevator will take too long, and I need her in my arms right now. I need to know she's safe and that I can keep her that way. For the first time since learning about Frankie's identity and my true mission, the desire to protect her comes with a swift kick of urgency. She's been in danger this entire time, and only now do I fully realize it.

By the time I reach the cabin door, my lungs are on fire and I can't catch my breath. I fling open the door and find her standing by the long desk beneath the television. Four champagne flutes tower on top, accompanied by the tainted bottle of Bollinger.

But I can only focus on her. I rush forward and take her into my arms.

"Is everything okay?" she mumbles into my chest as I smash her against me.

"No, but it will be." I place a kiss on top of her head. Before I can say anything else, someone knocks on the door.

I'll have to tell her what I've learned after they leave. Right now, we have a kill to take and a man to save.

Chapter Thirty-Three

Frankie

Amber sits on the edge of the bed, a filled champagne flute in her right hand. As she prattles on about how wonderful *Chad* has been, I pray she doesn't study the bubbling liquid too closely. I stirred the glob of semen as best I could, but it's definitely still visible. The goo dances in the liquid, getting bounced to hell and back by bubbles as she talks.

I raise my glass and pretend to sip, and Maverick does the same. I hope it encourages her to follow suit, but only Ice Pick takes the bait. He tips back his glass and downs it in one swallow.

He smacks his lips and looks at the glass. "Whew, that's got a little tang to it, huh?"

My cheeks blaze red. "It's vintage. Sometimes the, uh, the fruit . . ."

Fuck, I don't know where I'm going with this. Is champagne even made with fruit?

"The grapes can end up a little tangy," Maverick says, swooping in to save the day.

"Don't worry, baby." Amber tickles Ice Pick's mustache, which is both weird and unsettling. "Mama will teach you all about the finer things when we get back on dry land."

Mama?

Hearing her talk made me feel like I was going to puke, but when she finally sips the champagne, my stomach convulses. A large glob slides into her gaping maw, and she swallows.

Amber purses her lips and clears her throat. "Yes, that tang is indicative of the year, darling. I once shared a glass with my late husband to celebrate a particularly sought after stud I acquired."

"Stud? Do you breed horses?" I ask. "I noticed your bracelet has a horse on it, so I just assumed."

"Goodness, no. This was a gift from my boss." She turns the bracelet, showing it to me, but I don't need to see it. Mine was a gift from my boss as well. "I breed show dogs. Imported Anatolian shepherds, to be precise. We purchased Sans Marko Bootcut Presentation. I'm sure you've heard of him. He championed very young."

"Oh, did you show him yourself?" Maverick asks.

She takes another sip. "Me? Show my own dogs? Never. I just breed the shit out of them and post the puppy videos all over social media. It's a great side hustle, and I've nearly made enough to retire from my desk job." She raises the glass and wiggles it. "Is there any more champagne?"

"I'll fill that for you," I say with a sweet smile. The urge to kill her is growing by the second. Maybe Ice Pick will let each of us get a stab in.

I'm getting turned on just thinking about it.

I pull the bottle of champagne from the fridge and

dump another globby mixture into her glass. It's the last of the semen, but that's okay. It's time to move to phase two of my plan.

Reaching into my pocket, I feel around for the glass vial. Cat was very kind to share some of her personal stash with me, and thanks to my years as a federal agent, I know just how effective a higher dose of scopolamine can be. In just a few minutes, this bitch will sing like a goddamn canary.

After breaking open the vial and dumping the liquid into the glass, I grab a stirring stick and give the liquid a good spin before handing the mixture to her. She looks a bit confused as she glares at the stirring stick, so I wave her off.

"No worries," I say. "It's a little trick I picked up in college. Makes the bubbles more . . . bubbly."

She raises her eyebrows as she takes a sip, then nods. "Oh, wow! It really does!"

No the fuck it doesn't. God, I hate her.

"How about that card game?" Ice Pick rubs his hands together. "I'm feeling lucky."

"Not yet, but you will be," Amber slurs. The champagne is already working its magic, meaning she's a fucking lightweight from hell. When the drugs kick in, we are in for a show.

"Sorry, pal. Couldn't find any cards," Maverick says with a show of his empty hands. "Looks like we'll just have to settle for good old conversation."

"Maybe I could go find some." Ice Pick rises to stand, but Maverick and I both jump up to stop him.

"No!" we say in unison, earning suspicious looks from both of our guests.

Maverick places a hand on Ice Pick's shoulder, forcing him to sit again. "We just want to hang out and catch up.

We can find some cards in a bit. The night is young, right?" He clears his throat. "Tell us more about your dogs, Amber."

"Nothing much to tell. To be honest, I don't know much about them. I pay my staff to handle them." She finishes the second glass in one swallow, come globs and all. "I only go around them for filming. I used to film the births, but I had to stop." With a roll of her eyes, she holds her glass toward me again, and I take it for a refill. "I mean, excuse the flippity fuck out of me for wanting to pull the puppies out as quickly as possible. I just want to see how much money I'll be able to make before crawling back into bed. The bitches eventually wised up and started whelping when I'm away from home. Grand Duchess Tool Biscuit is probably popping out dollar signs as we speak."

I pass the filled glass back to her—after adding another dash of scopolamine. She'll be fine. I think. "Can't pulling the puppies like that . . . hurt them?"

"Who cares? Half my breeding stock has genetic issues, anyway. Pulling the puppies gives me a fallback position. I just pretend I made a mistake and that the hip dysplasia was my fault. Works every"—she hiccups—"time."

I study her pupils as she talks. They haven't quite blown as wide as I'd expect from the dose of meds, but they're close. I can't stomach any more talk about the animal abuse, though, so I change topics.

"Tell us what you like about our Chad," I say as I scrunch my nose at Amber and try to look cutesy.

"Bless you," Ice Pick says.

I cock my head at him.

"Oh, sorry," he says. "Thought you had to sneeze."

Note to self: don't try to look cutesy ever again.

"Well, I needed someone who would talk," she says, and my ears swivel toward her. "He seemed like a talker, so I went with it. You practically put the perfect imbecile right into my hands."

I spare a look at Maverick, and he nods.

"Wait, are you saying Ice Pick—Chad—is an idiot?" I ask.

"Yeah, is that what you're saying?" Ice Pick adds.

As Amber downs the third full glass, I regret putting that extra dose inside. She clearly didn't need it.

"Did you actually think I liked fucking you? Ugh, it was terrible. Like masturbating with a cocktail sausage." In a fit of giggles, she turns to me and sobers just as quickly. "Want to know the worst part? I still can't get him to give up his serial killer friends. I've faked orgasm after orgasm for nothing." Her grin reappears, widening until I fear her face will crack. "But that's okay, because now I'm here. Now I know what those pretty purple wristbands mean."

Tears fill Ice Pick's eyes as he sits on the edge of the bed. His hands form fists in his lap, and the champagne flute shatters in his grip.

"Permission granted," Maverick says.

Ice looks at his hands. "It ain't an ice pick, but I guess it'll do."

"We thought of that," I say as I slide an ice pick into his hand.

Amber places her palm to her chest and giggles through a hiccup. "What do you—"

Ice Pick plunges the stiff metal shaft into her chest, right through her hand. With the way the rod sinks into her body without resistance, he must have missed every bone and driven that pointed end right past her finger bones and rib cage. Amber's mouth opens in a scream, but Ice silences her by plunging the handle a little deeper. Her cry chokes off as she weakly grips his wrist with her free hand.

"Why?" she whimpers.

"That was for Sans Marko Bootcut Presentation. And this is for me." He pushes one more time, and we hear an audible pop as the ice pick sinks to the handle.

Amber's head lolls to the side, and her eyes cease to see what's in front of her. Which is a real shame, because I'm giving her the fucking finger as she makes her exit from this world.

Good fucking riddance.

Ice Pick uses his feet to kick her body off the bed, and Maverick and I step over her to sit beside him, one of us on each side. We wrap our arms around him and embrace him so that he doesn't have to feel so alone.

"Damn, I thought she was the one," Ice Pick mumbles. "I can't be with a woman who abuses animals, though. There are some real sickos in this world."

I blink and stare at the wall. "So we didn't need to prove that she was a fed?"

He shakes his head. "No, I figured she was. Just like you, Frankie. But I—"

"Hold it," Maverick says. "Frankie isn't a fed. She's one of us."

Ice turns his head and gives Maverick a dramatic wink. "*Right*. One of us."

"You weren't on the ship," I add. "You didn't see the way I tortured one of the feds we discovered."

Maverick points at me. "That's true. Then she came back here and fucked me stupid because it turned her on so much. Definitely not fed behavior."

"It's okay, guys. Your secret is safe with me. No need to lay it on so thick." He shrugs out of our hug and rises to his feet. "But thanks. You guys saved me from a lot of heartache."

As he leaves the room, I'm not so sure we saved him from the heartache. He looks as if his heart aches quite a bit. But at least we saved him from his eventual demise, because she definitely had a lot of hate in her heart. And as I clean up the glass as Maverick goes to get the crew to dispose of the body, I wonder if I'll wear that same look at the end of this trip.

I can't think about that right now. That's a problem for later. For now, I want to check out that bracelet a little more closely. If the women received a bracelet, that means the men had something of their own too. Castle wasn't wearing any jewelry, but he was Cattle. Maybe they took their items away.

Men come to remove the body as I sit on the bed with the bracelet in my hands, turning it over and looking for any type of listening device, but I see nothing. The small horse charm isn't large enough to hold much more than—

"A tracking device," I whisper.

I dig through my bag and find my matching bracelet, then walk to the balcony and toss both into the ocean. If King wants to know where I am, he can come and find me. I'll be fucking ready for him.

Chapter Thirty-Four

Maverick

By the time I return to the room with a disposal crew, Frankie has already swapped her attire for something more comfortable. She stands on the balcony, resting her arms on the railing as she stares at the ocean. The wind whips through her hair. She squints into the breeze, ever defiant, even against Mother Nature.

I push the sliding glass door aside and join her. She sighs as I rest my hand against her opposite hip.

"That worked out pretty well, huh?" she says.

"That it did, thanks to you. What did you put in her drink?"

"Some of Cat's motion-sickness medication. Scopolamine. But I don't think it would have loosened her tongue that quickly. I think the bitch wasn't used to high-dollar champagne that goes down like water."

"And semen."

Frankie laughs, and the sound soothes my soul. "That too."

A loud thump comes from inside, and we turn in time to see the workers bump Amber's limp body against every surface. Good. I hope they toss her into the ocean, and I hope her poor dogs end up in loving homes where they won't be bred to death for content.

"This ordeal made me wonder why we don't trade the yellow Cattle for animal abusers," I say as we watch the bitch disappear through the door and out of our lives forever. "Red are the rapists. Pink are the child abusers. Yellow could be for the animals."

Frankie nods and rubs her arms. "Cat would love that. Have you had to sit through her photo presentation of Shorty and Mr. Whiskers? I think she'd kill for those cats, confession notwithstanding."

We step into the room and check the bed for any bloodstains, but it's clean. At least the bitch was polite enough to bleed out inside her abdomen. I'll be sure to send a thank-you card.

As I begin undressing for bed, I realize Frankie is watching me. Intently. Her icy-blue gaze burns a hole through my back, so I ease off my shirt as slowly as possible as I enjoy the heat. She shifts on the bed, snagging her bottom lip between her teeth in that cute way that drives me wild.

"Stop doing that," I warn. "I imagine your pussy is very sore from earlier, but I won't be able to hold back if you keep looking at me that way."

"Ooh, I'm so scared," she says with a mocking bite to her tone.

I run the pliable leather through the belt loops as I whip off my belt, then crack it against my palm. "I've never been the type to force a woman into submission, but you're asking for it, sweetheart. That bratty, bossy attitude makes me want to knock you down a few pegs sometimes."

Her jaw drops, and I worry I've offended her, but then her lips curve into a wide smile. She gets on her hands and knees on the bed and crawls toward the edge.

"I've never been submissive before. Never even considered it." She nibbles her bottom lip again, and my limp cock begins to ache at the base. "Well, until now."

I step closer to the bed. My belt remains in my right hand, but I use the left to gather her hair behind her skull. Pulling the strands taut, I tip her head back.

"Is this something you'd like to explore?" I ask. "I think it's something I'd like to try. Very much."

A moment of uncertainty flits through her eyes. I get it. This is so far out of my comfort zone, but that's what's turning me on. I only hope she feels the same, but asking a woman like her to kneel before me . . . If she says no, I won't be offended.

Her eyes close, and she winces as I tighten my grip on her hair. My instincts tell me I'm being too rough, that this is wrong.

But then she moans.

"I think I'd like to try it too," she says. "Just . . . no punches or anything, yeah? I'm still sore from Castle beating the fuck out of me."

I give her cheek a light tap, testing the waters.

"Harder," she says with a grin. "I might be bratty, but I'm no baby, Maverick. You can punish me if you want."

She bites her fucking lip again, and punishment has never sounded so good. I drag her head closer to my abdomen. Her tongue rushes toward my skin, but I snatch her back again.

"I didn't tell you taste, sweetheart."

She groans and tries again, but I pull her away and give her cheek another light slap.

"Not until I tell you. Now be a good girl and free my cock."

I release her head, and she moves to the floor. On her knees, she begins unfastening my pants. I watch as her fingers work open the button, then lower the zipper. We're both a bit shocked when my cock bounces up a bit as the pants fall away. I've managed a decent semi . . . without any pain.

If I think about it too much, I'm liable to lose whatever magic is currently happening, so I turn my attention back to the beautiful woman kneeling before me. She seems to realize as much herself, because she just nibbles her lip and waits patiently for instruction.

"Suck me," I demand. "I don't care if it's soft. Suck me until I'm hard, even if it takes all night."

I grab the back of her head once more and snatch her face toward my dick. Her lips part, and the surprise on her face as I force my way into her mouth is fucking heavenly. She moans and drives a hand between her legs, but I tighten my grip on her hair until she screams.

"I didn't say you could touch yourself. Be good, sweetheart. I don't like punishing you."

Tears slip from the outer corners of her eyes as she nods and removes her hand from her shorts, but I don't miss the way her fingertips glisten. She's getting as much out of this as I am, and that makes it even better. The silent permission and trust that passes between us elevates the feeling of her tongue as it swirls in gentle circles over the head of my cock.

And I begin to grow hard.

She pulls her mouth off my dick and looks up at me.

"Please may I touch myself? I promise I won't come until you let me."

"No, I won't allow it. Now suck me." I drive her head into my lap again, and she moans around my dick.

Her hands go to my thighs, and she tries to push away. I'm not sure if she's actually fighting it or if she's simply playing out a fantasy of her own. What the fuck do I do? If I stop, that might break the immersion, but if she's uncomfortable, I won't be able to enjoy myself. Her absolute trust is what makes this so amazing, and I don't want to lose it.

I ease back her head and look into her eyes. "If you want me to stop, you need to ask like a good girl. If you don't explicitly tell me to stop, I won't. Do you understand?"

Oh, she definitely understands. She nods and opens her mouth again, begging me to keep going, and I'm more than happy to oblige, now that we've gotten that out of the way. Using her hair as a lead, I place her back on my dick where she belongs.

The fight resumes, and every time Frankie struggles for breath, my dick hardens a little more in her mouth. Guilt nips at my heels, though. It was easier to accept abusing myself to get hard.

But then I look down at Frankie and see the way she's enjoying this, and maybe I don't have to feel bad. A dark spot marks the crotch of her shorts. She's so turned on that she's soaked herself. Fucking literally. And who am I to deny the woman some pleasure?

When she realizes I'm watching her, she lets out a low moan and tries to touch herself again. I snatch her up by her arm and toss her to the bed. She looks up at me with a wildfire blazing in her eyes. It seems I'm not the only one who's had some feral part of their sexual psyche unlocked.

"I told you to stop, sweetheart. Take off your shorts and

turn over. I'll have to punish you now." I crack the belt against my thigh, and the sharp sting jumps straight to my dick. My cock jumps, and her eyes shine with desire as she notices.

She stands near the foot of the bed and slowly lowers her shorts as she looks at me over her shoulder. Fuck, she's not even wearing panties. As she bends to step out of the shorts, I get a beautiful back view of her glistening slit, and I can't wait to feel her wrapped around me. When she's undressed her lower half, she lies on the bed and grips the comforter, bracing herself.

I raise the belt and bring it across her ass. The leather makes a loud *crack* as it collides with her skin, and she yelps. Her fingers tighten in the blanket, and I watch as a red welt blossoms on her left cheek. I bend and kiss the mark before standing and bringing the belt down again.

Her head whips back, and she cries out. "Fuck!"

She didn't say to stop, though.

I whip her once more, then run my hand over the marks. Her skin heats like fire beneath my touch, but she lets out a moan to reassure me. This is okay, that moan says. This is more than okay.

This is *everything*.

Then I take the belt and wrap it around her neck from behind.

Chapter Thirty-Five

Frankie

Panic ignites every nerve ending as the leather pulls tight against my skin. My fears about fucking a serial killer mostly revolved around falling in love and getting ditched like my mother. Never once did I consider becoming one of their victims. I'm considering it now, though.

And I'm not against it.

Does being choked damn near to death sound like a good time? No. But neither did murdering people, and look what I've learned by trying new things. So I let him do it. I put my trust in him as he pulls back on the strap and stops the blood from traveling to my brain.

"How far can you arch that back before it hurts?" he asks, and the gravel in his voice makes my pussy clench. "Oh, sweetheart . . . that's beautiful. Your pussy is so thick that it pokes between your thighs. It's *begging* to be touched."

His thumb drags through my slit as stars dance in front

of my eyes. From the pleasure or the impending blackout, I can't tell. Or care. I just live in this moment, enjoying the way the near-death experience heightens every sensation.

He releases the belt, and I drop back to the mattress, gasping for air. I could still breathe in that position, but my brain is so hungry for oxygen.

His arm glides beneath my stomach, and he raises my ass in the air as he steps behind me. I brace for him to enter me, but the belt cracks against my ass again. The pain bolts up my back, and I nearly collapse, but his soft kiss follows. He traces the fiery welts with his tongue, blowing the damp spots to cool the burn.

"I want you inside me so bad," I plead, knowing he won't give me what I so desperately desire.

"This isn't about you for once. Now be quiet. Good girls only speak when spoken to." He cracks the belt on my ass again, but no gentle kisses follow this strike. I almost like it better this way. It feels as if I'm really in trouble.

"Please fuck me," I beg, and I'm rewarded with the belt looping around my throat again. He snatches back, and I'm forced to look at the ceiling.

His hand caresses my cheek—on my face this time— before giving it a gentle slap. "Haven't I focused on your pleasure enough? You're being so selfish. Now it's my turn."

I want to cry out as he pushes inside me, but the sound leaving my throat comes out strangled and pathetic. It's kind of hot, not gonna lie. Allowing myself to be this weak and pitiful is a nice respite from always making decisions and having the control. I've never understood women who wanted to be used, but now that I've been with a man I trust?

Bitches, I get it.

My mind disconnects as he selfishly pummels my

pussy. I'm no longer a woman. Instead, I'm every sensation in my body. I'm every nerve ending, every sigh, every thread of pleasure. He makes this possible for me, by giving me a safe place to let go and just fucking *feel*. I don't have to think. He's doing that part for both of us.

Right before I black out, he releases the belt, and I collapse in a gasping heap. He tosses the belt to the side and grips my hips with both hands. Turning my head to the side, I watch as his neck cranes back, and I can barely breathe when I see the intense pleasure written on his face.

He looks down at me and smirks. His hand travels up my back, and he grips the back of my head, using my hair like a pull string. My scalp prickles with pain as he tightens his hold, and my back arches of its own volition.

"Fucking perfect, sweetheart," he breathes. "Keep your ass just like that. Let me watch how your pussy devours me."

His thumb gently rolls over my back entrance as he watches the disappearing act between my legs. I want to touch myself so badly, but I don't think he'll let me.

"May I please make myself come now?" I ask. "This feels so good, and I'm already so close."

He releases my hair and pinches the sensitive skin of my thighs as he pulls me snug against him in a harsh thrust. "When you come, I can't hold out anymore. You're a fucking goddess, Frankie, and when I hear those sweet sounds coming from that filthy mouth, my cock just wants to fill you. I'm not ready for that yet, so no, you cannot come."

He pulls out of me and flips me onto my back, manhandling me in a way no one has dared try before. I gasp and look up at him, realizing for the first time that the control he had might be slipping. He smirks down at me, reveling in my genuine fear.

"Spread your legs," he demands, and I shake my head. He places his hands on my knees. "We didn't have much dinner, and I've worked up quite the appetite. Now spread your legs and let me fucking eat."

He wrenches my legs apart—though I don't put up much of a fight—and licks his full lips before lapping up the arousal dripping from my V to my A.

"You taste like heaven," he groans before diving in again.

My hands move to his hair, but he swats my fingers away.

"Unless you want me to get the handcuffs, keep your hands above your waist." He studies my chest. "Better yet, play with your tits. Pinch those beautiful nipples until I tell you to stop."

My hands shoot to my chest because fuck being hand-cuffed. He can toss me around, spank me and choke me, but I draw the line at being bound in any way. I might only be exploring my upper limits, but some things we just know about ourselves.

As I pinch, tweak, and twist the sensitive nubs, Maverick drops his mouth to my pussy and groans. His tongue feels almost cold against my needy heat, and the contrasting sensations send goosebumps over my skin. Then he sucks my clit, and I lose all function. My thighs quiver, and the orgasm knocks at the door.

He raises his head and slaps my pussy. "I said you couldn't come. Don't disobey me now, sweetheart. Fight it."

Two thick fingers push inside me and tease the upper wall of my pussy. When his lips form a seal around my clit again, my soul evacuates my body. I fight the orgasm with every fiber of my being, but it's a battle I can't win. Not when he's stroking that hidden place inside me.

But just when I'm about to topple over the edge, he pulls away and leaves me feeling empty and almost numb.

"Wait, no! Come ba—"

My voice cuts off as the belt clamps over my neck. His hips push between my thighs, and his cock rests against my soaked entrance as he leans his weight into his hands on either side of my throat. The leather sinks into my skin, and I can't breathe.

"Make yourself come now." He smiles down at me, but the look in his eyes terrifies me as he whispers, "I won't release this belt until you coat my cock in your pleasure."

I didn't have "orgasm or die" on my bingo card this year, but I'm not mad about it.

My hand moves between my legs, and I push the tip of his dick inside me. Realizing what I need, he thrusts forward until his thighs bump against my ass. My eyes squeeze shut as a pleasurable pain drives through my abdomen. Nodding, I move my fingertips to my clit.

"Oh, good girl," he breathes as he thrusts in and out of me, all while keeping a dizzying pressure on the belt. "Touch yourself. Don't stop until you milk me of everything."

His cock jerks inside me, and I know he's fighting the urge to fill me. That thought pushes me over the edge. With a silent scream, I let go and fall. My hands and legs do weird shit, and I have no control or care. Does my O face look ridiculous? Doesn't matter. I don't exist. I have been replaced by sheer intensity and explosion.

I rip my hand away from my pussy, afraid I'll never stop coming if I don't. I'm also slightly panicking because I kind of need to breathe soon. Maverick stares into my face as he continues pumping into me, but he hasn't let up on the belt.

My hands fly to his wrists, and I peer into his green eyes.

"Do you trust me?" he asks.

I do.

My hands fall away.

"Fuck," he grunts, and the pressure on my neck intensifies. As does my need to breathe.

A ringing sound fills my ears, and a white haze creeps over my vision, but I stay calm. Because I trust him. Despite knowing what he's capable of, I also know I'm safe in his care. He isn't like King or Castle. He won't betray that trust.

His hips stutter, and heat jets inside me as he stalls. The pressure in my head increases until I'm certain something will burst, but then he pulls the belt away. My hands fly above my head, and I suck in air as he stands upright. Though *stands* is a bit of a stretch, as he sort of totters in place before sitting on the edge of the bed.

"Holy shit," he groans as he flops onto his back. "That . . . was fucking incredible."

I smile to myself and preen under the compliment. Same, dude. Same.

Chapter Thirty-Six

Frankie

There is a scene from *Gone with the Wind* that I never really understood until this moment. In it, we see a pissed-off Scarlet being carted upstairs by a belligerent Rhett. We then see her in bed the next morning, happy as a clam as she hums a little song and fiddles with her hair or her nightgown or something. I always wondered what he did to change her mood, how throwing her around like that would be something to soothe her instead of angering her further.

As I munch on strips of bacon in bed the morning after a night of being bossed around, I get it.

We've hardly slept, yet I've never felt more refreshed or at peace. The late-night hours were spent exploring this new and violent territory, and sleep seemed less important than chasing the next orgasm. I'm sore, but I'm satisfied in a way I've never known before.

"Was that the first time?" I ask Maverick as he swallows some orange juice.

His eyebrows rise. "First time . . . ?"

"Getting hard without getting hurt."

"Yes. But it was also my first time taking charge like that. Maybe it's the control I needed . . ."

I point at him with another strip of bacon. "That's exactly what I was thinking. Whatever psychological wound you have, it centers on needing either pain or control to achieve an erection. But hey, at least you have options now."

"Not when I masturbate. What am I supposed to do, boss my dick around? I already choke the shit out of it."

I nearly spit orange juice when I see how serious he is.

"Are you okay after last night?" he asks. "We didn't really talk about any of that beforehand, and then we both crashed, so I didn't exactly handle the aftercare very well either."

I pin him with a deadpan stare. "Thank you for checking in, but I'd like to think that the explosive orgasms would have been a sign that I was great with it."

"Is it . . . something you'd like to do again?"

Could his anxiety be any more adorable?

I push my plate aside and crawl closer to him. "It's something I'd very much like to do again. Maybe even right now."

He grips the back of my head and pulls my hair. "Say less."

His mouth moves to my throat, where he nips the sensitive skin. My pussy is so sore already, but I can sit on an ice pack later. I need to make up for lost time—all the years spent denying myself the wonders of a skilled and rough lover.

Someone knocks on the door, and we stare at each other as a silent message passes between us: *Let them knock.* I pull his hand to my breast as his mouth dips to my collarbone.

Knock, knock, knock.

We quietly groan and put some space between us. As I smooth the wrinkles in my night shirt, he goes to the door. It creaks open, and Eve rushes into the room. Oblivious, she plops down on the bed and plucks a strip of bacon from my plate.

"Pork?" she asks as she sniffs the strip.

I nod, and she takes a bite.

"Sorry. I made the mistake of trying Chef's special this morning." She grimaces, then shoves the rest of the bacon strip into her mouth. "Needless to say, I'm fucking starving now. Work keeps me on a strict diet, so I only get to eat whatever I want on these retreats, and acid-tenderized federal agent ain't it."

"He served the guy I—"

Eve nods at me and reaches for the toast on my plate. "You don't mind, do you?"

I genuinely don't, so I push the plate closer to her. "Knock yourself out."

She grabs the little pot of jam and slathers some on the toast. "And yes, Chef Maurice served the guy you killed as our breakfast. When we asked if it's even safe to eat meat that's been soaking in fucking sulfuric acid, he assured us it was properly rinsed."

"I wouldn't have taken that chance either," Maverick says.

Eve glances around. "Did you guys get a bottle of Bollinger? I want to make a mimosa."

"You don't want our Bollinger," I say as I share a look with Maverick. "It's tainted."

"Shit, if y'all were in here doing the nasty with a bottle

of vintage, you've been hanging around with Bennett too long. Food is for eating, not fucking."

"We definitely weren't fucking it," Maverick mutters.

I explain what happened last night with Amber and Ice Pick.

"Damn, I hate that for Ice." Eve grabs a napkin and cleans the jam and toast crumbs from her fingers. "Are you guys coming to the event this morning? That's the reason I stopped by, despite also raiding your pantry."

"What's the event?" I ask, excitement thrumming inside me. I only have a few days left to explore this new murderous side of myself, and I want to make the most of it.

Maverick's hand lands on my shoulder, giving it a gentle squeeze. "Didn't you say you wanted to stay in the room today?"

Eve scoffs and rises to stand. "You can dick her down later, lover boy. Jim set up a beach relay race, and you aren't fucking up our all-girls team this time. Cat and Kindra already planned our outfits, and I approved them." She looks me in the eye. "You ready to kick their asses, honey?"

"Born ready." I smirk at Maverick, but he looks less than enthused. I turn back to Eve. "I'll be there. Just tell me where and when."

She glances at the clock above the bathroom doorway. "We have to be on deck in an hour, so the sooner you get to Kindra's room, the better. Maverick needs to go to Cat's room to meet with the—"

"I'm not going."

Eve and I turn to look at him, both of us shocked.

"What the fuck do you mean? Yes you are." Eve folds her arms over her chest and pops out her hip. "Me, Kindra, Cat, and Frankie. Aven, Ezra, Bennett, and you. That's the way this works, and you don't have a choice in the matter."

I place a hand on Eve's shoulder. "Give me a second to talk to him. I'll meet you in Kindra's room shortly."

With an exasperated sigh, Eve agrees and tells me Kindra's room number. I walk her to the door, then return to Maverick. He sits on the edge of the bed as he twirls a bit of ripped napkin between his fingers. I take a seat beside him and place my hand on his knee.

"Hey, what's bugging you?" I ask.

He shakes his head and keeps twirling the napkin.

"Talk to me. I can't very well help you if you don't tell me what's wrong."

With a sigh, he finally looks at me. "*You* are what's wrong, sweetheart. We're changing you, and I don't want you to return from this trip disliking who you've become. Killing people and having fun doing it . . . This isn't who you are. This is who *we* are."

"Maybe this is who I've been all along."

He looks away from me, the fight gone from his eyes. His mouth opens, then closes, and he shakes his head. "I'm not going to the relay race, Frankie, and I don't think you should either. You're making a mistake. Please . . . stay here with me. You can justify the other kills you've made here, but you can't justify what you'll be expected to do today."

"I'll learn to live with it." Frustration bubbles over, and I stand and head for the door before I say something I'll regret. I exit the cabin without so much as a look over my shoulder.

He'll either show up or he won't, but I'm gonna be there.

Sand squishes through my toes as I walk along the shore. The boat that dropped us off speeds away to pick up the next group of participants, its engine buzzing like billions of pissed-off mosquitos. Kindra bends at the waist and snags a shell from the oncoming tide.

"It's got the perfect little hole," she says as she holds it up to the sunshine, and she's right. A circular area has been worn through the flat shell.

Eve laughs and looks at me. "I know someone else who has the perfect little hole."

"Eve!" I swat her arm. "What the fuck do you mean by that?"

She points down the beach, and I follow her gaze until my eyes land on a small group of men. Maverick stands among them.

"You convinced him to come when he didn't want to," Eve says. "I know him well enough to know that's saying something. Maverick says what he means, and if he didn't want to come, he wouldn't have. Not without some serious convincing."

"I didn't use any of my holes this time," I say. "I don't think it's that serious, though. Maybe he just had a bad case of FOMO."

Kindra pulls off her necklace and runs the slender chain through the hole in the shell, turning it into a charm to accompany the silver hand-shaped charm already dangling from her neck. She grips the silver hand and gives it a shake. "These men show their affection in weird ways. Ezra proposed with a disembodied hand inside a pumpkin."

"Bennett tried to make my life a living hell because he had a crush on me. Then he shoved a turkey leg in my ass." Cat shrugs. "Maverick showed up because he's got it bad, girl. Just accept it."

As we dressed in our matching outfits—purple crop tops, black fingerless gloves, skin-tight black shorts—I explained Maverick's reluctance to join us. I didn't include the details about why, though. Specifically, the facts surrounding my employment and that Maverick doesn't want me to lose myself. Friendships haven't come easy in my life, and I really like these girls. If they find out I'm a fed, I'll lose their trust. I'll have to tell them eventually, just not right now.

"So, what are we doing today?" I look down the beach, but I don't see any event stations. The Cattle aren't even present.

"Enjoying being on solid ground." Cat flops down in the sand. "I couldn't care less what the rest of the day entails. Just leave me on the beach."

Kindra smiles and rolls her eyes. "It's a relay race. That's all we know. If it's like the Olympics on the island, we'll take turns killing Cattle. Just be forewarned that things aren't always what they seem."

"What do you mean?"

"You might see a chainsaw, only to grab it and discover it doesn't have any gas," Cat says.

"Have a backup plan in place, honey," Eve says with a wink. "Jim sneaks in little tricks to make it more interesting, and we have to roll with it. I think you'll be just fine, though."

The tiny boat speeds toward the island and drops off another round of passengers. Looking around, I realize we're the only group who dressed up, and I'm feeling a smidge foolish. Especially when I glance down the beach and spot Maverick staring at me.

Bennett stands to his left, Aven to his right, but it's as if he's standing all alone. His face is all I see. The wind whips over his hair—it can't very well whip through it with all that product keeping it in place—and he squints at me. He's being a stubborn dick about this murder BS, but I still want to rip off his light button-up and wrap my legs around his waist.

But there's no time to think about it as Jim appears from the wooded area further inland. He motions us closer, and we all gather around. Maverick makes sure to stand beside me, and the heat of skin makes me shiver.

"Last chance to back out," he mutters. "We aren't on the same team, so I can't save you if you choke. But I can stop this before it even begins. Just say the word."

Unless he has a time machine that can take me back to the moment I accepted this assignment, that seems unlikely. That's when this began, and there's no stopping it now.

I shake my head. "You asked me to trust you. I want the same. Can *you* just trust *me?*" I turn and meet his gaze. "Please?"

He sighs but doesn't answer.

Jim begins explaining how the game will work, which silences any further conversation between us. For now. I'm sure Maverick will want to talk more about this when we're back on the ship. What will it take for him to accept that I've chosen a new path?

When Jim finishes explaining the rules, we follow him through the thick brush to the other side of the small island —to "keep us out of view," as he explained. I think he just did this for extra suspense on our part, because I'm frothing at the mouth to see the killing field by the time the trees break apart.

We step onto a stretch of sand that looks much like the one we just left. The main difference is the buzz of activity. Different stations have been positioned along the shore, with a few Cattle secured at every post. Most have their lips sewn shut, but a few have been left to scream. And scream they do.

"I want the talker," Cat says, and we nod in agreement, understanding that she needs the Cattle's crime if she wants to make the kill.

That part was important to me at first too. Now . . . I just want to shed some blood.

We take a moment to study the course. The talker for our lane is situated at the start, at station one. It's just the Cattle, a plastic sand pail, and a tiny plastic shovel. The next station is a bat sticking out of the sand, with Cattle sitting in a line a little further down. They're spread a fair distance apart, though, which makes me think the bat will be the murder weapon.

"Did any of you play softball in school?" I ask. "I wasn't athletically inclined."

"The only balls I caught were with my mouth," Eve says. "Before I was comfortable with my sexuality, I tried to mask by being promiscuous with boys. My best friend was gay, and I saw the way everyone said it was just a phase. I wasn't about to get that lecture." She shudders.

Kindra stares down the beach and understands what I'm getting at. "I was on the golf team. It's not a bat, but I'm pretty good at hitting a small target at high speed."

"Golf?" Cat and I say in unison, and that earns a laugh from all of us.

"Yes, *golf*," Kindra says with a giggle. "I wasn't good enough for the PGA, but I think I can whack a seated man's head just fine."

I look back at Eve. "I can't see further down the beach. Are you okay with you and I taking the last two stations, even though we don't know what they'll be?"

"I don't know that we have much of an option." Eve blows out a breath and holds her hair away from her neck. "If we want to beat the boys, we need to match ourselves to the tasks. That's easy with the first two."

"You'll have to run all the way down the beach," Cat points out. "This isn't a traditional relay. We won't be tagging you in further along."

Eve's eyes light up. "I ran track all four years of high school, so that goes in our favor."

"Don't look at me," Kindra says with a jiggle of her apron stomach. "My man likes my girlish figure, and I don't exactly participate in activities that would alter it. I'm best at station two."

"Eve, you take the fourth station. I'll take the third," I say, and the girls nod.

With a plan in place, we take our starting positions and wait for Jim to drop the checkered flag. The boys do the same in the lane beside ours, choosing a starting order of Ezra, Aven, Maverick, and Bennett.

"Good luck!" I say to Maverick.

With a deep sigh and a shake of his head, he gives me a sad smile. "Good luck."

Then Jim drops the flag, and we're off.

Chapter Thirty-Seven

Maverick

With a gleeful grin, Jim raises the bullhorn in his hand as the first contestants race toward the bellowing Cattle. "Station one!" he yells, not realizing that he doesn't need to shout into a device that is literally made to amplify your voice. Feedback screams through the speaker, and the racing Sinners cover their ears.

"Keep running!" Aven shouts.

Jim jiggles the bullhorn, then raises it again. "Sorry! Station one, you must use the shovel to dig a pit. You must use the pail to fill your pit with water, then drown your Cattle. You may not use anything else, and you must work alone."

"Jesus fucking Christ, how?" Cat screams as she drops to her knees and begins digging.

I get what she's saying, though. She weighs maybe as much as her Cattle's left quad. If she can even dig the hole deep enough, how will she ever get his head into it?

As she scoops sand, she speaks with the man on his

knees beside her. Unfortunately, he isn't speaking back, which is going to make this problem even greater. She's the Confessor. If he won't talk, she can't kill.

"Are we allowed to talk to our teammates?" Frankie yells toward Jim.

He raises the bullhorn once more. "You may talk to your team, but be mindful! Everyone else will hear whatever you say because you may not cross the red line until it's time to run to your station!"

"Cat, just . . . keep digging!" she screams.

I nibble my thumbnail and look at her Cattle. He stares out at the ocean, as if he isn't at all bothered by what's happening around him. Stepping to the side, I spot the band on his wrist. It's red.

Okay, sexual crime. The victim was an adult.

Studying his exposed skin, I spy Jesus' crying face peeking from the top of his t-shirt. He doesn't exactly strike me as the religious type, what with the contrasting satanic imagery scrawled over his right hand, so I can only assume someone in his life is. Probably his mother.

"How did she feel when she found out her baby boy was a rapist?" Frankie yells toward the man as Cat continues to dig. She figured it out as quickly as I did, though that's no surprise, given her career choice. And fuck, she was made for this.

The man's head twitches to the side, but he continues staring at the ocean.

"Did she cry?" I add, hoping to goad him into a response. "I bet you broke your mama's soul when she saw—"

"Shut your mouth!" the Cattle screams. He moves to charge toward me, but a chain hidden in the sand holds him back. As it snatches taut, he falls onto his face.

Frankie smirks at him. "I'd tell you to come shut it for me, but you seem a little . . . tied up."

The girls giggle in their line, and I'm pleased when I look up and see Frankie smiling at me. Hopefully she can forgive me for my sour mood earlier. My stance hasn't changed, but my approach has. My mother always said you catch more flies with honey than vinegar.

Frankie isn't a fly any more than she's a serial killer, but I hope the principle still applies. I also hope that when she's faced with the decision to end someone's life, she hesitates. That's all I need. If she gets to her station and pauses for even a second, I'll keep clinging to the shred of hope that I can save her from herself.

"What the fuck are you doing?" Bennett whispers. "Don't help them."

I shrug him off and turn my attention back to the competition. Cat is making good progress with her sand hole, but Ezra has pulled pretty far ahead of her. He's already on his third trip to the ocean. Peering down the line, I see that everyone else is miles behind.

Grim and Rosie scream from the sidelines as their brain-cell-deficient teammate attempts to drown their Cattle with the bucket. That's it. Just the bucket filled with water. Despite twelve trips to the ocean and back, their teammate still hasn't realized that the water just falls out every time it's tipped over the Cattle's head. It doesn't help that Grim screams in German, and poor Rosie's screams can't be heard by anyone but Grim.

In the next lane, Ice Pick sits on his ass, dragging the shovel through the dirt and crying. His team walked off a few seconds ago, and I don't think he noticed. I guess he's taking the Amber situation harder than we realized.

I glance back at Ezra and Cat. It'll be a minute before I

need to run for my station. Frankie is locked in, watching as Cat hauls bucket after bucket to the slanted pit she's dug. She should be fine for a moment.

"Hey, I'll be right back," I say to Bennett.

He waves me off, too focused on the event to spare me two seconds of his attention.

Shaking my head, I hurry over to Ice Pick. I squat beside him and place a hand on his shoulder. "Ice, talk to me, man."

He blinks and swipes his hands over his eyes, then runs his hairy forearm under his nose. When he finally realizes it's me, he smiles. "Oh, hey. Sorry I lost it for the team. I just . . ."

His lower lip quivers, and I haven't been this tempted to comfort a grown man in my entire life.

Oh . . . fuck what the guys think.

I lean forward and pull Ice Pick in for a hug. I regret it when I take a breath in, but that's okay. He's sad, and sometimes it's tough to shower when we're sad.

Deodorant would have been nice, but—

"Ice, I'm sorry we killed your girlfriend." I pat his back and try to think of something more eloquent to say. "I mean, *we* didn't kill her. But we kind of set it up so that *you* would want to kill her."

Okay, that sounded better in my head, but I'm pretty sure it only made things worse. His shoulders shake as he starts to cry. Loudly.

I glance around to see if anyone has noticed, but each lane is hyper-focused on their own team. Even Ice Pick's ex-teammates have gathered near Jim to root for their favorites.

Grim's teammate has finally started digging a hole, and Ezra has damn near drowned his Cattle. The Confessor isn't far behind him. Cat's sloped design proves genius, and she's able to slide her squirming Cattle down the sandy bank until his nose and mouth dip below the water.

When Ice Pick finally pulls back to take a breath, I see that he left a large snot stain on my shirt. Lovely. He swipes it with his hand and apologizes.

"It's fine, but I need to get back to my team. Come with me, okay?" I get to my feet and dust the sand from my knees, then reach out for him. I'm surprised when he slips his hand in mine and smiles as he allows me to help him stand. "You'll be all right. It doesn't feel like it right now, but you will. Just . . . if you ever need someone to talk to, come to me. Yeah?"

Ice Pick chuckles and eases his hand out of mine. "Don't go getting mushy on me, kid." He looks at me and sobers. "But yeah. If I ever need someone to talk to, it'll be you."

We turn to walk back to the group and nearly bump into Frankie.

"Sorry," she whispers, and when I see that adorably sheepish smirk, I almost believe she is.

"I'll meet you over there," I tell Ice Pick. "Go stand with Aven."

Ice Pick nods, swiping the residual tears from his eyes as he hurries to join the boys.

"That was incredibly sweet," Frankie says as she steps into me. "It's kind of hot to see you nurture someone's brokenness after the way you broke me last night."

A breeze kicks up and sends her hair around her face. She laughs and brushes it away, and I'm stunned by how beautiful she is. I'm so taken aback that I can't even form words.

She glances over her shoulder. "Cat's nearly done, and

Aven's already running for the bat. Maybe we should get back to it."

I place my fingers under her chin and gently force her to look at me. "And you're certain this is what you want to do?"

"Are you trying to talk me out of it again?"

"No, if you want to do it, I won't fight you on it."

Momentary panic flits through her eyes. "Do you plan to punish me later by not punishing me at all if I go through with it?"

A laugh bursts out of me. I can't help it. She's genuinely worried I won't toss her around if she commits to the game. "Sweetheart, punishing you in that way would only be a punishment to myself. My concern is only for you and what this could do to you on a mental level. Just . . . Just remember that you don't have to do it if you don't want to. If you get to your station and have second thoughts, just—"

Bullhorn feedback cuts off the end of my sentence, as well as my train of thought. "At station two, you must place your forehead on the upright bat and spin *fifty* times!" Jim screeches. "Once you've completed the appropriate amount of revolutions, you may snatch up the bat and use it to beat your Cattle senseless!"

"We gotta get back in line," Frankie says. She stands on tiptoes and places a soft kiss on my lips. "Just trust me, Maverick. I'll do what's best for me, even if that means walking away from the kill. I just need to know that my decision won't change how you feel about me, regardless of the outcome."

I could end it all here. As she looks up at me with those crystal-blue eyes, I can see that telling her it would change how I feel would be enough to stop her madness.

But I have to be honest with her.

And myself.

"Nothing will change how I feel about you," I admit. "I don't know what this is, but I'm not ready to stop exploring what it could be. Your profession doesn't matter to me. I just don't want you to wake up one day and resent me for not stopping you."

"Sometimes it has to be enough to know you tried." She shrugs her shoulders. "I'm not an easy woman to get along with, and it's partly because I'm stubborn. At my age, I'm pretty set in my ways. If I want to do something, I do it, and you can't stop me. That's the entire reason my division wants me dead."

"Because you forced your way into male spaces?"

She shakes her head. "No, not male spaces so much as spaces I really don't belong in. I see that now. I wasn't cut out for the job, and King knew it. He blocked every attempt I made to get into his castle, but nepotism won the day."

"I thought your mother didn't want you in this line of work?"

"She didn't, but remember what I said about being really stubborn? Yeah. I'm pretty sure she pulled the strings just to shut me up."

"Frankie, it's almost time!" Eve yells toward us.

We glance down the lanes. Blood coats the sand as Aven raises and lowers the bat on his Cattle's head. His victim is clearly dead, but he's lost to the violence. Kindra, on the other hand, stands patiently beside her Cattle as one of the crew checks for a pulse.

"Shit," Frankie says. "I gotta get over there. We'll continue this later."

She stands on tiptoes and gives my cheek another peck before hurrying back to Eve's side. Just like that, hope evaporates from my heart. There will be no hesitation on

Frankie's part. I can tell that much from the determined way she stares down the lane, practically raring to rush across the sand and make a kill.

As I stare down the lane, I can only think one thing: I have to save Frankie before she reaches the point of no return. We're approaching that deadline, but I still have time. Two more nights, to be exact. When Frankie leaves this ship, she'll do so with her head on straight, even if that means I have to rip out my heart to make it happen.

Chapter Thirty-Eight

Maverick

Despite Aven's reluctance to stop beating a dead horse, Frankie and I still manage to race down the beach at roughly the same time. I'm a few seconds ahead of her, so I quickly formulate a plan as Jim shouts instructions from the bullhorn.

"Station three, welcome to the beach picnic! The rules are simple. Using only the items provided in your picnic basket, you must prepare a wonderful spread. Drape your blanket on the sand, and don't forget to grab your special guest!"

He motions toward the water, to a few surfboards bobbing in the waves. I hadn't given them a second thought before now, but as I look closely, I see Cattle strapped to each one. Naked, shivering Cattle.

"If your Cattle dies on the journey to the picnic, your team will be disqualified," Jim adds. "All kills must be taken on the picnic blanket to count, and the blanket must remain in your lane!"

With a groan, I look at the ocean. I'm not a terrible swimmer, but I don't know about Frankie. Cutting through the waves will be a major pain in the ass, but it's also exhausting.

"You better not lose this for us, blondie!" Bennett yells toward me. Probably because I'm simply standing here and watching as Frankie races toward the water like some Baywatch daydream.

She rips off her shirt as I hurry after her. It flies behind her and lands in my face, ruining my perfect view. I'm glad when she doesn't strip further. Bennett isn't the only one with a possessive streak. The idea is a good one, though, so I steal it. As I run, I rip off my clothes until I'm down to my boxers.

Frankie is all giggles and smiles as she dives into the water, but I'm increasingly nervous about the distance. While it doesn't seem that far on land, treading water for that length of time is nothing to sniff at, and we'll have squirming passengers to tend to on the return trip.

Cheers erupt behind us as another team finishes the second station. I wade into the water until it reaches my knees. Then I begin the swim.

I was wrong to worry about Frankie. She reaches the surfboards, chooses one, and begins paddling toward shore. I was right to worry about myself, though, because I still have several yards to go, and I'm already winded.

"You good?" Frankie asks as we pass in the water. She even stops kicking her legs as she swipes the water from her face.

I grunt and force a smile. "Never been better, sweetheart. Just giving you a little head start."

"Right," she drawls as she kicks toward shore.

Setting my jaw, I try not to think about the horrible pain

digging into my arms and legs. Exhaustion is already setting in by the time I reach the surfboards, and I'm more than happy to rest a moment as I catch my breath. Bennett stomps his feet and screams at me when he realizes I'm resting, but that's fine. I can't hear him all the way out here.

I can't rest for long, though. As I look at the waves crashing onto the beach, I see another participant diving into the water. I don't mind losing to Frankie, but I refuse to be bested by a no name. As I study the Cattle on the surfboards, I don't see any advantage to be had, so I settle on the surfboard I currently cling to. The man strapped to it doesn't seem to mind, not that he could tell me if he did. He appears to be unconscious.

At least . . . I hope that's the case.

I'm too fucking tired to check for a pulse, so I start paddling. The return trip is easier once I'm out of the current. The waves push me toward shore. When I finally feel the sand beneath my feet, I change modes from Mermaid Maverick to Land Maverick, and despite the way my arms and legs feel like massive cement weights, Land Maverick is much faster. I move to the front of the board and grip the modified, reinforced wrist strap as I wrestle the Cattle out of the surf.

To my right, Frankie grunts and groans as she tries to yank her Cattle to the picnic area. Despite her best efforts, she's made little progress since leaving the water. Her face has gone red with the effort, and my heart is breaking as I witness the desperation in her eyes. She turns her head so that I can't see the tears of frustration.

I have a choice to make at this moment. Helping her would mean going against what I want, and what I want is for Frankie to leave this beach without making a kill. I'm so scared that if she does it, she'll regret it later.

But if I don't help her right now, I'll regret it.

I drop my wrist strap and rush to her side. Bennett screams and shouts his displeasure behind me, but I ignore him as I get behind Frankie's surfboard and push.

"What are you doing?" she asks, though she doesn't stop pulling that strap with everything she has. "I thought you . . . didn't want me . . . to make . . . the kill." With another tug, she falls to her ass. "Fuck! Why is this so goddamn hard?"

I move to the front of the board and grab the wrist strap from her. "That's why I'm helping. Because it's hard. If I'd needed help in the water, you'd have done the same."

Frankie doesn't respond.

I give the board another yank, clearing a small dune that would have been in her way. "Right?"

"Totally," she says.

Why don't I believe her?

I haul the surfboard the rest of the way to her station, then turn to face her. "In the spirit of fairness, it would be nice if you waited to begin. You know, to give me a chance to catch up."

"I still have to get him on the blanket," she says as she kneels beside the surfboard and begins unstrapping the nude man. "You have plenty of time to catch up."

Again, why don't I believe her?

I rush back to my surfboard, but the Cattle isn't there. I guess I didn't need to worry about him being dead after all. Bennett's screams finally register in my head, and I look down the beach as a bare butt races toward a rocky outcropping.

Catching up with him isn't hard to do, as his legs are chained so that he can't get a good stride. Restraining him, however, will be interesting. As I mentioned, he's very much naked, and I don't cherish the thought of his cock and balls bouncing against me as I carry him down the beach. Dragging his dead body by the foot would be preferable, but he can't be killed away from the picnic blanket.

Can't be killed, but Jim didn't say he had to be fighting fit.

I grab a nearby rock, aim for his head, and send it. The large stone smacks the side of his head, and down he goes. He scrambles to get up again, but I'm already on him with another rock in hand.

It's not my finest moment, but I straddle his waist and proceed to bludgeon him with the rock. Again, Jim said we had to use the items in the picnic basket to kill our Cattle, but he didn't say we couldn't use other things to incapacitate them. I bring the stone down on his skull until he finally lies still. The last strike misses, though, and I end up caving in his nose and part of his right eye socket.

"Sorry about that, buddy," I say as I grip his leg and start dragging him down the beach.

It all works out in the end, though, because Frankie is still struggling to get her Cattle onto the blanket. Whatever drugs Jim gave them are starting to wear off. The man occasionally groans and tries to roll away, much to Frankie's growing frustration.

"Please be still," she pleads. "I'll make it quick."

I drop my guy's leg and pull the blanket out of the picnic basket, then spread the red-and-white fabric over the sand. With a few quick tugs, I've got him on the blanket.

"How the fuck am I supposed to kill him with a fucking baguette?" Frankie screeches.

I look up as she flings things from the picnic basket, each item less murdery than the last. "A few more hours in the sun and that potato salad might do the trick."

"I'd have more luck trying to kill him with my bare hands," Frankie laments. "Do we all have the same shit?"

Opening my basket, I spy three butcher knives and a hand grenade. "Uh . . . keep digging. Maybe there's something."

"Ah ha!" she says, and I expect her to pull a Ruger from the basket. Instead, she produces a corkscrew, which she then tries to shove into the man's chest.

No hesitation.

Well, there goes my last ounce of hope.

"Try twisting," I say as I show her what I mean.

"Easy for you to say with a knife in your fucking hand." She puts all of her weight behind the corkscrew as she twists to the right. Something pops, and she sinks down. The Cattle groans and turns his head. Frankie looks at me. "Shouldn't he be dead?" she whispers.

"Why are you letting her win?" Bennett screams.

My gaze bounces between Frankie and Bennett. "Listen, you'll need to hurry this up. There's only so much stalling I can do before Bennett takes *me* out on this picnic blanket."

"Wait, you're trying to let me win?" Frankie sits back, and her Cattle begins to sit up.

"Hey, you need to finish him off."

"No. If I'm going to win this leg, I want to win fair and square."

The dazed man looks at me, then down at the bloody man on my blanket. He blinks and then squints at the knife in my hand before looking down at the corkscrew rammed in his chest.

"Okay, but take him out before he comes around. You won't stand a chance if—"

Frankie places her hands on the man's shoulders and

lowers him to the blanket, and he complies without complaint. "First you don't want me to kill anyone. Now I'm not doing it quickly enough. Make up your mind!" She slams her fist onto the corkscrew, and the man coughs up some blood.

"You, uh . . . It's a lung shot. He'll take a bit to die from that." I step over my Cattle and slit his throat. Blood jets from his carotid and coats my chest in red. I look back, toward the start of the race. "Can I get a check?"

"Drat," Frankie mutters as she tries to wrestle the corkscrew free. When tugging doesn't work, she places her feet to either side of it to give her some leverage, and she yanks some more.

"Remember, sweetheart?" I turn my wrist, spinning the knife in my hand. "Give it a twist."

She grits her teeth and looks up at me. "This is what I'm gonna do to your nuts later." With that, she gives the tool another yanking, but with a twist this time, and it pops free. Blood trickles from the small wound.

Jim trots up and reconsiders kneeling to check my guy's pulse. "Was the bludgeoning wholly necessary? So much blood. I'll put my cleaners' kids through college after this trip."

A guttural scream comes from Frankie, and I turn in time to see her straddle the man and drive the corkscrew into his eye. "Why won't you fucking die already?"

"You might have better luck if you flip him around and use the same force on his neck. Right at the base of the—"

She yanks out the corkscrew and tosses it aside. "Do not mansplain murder to me, please."

Jim stands up and nods. "He's dead." Then he raises the bullhorn, and right in my ear, he says, "Station four!"

Bennett tears past me, and I'm grateful because it

means Jim aims the bullhorn away from my fucking ear. Whatever rules he lays down, I don't hear them. I doubt I'll ever hear anything again.

But then I do hear something. Female voices shouting and encouraging Frankie to keep going. As I peer down her lane, I see Cat, Kindra, and Eve jumping up and down and cheering her on. No wonder she wants to be part of this so badly. It's the power of finding your tribe.

I turn back to Frankie. She's abandoned the corkscrew in favor of the glass bowl the potato salad came in. As she smashes it beneath the blanket, then pulls out a large, sharp shard, I'm in awe of her resourcefulness. When she wraps the sharp edges with the cloth napkins from inside the basket, then drives the curved glass into his neck, I'm taken aback by her ferocity. It's like watching your house cat tear the head off a bird. You know they're capable of it, but you're still fucking shocked when it happens in front of you.

Watching her face, I wait for the remorse to light her eyes. I study her and hold my breath as she eases the glass from his throat. Blood rushes out and coats her hands to the tempo of a heartbeat, and still the look on her face hasn't changed. Then her lips curve into a smile, and she flops onto her ass.

"Amazing," she says, and I recognize that look in her eyes. It's the self-satisfaction after removing a filthy smudge from your window on the world. It's the comedown after release. It's the end of what you were and the beginning of what you will be.

And it's all my fault.

Chapter Thirty-Nine

Frankie

Water coils around the drain, washing the blood away. Such a shame. I loved the way it painted his skin seconds ago. He seemed eager to get it off, though, so I didn't complain when he asked if I wanted to shower together.

I lather my hair with mint-scented shampoo. The tea-tree oils help soothe my scalp, which is often itchy and dry. Maverick's hands replace my own, and I moan as he massages the tingle into my head.

"That feels amazing," I whisper.

"Better than the kill?"

I close my eyes and remember what it felt like to watch that piece of shit take his last breath. It would have been more enjoyable if he'd been conscious enough to realize what was happening, but it was still nice.

It can't compete with Maverick's body heat behind me, though.

I reach back and grip his soft cock. "No, this is definitely better. I don't think much else can compare."

He gently spins me and places my head beneath the shower's spray. His hands firm on my waist, holding my lower half against him as I rinse the shampoo from my hair. I crane my neck and close my eyes so that I don't end up blind. One time, I thought I had slathered my pussy stubble with shaving gel, only to realize seconds later that I had used the tea-tree shampoo. If it burned my meat flaps that badly, I can only imagine what it would do to my eyes.

"I'm glad to hear I'm not second best," he says before dipping down and nipping my neck. His tongue explores my skin, sending tingles through my limbs. "How about we skip the event this afternoon? Instead of riding jet skis and drowning assholes, we could ride each other."

"That sounds amazing . . ."

His lips stop working their magic, and he stands upright and looks me in the eye. "But?"

I bite my bottom lip. "I kind of told the girls I'd go. I don't want to disappoint them."

His concern fades, replaced by a soft smile. "I wouldn't want you to disappoint them, either. I'm glad you've made friends. They're really good people, and I know they'll keep you safe."

"About that . . ." I swipe the water from my face and swap places so that he can wash his hair. "I'll eventually have to tell them that I was a fed, but I don't know how. Or when. I feel like I'm lying to them, and I don't want them to feel betrayed once they learn the truth."

"*Was* a fed? Frankie, that's your livelihood. You've dedicated years of your life to your job, and now you want to throw it all away?"

"I thought you were letting this go." I fold my arms over

my chest. "I can't be a killer and a fed. If I have to choose, I'm picking the thing that makes me happiest. I've made friends here. And more."

He sighs and dumps an ungodly amount of shampoo into his palm. Then I remember how much product he puts in his hair, and I wonder if it's enough.

"That's why I'm so worried about you," he finally says after a lengthy lather and rinse. "We *are* something more, and that means I care about you. It means I want what's best for you, and I'm not sure this life is it."

"Shouldn't I be the one to make that decision?"

"You're right."

I open my mouth to argue, but then I realize he just agreed with me. The shock is immediate. "Come again?"

"I said that you are correct. It's your life, and you have to choose what's best for you." He leans down and cuts off the water, then swipes his hand down his face so that he can see. Then he steps forward, fresh hunger in his eyes. "Right now, though, I want to do what's best for me."

He takes another step forward, forcing my back against the shower wall. He places one arm beside my head, caging me in. His other hand reaches up to brush the damp strands of hair from my cheek.

"Right now, I just want to sink inside you. I don't want to think. I just want to feel." He leans down and captures my mouth in a kiss that silences my brain. His hand glides behind my neck, squeezing and pulling me closer. I don't think I could get away from him if I wanted to, and that's a fucking turn on.

I pull back. "Get rough with me."

"How rough are we talking?" He smirks, and I want to melt. Does he have to be so fucking hot?

I push against his chest and step out of the shower. "No limits. Safe word is pineapple."

"Wow, you really are fitting in."

For once in my life, yeah, I am. That's why I can't give this up.

I run the towel over my head and body, doing just enough so that I don't stick to the comforter when we finally make it to the bed. He does the same, and we're tangled in each other's arms seconds later. We don't make it as far as the bed, though.

He picks me up by my waist and sets my ass on the bathroom counter, to the right of the sink. His eyes are glued to the warm place between my legs as he drops to his knees and swipes his tongue through my slit.

"Fuck, you are delicious," he growls before diving in again.

I run my fingers through his damp hair as I watch him feast. It's a beautiful sight, really. His eyes are closed, and he looks as if he's genuinely satisfied with his meal. Gentle groans spill past his lips, where they vibrate against my clit.

He pulls his head away from me and looks into my eyes. Grabbing my ass in an almost painful grip, he snatches me closer to the edge. I tip back and catch myself with my hands just before my head smacks against the large mirror.

Then he dips down and . . . oh my fucking—

"Maverick!" I try to push his mouth away from my asshole, but he's too strong. "This is unsanitary! I shit from there!"

"So fucking dirty," he says before diving back in.

God, and I can't stop him because it feels so good. It's like having my pussy eaten, but better because this is so fucking wrong. His tongue teases places I've never touched with bare fingers.

He nips my inner thigh to the point of pain, then leans back. "Make sure you pay attention. You get to do me next."

"Wait, what?"

He smirks and kisses my thigh. "I'm kidding, sweetheart. Now shut up and let me worship you."

His mouth melds with my ass again, and I let it happen. I can't deny how good it feels, even though it still grosses me out. At least it was after a shower and I don't have to worry about any natural but very unflattering aromas.

It's clearly working, though, because arousal drips from my opening to my asshole. Maverick groans again as the liquid coats his tastebuds. His fingers sink into my thighs. But when he rises to stand, his dick is still limp. I can remedy that by providing pain, but I think I'd rather see if getting him to take control might help matters. I close my thighs.

"I didn't say I was finished with you." He steps closer, but I keep my knees together. "Sweetheart, don't be a bad girl. Let me see how wet you are for me."

Nibbling my bottom lip, I smirk and turn my head away from him.

"Oh, someone's being difficult." He grips my knees and wrenches my legs apart in a show of strength. A whimper squeaks out of me, lighting a fire in his eyes. "Bad girls don't get their ass eaten. Do I need to remind you who's boss here?"

With a grin, I nod and close my legs again.

He rushes forward and hoists me over his shoulder. I yelp, genuinely surprised at his raw power as he carries me to the bed and tosses me to the mattress. After bouncing twice, I finally settle.

Maverick is on me immediately. Taking a wrist in each hand, he holds my arms above my head as his pelvis pins me to the bed. He grinds his cock through my wetness, and I'm pleased to feel the way it's firming against me. I wiggle against him in a feigned struggle, but I'd be lying if I said I didn't feel a little panicked right now. Despite knowing I'm only one word away from stopping this, he feels unstoppable.

His mouth dips to my collarbone, but instead of the gentle nips and kisses I'm used to, he clamps down on my skin with his teeth. I cry out, and my arms instinctively jerk downward in an attempt to stop the pain, but his hold is too strong. Then his teeth release, and his tongue slides over the area, taking away the pain.

When he leans back, I try to close my knees, but his hand whips between my legs and stops me. He palms my pussy, placing sweet pressure against my clit. "Do you need to be spanked, sweetheart? Is that the only way to get what I want?"

Recalling the sweet heat of the belt, I nod. "Yes, I definitely need to be taught a lesson. I am bad."

"So bad." He smirks and releases my arms so that he can get the belt. "When I get back to that bed, I expect you to be standing with your hands on the mattress."

I scramble off the bed and get into position. Seconds later, his heat closes in on my backside. The belt cracks over my skin without warning, and I clutch the comforter as I bite back a scream.

"That was for closing your legs," he says, his voice deep and gravelly. The leather sings over my skin a second time.

I grit my teeth and wait for the pain to pass before I say, "And what was that one for?"

"That was for making me fall so hard for you."

The belt loops around my neck, and he pulls back on the strap as he enters me. My head snatches back, forcing me to look at the ceiling as pleasure crawls up my spine. His cock forces its way inside me. My pussy wasn't quite ready for the intrusion, but something about the resistance turns me on.

A sharp pain bolts through my lower half with each thrust. Each aching jab also tightens the pressure on my neck, pinching my skin. My nipples brush against the comforter with every pass of his hips. His free hand grips my right hip, his fingertips digging into my skin. I feel so much at once, yet I can't focus on anything. It frees my mind in a way I've never experienced before Maverick.

I drive my hand between my legs, and Maverick releases my hip to snatch my wrist behind my back.

"You . . . didn't ask . . . for . . . permission," he grunts between thrusts.

"Please let me come." My god, I sound so pathetic.

He drops my wrist and tightens his hold on the belt, yanking my head until I'm practically looking at him. "Get on your knees, sweetheart. I'll tell you when I want you to come."

He pulls the belt away from my skin, and I scramble to the floor like a dog. If he tells me to roll over so he can scratch my belly, I just might listen.

"Place your hands on your knees, then look up at me and open your mouth. No matter what happens, your hands are not to leave your knees. Do you understand?"

My hands go to my knees, and I nod as I part my lips.

"Tongue out, sweetheart. And don't take your eyes off my face."

I stick out my tongue, making more room in my mouth for his massive dick, which he slides to the back of my throat. My eyes slam shut as a gag wracks my body, and my hands fly to his thighs.

He gives my cheek a gentle slap. "Eyes open and hands on knees."

My eyes flutter open, and my palms clamp on my knees. Tears stream down my cheeks, but I fight the urge to gag again.

"Oh, good girl," he coos as he grips the back of my head and picks up the pace. "Take me, just like that, all the way down your tight throat."

Breathing through my nose, I try to guard my teeth as he skull fucks the living shit out of me. He tips back his head and moans, his fingers digging into my scalp. After a few more rough thrusts, he pulls out of my mouth, raises his cock out of the way, and pushes my mouth to his nuts.

"Suck," he commands.

I open my mouth and gingerly take the smooth skin past my lips. My tongue swirls over his left nut as I provide some suction, and he rewards me with a low groan. The hand gripping his cock begins to move up and down his shaft.

"Fuck, I can't last," he says through gritted teeth. He pulls my head away and motions for me to stand. "I need to fill you now. Get against the wall."

I look around for a wall with enough space, but there are paintings and pictures everywhere I turn. Then my eyes land on the balcony door. I head that direction, but that gives Maverick another idea.

"On second thought, go onto the balcony." A devilish gleam lights his eyes. "I want everyone to see you."

Chapter Forty

Maverick

Frankie's eyes widen as the submission leaves her body. "Excuse me, what? You . . . *want* people to see me? What happened to the possession?"

I step into her, pinning her perfect ass against the glass door, and I wish I could split myself in half so I could both witness and experience her from all sides. "Oh, I'm definitely still possessive, but unlike Bennett, I don't mind if people admire my toys. So long as I'm the only one playing with them."

I brush the hair out of her face and kiss her. The fear that I've ruined the moment dissipates when she kisses me back. Then her hands slither behind her, and she pulls the door to the side.

Salty sea air tangles within her hair as she steps backward onto the balcony. She keeps moving until her back hits the railing. Her worries about being seen were unfounded, as the only eyes privy to our intimacy are those in the water. Unfortunately, whoever stays in the rooms next to ours is about to get one hell of a concert. Metal clinks against ceramic to our left, so I can only assume they're having their afternoon tea on the balcony.

Frankie hears the clanking as well. She clamps her lips shut, refusing to make a peep as I tweak her nipple.

This won't do. I bend down and place my lips beside her ear. "I want to hear you beg for it, sweetheart. Tell me what you want."

She reaches between us and grips my throbbing cock.

I grit my teeth and suck air as I step into her to ease the painful ache from her tugging. The pain only hardens me further. "Use your words. Say it aloud and raise your voice so I can hear you over the waves."

"You mean raise my voice so our neighbor can hear," she mutters.

I shrug and turn to walk away.

"Wait!" Frankie shouts, and I turn back to her with a smirk. "Please . . . fuck me."

Cocking my head to the side, I study her. "What was that? I couldn't quite hear you."

Pursing her lips, she stomps her little foot and screams internally. "Please fuck me!" she shouts, and the clinking stops. Seconds later, the neighbor's balcony door slides open and shut.

Frankie covers her blazing-red face and groans, but she's about to make that sound for a different reason. Having gotten what I wanted, I step into her and pick her up. She wraps her arms around my neck in a panic as I stride closer to the balcony railing.

"What are you doing?" she squeals as she dares to glance down. Dark waters look back at her.

"Giving you what you asked for. Now place your hands on the railing and hold on tight."

She seems unsure, but she eventually stretches her arms out to the sides of her body. Gripping her legs, I take a step back and line myself up with her entrance. I can't resist raising and lowering her hips a few times, which drags my cock through her pleasure.

Frankie whimpers each time my dick grinds over that sensitive place at the apex of her slit. Her hips roll, begging me to impale her and end her suffering. I adore the way she writhes in my arms. I bask in her greed as she begs for pleasure only I can provide.

"I want you inside me," she quietly pleads.

"Louder."

She closes her eyes. "I want you inside me."

"You must not want it enough because that's still pretty quiet."

"Would you please fuck me before I lose my shit?" she screams, and the neighbor to our other side decides they've had enough as well. The door opens and closes.

At least she obeyed this time. I reward her by raising her hips and lowering her onto my cock. She hisses and drops her head back as I give her all of me.

"Do you want to come now, sweetheart?"

She nibbles her lip and nods at me, and my dick jumps inside her.

"Tell me," I demand.

"I want to come. *Please* make me come."

Desperation drips from every word, and I try to think of anything other than the perfection before me. The fear was always the inability to satisfy her because I couldn't get it up, not because I'm a two-pump chump. I never imagined fucking my ideal woman would come with such a drawback.

It's the emotional connection.

Is it? Is this why erections come easily with her? Is this why I finish at an embarrassing pace? Is this why I'm looking into her piercing eyes and wondering what it would be like to come home to her at the end of a long day?

"Fuck, I'm so close." She adjusts her grip on the balcony. Her arms have begun to shake, and I don't think she'll be able to support herself much longer.

I pull out of her and drop into one of the armless chairs. "Ride me," I demand.

Frankie straddles my lap and leans back so that I can enter her again. We moan together as I sink into her heat. Her hands wind around my neck, and her hips begin to roll. Warm breath rushes out of her each time I bottom out.

My hands move to her ass, where I squeeze and encourage her to ride me harder and faster. She complies, and her hips begin to buck rather than roll. Whimpers become cries of pleasure as her body quivers. Her grip firms on my shoulders, pinching the skin until it feels as if she'll rip the muscles from my bones. The pain melds with her frantic sounds as she comes on my cock, squeezing and drawing the come from my balls. I let out a groan as I fill her, unable to hold back another second.

The gentle sound of applause cuts through our post-orgasm haze, and we turn toward the sound. Apparently, the balcony door didn't signal our neighbor's exit. Our neighbor came to bear witness.

Frankie covers her face and groans as more applause joins in, and the embarrassment is setting in for me as well. It only gets worse when we attempt a quiet exit. As Frankie gets off my lap, the chair legs scrape against the floor, and it sounds as if we've just blown wind. Giggles erupt from every direction.

"It wasn't a fart!" I shout. "It was the chair!"

"Or a queef," a man titters from nearby.

I try to repeat the sound, but of course the chair refuses to cooperate this time.

"Let's just slink away." Frankie looks at the chair. "Quietly this time."

We hurry back into the cabin to lick our wounds. I thought a little exhibitionism would be fun, but maybe that's one kink I can cross off my list. The feeling seems to be mutual. You could cook eggs on Frankie's fiery cheeks.

Frankie waddles to the bathroom to clean up as I step into some boxers and flop on the bed. She throws on a baggy t-shirt and some joggers before joining me. Her body sidles up to mine, fitting like a missing puzzle piece against me as I drape an arm over her shoulder and kiss the top of her head.

"You were amazing," I whisper against her soft hair.

"Our audience seemed to think we were both pretty amazing," she says with a laugh. "I can't believe I did that."

She opens her mouth in the most adorable yawn, and I hug her a little tighter. I can't help it. Even though she's practically on top of me, it feels like we aren't close enough. This is such a foreign feeling, but I want it to become familiar. I want more of these little moments of peace with a beautiful woman in my arms. Not just any beautiful woman, though.

It has to be her.

And it can't be.

Chapter Forty-One

Maverick

I let her sleep for a few hours while I hold her, but I keep a close eye on the clock as she snores in my arms. Part of me wants to be selfish and keep her in the room, all to myself, but she really has her heart set on an afternoon with the girls, so I give her a little nudge. Her head rises, and a long string of drool connects my bare chest to her lips.

"Shit, did I fall asleep? What time is it?" She sits up and looks around, her hand clamped to her head.

I smile and stroke her shoulder. "You didn't miss anything. I woke you up in time."

"Thanks. I guess I needed that nap." Raising her arms above her head, she stretches with a groan, then rises from the bed and strides to the closet, where she begins digging through her bag. "Are you coming with?"

She pulls a skimpy silver bikini from the shadows, and my mouth begins to water.

"Yep, I can definitely join you," I say as I leap to my

feet. I'm not missing a second of Frankie wearing those tiny scraps of fabric.

I throw on a pair of swim trunks and go to the bathroom sink. Right as I begin brushing my teeth, someone knocks on the door. I move to answer it, but Frankie waves me off.

"I'll get it," she says. "It's probably one of the girls."

With a nod, I go back to the sink. The door creaks open seconds later, but instead of a greeting, I hear Frankie gasp.

"King?" she shouts. "Why the fuck are you here?"

"Well, that's no way to talk to your boss," a male voice answers. A *British* male voice.

I spit into the sink, then quickly rinse my mouth with water before leaning past the alcove's edge and sneaking a peek at this visitor. He's tall, with a thick shock of salt-and-pepper hair atop his head. A trimmed beard graces the manliest jawline I've ever seen, and he peers back at me with oddly hypnotic dark eyes.

"Many apologies. I didn't know you'd have company." He gives me a nod. "Still, this meeting can't be helped. Your tracker went offline, and naturally, I became concerned."

Frankie pushes out her lower lip in a faux pout. "Aw, so sorry I concerned you, but wasn't the entire point of this trip to get rid of me?" She drops the act and rolls her eyes. "You came to make sure the job was done, nothing more."

She goes to shove the door closed, but he stops it with his black dress shoe. After firming his grip on the door's edge, he pushes it wide and steps into the cabin. Frankie begins to backpedal, and I dart between them.

"I don't know what sort of agreement you have with Jim, but I vowed to protect her," I say. Using my arms as a blockade against the narrow walls, I halt his forward movement. "I suggest you leave the room if you want to make it off this ship in one piece."

King straightens to his full height and adjusts his tie with a smirk that holds no amusement. "Young man, I appreciate your tenacity where my little Ghost is concerned, but I have no plans to harm her, I assure you."

"Then why was I sent on this mission?" Frankie ducks beneath my arm and approaches King. "Castle told me everything. We were sent here to die because you wanted to get rid of us. I can understand getting rid of him and Amber, but why me? What the fuck have I done that would warrant signing my life away?"

King rubs the thick stubble running along his jawline. "Is that what you think happened? You believed I orchestrated this to end your life?" He shakes his head and utters a single chuff.

"What was she supposed to assume?" I ask. "If everyone else was here to be eliminated, what was her purpose?"

"Unfortunately, it's not my place to say."

"Then whose place is it?" Frankie asks. "You're my director. If not you, then who?"

King shrugs his shoulders and clasps his hands together. "I'm not at liberty to say."

"Bullshit." Frankie ducks under my arm again, appearing seconds later with her badge in hand. She throws it at the man, and he winces as he catches it against his chest. "I quit. I'll send in my resignation letter the moment I return home. After that, wipe me from the system and forget I ever existed."

"That's not what I want, Ghost."

"Don't fucking call me that!"

He winces again. "I've come to offer you a promotion. The only catch—"

"Fuck you and your catches. God, I can't believe I ever looked up to you." With tears in her eyes, she pushes past

King and exits the cabin. I move to follow her, but he grips my arm and holds me in place.

"Let her go and give her some time," he says. "Jim told me you just want what's best for her, and we both know that means steering her back to her post. In fact, it's probably best you let me take it from here. I'll gather her things and—"

"Gather her things? What, you plan to kidnap her off the ship?" I yank my arm out of his hold. "No. I won't let you take her."

"The experiment had its desired effect, but she's gone a little too far into your world. Nothing we can't fix with a little reprogramming."

"A little . . . *reprogramming*?" I blink my eyes as if that will clear the cotton from my ears, because there's no way I heard him correctly. "She's not a fucking robot. She's a human being, and you aren't reprogramming shit."

He cocks his head and studies me. "Funny. You didn't seem to have a problem with it when you were sleeping with her. Wasn't that a form of reprogramming?" He sighs and shakes his head as he stuffs his hands into his pockets. "I wanted her to develop a compassion for the art of what you and your friends do. I never wanted her to become the artist."

"Why would you want her to have compassion for us?"

"To make her better at her job. Her bloody mother kept her locked away in a tall tower." His mask cracks, and the frustration shows through. "She's the reason Frankie never received any field assignments, which means she lacked the necessary experience for the jobs she'd have been best at. I saw her potential, and when I created my division a few years ago, Frankie was the first prospect on my radar. Sending her on this trip wasn't my decision, however. This was miles above my head. Using my connections, I did what I could to protect her. You have to see that."

The fight drains from my body because I see it. He's telling the truth. Jim wouldn't have given him carte blanche on this ship unless he trusted him, and I also realize King and I aren't so different. He wants the same thing I do. For Frankie to be happy.

We both know this life won't bring her that.

"What do you need me to do?" I ask.

"I was hoping I could bring you around. Jim was right about you."

As he drapes his arm over my shoulder and leads me to the balcony, my stomach is already swaying. Before he even has a chance to speak, I know what he's about to say. I know what I'll be asked to do.

And because I know it's the right thing for Frankie, I'll do it.

Frankie

Tears soak my cheeks as I hide in an alcove and cry like the little bitch that I am. I'm supposed to be made of tougher stuff than this, but it seems I'll always melt under pressure. My strength can only carry me so far, and I've reached the outer limits.

The implications of King's words grind salt into festering wounds. I grimace and open my mouth in a silent scream. I envy women who cry loudly. My emotional pain yearns for a voice.

It's the finality of it all that's affecting me so much. I planned to quit when we got back, but seeing King just set me off. Being reminded of the way the department used me and lied to me struck a match beside a powder keg, and there would be no more waiting. I had to rip off the Band-Aid and allow the explosion to occur.

But if quitting was the right decision, why do I feel so terrible?

Wrapping my arms around my midsection, I clutch

myself and try to slow the rapid beat of my heart by breathing in through my nose and out through my mouth. It's not working. The finality of tossing the ashes of my life off the side of a cliff has registered, and I feel as if I'm grieving.

I glance at the clock above the bar in the lounge across from my hiding place. Twenty minutes have passed since I raced out of the room. Surely Maverick has run King off by now, and I can think of no better place to heal than in my lover's arms.

After a quick stop by a bathroom to splash some water on my swollen eyes, I hurry to the elevator and make a beeline for the room. The sooner I can take a deep breath and feel safe, the better.

When I enter the cabin, Maverick is seated on the bed, facing the balcony overlooking the ocean. The parted curtains let the afternoon sunshine into the room. In the distance, a small boat ferries a group of people toward a gaggle of jet skis. They're too far away to make out details, but I hope it's the girls. And I hope they're having an amazing time. I'm a little sad that I missed out, but there will be other trips.

Thinking of what I have to look forward to in my new life softens the blow a little, but fuck, this still hurts.

I step closer to the bed. "Where'd the asshole go?"

"He went to see Jim." Maverick doesn't turn around as he answers me, and I don't like the flat tone of his voice. "Said he'd be in his room when you were ready to depart."

"He's lost his mind if he thinks I'm going anywhere with him. Even if he didn't send the order down the pipe, he could have told me the truth about the mission." I open the closet to grab my bag, but it isn't there. "Where's my shit?"

"King already loaded your things into the helicopter."

I roll my eyes and go to the bed. "Well, he can unload them. I'm not leaving this ship until the final—"

"You should accept the promotion."

I drop onto the bed and bury my face in a pillow so I can scream. "Why won't anyone listen when I speak? I don't want to be a fed anymore. I want to be a fucking serial killer, and I'm not changing my mind!"

He finally turns to face me, and I don't like that look in his eyes. I don't even recognize him. "You want to be a serial killer because I've made you believe I have feelings for you. In truth, I don't. Like you, I was simply following orders from a superior, and now that the mission is over, I can stop pretending."

"Maverick, you don't mean that." I sit up and laugh because if I don't, I'll cry. "I profile people for a living. I can tell when someone is lying."

"I do mean it, Frankie." He turns back to the window. "Let's stop pretending now. For both our sakes."

Tears prick my eyes again, but I swallow them down. "You are so full of shit. My pussy is still sore from you dicking me down a few hours ago, so don't try to feed me some bullshit about how you don't have feelings for me. I'm not stupid. You're trying to do something you feel is selfless, but you're only hurting both of us."

"I'm sorry you're struggling to accept—"

"Fuck you!" I throw the pillow at his head, and he rocks forward when it connects with the back of his skull. It's not enough, so I grab another and start beating him with it. "Fuck you, fuck you, *fuck you!*"

He sits stoically and takes his beating, which does nothing to dissipate the rage roiling through my veins. I want him to hurt as badly as I hurt right now, but his face is a blank mask. Short of stabbing him to death, I don't know what I can do that will allow him to feel what I'm feeling. Because this heartbreak feels like dying.

"You want me to leave? Fine. I'll fucking leave." I get off the bed and smooth my shirt, giving him a few extra seconds to change his mind. When he keeps staring at the water, I realize I'm fighting a losing battle. Maybe he's telling the truth and this was all imagined on my end.

With my heart shattering into millions of pieces, I turn and leave the cabin again. I pause just outside the door and close my eyes, all while screaming in my head. I mentally beg him to come for me, to save me from the anguish.

He doesn't.

My life is currently in pieces, and if Maverick won't help me put the pieces back together, I'll just have to do it myself.

And it starts with King.

With each step I take toward Jim's room, a bit more confidence ebbs into me. The pieces of armor fall into place, and the emotional pain recedes to make way for the stoicism my line of work requires. I shift, becoming the unfeeling creature I guess I'm forced to remain.

Maybe it's for the best. Feeling things hasn't exactly worked out for me.

I take the elevator and wind through corridors until I can rap my knuckles against the large wooden door. Jim says I may enter, and as I step into the room, I'm assaulted by a thick cloud of cigar smoke. King and Jim recline in large leather chairs by a fake fireplace. Each man clutches a long cigar, which they seem to chew more than smoke.

"Frankie, my dear girl," Jim says as he sits forward. "Come, take a seat, take a seat." He motions toward a delicate pink chaise lounge against the wall.

I stroll toward it and sit, all while wishing I'd worn my

black pantsuit to this meeting. It's hard to take myself seriously when I'm dressed in a baggy shirt and joggers, but I didn't exactly have a choice since someone spirited away my things.

"Have you had a chance to think about the promotion?" King asks. He plucks a glass of something golden from the side table and swirls the liquid. "If you're concerned about things you've done on the trip, consider it water under the bridge."

"And what if I want to keep doing these things?"

King sips his drink, then slides the glass onto the table. "I was hoping you'd find these activities less than desirable, but given your breeding, I suppose this was to be expected."

"My breeding?"

"Your father," Jim says. "Terrible business, that."

"Terrible . . ." I look between them. "Do you know who my father is?"

King sits forward now. "Of course we do. You'll find there isn't much we don't know."

"Who is he?"

"If you want to know that, you'll have to ask your mother. In fact, I think you'll find she has the answers to so *many* of your questions." King drags his finger around the lip of the glass on the side table. "I hear she's quite cunning."

"You're that high up in the bureau, and you've only *heard* of my mother?" My eyebrow rises. "Why don't I believe you?"

"Oh, we've spoken a few times." He smirks and raises his glass toward me. "Do you drink, Frankie?"

"Where are my manners?" Jim stands and fetches another glass. While he's busy at the side table, King leans forward and speaks softly.

"I apologize for getting you here under a guise, but it really was the best way to give you the insight you need. This decision wasn't made lightly, Frankie. When you learn who your father is . . ." He shakes his head and leans back in his seat. "You'll need friends when you fall from high places, and I was merely setting you up with a soft place to land."

"Can you stop being so goddamn cryptic and just come out with it? Who the fuck is my father? Why the fuck was I sent here? You say you went along with it, but who sent the order? And if I wasn't meant to die—"

"Tell her that part, at the very least," Jim says as he places the glass into my hand.

"You don't think it best she hears everything from the nag herself?" King asks.

Jim blows out a breath and drops into his chair. "Maybe not that bit, old man, but it all ties together too tightly to untangle now, doesn't it?"

I'm not a big drinker, but I'd chug a bottle of vintage *Ball*inger if it were in my hand right now. Anything to ease the burgeoning annoyance in my soul. I tip back the drink and swallow the liquid in two gulps.

"You're driving the poor thing to drink," Jim says with a cluck of his tongue.

"I'm glad you two find this so entertaining." I stand and move to the side table to pour another glass of something strong. "Meanwhile, this is my fucking life. You send me here and completely upend my world, then swoop in and expect it to turn right-side up again."

"Maybe not right-side up," King says. "More like giving you a new perspective. You can stroll along a slightly tilted axis while remaining upright, you know. How do you think I've managed for so long?"

I knock back another glass, then fill a third. "So you're a killer too? Will wonders never fucking cease."

"Does that bother you? Considering your new hobbies, I wouldn't think it would." King studies me over the rim of his drink.

A wave of dizziness sweeps through me, and I push the glass aside. I've had enough—in more ways than one.

"Whatever. None of this matters. I came here to tell you —" I go to take a step forward and nearly fall when my legs don't want to cooperate. Gripping the edge of the table, I gather myself and wobble to the chaise lounge. "I came here to tell you I meant what I said. I quit, and I have no desire to continue my employment. I—"

The room spins, and I nearly collapse on the small couch. I take a seat and suck in a deep breath as I try to appear more composed than I feel.

"I suppose I can give her that much." King's voice filters through a haze as a black vignette creeps over my eyes. He leans closer, and his dark eyes become pits I'm falling into. When his voice comes out in a ragged whisper, the words freeze the blood in my veins. "You weren't sent here to die, Ghost. You were sent as bait."

Chapter Forty-Three

Maverick

Normies and Sinners alike crowd the upper deck as the helicopter rises from a higher plateau and shrinks before disappearing over the horizon. Everyone else came out to be nosy. I came out to say goodbye.

King was right. The only thing tying her so tightly to this lifestyle has been me. I'd begun imagining her in our world, but she doesn't belong here. It would be like keeping a dolphin on dry land. Sure, she can breathe oxygen, but she'll eventually become a dry, screaming, miserable husk of what she once was.

Frankie is a fed. It's in her blood. I am a killer. It's in my blood. We were never meant to be.

Ice Pick stands nearby, a beer in his right hand as he leans over the railing and spits on the lower deck. If anyone can understand my heartbreak, it's him, so I hurry to join him. Misery loves company, after all.

"How you holding up, buddy?" I ask as I slap my palm

against his back. "Maybe we could go to the bar this evening and do a little prowling?" I have zero desire to prowl for anything, but playing wingman doesn't sound so bad.

He takes a swig of beer and smacks his lips. "No can do, I'm afraid. You remember the brunette that was fighting for me on the beach?"

I nod.

"Turns out, she's definitely not a fed. We've got a date tonight." He laughs and wiggles his eyebrows at me. "Looks like someone's in for three inches of *hard* rain tonight."

"Oh, wow . . . good for you, man." I clap him on the back again and try to get the mental image of his hard "rain" out of my head.

He glances past me, then looks the other direction. "Where's Frankie? She's really good at judging people just by talking to them for a second, and I want her opinion."

"She, uh . . . She went home, Ice. I don't think we'll be seeing her again."

"Yeah, right. The way she looks at you? I don't think wild horses will keep her away."

Well, this definitely isn't helping me feel any better.

Cat, Bennett, and Eve sit on the lounge chairs a few feet away. Eve gives me a wave when she spots me, and I leave Ice Pick in hopes of calmer waters. I head over to the trio and take a seat at the foot of Eve's chair.

"How'd the jet ski rides go?" I ask.

Bennett kisses Cat's shoulder and whispers something in her ear, seemingly oblivious to my question. Cat giggles and pushes his head away before turning to me.

"We had a good time. Bennett's just being a perv now because watching me kill turns him on." She giggles again and removes his hand, which was creeping up her thigh. "Where's Frankie? We missed you guys."

"We waited as long as we could before taking off," Eve adds.

I squeeze the back of my neck. It seems I'll have to answer this question everywhere I go. Luckily, Grim, Rose, and Kindra appear further down the deck, with Ezra hot on their heels. If I can get everyone in one place, maybe I can just say it once more and be done with it.

"There's something you guys should know about Frankie," I say, trying to stall a little to give everyone time to get here.

Eve flicks her hair over her shoulder, then straightens the crooked strap of her bikini top. "What, she's a fed? Honey, we already knew that. I clocked her the moment I met her."

"How did you . . . ?" I blink, completely taken aback.

Cat laughs. "How did you *not* know?"

"What, that Frankie was an agent?" Kindra says as they approach us. "We kind of figured."

"Did everyone know?" I ask.

Rose nods and signs something to Grim, and he relays the message to the rest of us. "Yes, as Rose says, only a man without eyes would have missed it."

The smile drops from Eve's face. "Don't tell me you broke it off when she told you."

"No, I knew from the beginning. Jim set me up to protect her, so I've spent the entire time trying to keep her identity a secret." I squeeze my neck again to relieve the tension trapped in my muscles. "I figured if you guys knew, you'd try to kill her. Or worse, you'd ostracize her."

Ezra scoffs. "We let Bennett hang around. A federal agent can't be worse than *him*."

Everyone laughs at that, even Bennett. Everyone but me. Frankie feared the girls wouldn't like her anymore once they knew the truth, and to be honest, I thought the same. Now I see that none of that mattered to them.

But this was for the best, and I know my friends will understand too.

"So where is she? Hopefully she isn't hiding because she's worried about what we'll think, the poor dear," Cat says. "Should we keep the jokes to a minimum? Is she sensitive about it? Gosh, I hope we haven't fucked up and upset her in any way."

I shake my head and take a deep breath. "No, I'm sure she had no hard feelings when she left."

"Left?" the girls say in unison.

"What the fuck do you mean, when she *left*?" Eve nearly shouts at me.

I explain what happened with King, how he showed up to take her home, complete with a shiny new promotion. No detail is spared, including my feelings about how this is best for her and how much it's hurting me. The last part isn't easy, especially since the guys are here. Grim eventually wanders off, made too uncomfortable once the talk turns to feelings.

"But you told her how you feel about her, right?" Kindra asks. "I mean, you confessed all this to her and let her decide, and this is the choice she made, so there's really no reason for you to feel bad."

Ezra drops his hand to my shoulder and gives it a hard squeeze. "Bad business, that. But as Kindra said, you told her how you feel. If that wasn't enough for her, good riddance."

"Well, no," I admit. "I worried if I told her how I felt, it might manipulate her into—"

Hands smack me from all sides.

"Are you fucking stupid?" Cat shouts.

"Have our late-night talks taught you nothing?" Eve demands.

Kindra shakes her head. "I am so disappointed in you."

Even Rosie speaks volumes with the scowl on her face.

"Really stupid move, kid," Bennett says with a shake of his head. "Even I knew enough to pour out my heart when it really mattered."

I scoot away from the group and turn to face them. I'm beginning to feel like a wounded wildebeest surrounded by a pride of hungry lions. They each take nips, but I'm already bleeding. I have no fight left.

"I'm glad to know each of you would have made better decisions, but these are the choices I made, and I'm happy with them. If you knew how much her career meant to her, you'd understand." Emotions bubble beneath my skin, but I push them down. "This was for the best. It wasn't an easy call to make, but I fucking made it."

Eve shakes her head. "Honey, sometimes it's best to let people make that call themselves. You might not regret keeping your feelings hidden right now, but you will."

"Well, we'll just have to fix this when we get back," Kindra says with a flick of her wrist. "Ezra can find her. Then we'll all tell her the truth. That Maverick is a massive idiot who self-sabotages because it's easier to hurt himself than to allow someone else the opportunity."

My jaw drops. "That's not—"

"I can back that up," Eve says with a nod.

My eyes widen. "You're supposed to be on my side!"

"Are there any feds still alive on this vessel?" Ezra asks. "We could grill them for more info about her. Might make it easier to track her down."

Bennett nods. "Good idea. I'll ask—"

"Wait!" I hold up my hands in a physical attempt to

stop the insanity. Their heads turn to me, and I'm grateful when their mouths close. "Guys, Frankie was the best and worst thing to ever happen to me. She showed me what I'm capable of having, but she also showed me why it's best I don't have it. This is better for her."

Eve places a hand on my arm. "That's why we want to help. We've seen how happy she makes you. You're the sunshine in everyone else's day, so it was nice to see you get blasted with the radioactive rays for once."

"I appreciate it, more than you guys realize, but . . . let it go. For me."

The group heaves a collective sigh, then murmurs their agreement. They'll drop it.

Now I just have to figure out how to let it go myself.

Chapter Forty-Four

Frankie

Time is a funny thing. I've been back in Virginia for over a week, but it feels like months have passed. Being sequestered in a government facility for one hell of a debrief tends to have that effect, I suppose. Now my jail sentence is coming to an end.

King has been nothing but kind, and I regret my cold demeanor toward him on the ship. I also regret that he was forced to drug me, which gave me a nasty headache for hours after waking, but at least my good sense has begun to return.

And now I realize that Maverick was right.

As I stepped into my pantsuit and smoothed the white undershirt a few hours ago, I cloaked myself in the familiar armor that reminds me who I am, and I am a federal agent. King has been helping me remember that. When I arrived at my room, all the cases I've worked to a successful outcome were laid on the bed. Filtering through the paperwork was a swift slap to the face, but King's words were a balm to the wound.

"We all have a place in the food chain. Some of us were meant to focus on the prey. Some were meant to focus on the predator."

We are the shepherds. The average citizens are the livestock we must protect. Those who would kill the livestock are the wolves, but those who kill the wolves? The killers we let slip through our fingers are the livestock guardians, and they are the people who I will miss more than I have any right to.

But now I understand why we let some of them go.

King has explained a lot in that tiny room over the course of the last few days. Everything I learned about the plan was correct. Ten agents had been sent to their deaths so that their respective departments could sweep out the trash. When King saw that my name had been added to the list, he initially planned to remove me. That's when he found out why I'd been sent, and by whom, and he decided it was best to let me go.

King and I never had many interactions before this assignment, but he was someone I'd always admired. My view of King changed on the ship, and he became someone I hated, but my view of him shifted once more with each meal we shared in my room. Both versions were incorrect in my mind, and the real King is someone I neither admire nor hate, but I respect him. The admiration will return, I'm sure. Especially since I've decided to take the promotion.

It wasn't an easy decision, but Maverick was correct in more ways than one. My fast attachment to him clouded my mind, but he helped clear the fog in the end. His cruelty was a kindness. I see that now. It doesn't lessen the hurt, but time heals all wounds, right?

I'm currently preparing to heal a wound right now. I sit at a vanity in my tiny jail cell—a locked bedroom in a secret government facility—applying makeup as King stands behind me and tries to give me the last pieces of the puzzle in his grasp. Well, the pieces he's willing to part with. He still skirts certain questions, telling me my mother will need to provide those answers.

"When I did a bit more digging, I discovered your decidedly dark lineage. Have you ever heard of the Butcher of Greenthorn?"

I lower the mascara and glare at him in the mirror. "The British serial killer in the seventies who slaughtered three families? *That's* my fucking father?"

"What about the Witch of Windsor?"

My eyebrows pull together. "Wait, that's a woman. Are you saying I'm adopted?"

King tips his head back and laughs. "I'm saying your father is such a notorious killer that he has many names. He's prolific in ways you can't imagine. But that's why I chose to send you on the cruise. I allowed you to go so that I could move you up in my particular division. It was important for me to know you could work with killers. But I also had to know if you had the same . . . sickness as your father."

I nibble my lip and look at the floor. "If that was the test, I'll be honest and tell you I failed pretty miserably. I . . . killed Castle."

"And enjoyed it?"

A pain grips my heart as my ugliness is laid bare. "Yeah."

"What did you enjoy about it?" He takes a seat in a side chair, looking like a therapist settling in to pick my brain apart. "*Why* was it enjoyable?"

"Because he was a piece of shit," I mutter. "He hurt

people. He tried to hurt me, but he didn't get far. Maverick bashed the door in and—"

My throat closes off as the memory grips me in a chokehold. The fear doesn't prevail, though. I'm stifled by the memory of Maverick's beautiful face and the rage reflected in his green eyes. I'm silenced by the anguish of the feelings I still have for him.

Was it really all pretend?

"Maverick stopped him," I finish.

King nods. "Well, there's your answer. You killed for a pretty good reason. It's the same reason for most of my kills."

"Most?"

An alarm blares from King's phone, and he raises the device to shut it off. "It's time," he says. "Just remember what we discussed. No matter how you feel when you learn the truth, you do not have authorization to take a kill. Do you understand?"

I smirk and roll my eyes. "Whatever she has to say, I doubt I'll want to kill her, King. She's my mother."

I pull the black sedan into a parking spot toward the back of Deluca's. King thought it best I not drive my flashy red sports car, though he wouldn't say why. My mother should be expecting me, so it's not as if my arrival will surprise her. Before I left for the cruise, we settled on a time and a place.

My hand moves to the pistol on my hip, but it isn't there. Another one of King's conditions. It seems his trust in my willpower has slipped, but he has nothing to fear.

Nothing my mother says will make me want to kill her. She's all I've ever had, and while she isn't the most feeling person, I know she feels the same about me.

A hostess greets me in the front room of the large manor that's been transitioned into an Italian restaurant. My mother and I eat here often enough that I recognize her, but she seems shocked to see me.

"Table for two in the Peacock Room?" I say with a smile.

She smiles back and grabs a menu before leading me down the parquet hallways until we reach a large wooden door. Pushing it open, she reveals a lavish room that feels more familiar to me than my bedroom at home. Royal-blue carpets cover the floor, and a massive painting of a peacock looms above a blue marble fireplace. It's too warm for a fire now, but in winter, it provides a romantic glow.

My mother isn't seated at the small table at the center of the room, but a single nearly empty wineglass whispers of her presence. She must have gone to the bathroom.

I thank the hostess and pluck the menu from her fingers before taking a seat. I get another shock when I spot the appetizer on the side table. It's a massive plate of fried zucchini blossoms. I hate those, and my mother knows it.

An uneasy feeling slides over me as I give my wine order to the waiter who appears seconds later. Despite setting this up before ever leaving the mainland, it appears my mother isn't expecting me.

When the waiter returns with my wine, he asks if I'd like to order anything while I wait. My appetite has taken a sudden downward turn, so I decline. Anxiety takes up too much space in my stomach for me to hold anything else. If I try, I'll likely expel it from one end or the other.

The door finally creaks open after several tense minutes, and my mother appears. She's too busy fussing with some stain on her camel-colored blouse to notice my presence, but when she finally looks up, I couldn't have prepared myself for the shock on her face. She looks as if she's seen a ghost. How fitting.

"I take it you weren't expecting me?" I try to temper my voice, but it comes out shaky. After clearing my throat, I try again, and I'm pleased when I sound more sure of myself. "We set the date in advance, and I never miss a date at Deluca's."

She schools her face, reining in the brief slip of emotion that is so unlike her. "I wasn't sure you'd return at all, but I'm glad you have. How was your trip?"

No smiles are forced on her end. She strides to the table and sits as if nothing is amiss.

"The trip was eventful. What I can't figure out is who sent me, though. King said it wasn't him."

"King said it wasn't him, huh? I'd like to meet that smug piece of shit and give him a swift kick in the ass."

"He said it wasn't his place to answer every question. He said I should ask you."

My mother scoops up her wineglass and downs the remains. "What does it matter now? You survived and you completed your mission."

"So why do you sound so disappointed?" My stomach lurches as the question fires from my mouth. I can't help it. King tried to warn me, and Jim even hinted that my mother is someone I'm not that familiar with, but experiencing it now is a shock to my system.

How long have I lived with this stranger? Why haven't I noticed her coldness before now? It has nothing to do with a lack of affection and everything to do with a lack of give a fuck. I've made excuses for this woman's unfeeling demeanor my entire life, and now I see her for what she truly is.

She glances around, looking anywhere but at me. "Where is the waiter? I need more wine."

"Mom, who sent me on the cruise?"

"I told you, none of this matters. I'm tired of the questions."

"Who sent me?"

She finally looks at me. "I did. I sent you. There. Are you happy?"

My world tries to tilt off of its axis, but I grip the table and hold steady. If I want answers, I'll need to keep my composure. "King said I was bait. Who were you trying to bait out? And why couldn't you tell me?"

"What does it matter now? It didn't work, did it? Daddy didn't come save his little lamb." With a guttural scream, she turns and launches her wineglass at the empty fireplace. The glass explodes when it connects with the marble. "I just want to see him once more, to ask him why I wasn't enough. Why wasn't I enough? Why?"

My grip on the table tightens. My mother sent me into a dangerous situation in an attempt to bait out my serial-killer father so that she could get some fucking *closure*? As a woman, I get it. That ghosting shit is fucking annoying. But did she ever love me as a daughter, or was I always her little bargaining chip?

"I never wanted a child. In fact, I made an appointment to get rid of you the moment I learned I had a filthy parasite inside me. That's when I learned your father's little secret. That he has a weakness, and it's his disgusting offspring."

She swipes her nose and shakes her head, sending her short gray hair wobbling. "He showed up at the clinic and begged me to keep you. It was the only time I saw fear in that man's eyes, though I never saw him again after that. Not for lack of trying."

"The . . . skydiving lessons weren't because you thought five-year-olds needed life experiences?"

My mother scoffs and folds her arms over her chest. "I'm surprised it took you this long to figure out that I've been putting you in harm's way as often as possible. And look what good it's done me. I have nothing to show for it, and you're still here."

I didn't see it because I didn't know I was supposed to look. A mother should care about her child. I took that at face value.

"Mom, I—"

"I think you can stop calling me that. Though I gave birth to you, I have no attachments, so you can free yourself from yours as well." She drops her forehead to the table and waves me away. "Leave. And tell the waiter to bring more wine."

Now I understand why King was adamant that I leave my service pistol behind. Now I know why he needed to remind me that taking this kill wouldn't be authorized. Because if that cruise taught me anything, it's that murder is definitely a fucking option.

The butter knife gleams, practically begging me to reach out and grab it so that I can ram it into my mother's spine. I suddenly wish I was back on the boat, with one million torture options at my disposal and a lack of moral compass for as far as the eye can see.

I rise to leave. That's when I hear a bit of shuffling within the massive wardrobe at the back of the room. My mother's head pops up from the table, and we're both shocked when Cat and Bennett stumble from the doors as they fly open.

"Lady, you're a real piece of shit," Bennett says, "and that's saying something, coming from me."

"What the fuck are you two doing in here?" a deep British voice demands.

All of us turn toward the flowing blue curtains draped over the window as Kindra and Ezra emerge from behind them. Kindra gives me a little wave.

"We could ask the same of you two," Cat says.

We nearly jump out of our skin as Eve's voice joins the party. "Can someone give me a hand? I'm wedged behind this weird purple sofa thing."

"What are all of you doing here?" I ask as I spin around and see all of my serial-killer friends.

"Honey, I don't know about the rest of them, but I showed up to kill this bitch." Eve clambers over the couch once Ezra and Bennett move it away from the wall. "Jim told us how she used you, and I had a friend of mine hack into her phone so I could learn her schedule. I paid the owner of this place a large chunk of my last paycheck so that I could hide out before she arrived."

"We've been in this wardrobe since last night," Cat says. "We had Ezra do a little digging, and that's how we learned she liked this place. She usually eats here every Wednesday."

"Since I already had the info, Kindra and I thought we'd stake it out today, not realizing everyone would show up." Ezra laughs and looks around.

Not everyone showed up, though. As I look around the room, one face is blatantly absent.

Eve realizes what I'm looking for, and she comes to my

side and places her hand on my shoulder. "He'll come around, honey. He just needs some time to realize that sometimes you can be both things."

"So I was right? He only said those things to—"

"To protect you," Maverick says.

The group spins to face the door as Maverick steps into the room. The air leaves my lungs as he moves toward me.

"I thought I had to hurt you to help you, but you were right. I was only hurting the both of us. I'm sorry I said you didn't mean anything to me. Frankie, you mean *everything* to me."

"You said she didn't mean anything to you? What the fuck were you thinking?" Eve shouts.

He ignores her and keeps looking into my eyes. "Jim finally told me everything. About your mother and what she did. About who your father is. I was foolish to think I knew best, and I never should have let you walk away without telling you everything first. So I'm telling you now. I'm crazy about you, sweetheart. You've opened doors I've kept shut for so long, and I want to walk through them with you. I can't change who I am and what I do, and I don't want to change anything about you, either. That was my fear. When I saw you getting excited over the kills, I worried we were changing you."

"What did you people expect?" my mother screeches from her seat. "Considering who donated her sperm, it shouldn't come as a shock. All of his spawn come out as killers. I've kept track of them, and at least two have given in to their urges." She sneers at me. "Well, I guess it's three now."

"I completely forgot this bitch was still in the room," Eve says with a sigh. "Can we kill her yet?"

"Not until she tells me who my father is." Nudging

Bennett out of the way, I stand beside the woman who gave me life. Despite literally being surrounded by serial killers, she shows no fear. She must know that King wouldn't authorize the kill. Or couldn't.

"I had to tip the valet. Am I late? What did I miss?" Jim says as he enters the room, and now our party feels complete.

"Tell me my father's name," I demand of my mother.

She scoffs and folds her arms over her chest, yet she says nothing.

"Why are you being so cagey now? Your little plan doesn't even make sense. If you changed my name so many times, how was my father supposed to know who I was?"

"He's an incredibly intelligent man. If I'd put the name Francesca on everything, he'd have seen right through my plan." She shakes her head and grits her teeth before continuing. "I had to make it look like I didn't want you found, but I knew he knew who you were. He always knew."

"Who is my father?" I ask again.

My mother raises her chin and licks her lips. "I'll never tell you. That secret will go with me to my grave."

"I wasn't asking you." I turn to face Jim. "Who is my father?"

Jim claps his hands and bounces on the tips of his toes. "Oh, goody! I was hoping she'd be her usual churlish self. If she won't tell you, then I feel it's my duty to do so."

"Madigan, if you tell her, I'll bury you. I have the evidence to do it." My mother's icy eyes level on Jim.

Jim blinks at her and smiles. "Oh, be quiet, witch. You have no power here. Our dear Frankie has a right to know that her last name isn't Grant or any of the other fabricated identities you've concocted over the years."

I take a deep breath as I prepare to hear the next words

out of Jim's mouth, but I'm still nearly knocked off my feet when he finally makes the big reveal.

"Her last name is one she's learned on this trip, for she shares it with two of our very own." Jim looks at me with a genuine smile, pride gleaming in his eyes. "Frankie, your last name is Carter."

Chapter Forty-Five

Maverick

Ezra's head turns toward Frankie, but Bennett's head swivels in my direction. I know what he's going to say before the words leave his angry mouth.

"You've been fucking my *sister*?" He chases me around the table as everyone else tries to process the news. "When I get my hands on you—"

Frankie steps into his path, stopping him. "Hey, I appreciate the familial backup, but I'm technically your *older* sister, so I don't need protecting."

"God, how did we ever miss it before now?" Ezra says as he steps closer to them, and he's right. The resemblance is uncanny, especially the eye shape and their noses—though I'm glad Frankie is decidedly still very feminine. If the resemblance were too spot on, I'd feel like I was fucking my guy friends.

The group crowds around, and congratulations are

shared at Frankie finding family on the day she lost her mother. Speaking of the hag, she sits at the table with a sour expression on her face. She stands to make her escape while everyone is occupied, but I step into her path before she can reach the door.

"Where do you think you're going?" I place a hand on her shoulder and spin her to face the mess she's created. "Surely you didn't think we'd just let you walk out of here. After what you've put my girl through, that isn't an option."

Frankie frowns as she looks at us. "Unfortunately, I don't have a choice. King wouldn't authorize the kill, so we have to let her walk."

Bennett clucks his tongue and steps beside his sister, which is still weird to say. I don't know how I'll ever get used to it. He drapes his thick arm over her shoulder and looks at her mother, who I hold in place.

"You're thinking of this the wrong way," Bennett says. "Sure, you'd need clearance from a superior to take a government-sanctioned kill, but you have the benefit of walking between two worlds here. As a fed, you answer to King, but as a Carter, you answer to someone else."

Realization dawns in Frankie's eyes, and she shifts her gaze from her mother to the man standing off to the side. "Jim, permission to kill Monica Grant?"

Jim rocks on his heels with a wide smile on his face. "Permission granted."

"What? No! You don't have the power to do that!" Frankie's mother drops to the floor, and I'm not sure if it was intentional or if her legs ceased to work. She scrambles for the door, crawling on her hands and knees. "She's my daughter. She won't kill me!"

She doesn't believe her own words. That much is clear from the frantic way she struggles with the knob, which Jim must have locked—or had someone else lock—behind him. Like a pack of jackals, we descend, closing her in on all sides.

"Your daughter?" Frankie shakes her head as she looks down at the woman. "I think you can stop calling me that now. Though you gave birth to me, I have no attachments, so you can free yourself from yours as well."

With a wild look in her eyes, Frankie's mother spins to face us. "You'll regret this. All of you. I'm not like your usual victims. I'm important!"

"I learned something on my trip," Frankie says. "You have surrounded yourself with a whole lot of nothing. No friends. No lover. Now you don't even have a daughter. No, I'd say you're about as unimportant as it gets."

I chuckle. "Damn, sweetheart. That's cold."

"Yes, well, I'm only giving her what she gave me for the entirety of my childhood. Ice. Distance. A complete lack of emotion." Frankie shrugs and looks her mother up and down. "Experiencing a little warmth has a way of opening eyes."

"He'll leave you too," her mother says. "Just like your father left me. You're only perpetuating the cycle. They're incapable of love!"

"No, mother. That's you."

Frankie raises a butter knife she'd kept hidden in her hand. She brings it down, ramming it deep into her mother's chest. The woman clutches the inches of silver remaining outside her body and slumps against the door. With wide eyes, she crumples to the floor.

There are no parting words, no death-bed confessions. Her mother gasps a few times, and then she's gone. She takes an oppressive air with her, but she leaves behind a final smell that could clear a cattle barn.

Bennett gags as we all take a step away from the body. "Jesus wept. What the fuck did this bitch eat for her last meal? It smells like she's been dead for a week already."

"I thought I was done puking," Cat groans.

Frankie rubs her arms and looks down at the body. "I guess she couldn't keep the rot inside anymore." Her nose wrinkles, and she covers her mouth. "Fuck, that really is bad. Let's get out of here."

Jim unlocks the door, and we file out of the room, careful to step over the corpse. Once we're in the hall and away from the smell, I grab Frankie's arm and hold her back as the rest of the group leaves the manor restaurant in a flurry of excitement.

"I meant what I said," I whisper. "I was wrong for lying to you about how I felt. Can you forgive me?"

She nibbles her bottom lip and smiles. "I'm not okay with the way you handled things, but I won't stop you from trying to make it up to me." She steps into me and walks her fingers up my chest. When she reaches my neck, her hand slithers behind my head and pulls me closer. "You can start by kissing me."

More than happy to oblige, I press my lips to hers, and my world feels complete again. "I'm sorry I ever doubted you. If you want to be a killer, I won't try to stop you."

"That's the most beautiful part." Her blue eyes glisten as she looks up at me. "King's division is essentially made up of sympathizers—people who work with and turn a blind eye to certain serial killers. I'm free to explore my new hobby as long as I stick to some guidelines. Oddly enough, they're the same rules you guys already live by."

"I just didn't want to change you."

She shrugs. "Maybe change isn't always a bad thing.

The road I was on wasn't a good one. I was becoming my mother, and that isn't what I want for my life."

"And what do you want?"

Frankie glances at the watch on her wrist and sighs. "Right now? An orgasm. How much time do you have?"

"I was due to get on a plane in a few hours, headed for Texas to look for the missing Carter sister, but I think the trip is off now."

Frankie looks down the hall, toward the door to the restaurant's sprawling front lawn. "Right. I have . . . brothers. That feels so weird. And they've been looking for me?"

"Well, they've been looking for Luisa G., and I'm really hoping that's you."

She smiles and shakes her head. "My mother had this planned from the start. Luisa on the birth certificate. Eileen on the social security card."

"It worked. You weren't even in Texas." I shake my head and laugh. "Looks like you gained a lot on this trip, though. Some family and friends. A new hobby. A promotion."

"A boyfriend?"

I smile down at her and plant a kiss on her nose. "Yes, you gained one of those too. You'll have to be patient with me, though. I've never done this before."

"We can figure it out together." She stands on her tiptoes and places a kiss on my lips.

The manor door swings open, and Eve peeks through the gap. "Jim made reservations at that hot new restaurant in Miami. You guys in?"

"Miami? Why would we drive for hours just to eat?" Frankie looks up at me.

"The perks of Jim's private jet. Unless . . . you wanna get some takeout and show me your place?" I wiggle my eyebrows at her. "I think that orgasm is very possible."

"We'll take a raincheck!" Frankie calls toward Eve.

Eve giggles and closes the door, but not before Bennett shouts something about me keeping my hands off his sister.

"He'll get used to it," I say to Frankie.

"He'd better," she says as she looks up at me. "I don't plan on going anywhere."

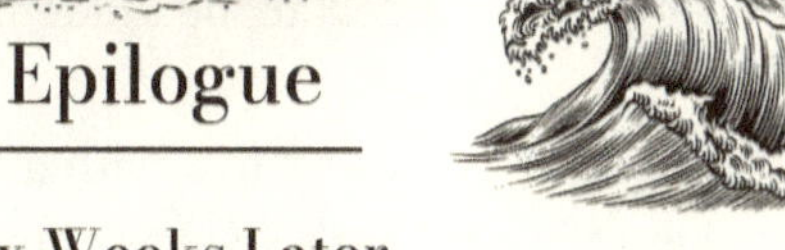

Epilogue

Six Weeks Later

Frankie

The donation truck pulls away from the curb, filled with all the things that remind me of my mother. When I move in with Maverick and Eve, I'll paint every wall in their apartment with a splash of color, just to keep that woman's memory at bay. But I guess I need to stop calling it *their* apartment. It's ours now. I signed the lease last week, and King okayed the move to New York with his blessing. Remote work isn't unheard of in these post-Covid settings, after all.

The Midnight Masochist and I have gotten very close since that fateful dinner. He's divulged his painful histories to me, and I now know the full story behind his scar. I shared my strange upbringing—all the little things I once thought were my mother's quirks. Now I know they were merely ways to put me in danger to try and bring my father out of the woodwork. Too bad it didn't work.

Maverick pulls into the driveway as I'm turning to lock up. The house holds no fond memories, so I'm happy to leave. All the memories I need wait somewhere in the future.

"Hey, sweetheart. Need a ride?" he says through the lowered window of my red sports car. He looks amazing behind the wheel.

"More like I need to be ridden," I mutter under my breath.

It's a wonder I don't live with a constant UTI, considering how often we fuck. It's been almost six hours since our last session, and I'm ready to go again.

After locking the door for the last time, I hurry to the car and slide into the passenger's side. Much like our sex life, we take turns being in the driver's seat. We like it this way.

"Did Jim tell you what he bought?" I ask.

Maverick shakes his head and backs out of the driveway. "No, you know how he is. I'm just glad he didn't try to rope me into this one. I've had just about enough of his schemes."

I buckle my seatbelt as he pulls off the side street and onto the main road. "Hey, that's no fair. I just joined the crew, so you can't stop going to the events now. I'm already ready for whatever comes next."

"Oh, not to worry. We'll definitely attend whatever he plans." He slides his hand onto my thigh and gives it a squeeze. "I'm just glad we'll be there as guests instead of test subjects this time."

After a few more turns, we arrive at Deluca's. Dining here seemed a fitting goodbye to Virginia and my old life. Jim even booked the Peacock Room, though he requested a larger table for our party. It'll be nice to share the meal with family and friends.

Inside the restaurant, we find everyone already waiting. King and Jim hover by the fireplace, sipping golden drinks and chatting. Cat and Bennett whisper and grin as they peruse the menu. I wonder if they're talking about how to use the different dishes in the bedroom. Kindra, Ezra, and Eve look up as we enter, all three of them wearing the biggest smiles. I'm still getting used to this, but it's a good feeling, even if it's a little awkward.

"She's here. Can you finally tell us about your big purchase?" Bennett asks Jim as he pushes the menu away from him.

A mischievous gleam flits through Jim's eyes as he grins at us. "Are you sure that's the secret you want to pluck from the box? I recently came into possession of a much juicier tidbit."

"Can't you give them both?" King sips his drink, then shakes his head. "What am I saying? Where's the fun in that?"

The two men laugh at their little inside joke. It's strange to see King laugh at all, but I've seen a side of him that most in the department will never witness, not even the select trustees in our division. We're part of an inner circle that most couldn't understand.

"I'll be kind and let them choose. We'll take a vote," Jim says, and we all groan. "Don't be spoilsports, now. The choice is a simple one. Do you want to hear more about my recent acquisition, or would you like to learn a tasty little secret we recovered from Frankie's mother's laptop?"

Personally, I'm finished hearing about my mother's dirty dealings. She was a woman obsessed. Her every waking moment was filled with the search for my father. She tracked his trail all over Europe and Asia, finding evidence of his work as recently as three years ago. That must have been why she took that trip to the Alps a couple of years back. She thought she was close to finding him.

Maybe King and Jim finished her life's work for her.

Everyone around the table seems to come to this conclusion as well. Their eyes turn to me, realizing that what Jim knows might have something to do with my father's location.

"Don't look at me," I say. "I'm not the only one who has a dog in the fight. He's their father too." I motion between Ezra and Bennett. "I have no desire to know a man who had no desire to know me, but they deserve a say."

Ezra shifts uncomfortably in his seat, but he says nothing. Kindra places a hand on his arm in a show of support.

"I'm with Frankie," Bennett says. "He hasn't made an effort, so I really don't give a shit about meeting him. We found our sister, and that's all I cared about."

My heart squeezes in my chest. Having brothers has been an interesting experience. It's something I didn't know I'd been missing, but those two men have filled an empty space in my soul. They all have. Kindra, Cat, and Eve have become like sisters. Jim and King are the fathers I never had. The void created by my mother has been filled to the point of bursting.

Ezra nods and adjusts his glasses on his nose. "They're right. I think it's more difficult for me because he came around when I was young. He took me to Dover." He clears his throat as emotion overcomes him. "But I can't remember his voice. I know he spoke to me, but I can't recall what was said. His face is a blank slate, and I don't know that I need to change that."

Eve shrugs. "Then it's settled. Tell us about the next trip!"

"Are you sure? No take-backsies . . ." Jim rocks on his heels, dragging out the anticipation as Maverick and I take a seat at the table. When no one budges, he and King join us at the table as well. "Very well. If the decision is made, then I'm happy to inform all of you that this fall, we'll be enjoying a week at Laughter Park."

Cat sputters on her glass of water. "The amusement park that closed down six years ago? What are we gonna do on a bunch of abandoned rides?"

"Wait, that's just off the Carolina coast. Isn't it a bit risky to operate so close to the unsuspecting public?" I pause, giving Jim time to answer, but the door swings open and a familiar figure steps into the room. "Gary?"

The little bug-eyed man is hard to mistake, what with all his scars and that spiked hair that shows his scalp. His skull is a bit misshapen on one side now, and I feel a bit guilty about that.

Ezra and Bennett jump from the table, nearly knocking it down with their enthusiasm. A steak knife gleams in Ezra's fist, but I don't know what Bennett expects to accomplish with that breadbasket. Not wanting to find out, I leap from my seat and stand in front of the terrified man as everything clicks into place.

"He's not who you think he is!" I shout at my brothers. "You snatched him by mistake. You were after his twin!"

The men lower their weapons and look at each other.

"Twin?" Ezra asks. "That's impossible."

"It's the truth. You can ask Jim!" Gary peeks out from behind me. "Ezra, when you mentioned that football game at the bar, you were talking about my brother. I never did anything great like he did. I never scored a touchdown or even had any friends to invite me to a poker game. When you said all that, I lied because I was excited to see what it was like to be popular. My name . . . isn't even Gary."

Jim explains Gary's ordeal, and the men burst into another argument. Ezra keeps saying it's impossible, that he would never make that sort of mistake. Bennett laments that it doesn't matter and he just wants to end his life.

King taps his wineglass, calling for order. "It happens to the best of us, lads. Sometimes we get it wrong. Nothing to do now but accept it and move on."

"That's why I came in here," Gary says. He gathers his courage and steps out from behind me. "I know how much you guys wanted to kill me because you thought I was my brother."

"Pretty bold of him to assume that's why *I* wanted to kill him," Bennett mutters.

"I wanted to help," Gary adds. "Jim has done a lot for me, and I wanted to show you guys that I'm not mad about what happened. So, I convinced my brother I wanted to patch things up. He's right outside."

As a group, we stand from the table and follow the little man to the front lawn. We pour from the building as a group and spot Gary's carbon copy in the circular drive. He gives his brother a little wave, then gets a bit nervous when he sees the crowd behind him.

"Long time no see." He holds his hand out to Gary, who doesn't accept the handshake. He lowers his hand and clears his throat. "I, uh . . . Who are all these people?"

Gary turns to us. "Do you want to kill him here, or should we take him inside?"

"We usually don't announce our plans, old chap, but here is fine. Jim has the staff on payroll now." Ezra takes a step toward the man.

Gary's brother flinches and takes a step back. "Kill me? What are you talking about? You said you wanted to have dinner and catch up. I flew all the way to Virginia for this."

"We'll be sure to pay for your return trip," I say. "In a pine box, of course."

Eve and Kindra chuckle beside me.

Something cold slides into my palm, and I look down as Ezra pushes the steak knife into my grasp. "You should do it," he says.

"The fuck she should!" Bennett bellows. "Gary was my kill to take on the island, so this is my kill to take now."

"She hasn't gotten to kill as much as we have. Let her have a turn," Ezra says.

Bennett groans and turns to Jim. "Tell them it's my turn! Ezra can't go back on his deal."

"Settle down, children, settle down." Jim points toward the woods. "No one will get the chance to kill him if he gets away."

We turn and look as Gary's brother disappears into the trees.

"Get him!" I shout, and we take off running.

Like a pack of wolves, we race through the woods in pursuit of a kill. I glance to my side with a breathless smile. Maverick runs beside me, hyper-focused on the stumpy-legged man tootling away from us. To my right and just behind me, the girls give chase with giggles and feminine war cries. My brothers continue bickering as they pick their way through the thick brush, and Jim and King bring up the rear.

Maverick sees an opening and darts forward to tackle the man to the ground. The girls descend, each of them taking a limb and pinning it to the leaf litter.

"He's mine!" Bennett yells as he comes to a stop. He holds up a finger, then plants his hands on his knees. "Just as soon as I catch my breath."

The man writhes on the ground, bucking beneath the women like a demon being doused with holy water. If his head starts to spin as pea soup spews from his asshole, I won't be surprised.

"Take the kill," Maverick says beside me.

I shake my head. "I just found my brothers. I'm not about to piss one off now."

"He's giving it to you," Cat whispers. "He's not really out of breath. He's just incapable of openly being a nice guy. We're working on it."

Despite the whispering, Bennett hears her. He purses his lips and stops pretending he can't breathe. With a scowl, he stands upright, folds his arms over his chest, and looks away. "Merry Christmas."

I grip the knife a little tighter and look back at Maverick. He's told me he doesn't care that I've chosen to be a killer, but that hasn't been tested yet. I've been too busy acclimating to my new position at work to partake in my new hobby. I worry he's just being strong for me.

"Honey, if you're gonna do it, now's the time," Eve says as she struggles to hold her grip on the man's leg.

There's only one way to find out if this will change the way Maverick feels about me. With a smile, I step forward and plunge the knife into the man's stomach, dragging to the side with all my weight. He screams as the serrated blade claws over his internal organs, which then burst from the seam in his abdomen in a rush of red and pink.

"He hurt children," Ezra says behind me. "Drag it out a bit if you can."

"With pleasure," I murmur as I grip a rope of intestines and drag it from his guts. Once I have enough pulled from his insides, I start shoving it into his gaping mouth.

Unfortunately, he passes out soon after, but that's okay. While he's unconscious, I slash the thumping stretch of skin on his neck. A red trickle burbles out, and he gasps a bit before going still.

A small round of applause erupts from the group as we stand from the murder. I turn to Maverick, but my heart refuses to beat when I see the look on his face. He isn't clapping. He isn't even smiling. He looks upset.

The worry fades as he pulls me against him and whispers in my ear. "That was the most beautiful thing I've ever seen, and when we get home, I'm going to reward you for it."

"Glad I'm heading out for a trip tonight," Eve says with a giggle. "You little sadists will have the place all to yourselves. Just keep the fucking out of my room. Deal?"

My cheeks blaze red.

"Could we maybe not talk about my sister's sex life in my presence? Thanks." Bennett gags and rolls his eyes.

Ezra plants a hand on my shoulder and gives it a squeeze. "That was a good kill, Frankie. Worthy of the Carter name."

"Thanks."

The group is all smiles as they turn and head back toward the manor, the excitement over. Maverick and I linger behind, looking into each other's eyes as the footsteps fade. I'm glad Gary wasn't here to witness his brother's demise. He had the forethought to stay put.

"I was worried you'd be upset," I say once I'm sure the others are out of earshot.

He cocks his head and stares at me. "Upset?"

"You never wanted me to be a killer. I know we've talked about it, and you say you're okay with it, but I wasn't sure you meant it."

"Do I have a habit of saying things I don't mean?"

I smirk. "There was that one time . . ."

"Okay, okay, but that was for a good reason." He brushes my hair away from my cheek and places a gentle kiss on my lips. "It was never that I didn't want you to kill. I just wanted you to be happy."

"Then kiss me again," I say, and he does. "That's all I need. Your support. No matter what my decisions are, I just need to know you support them. Can you do that?"

"Always."

"Then I'll always be happy."

"Even when we're barreling down a roller coaster hill at an amusement park that likely hasn't seen an inspection since before the pandemic?"

I wince. "Okay, maybe that's a little much . . . but as long as you're with me, I think I'll get through it."

"That's what I like to hear, sweetheart."

He takes my hand, and we head toward the others. We head toward family, friends, and a lot of unknowns. But we're heading toward them together.

Check out book four, *Slaughter Park*, the next stop in the Slaycation series: Books2read.com/SlaughterPark

If you want to stay with dark-lite, check out these stories.
Stranger Session: Books2read.com/StrangerSession
Her Fantasy: Books2read.com/HerFantasy
Last Mistake: Books2read.com/LastMistake
Protect Me: Books2read.com/ProtectMeNovella
Dark Decisions: Books2read.com/DarkDecisions

If you're ready to dive into darker reads, make sure you check out Lauren's dark, hitchhiker romance standalones in the Ride or Die series. These can be read in any order.

Hitched: Books2read.com/Hitched
Along for the Ride: Books2read.com/MFMHitchhiker
Driving my Obsession: Books2read.com/
DrivingmyObsession
Across State Lines: Books2read.com/AcrossStateLines
Don't Stop: Books2read.com/Dont-Stop

Connect with Lauren

Don't miss a thing from Lauren Biel! Check out all of her books, social media connections, and other important information at Campsite.bio/LaurenBielAuthor and Lauren Biel.com

Acknowledgments

To my VIP gals (Jessie, Nikita, Lexi, Grace, and Kim), thank you for always being there for me!

Thank you to my husband for supporting me on this journey.

Brooke, my editor, you're the best and I *still* couldn't have done this without you!

Thank you to my valued Patrons. Your contribution helped make this book happen!

Adrianna K, Mickayla F, Patricia W, Jessica D, Stephanie R, Abby R, Kelle T, Heather B, Shahalie, Ashley M, Laura F, Megan L, Leslie M, Kim R, Curvy Pear, Ashley S, Nikkie B, Rebecca C, Kaat, Emily S, Kimberly G, A.Reads, Cplay, Danielle N, Sunshine_the_Bookie, Sara M, Harley B, Heather M, Bonnie F, Marguerite, PaigeeBear, Tiffany M, Tara H, Vikki S, Amanda T, Suzy A, Andie J, Lisa W, Court's Bookshelf, Nicholetta88, Emily S, Sheena E, Queen Ilmaree, SerenaLorraine, AprilCoats, Heather S, Jennifer S, Just Jen Here, Mikasa_Kuchiki, Jada W, Briyanna M, Jesi D, Charmaine B, Michelle, Christy P, Dani C, Kayla T, Arnica S, Cassi K, Gumdrop, Maxine T, Barrie, Alexandria R, Leslie W, Kayla M, Marisa K, Smitty,

Brooke, Ashley P, Mandy G, Bailey A, Anna S, Shelby F, Tiannah J, Sharee S, Courtney P, Kristiana B, Vero A, Chelle, Sara S, Samantha R, Jessica G, Kimberly S, Tabitha F, JesStenger, Lindsey S, Laura T, Joanna, Nicole M, Nineette W, BoneDaddyAshe, Kimberly B

Also by Lauren Biel

To view Lauren Biel's complete list of books, visit: https://laurenbiel.com/laurenbielbooks/

About the Author

Lauren Biel is the author of many dark romance books, with several more titles in the works. When she's not working, she's writing. When she's not writing, she's spending time with her husband, her friends, or her pets. You might also find her on a horseback trail ride or sitting beside a waterfall in Upstate New York. When reading her work, expect the unexpected. To be the first to know about her upcoming titles, please visit www.LaurenBiel.com.